More books by S.M. LaViolette & Minerva Spencer

THE ACADEMY OF LOVE SERIES
The Music of Love
A Figure of Love
A Portrait of Love
The Language of Love*

THE OUTCASTS SERIES
Dangerous
Barbarous
Scandalous

THE REBELS OF THE *TON*
Notorious
Outrageous*
Infamous*

THE MASQUERADERS
The Footman
The Postilion*
The Bastard*

THE SEDUCERS
Melissa and The Vicar
Joss and The Countess
Hugo and The Maiden*

VICTORIAN DECADENCE
His Harlot
His Valet
His Countess
Her Master*
Her Beast*

ANTHOLOGIES:

THE ARRANGEMENT

*upcoming books

S.M. LAVIOLETTE

Crooked
Sixpence
CS
P
Press

CROOKED SIXPENCE BOOKS are published by

CROOKED SIXPENCE PRESS

2 State Road 230
El Prado, NM 87529

First printing March 2021
10 9 8 7 6 5 4 3 2 1

Photo stock by Period Images
Printed in the United States of America

Chapter One

Scotland
November 1811

*B*enedicta Elizabeth Norah Winslow de Montfort, tenth Duchess of Wake, tiptoed quietly—as quietly as it was possible to do wearing top boots—toward the servant staircase.

The house was silent except for the settling of ancient timbers, as it should be at three in the morning. The only occupants—other than servants—were Benna's cousin Michael and his loathsome friend, Viscount Fenwick.

Life had changed drastically in the two weeks since her brother David's death.

Not only did she miss David—although she had seen little enough of him in the three years since he'd inherited the title—but her happy, predictable routine had been smashed to flinders thanks to the arrival of her cousin and now legal guardian, Michael de Montfort, the Earl of Norland.

Michael had only taken control of Wake House a scant two weeks ago but already his changes were profound—not to mention unwelcome.

He'd begun replacing servants with people he'd brought from his estate in Northumberland. Not just the footmen and grooms, but old family retainers like Mrs. Hotchkiss, the housekeeper, and Clavering, the butler.

Benna scarcely saw a familiar face as she walked the house and grounds.

And now, ominously, Michael was making noises about replacing Old Tom, the stablemaster—a man who'd been more like a fond uncle to Benna than a servant. Tom had grown up on the estate and had once run barefoot and wild with Benna's own father when the duke had been a lad.

To think of Tom not being part of her life was simply unbearable.

The other change Michael had imposed had to do with Benna, herself.

Ever since Benna could remember she'd been left to her own devices. And she liked it that way.

When it came to her doting father, Benna had needed to exert minimal effort to twist him around her finger. While the duke might have wished that the only daughter of his beloved wife had resembled that deceased beauty more than his own pale, tall, gangly person, he'd never made Benna feel that she was a disappointment to him.

Because horses had been the duke's only passion after the death of his wife, he found nothing amiss in Benna's desire to spend more time in the stables than in the schoolroom.

Since the age of twelve—after Benna had saved her father's favorite hunter by prudently and competently fomenting the poor beast's injured hock—the duke had all but put her in charge of the stables during his frequent absences from Wake House.

David, who'd inherited the unenviable task of running herd on Benna after their father's death, had not been nearly as sanguine about her breeches, string of fifteen slapping hunters, or the fact that her closest—nay, her only—companion was Wake House's crusty old stable master, Tom Barnum.

"Father gave you your head for far too long and now you are unmanageable, Benna," David had shouted that last time he'd come home to visit, only three months before he'd died in a freak accident hunting with the Quorn.

"I warn you, Benna, I won't be ruled by your tantrums like Papa was. You had better prepare to find yourself a husband next year in London, my girl, because I shan't have you haunting the stables in your ridiculous garb and behaving like another one of my grooms after I am married."

David's betrothed. Lady Louisa—a so-called *diamond of the first water*—was a woman Benna had never met.

When Benna had asked when she would meet the nonpareil, her brother's answer had crushed her. "I'm too embarrassed to bring her for a visit and expose her to your hoydenish behavior. You've run wild for a long time, Benna, but I shall break you to bridle by the time I bring my wife home."

Even at the time Benna had deeply regretted throwing the porcelain statuette at his head. Not because she had liked the gruesome thing—a maudlin rendering of a goose girl with her adoring gaggle—but because that blazing row was the last memory she had of David.

Now he was gone, and she was the head of their ever-shrinking family.

Thanks to an ancient and unusual remainder in the Wake dukedom's royal patent, Benna had inherited the title of duchess from her brother, although all the subsidiary titles had passed to her cousin Michael, Benna's heir presumptive in addition to being her guardian.

It took less than a week of daily exposure to Michael's reign to discover that he was not put off by either her temper or her stubbornness.

They'd first locked horns the day after David's funeral, when Benna had burst into her cousin's study—which should have been *her* study after her brother's death—and demanded to see a copy of David's will.

As a minor, Benna had been excluded from attending the formal reading, which had taken place with only Michael and David's new solicitor in attendance. Why her brother had sacked the solicitors their father and grandfather had used—the London firm of Norris and Ridgewick—Benna did not know.

Michael had smirked, visibly amused by her demand. "You're not entitled to anything, my dear child, but I will kindly—this once—appease your curiosity and allow you to look at your brother's will."

Benna was still horrified by what she'd read. The terms of the trust—the corpus of which would only be available to her on her twenty-fifth birthday—had not surprised her since her father had been the one to establish it.

But why, in the name of God David—her legal guardian after her father's death—had chosen Michael for that role, she would never know.

Her brother had known how much Benna despised their arrogant, far-too-domineering cousin, and yet he'd granted Michael total authority over her person and future.

The morning after that first clash with Michael Benna had gone down to the stables early, as was her practice, intending to put her new hunter through its paces.

She'd arrived to find Michael's loathsome servant Diggle blocking the entrance to the horse stalls.

"'Is lordship wants to see you, sharpish."

Benna had been thunderstruck; never had a servant looked at her so insolently or spoken so disrespectfully. "You will address me with respect in my own home, or you may pack your belongings and be gone."

Diggle had only laughed.

And when Benna had tried to push past him, he'd grabbed her upper arm with a hand as big as the huge bronze sundial in the parterre garden. "I'm to bring ye."

Then the brute had *dragged* her all the way back to the study, where Michael had the audacity to make her stand on the carpet in front of his desk—like a recalcitrant child—while he'd laid down what he called the *new law*.

No more spending her days in the stables, no more wearing breeches, no more hunting, and absolutely no riding without one of his grooms in attendance.

"Lastly," he'd said, with a hateful smirk, "at least for now, if you wish to go for a ride, you will do so wearing a proper habit. I am arranging for a dressmaker to come out and fit you for appropriate clothing."

Benna had looked right into Michael's eyes and enunciated, "Go. Straight. To. Hell." She'd then marched back to the stables and gone about her usual routine.

The next day, when she'd gone to ride, she discovered that Spitfire, her new gelding, was missing.

Benna had found her cousin in the breakfast room, along with Viscount Fenwick.

"Tom says you sold Spitfire?"

Michael had winced. "There is no need to shout."

"There is *every* need," she'd shouted again. "Those horses are *my* property."

"I'm afraid not, my dear. Or do you need to peruse the document granting me power over you and every item on this property?"

"Why are you *doing* this?" Benna had been ashamed of the pleading note that had crept into her voice.

"I will sell a horse each time you disobey me," he'd said in a cool, superior tone that had stoked the rage burning inside her. "If I were you, dear cousin," he'd added, his gaze on her hand, which was moving toward a crystal vase on the nearby console table, "I would not get any ideas about hurling that at my head."

Benna had snatched back her hand, almost chewing out her own tongue trying to keep it behind her teeth.

As she'd flung herself out of the room, she'd heard her cousin and Fenwick chortling behind her.

Michael had sold off seven of her hunters in only two weeks.

Finally, Benna had stopped riding in the mornings—she refused to go with any of Michael's despicable grooms accompanying her— but she'd found a way around the embargo by sneaking out at night.

That pleasure, however, would be taken from her as the moon waned.

Terrified that she might lose the rest of her horses, she now grudgingly spent the daylight hours wearing a putrid dress, dining with her cousin and his vile friend, and studying under the tutelage of a prosy curate that Michael brought with him from Northumberland.

A sudden snatch of conversation jolted her from her furious musing, "—good God, Norland, you can't be serious!"

Benna recognized the slurred voice as belonging to Viscount Fenwick.

She froze on the second-floor landing.

"Christ, Fenwick." Michael sounded so loud that Benna assumed the men must be on the other side of the panel that served as a hidden door to the servant stairs. "If you don't keep your bloody voice down, they'll be able to hear you in London."

"How old is the chit, anyway?" Fenwick asked, his voice already becoming dim as their footsteps moved past.

"She'll be seventeen in a few weeks."

"That's a bit young, isn't it? Don't you think the trustees will—"

Benna mashed her ear against the wood, but all she could hear was a distant murmur, and then the closing of a door. They must have retired to the library.

And they had been talking about *her*.

5

Benna chewed her lip and stood staring blankly at the candlestick in her hand.

Go to your room, the voice of reason ordered.

She knew she should listen.

But, instead, she opened the door a crack, made sure there was nobody loitering—like the odious Diggle—and sped down the wide corridor to the section of hallway that was three panels away from the double doors to the library.

Benna located the small catch easily and opened the door to the narrow corridor that ran alongside the library, leading to one of the bigger priest holes in a house that was littered with them.

The servants knew about this hideaway, of course, but nobody else knew the *real* secret of the room: that it was actually a double hole, two secret rooms, one behind the other.

The main priest hole was large enough to have a cot, chair, and table. At the back of the room was a section of paneling that swung up when shoved at the bottom. By turning sideways, she could ease her body into the second room, which was far smaller than the first, barely a cupboard with a single chair.

Benna had discovered the second room completely by accident. As a girl, she'd enjoyed spending time in the cozy room and had once accidentally dropped the book she'd been reading. When she bent down to get it, she'd leaned against the panel.

That had been years ago, and she'd never seen any sign of use in the room and hadn't told even her brother of its existence.

Benna left her candle in the outer priest hole and felt her way by touch into the inner sanctum. On the wall was a raised piece of wood that covered a peep.

Benna slid the wood aside slowly.

"—yes, of course I know that, old man." Fenwick's voice was so loud it sounded like he'd stepped into the priest's hole with her. "What I still don't understand is how you talked poor old David into putting the girl—along with everything else—into your hands." He gave a raucous chuckle. "Fairly reeks of the Princes in the Tower, don't it? I daresay David's old windsuckers would have had something to say about appointing you guardian if you hadn't convinced David to give them the sack and hire your man. Too bad about the trust though, eh?" he taunted.

Benna frowned. What did he mean, *too bad about the trust?* Too bad about it, how?

Fenwick was in a chair not far from the mantelpiece, the back of his head to her. The peep was tucked within an especially elaborate piece of scrolling.

Michael sat directly across from him.

"You don't need to know about any of that, dear Dickie," her cousin said, his gaze fixed on something Benna could not see, his handsome face wearing a cold, pitiless expression that made her shiver. "All I want from you is to stand witness to the affair."

"You know me, old chap, always glad to help out a friend in need."

Michael's full lips twisted into a mocking smile and he turned until he was staring at his friend, and therefore looking directly at the peep. "Your helpfulness is one of the characteristics I like most about you, Fenwick."

Even though she couldn't see the viscount's face, she could tell by the way his shoulders stiffened that he didn't care for the other man's innuendo. "You needn't come the ugly with me, Norland. I'd help whether or not you knew about the other thing."

"To be sure, Dickie, old chap," he soothed. "I did not mean to cast aspersions. By the by, how goes that business—*the other thing*, as you so quaintly call it? Is it still as lucrative as it was when your dear, departed brother was, er, extorting money for God and country?"

"It's not me we're here to talk about," Fenwick snapped. "When do you want me back here?"

"Oh, I shall be ready for you before you leave, my good man." Michael raised a glass and took a sip. "It turns out that dear Benna's way of going on has quite played into my hands. The last time she went anywhere was with my uncle when she was barely a girl. Nobody else in our family has seen her in years. The people in town see her, of course, but all they see is a tall, skinny, towheaded woman. None of them would be able to describe her more fully that that. She has no friends and has shocked and alienated all the local mamas by dressing and behaving like a man. Best of all, rumors abound about her infamous temper tantrums with her brother. I've already got five witnesses willing to swear she's become even more volatile and unstable since David's passing." One side of his mouth pulled up. "Thanks to my cousin David's ironclad will, Norris and Ridgewick will be at *point non plus* if they dare to challenge me. They may have their hooks in the trust, but my little cousin is all mine."

7

Benna let out a shaky breath and forced herself to inhale, her body trembling.

Michael smirked and sipped his brandy. "I've been seeding word of her instability for over a year now. By the time the marriage is known I shall be viewed as the hero of the matter—sacrificing myself for the future of the de Montfort family. And then once dear little Benna has been persuaded to—"

Fenwick snorted. "Not so little. She might be a bean pole but she's almost as tall as you, Norland. How will you take care of her when you're done?" he asked, his tone sly. "The one thing everyone in these parts agrees on is that she's a spanking rider—far better than poor David. It won't be so easy to arrange for *her* to take a convenient fall."

Benna bit her lower lip in time to hold in a gasp.

Michael's mouth tightened, his eyes glinting dangerously. "You had better learn to mind your tongue, Fenwick. I shouldn't want somebody to cut it out for you."

For a long moment the only sound in the room was the crackling of the fire.

Michael pinned Fenwick with cold blue eyes. What the viscount was looking at, Benna had no clue.

It was Fenwick who broke the silence. "I still don't see how you're going to get her up to scratch. A right willful baggage from what I've seen."

"Benna has been too long indulged, first by her father, and then by David." Michael's features tightened until his handsome face was a cruel mask. "Never fear, my dear Fenwick. I shall bring her to heel with very little effort. Besides, it will hardly matter what she says or does."

Fenwick chuckled. "You've got a parson in your pocket?"

Michael cocked his head at his so-called friend, his expression anything but friendly. "So curious you are about my affairs, dear Dickie. But I believe you don't need all the details. All you need is to be sober enough to stand upright this coming Monday."

Fenwick said nothing, but his white knuckles around the glass told Benna how much he liked being spoken to so contemptuously.

"As soon as we are wed my man Diggle shall take Benna to a place where she will be safely—and quietly—kept."

"Oh? Where?"

"Never you mind. Suffice it to say that I've got somewhere secure I can tuck her away until I need her."

Benna's breath froze in her lungs.

Fenwick chuckled and Benna heard a grudging—but nervous—admiration in the other man's braying laughter. The viscount raised his glass. "Here's to you, Norland—a more heartless bastard I hope never to meet."

Benna pushed the wooden cover closed with a shaky hand and slid to the floor.

Good God. She'd always thought Michael was loathsome but she'd not dreamed he'd stoop to *murder*.

Everyone had believed David's death was an accident. His hunter had been found, dying, near David's body. Her brother's head had been crushed by the stone wall he'd apparently been trying to jump.

Based on Fenwick's not very subtle ribbing she now had to wonder; had Michael engineered David's death?

Had her brother signed his own death warrant when he'd re-written his will giving Michael control over not only Benna, but, by extension, the dukedom?

If Michael planned to force her to marry him and lock her away then the thought that he might also be a murderer was not so farfetched.

It must have been difficult to murder a man during a crowded hunt.

It would be far simpler to kill a reclusive duchess who'd not left her remote estate since she was twelve.

All these years living her life the way she wanted had, apparently, led to a situation where it would be all too easy for Michael to make Benna disappear.

She didn't know where Michael planned to "tuck her away" but she could easily guess.

Bumpkin though she was, she knew of those quiet houses in the country, set away from towns and busy roads, places where inconvenient or embarrassing family members could be stored like unwanted pieces of furniture, away from the prying eyes of society. Indeed, when she was younger, she recalled hearing murmurs of an aunt on her mother's side who was locked away.

What had happened to that woman? Benna didn't even know her name. Was she still alive? Did anyone remember her? Did anyone care?

A strange sound assaulted her and Benna realized her teeth were chattering. Not from cold, but from fear.

Good God. What am I going to do? Who can I tell? Who would even believe me, not to mention help me?

Hot tears trailed down her cheeks and she angrily brushed them away with the heel of her hand.

It was already early Wednesday morning and he'd said they'd marry sometime on Monday.

Benna swallowed, almost choking on her fear. *I've got less than six days to stop him.*

Chapter Two

Cornwall
1817
Six Years Later

*B*enna pitchforked the last of the ancient, rotting straw from the stall into the rickety wheelbarrow and then paused to catch her breath.

She didn't mind the smell of fresh horse droppings, but the Earl of Trebolton's stables stank of damp, neglect, and decay; it was clear they'd not been cleaned in years.

Everyone in the area knew that the new earl was terribly short of money, hence his willingness to hire somebody like youthful Ben Piddock as his stable master-cum-groom-cum-postilion-cum-stable lad and so forth.

Thanks to Lord Trebolton, Benna was king—or queen—of all she surveyed: dozens of dirty stalls; a tack room filled with cobwebs and crumbling leather; a defunct smithy and forge; two enormous, empty stable blocks; five horses, four of which were ancient carriage horses who could barely haul themselves, not to mention an actual vehicle; and one cantankerous mule named Hector.

Bringing the Trebolton stables back to life was a job that would have kept a dozen employees busy.

In the month she'd been working for the earl she'd repaired broken stall doors, dug up rotting posts and cross-pieces on the outdoor enclosures, replaced cracked and missing roofing tiles, and handled dozens of other small projects. It was hard work—harder than anything she'd done in the almost six years since she'd left Wake House, but Benna adored her job.

Not to mention your employer.

Benna grimaced at the familiar, unwanted voice. Even though she had not seen Geoffrey Morecambe for almost a year, her ex-employer's voice had become an annoyingly persistent presence in her head.

She knew that she shouldn't engage phantom Geoffrey in conversation. Not only had arguing with him in real life been pointless, but she also suspected that bickering with one's own mind was not a badge of sanity.

But it wasn't as if she had anyone else to talk to, so …

So what if I find the earl appealing? she retorted. *It's not as if I have any plans to act on my attraction.*

Which is just as well, considering how matters ended the last time you let yourself be guided by infatuation.

Thank you, Geoffrey. I hardly need reminding of that disaster.

"Hallo? Ben? Are you in there? *Ben?*"

Benna jolted at the new voice, which came from out in the corridor, rather than inside her head. And it belonged to the earl's eldest niece, Lady Catherine.

"Blast and damn," Benna whispered.

"My uncle has need of you, Ben," Lady Catherine's voice floated down the dank, dim passage to where Benna stood frozen with indecision.

Did Lord Trebolton really want to see her or was Catherine employing her uncle's name the way hunters used beaters to flush out game?

"He says it is important, Ben."

Benna ground her teeth. "I'll be right there, my lady," she called back using the low, gruff voice that was second nature to her after masquerading as a man for so long.

Benna leaned the pitchfork against the wall, wiped her filthy hands on her woolen breeches, and snatched up her coat, shrugging it on over her damp, sweaty shirt and vest.

Lastly, she tied on her red-checked neckcloth and shoved her hair off her brow before clapping her battered, dusty cap on her head.

She grimaced when she caught a whiff of her own body odor, which smelled a lot like the ancient manure and moldy old straw she'd just been pitchforking. She needed a wash. Badly.

Benna found Lady Catherine hovering around the front entrance to the stables, unwilling to step into the spider and rat-infested structure to find the object of her desire and persecution: Benna.

"Good afternoon, Lady Catherine." Benna doffed her cap to the earl's niece, who was about four years younger than her, keeping her expression polite but aloof.

Lady Catherine had the same dark hair and fair skin as her uncle but she'd inherited her mother's—a woman so reclusive that Benna had only seen her once—blue eyes and tip-tilted nose. At nineteen she should have been attending her second London Season rather than mooning over her uncle's tall, gawky stable master.

Lady Catherine's eyes roamed Benna's body with a fervency that made both their faces flush. Even after all these years, Benna still wasn't accustomed to the attention she received from other women.

"Come along," Lady Catherine ordered, visibly miffed at Benna's indifference.

Benna glanced at her hobnail work boots. "I'm covered in muck, my lady. Mayn't I—"

"No. You will come with me now." Lady Catherine spun on her heel and began to stride in an unladylike fashion across the weed-strewn drive that led from the stables to the house.

Benna followed, scuffing her feet as she went to knock off some of the dirt.

Lord Trebolton's house was as neglected as his stables. From the look of it, the original structure had been built during the early Tudor period but had been expanded so often it was now an architectural hotchpotch that sprawled over an acre or more.

The journey from the stables to the house cut through several distinct gardens—all of them overgrown and dormant at this time of year.

Lady Catherine strode several steps ahead, her hips swaying in a deliberate, exaggerated way that made Benna sigh.

Flirtatious females were not a new complication; Benna had dodged amorous inn maids and groping pub wenches almost nightly when she'd worked as a post boy.

But Lady Catherine was persecution on an entirely new level—although she'd thus far kept her hands to herself—and Benna lived in fear that the other woman's behavior would attract the notice of the earl and get her sacked.

She didn't want to lose this position because it was perfect for her in so many ways.

First, Lenshurst Park was remote and far, far away from Scotland.

Second, the earl was kind and too distracted to pay her much mind.

And third, he did not employ a lot of servants to wonder why a mere stripling with limited experience had landed such a plum position as his lordship's stable master.

As they mounted the gray slate steps to the house Benna darted past Lady Catherine to open the door. There were so few servants on the estate that there was nobody to spare for door opening, message delivering, or fetching and carrying, which was why the earl had used his niece as his emissary today.

Lady Catherine nodded slightly at Benna's gesture of respect and swept into the house like a grand dame.

Benna had to bite back a smile. Both Catherine and her younger sister Mariah were almost endearingly naïve. As far as Benna could tell, neither girl had ventured any farther than the small market town of Redruth.

Lady Catherine led her up two sets of stairs and down a long hallway with worn, ragged carpets on the floor, stopping in front of a beautifully carved wooden door that was dry, splintery, and crying out for a good oiling.

Almost six years of being a servant made Benna notice such things.

"He is expecting you," Lady Catherine said, casting a haughty look in Benna's direction before sweeping past her, the epitome of a great lady who'd been put upon to play the part of footman.

Benna removed her cap and scratched on the door as all the servants at Wake House had been trained to do. The duke had disliked loud or obtrusive sounds so the house servants had worn felt slippers over their shoes.

She glanced down at her second-hand, too-large boots and frowned. Well, there was nothing she could do about it now.

The muffled command, "Come," came from beyond the door.

Lord Trebolton's study was unexpectedly cramped, dark, and ill-situated, its only windows facing the east and offering a view of the stables.

The furniture and draperies were as tattered and worn as everything else on the estate.

Well, everything except the man who sat behind the big, scarred desk.

"Just a moment," he mumbled, his quill scratching across a page.

Take all the time you need, Benna wanted to say, visually gorging on his masculine perfection.

Jago Crewe, the ninth Earl of Trebolton, was the most attractive man she'd met in her almost twenty-three years. Handsomer even than Geoffrey Morecambe, a man who'd made at great deal of money off his resemblance to Apollo.

The earl was taller than Benna by perhaps an inch, his body elegant yet powerfully built. His hair was a brown so dark that it looked black against his pale skin. A strong jaw, straight nose, and generous lips created a classically handsome visage. But it was his eyes that were his true glory: sleepy, thickly lashed, and the color of rich nut-brown ale.

But Lord Trebolton was something far more impressive than a gorgeous mythical god; he was a genuine hero.

Benna had watched him singlehandedly save the lives of six men the day of the Redruth Mine cave-in.

In addition to his physical perfection and noble skills, he was also uniformly polite and kind to people of all orders.

Sounds like a dull dog to me, Geoffrey groused.

Benna thought the Earl of Trebolton was the closest thing she'd ever seen to a storybook hero.

Interestingly, the only time his warm expression had cooled was when the female members of the local gentry flung themselves at him—an occurrence that took place with almost laughable regularity.

It seemed that every eager mama with a marriageable daughter for miles around had flocked to Lenshurst over the past month, ostensibly to call on the retiring Lady Trebolton, but really hoping to get a look at the new earl, a man who'd been away from Cornwall for almost two decades.

For once, Benna was grateful that she was masquerading as a man since that was probably all that kept her from behaving just like all the other besotted females who fluttered around him like doves flocking to a dovecote.

You'd think that you would have learned by now never to fall for a pretty face, my dear.

Just shut up and go away, Geoff.

Never, my darling Benna. I'll be with you forever …

Sometimes Benna feared that was true.

She pulled her thoughts away from her past—and her hungry gaze from her employer—and looked around at the rest of the overstuffed, rather gloomy room.

To her right, in front of the hearth, was a chess table, the pieces set up and a game in progress.

Benna adored chess and had played often with David—back before he'd become too stuffy to play with his little sister—and later with Geoff, although he'd stopped playing her after she'd trounced him.

It was black's turn and Benna played out the next few moves for each side in her mind's eye.

"It is a game called chess."

She looked up to find the earl watching her, light glinting off his spectacles and hiding his eyes.

"Yes, my lord, I know."

His elegant black brows arched, disappearing beneath the glossy locks that fell over his forehead. "You play chess?"

"Yes, but not for some time."

"Well," he said, sitting back in his chair, his usually serious features shifting into an expression of wonder, "what a delightful surprise. I've been looking for somebody to pit my wits against since moving back home."

"I'm not very good," she lied.

"Nor am I."

Somehow, she didn't believe him.

"Perhaps we should have a game to see which of us is worse," he said, his tone teasing.

Benna stared; surely he was jesting?

He looked amused by her expression—likely one of shock—and allowed the matter to drop. "Why don't you have a seat, Ben. I've hardly spoken to you in the past month. Tell me, how is my stable progressing?"

Benna hesitated; what could she possibly say about the collection of ramshackle buildings that he would want to hear?

"It is quite all right," he said, reading her hesitation correctly. "I would have you speak plainly."

"There are now twelve stalls repaired and ready for occupants. Naturally Asclepius has the largest," she added, referring to Lord Trebolton's horse, a magnificent animal who resembled his magnificent master in both his dark coloring and regal bearing. "I've secured the fences around the turnout pens, and the larger arena. I'm still working on the close, smithy, tack room, remaining stalls, and lower paddock."

The earl's eyes widened with appreciation. "You are a whirlwind, Ben. I never expected even a fraction as much could be accomplished so soon. I am ashamed that it slipped my mind that you have no help in your monumental task." He pulled a wry face. "I have no excuse other than life's distractions. The first thing I am going to do is increase your wages and the second is authorize you to engage a groom and stable boy to assist you. As my stable master, you will choose your new employees."

Benna knew that he meant to be helpful, but the last thing she wanted was more servants in proximity.

"Thank you, my lord, that is most generous. But I am quite able to manage for myself—at least until there are more horses."

"I appreciate your attempt to practice economy on my behalf, Ben, but I'm afraid I'm rather set on my decision." He uttered the words in his usual soft-spoken fashion, but Benna recognized the steel beneath the velvet. The earl might have spent the last two decades living as a humble country doctor, but he was every inch an aristocrat. Lord Trebolton expected obedience from those in his employ, he simply had a gentler way of ensuring it.

After five years of taking orders from Geoffrey the earl was both easy and enjoyable to serve.

Benna dipped her chin. "Yes, my lord."

He rewarded her with one of his rare, intoxicating smiles, which left Benna feeling the way she had after drinking her first glass of gin.

"Which brings me to my second order of business: my nieces."

"Er, I'm sorry, sir? Did you say your nieces?"

"Yes. Neither of the girls have ridden since they outgrew their ponies, which my brother never replaced." The corners of his full lips turned down at his disclosure. "You have an excellent seat, so I am going to heap yet more duties on your shoulders and ask you to give them a few lessons—more in the nature of a refresher after so long—and also the mounting of them."

Selecting horses for his nieces would not be a problem, but lessons?

But, once again, Benna could see that he had made up his mind.

"It will be a pleasure to choose hacks for them, my lord." That, at least, was not a lie.

17

"I have business in Truro in three days' time. Normally I would ride rather than take a carriage but I anticipate doing quite a bit of shopping so I'll want you to have the coach made ready."

"Of course, my lord."

The Trebolton coach had not been used in some time and it would be a challenge to have the vehicle road-worthy in three days.

"There is an employment agency in Truro where you can arrange to interview some candidates for the new positions. You'll also find a small auction house where you can acquire my nieces' mounts, a gentle hack for the countess, a gig horse, and suitable replacements for our ancient carriage horses, which should be enjoying retirement rather than hauling that old bucket of a coach about."

"Yes, my lord."

Lord Trebolton rose and came out from behind his desk.

Benna shot to her feet and the earl laid a long, elegant hand on her shoulder. It was a gesture more suited to a father with his son than an employer to his servant.

His mesmerizing velvet brown eyes were only an inch above hers. "I want you to know how much I appreciate your hard work, Ben. Now that I have some idea of how matters stand with the estate there is no need for you to shoulder so much of the burden."

Although the earl had inherited his title almost a year ago, he had only resided at Lenshurst Park for a few months.

He gave Benna's shoulder a light squeeze. "Do not hesitate to tell me about any other needs you might have."

If only he knew what needs you really wanted him to address … Geoff snickered.

"Er, thank you, my lord," Benna said, her voice even lower than normal.

His hand tightened on her shoulder. "I'm afraid I've got one last duty to add to the towering pile." His perfect features became stern and forbidding. "I should warn you that it will be onerous. And possibly dangerous."

Benna goggled. "My lord?"

His expression shifted in an instant and he laughed, gave her shoulder one last squeeze, and dropped his hand. "I'm just teasing you, Ben. I want you to come up for a game of chess later this evening. Shall we say half past nine?"

Good Lord; he wanted her to come up to his study and spend time with him? Alone. Together.

Mocking laughter rang inside her head. *Pull your wits together, you gudgeon. He thinks you're a man, he doesn't fancy you.*

"Ben?" The earl's brows had knitted with concern.

"Er, nine-thirty, my lord. Yes. Tonight."

"Excellent. I shall see you then."

Benna pivoted on her heel and left in something of a daze, her shoulder on fire where the earl's hand had been, as though he had branded her skin.

***

Jago's fingers tingled from the sensation of the surprisingly fragile shoulder beneath his hand.

He'd known that Ben Piddock was slight, but he hadn't counted on the delicacy of the lad's build. Lord, how could such a slip of a person work so hard?

Jago hadn't spoken to the younger man much since engaging him a month ago, but he had watched him often from his study, whose east-facing window looked toward the stables.

The room was one of the few in the house with such an unfashionable view. It had been part of the steward's apartment when Jago had been a boy, back when the earldom could support such a luxury.

Day after day, Jago had seen the curly brown head bent over one task or another, setting new fenceposts and hauling away rotted sections, scampering around the slate roof of the stable as agilely as a squirrel, laboring with the vigor of three men.

Just yesterday he had watched Ben move an ancient trough toward the stables in painstaking degrees, using the old guard mule, Hector, a crotchety animal that nipped and kicked and fought Ben every step of the way.

Jago liked to think that if his mind hadn't been consumed with the disastrous estate he had inherited that he would have thought to hire help for Ben weeks ago, even though he could scarcely afford it.

His lips quirked as he recalled the boy's startled face when he'd asked him to come up to play chess. He'd looked poleaxed: as if Jago had asked him to sprint to Redruth naked.

Jago paused; something about Ben's startled expression had made him seem so *familiar*. It wasn't the first time he'd had the impression that he'd seen the lad before; the feeling seemed to get stronger, even though he got no closer to placing his face.

He shrugged off the nagging thought.

As for asking Ben to play chess? Well, he supposed it was strange behavior for an earl—playing a game with his servant—but it was the sort of thing he'd done whenever he pleased for the past eighteen years.

Jago found games a far more enjoyable pastime than dinner parties and vapid chatter—two activities he would need to reconcile himself to now that he would soon be reentering society.

But just because he'd had this new life foisted on him did not mean he had to give up on the old one, entirely. He could bloody well play chess with his stable master if he pleased; he would be damned if he gave up all the things he enjoyed just because he was now the head of an impoverished, crumbling earldom.

Speaking of that … Jago surveyed the piles of documents, papers, and ledgers scattered across his desk.

The Earls of Trebolton had always occupied the library in the past. But when Jago had returned to Lenshurst Park he'd discovered that the once-grand book room had been pillaged of furniture, drapes, artwork, and a great many of its books.

It had been far too dismal an atmosphere to work in, so he'd had his brother's massive mahogany desk and chair, as well as a large trestle table, moved into this all but empty room.

This hadn't been the only empty room at Lenshurst Park; there were dozens of others—mostly bedchambers—in the hundred and thirty room house, all stripped of their contents.

Jago saw that he'd unconsciously clenched his hands—an outward sign of the tension he felt whenever he thought about his family seat these days—and flexed his fingers on the carved arms of the massive chair.

It was a chair that he'd never thought he'd occupy. In Jago's mind this chair—this house, and everything in it—had belonged to his brother. Even now, almost a year after Cadan's death, it was still difficult to believe this was all his.

But Cadan was long buried; his older brother, his hero for the first eighteen years of his life, and a stranger for the next eighteen—dead.

When Jago had learned about his brother's death he'd come home to Lenshurst Park for the first time in eighteen years. He had remained for almost a month after the funeral, but he'd needed to return to his medical practice in the village of Trentham.

His brother's widow, Claire, had begged him not to go back to Trentham. "It is such a mess here, Jago, and the girls—well, they've grown wild and I can't make them mind me. And the house is just so—" She had begun crying at that point.

And Jago hadn't blamed her; the estate was a disaster.

But as sympathetic as he'd been, he couldn't stay. "I hope you understand, Claire, I am the only doctor for miles and I cannot simply leave Trentham."

It had taken nine long months to find a replacement physician for the small village where he'd lived for five happy years. During those months he'd made frequent trips to Cornwall to deal with the most pressing estate matters, but there had never been enough time to delve into the disorganized ledgers and mountains of bills.

At the time of Cadan's death Jago had not seen his sister-in-law for eighteen years—not since the night he'd left Lenshurst Park carrying only a small valise and portmanteau.

He'd been shocked at the changes the years had wrought on Claire's face and body.

When Jago left Cornwall Claire had just turned nineteen. Even back then—when they'd only been married two years—Claire and Cadan had already grown to despise one another.

Jago knew it was his brother who'd been largely to blame for their miserable marriage; Cadan had always resented that financial exigency had forced him to marry a woman from the merchant class and he had never let Claire forget that.

It had been an exceedingly unhappy household and his brother had spent far too much time in London, gambling away his wife's fortune.

And so it had fallen to Jago to befriend and comfort the lonely young woman, and he and Claire had become friendly, even though he never felt that he knew her well.

Jago had hoped that she would find solace in her children, but he'd learned, upon moving home, that both Cadan and Claire had ignored their two daughters, leaving them to all but raise themselves.

Not only that, but his sister-in-law had developed a terrible reliance on laudanum. Jago had been appalled when he'd discovered how much she consumed daily. He'd confronted her on the subject and had gradually helped her scale back her use.

Thankfully, Claire had seemed to welcome Jago's interference, rather than resent it.

"I am grateful for your help—and glad that you care enough to offer your assistance. I want to help you raise my daughters, Jago," she'd said, when he'd confronted her with her addiction. "I will do what I have to overcome my reliance."

As for the estate itself, Jago had believed that he'd finally discovered the depth of the financial problems months ago, but just this past week he'd found a letter from a bank—not their family bank—jumbled among bills, dunning notices, and heaps of other documents. The letter referred to a loan that would shortly come due.

A large loan.

Just thinking about the amount made him sick to his stomach.

Jago glanced at the clock on the mantle; it was two o'clock and he'd been at his desk since nine. It was time for something a bit more enjoyable.

He pushed up from his chair and went to the trestle table beneath the Tudor diamond-paned windows.

Spread out on the table's surface were the plans for the new hospital in Redruth. Just looking at the drawings was enough to soothe his frazzled nerves.

Jago had known that his days as a country doctor were numbered the moment he'd received word of Cadan's death. He would never practice medicine in the hospital he was designing. It was unheard of for an aristocrat to do something useful with his time, no matter how badly he needed money.

But while an earl was not allowed to pursue a career, he *would* be permitted to indulge in philanthropy.

Stephen Worth, the wealthy American banker who'd recently married Jago's dear friend Elinor had asked Jago to help him design a hospital that would be unlike any other in Britain: a hospital built by a doctor with doctoring in mind, rather than spiritual salvation or moral reformation.

As Jago gave his attention to the engrossing project the pressing troubles of the earldom fell away. He was in the process of correcting the architect's interpretation of a dispensary when the sound of a throat clearing startled him.

He turned to find Nance, his ancient butler, standing in the open doorway.

"I beg your pardon, my lord, but I knocked several times and there was no answer." Nance had been the butler at Lenshurst Park when Jago was a boy; the poor old codger deserved a pension and a cottage.

Unfortunately, Jago had neither for his aged servant, so he gave him an apologetic smile, instead. "I'm afraid I was deep in thought, Nance. Was there something you wanted?"

"Lady Trebolton is entertaining Mrs. Valera in the Yellow Salon and begs a moment of your time, my lord."

Jago jolted at the name *Valera*.

He shouldn't be surprised that Gloria Valera—formerly Gloria Bennett—was here. After all, she had left her card for him several times since he'd settled at Lenshurst Park.

Her persistent visits to the master of the house were not proper, but then Ria had never cared for anyone's rules but her own.

Jago had been dreading seeing her again after all these years. In fact, it was fair to say that he'd been dodging her. He was ashamed by his own cowardice and knew it was past time to face her.

"Thank you," he said to Nance, whose rheumy gaze was suddenly quite sharp. "I'll go directly."

Jago knew that Nance would remember Jago's youthful obsession with Ria. His butler would also know that the beautiful woman had been at the root of Jago's split with Cadan all those years ago.

He wasn't pleased at the thought of all that old scandal being stirred up again, but he knew there was nothing he could do to stop it.

Jago reached the Yellow Salon all too quickly. He pasted a smile on his face and opened the door to the pale pink and yellow-gold room that always left him vaguely bilious.

His sister-in-law sat facing the door and the first thing Jago noticed was her paler than usual complexion.

"Claire, my dear, how are you this afternoon?"

"I'm well, Jago. You see who has come to visit?" She gave him a nervous smile as her eyes darted toward the blazing fire she always kept burning in the stultifying salon.

Gloria's back was to the room and she appeared to be looking at something on the mantelpiece.

Always one to make the most of a dramatic moment, she turned slowly.

Time seemed to shift when he met her familiar green gaze and Jago huffed out a breath that must have been audible across the room.

Lush red lips curved in a way that used to knock the air from his lungs and apparently still did.

23

"Hello, Jago." Ria glided toward him, her tilted eyes glowing like emeralds and her hair the color of burning coals. Her face was every bit as arresting as it had been half a lifetime ago.

She stopped just out of reach, forcing him to close the distance between them if he was to take her extended hand.

"Mrs. Valera, what a pleasure to see you," he lied, bowing over her hand.

Her gloved fingers tightened when he would have pulled away. "Mrs. Valera? Why, we once used to be as close as brother and sister, Jago."

Brother and sister? Jago snorted. Hardly.

Her auburn-lashed lids dipped low. "You *used* to call me Ria." *You used to do a lot of things to me,* her wicked green gaze reminded him.

"I wasn't aware that you and Claire were acquainted," he said, trying to include his sister-in-law in the conversation—as it was *her* sitting room and she was mistress of the house, something that Ria seemed bent on ignoring.

"Oh yes, the countess and I are old friends, aren't we, my lady?" Ria asked, gracefully sinking into a chair close to where Jago was standing.

"Mrs. Valera has been kind enough to call … often," Claire said, avoiding Ria's question.

Jago bit back a smile at Claire's gentle set-down and lowered himself onto the settee beside her.

Ria's slight smile said she was amused rather than insulted by Claire's response. "That is true, my lady, and yet you have never been to Stanford Hall. I do hope you—both of you—will remedy that soon. You really must come and see my dear little home in the country."

Her *dear little home* was one of the largest houses in Cornwall.

When Claire merely smiled, Jago said, "I look forward to seeing it sometime."

Ria proceeded to tell Jago the gossip of the last eighteen years, doing her best to exclude the countess from the conversation.

As reclusive as Claire had always been, Jago wondered how much she knew about the voluptuous redheaded siren who had once beguiled almost every man in Cornwall—young or old, rich or poor, married or unmarried.

Interestingly, the only man who'd not been smitten by Ria was Cadan. Indeed, his brother had never missed an opportunity to denigrate her to Jago.

She's the bastard niece of our vicar, Jago. It hardly befits the son of an earl to be panting after her just like every other shop boy and footman in the area.

That had been the first time that Jago had struck his brother over Gloria Bennett.

He pulled his eyes from the dangerous perfection of Ria's heart-shaped face and glanced at Claire, who was looking paler than she'd been when he'd arrived.

"Shall I ring for tea?" he asked her when Ria stopped talking long enough for him to get a question in.

Claire opened her mouth.

"Not on my account," Ria said before Claire could answer. "As much as I'd love to stay and enjoy a comfortable coze with you, my lady," she cut the countess an insincere smile before turning back to Jago, "I just popped in to welcome dear Jago back to the neighborhood. I knew you'd not want to stand on ceremony with one of your oldest friends." She lowered her lashes and a delicate peachy stain washed across her high cheekbones.

He'd forgotten her astounding ability to summon either a blush or tears on demand. Even at nineteen she'd been a force of nature. Lord only knew what new tricks she'd learned in the intervening years.

"I don't know if you've heard, Jago, but I am now a widow." Her lush lower lip trembled and she blinked rapidly, as if struggling to contain her emotions.

Jago almost clapped. But instead, he said, "You have my deepest condolences."

"Although I have cast off my blacks I will always be in mourning for my dearest Henry."

Her dearest Henry? Even half-way across the country he'd read stories of the merry dance Ria had led her elderly, wealthy husband—a man whose death had left her one of the richest women in England.

"I've thought of you often over the years, Jago, and I've so regretted—" She bit her lip, as if she would like to say more, but then her eyes slid not so subtly to Claire, the source of her constraint.

The countess noticed the gesture and her pale cheeks flushed.

Jago stood. "Let me walk you out," he offered, already fatigued by her theatrics and annoyed by the way she was treating Claire.

"Oh, yes. Why, just listen to me—chattering when I really must be on my way. How kind you are to remind me, dear Jago."

Jago ignored her arch look and smiled warmly down at his sister-in-law. "I'll return shortly, Claire."

Ria waited until they were in the hallway before tucking her hand under his arm. "You can't imagine how delighted I was to hear you were back, Jago," she said, walking closer than necessary.

"I'm sure I can't. You know I've always lacked for imagination."

She gave a low, bawdy chuckle. "Oh darling, you can't still be angry with me, can you?"

Jago stopped in the middle of entry hall. Vermillion, amber, and emerald light from the stained-glass windows that flanked the front door bathed her glorious face.

Just like the windows—a pre-Henry VIII relic from when Lenshurst had been a monastery—Gloria Valera was a work of art. But there was nothing holy about her. Quite the opposite; she was an unholy menace to any man's peace of mind.

"Angry?" Jago repeated as he stared into eyes that could suck a man's soul from his body, even if he were vigilant. "Why would I possibly be angry, Gloria? Because I killed my best friend over you?"

Jago's anger stunned him. It had been eighteen years. *Eighteen years*. When would he be free of his fury and shame when it came to Brian's death?

Ria merely looked amused. "Oh no darling, I didn't mean any of *that*. I meant because I made you love me and then broke your little-boy heart." She laughed throatily at whatever she saw on his face.

Jago had to bite his tongue as he escorted her down the front steps.

Her liveried footman had opened the door to her carriage and Jago gladly handed her inside.

She took her time arranging her lush body on the cream leather seat, her sinuous movements those of a cat, her lashes lowered and her mobile features shifting into an almost convincing expression of longing when her eyes met his.

"I'm so delighted that you have come back, Jago."

"I am not the same man I was eighteen years ago, Ria."

Her lips curved at his unwitting use of her pet name and her hot eyes travelled over his body with an intimacy that was so shocking his face heated. "Well, thank goodness for that, darling. I have no interest in a mere boy"

Jago was no prude—he'd had more than a few lovers over the years—but his amours had never been emotional in nature—Ria herself had seen to that, decades ago. He wasn't a fool; he knew his appearance led women—especially younger and more impressionable women—to believe that he was some sort of storybook hero.

That was why he always chose older, experienced lovers, bluntly negotiating what he wanted in advance, making sure they knew he was interested only in mutual sexual gratification.

The few occasions when women had showed signs of becoming too attached Jago had immediately curtailed the arrangements.

He had no interest or tolerance for romance, *amour fou*, or passion. Not anymore.

And he most certainly had no intention of being lured into Ria's treacherous web a second time.

But even knowing all that, his body responded to the erotic promise in her eyes and he began to harden.

"I won't play your games, Ria. What do you want?" he asked coolly when she showed no sign of leaving.

"Then I shan't beat about the bush; I believe we could be very good for each other."

"Oh?"

Her eyes glinted at his dismissive tone, but her smile never faltered. "I know the state of affairs here, my dear." She paused, as if waiting for him to admit to being pockets-to-let. When he didn't speak, she continued, "I have what you need, Jago. And you have what I want." She gave his person a heated, lustful look.

Jago knew that what she desired was not his person, but his title. Even at the age of sixteen—the first time he'd met her—Ria had known what she wanted: wealth and status. She had already gained the first in abundance.

But status, he surmised, had proved far more elusive.

As exquisite and wealthy as she was, she was still the love child of a parlor maid and the widow of a man born and raised in the London stews.

That she could easily buy herself a title, Jago did not doubt. But it would likely come attached to an ancient syphilitic gambler who was more of a social pariah than she was.

Jago might not move in *tonnish* circles, but that wasn't because they were closed to him, but rather because he lacked any interest.

He snorted at her offer and shut the door with more force than was necessary. "Still the same old Ria, I see, willing to sacrifice everything and everyone to get what you want."

She rested her delicate fingers on the edge of the partially opened window. "It would be no great sacrifice to marry you, Jago."

The desire to tell that her that he'd been speaking of his own sacrifice was strong, but he kept his mouth shut. As much as Jago despised her, he could not afford, out of hand, to ignore what she was offering. He didn't wish to marry, but he strongly suspected that he would have to. Perhaps marrying the devil he knew was better than marrying a stranger. But he doubted it.

Rather than be offended when Jago didn't respond with flattery, she smiled. "Don't fall victim to your pride, Jago. Money is not the only thing I would bring to the table. If you are curious to explore what I mean, I would be delighted to provide you with a … sample."

He barked a laugh, more disgusted by his body's immediate reaction to her carnal offer than by the offer itself. "Still as persistent as ever, I see."

"Persistence is a virtue, my dear Jago."

"I didn't think you were interested in virtue, Ria."

She chuckled. "It has been so wonderful to see you again after all this time, Jago. Don't wait too long to pay me a visit."

Jago stepped away from the carriage. "Good day, Mrs. Valera."

Identical red-headed postilions in emerald and gold livery spurred the leaders and the coach leapt forward. It was a glossy black monstrosity, pulled by four black horses magnificent enough to draw the carriage of Satan himself.

Or, in this case, Satan herself.

Chapter Three

Scotland
1811
Six Years Earlier

What do you mean you won't prepare my carriage?"

The groom, Bannock—yet another of her cousin's new additions to the stables—eyed her up and down, his gaze insolent. Benna couldn't blame him; she looked like an idiot in the ruffly carriage dress Michael had ordered and she was now forced to wear.

"I want to speak to Tom." Benna was so furious she could barely force the words out.

"The old gaffer don't work here no more ... *Your Grace.*"

"*What?*"

Bannock smirked and nodded.

"What happened?"

"Got done for thievin'."

"That's a bloody lie," Benna shouted. "I want to talk to him. Now."

Bannock recoiled from her anger but made a quick recovery. "Well, ye *can't*. He left before first light, one step ahead of the sheriff."

"Left to go where?"

"Don't know. He's lucky his lordship didn't send the sheriff after him."

Benna couldn't even recall making the journey to the breakfast room, where she suspected Michael would be enjoying his usual leisurely meal.

Benna flung open the door to the cozy, sunny room, grimly pleased when both Michael and Fenwick jolted.

"Why good morning, Ben—"

"How dare you accuse Tom of stealing and sack him? How *dare* you?"

Michael gave her a smile that made her want to plant him a facer. "Not in front of our guest, my dear."

"He's not *my* guest. And this is *my* house and I am the mistress of it; I'll speak to whomever I please, whenever, however, and wherever I please."

Michael's smile never wavered, but fury darkened his eyes. "The old man was caught selling your brother's tack."

"That's a *goddamned* lie!" Benna raged.

Michael made a discreet gesture and the two footmen who'd been hovering—both of whom had come with her cousin—withdrew.

"Where is he now?" Benna had to force the words through clenched teeth.

"If he values his hide then he's many miles away—which is far better than he deserves."

"Who said he was stealing tack?"

"It hardly matters," he said coolly, "But, if you must know, it was Diggle who caught him."

"Diggle." Benna snorted. "Why am I not surprised." She wanted to launch herself onto her smirking cousin and scratch out his eyes.

Only with a herculean effort was she able to remind herself of how she'd discovered this disastrous news to begin with.

"One of your oafs—Bannock—refused to ready my carriage this morning."

"If you need to take a carriage somewhere, I shall be honored to accompany you, my dear." He'd turned back to his plate, buttering a slice of bread while Fenwick grinned, looking as if he were watching a particularly entertaining pantomime.

Benna scowled at the fool and pulled her gaze back to her cousin. "It just so happens that I don't want you to accompany me, *my dear.*"

Fenwick snorted, earning a disapproving glance from the earl.

"It is not appropriate for you to go jauntering about without somebody to accompany you."

"I *would* have somebody to accompany me if you'd not given poor Garvey the sack."

"Garvey? I presume you mean that ancient, witless maidservant who allowed you to run wild and unchecked."

"Garvey happened to be my mother's nurse, *my lord.*"

"Well, then it was time she was put out to pasture, *Your Grace*. You may take a carriage into town as long as you have Mrs. Blanchard accompany you."

Mrs. Blanchard was a horrid woman who'd appeared one morning in Benna's room, insisting that she was her new dresser. Benna was positive the woman was warming Michael's bed and had forbidden her to enter her chambers ever again.

"Mrs. Blanchard is a snoop who goes through my private things."

Michael laughed. "What in the world could a chit your age have to keep private?"

Benna ignored the odious question. "You've not heard the last from me on this matter, Michael. I'm going to get to the bottom of *Diggle's* monstrous accusation." Benna spun on her heel and flung the door open so hard that it bounced off the wall.

***

There was just enough moonlight that Benna could finish working on the rabbit's ears.

She'd begun whittling several years ago, when Tom had told her that she needed a way to vent some of her restless energy.

She'd been working her way through the animal kingdom ever since. When she'd begun this particular carving, only a month ago, she had looked forward to testing her skill on such an ambitious design.

Now, after living under Michael's thumb for more than two weeks, her normally steady hands were jerky and the fine details the work required seemed beyond her.

Before she accidentally cut off one of her fingers or ruined the carving entirely, she folded up her penny knife and slipped it and the small carving back into her coat pocket.

A quick glance at her watch told her it was three o'clock; she'd been waiting almost two hours. She stomped her boots and rubbed her hands together, her breath visible on the frosty air.

Benna glanced around the empty spinney, hope dying inside her. If Tom didn't come here tonight, she just didn't know—

"Your Grace."

Benna let out a mortifying squeak and spun around. "Tom!" She crossed the distance between them in two long strides and flung herself at him.

His stout body froze for an instant at her uncharacteristic behavior, but then he patted her on the back with one of his shovel-like hands. Although Tom was a good six inches shorter than her, he was heavy-boned and as round as a barrel.

"Here then, Your Grace," he muttered into her shoulder.

Benna reluctantly pulled away, rubbing at the tears of relief on her cheeks.

"No need for that, Lady Benna," he said in his gruff voice.

She smiled at the sound of her childhood name. "I was afraid you wouldn't come. Where are you staying? That rotten Diggle is the one who—"

"Shhh, now, my lady. Er, Your Grace," he hastily corrected. "It's not good for you to be so worked up, lass."

"I'm sorry, Tom. It's just that I'm so glad to see you. I thought you might have—" She frowned and pointed to a worn cloth bag at his feet. "What is that?" Her voice rose. "Are you leaving tonight?"

"I have to go, Your Grace, but I wanted to talk to you, first." His wrinkled old face seemed to collapse in on itself. "There's something foul goin' on, Lady Benna. It just ain't safe here—not for you. I don't want to leave you, but I don't know what to do."

Benna felt almost dizzy with relief at his words; she wasn't alone, after all.

"I overheard my cousin last night—that was why I came looking for you early this morning and found out you'd been sacked. He plans to force me to marry him, Tom. And afterward he's going to lock me up somewhere until he can—Well," she admitted, "I'm not sure what his plan entails, something to do with my trust, I daresay."

Tom didn't look surprised. "Oh, lass," he said, the words almost a groan.

"I know that he'd rather kill me but he obviously can't do so and inherit my trust." She scowled. "Or something like that. I've been such a fool, Tom. I never paid any attention to any of the details back when David explained it to me. I just don't recall what the terms are. But Michael is my guardian, so I daresay everything is under his control." She frowned. "Or perhaps he believes everything will automatically go to him after we are married?" Benna shook her head. "I don't know what the law is, but you can rest assured that he has looked into it."

Tom chewed his lower lip. "Well, I don't know nothin' about that, lass. But you've got that aunt and a few other cousins, can't you—"

"They are dependent on Michael and would never believe me, anyhow. After all, what proof do I have of anything? No, I need to get away from here—quickly. Where could I hide, Tom?"

"But this is madness, Lady Benna. Surely there must be some relative—or perhaps a family friend—"

"You know how things have been here. The last time I went anywhere was years ago. Since Papa died nobody but David, Michael, and a few of their friends have visited, and those I've avoided like the plague." She laughed and it sounded more than a little hysterical. "I'm only realizing now that living such an existence has left me terribly vulnerable." She groaned. "My God, Tom! He is going to do all this in less than a week and I can't think of any way to stop him other than to get away. And if you are gone, then who do I have to help me?"

He nodded. "I'm headin' to my older brother's place," he said. "You could come with?"

"I think that is the first place Michael will look—both for you *and* me—if I were to disappear right after you do."

"Aye, I reckon you're right. We could go somewhere else— London, maybe—and I can find work and take care of us while you do … well, whatever it is you need to do."

The thought of what he was suggesting was *terrifying*. But not as much as the thought of being married to Michael.

Benna's mind raced; she simply couldn't think straight with the fear of Michael hanging over her head. She met Tom's worried gaze. "I think that's a good idea. Papa's old solicitors are in London, Norris & Ridgewick. I met the old man once—Mr. Norris—when he came up from London a few years ago. He had dinner with us. I'm *sure* he would remember me. I know that David used somebody else for his new will, but I have a feeling my trust is still with Norris & Ridgewick—although I don't know anything for sure. Do you think we can get away without my cousin catching us?"

"He'll be looking for an older man and a young woman—not an old man and a lad."

Benna blinked. "What do you mean?"

"Remember when you came with me to the auction in Edinburgh?"

How could she forget? It was the last time she'd left Wake House. Her father had brought her along to visit her ailing grandmother—whom Benna hadn't seen since she was a toddler. But the old lady had died before they'd arrived. While the duke was busy with funeral matters Benna had dressed up in breeches and sneaked out with Tom, who'd taken her to the auction, where nobody had guessed that she was a girl. Not exactly an edifying experience for a thirteen-year-old girl to realize she could so easily pass for a boy, but …

"You really think I could do it?" she asked Tom.

"You'd have to cut your hair." He studied her, his expression thoughtful. "Even then, there's the color."

He meant the distinctive towhead white that she'd inherited from her father.

"Do you remember Miss Taverner?" Benna asked.

Tom's expression soured. "Oh, aye, *her.*"

Miss Taverner had been a horrid governess who'd left the duke's employ after less than three months, thanks to some encouragement from Benna. The woman had dyed her hair a jet black, which had made the ancient governess resemble a corpse.

"You could do that," Tom agreed. "But mebby don't dye it so dark. And you could say you're younger than seventeen to explain the lack of whiskers—I reckon you could pass for fifteen. Oh, and how about this?" He reached into his pocket and took out a familiar wooden case. "Here," he said, unfolding his spectacles, "Put these on."

Benna slid the glasses onto her nose. "Goodness," she said, the magnification making her dizzy.

Tom grinned, his face blurry. "You look nothin' like you, Your Grace."

"You'll have to stop calling me that, Tom. It's a dead giveaway." She squinted through the thick glass. "These might be a good disguise but I don't think I can walk without running into things." She removed them and handed them back.

"Oh, well, those're the strongest the oculist had. We could get some that wouldn't be so bad. I've got a bit-o-brass I saved up." He patted his pocket, where he must have put his money. "But not enough to keep you in comfort, your—er, lad. Can you get your hands on any—" He broke off and shook his head, "Lord. I can't believe the words I'm sayin'! If the old duke was here he'd—"

"If my father were here then I wouldn't have this problem. But he's not here, Tom. And what you're saying makes perfect sense, given my other options. I need to get away from Michael—and soon. As for money, I'm afraid I have none, but I've got a goodly amount of jewelry to sell." She frowned. "If I can find a way to get it out of the vault."

Tom nodded, his gaze abstracted "How long do you reckon you'll need to hide—and to what end?"

"I don't know," she admitted. "But I can't imagine I should need to stay hidden more than a few weeks."

"You think them solicitors will help? What if they believe you should be back with your guardian—since it's the law?"

Benna hadn't thought about that. Would Mr. Norris feel compelled to return her to Michael? What proof did she have of his plan?

Benna shook away the horrid questions, which seemed to be multiplying like rabbits even as she stood there. "I can think about that later. If not Mr. Norris then there has to be somebody I could go to for help, I just need to wrack my brains. I can't stay here and think about it. I might wake up tomorrow to find I'm on my way to some dreadful place with bars on the windows and—"

"Well, lookee 'oo I found 'ere—a convict and 'is accomplice."

Benna yelped and spun around.

Diggle stood at the head of the rough path that led to the spinney, grinning from ear to ear.

Benna glanced around wildly, looking for others.

"Naw, luv, just me." Diggle gave an ugly chuckle. "'Ardly need any 'elp pluckin' one old bird and a scrawny pullet." He lumbered toward them.

Tom reached out an arm and none-too-gently shoved Benna behind him. "Run, Your Grace."

"No, *Your Grace*," Diggle mocked, reaching beneath his drab duster and pulling out a cudgel. "You stay right where you are, luvvie."

Diggle was a hulking man but he moved so fast that he seemed a blur. His arm was only a flicker before the club connected to Tom's head with a sickening *thud.*

"Tom!" Benna screamed as the old man went down like a felled tree.

She dropped to her knees beside Tom's motionless body and leaned over until she felt a faint puff of warm air on her cheek. She almost wept with relief. "We need to get him to a doctor quickly or—"

A huge hand closed on her shoulder and lifted her to her feet as if she were a rag doll. "Nah, I fink we'll jest let nature take 'er course, Your Grace."

"Let me go you—you beast!" Benna squirmed and he twisted her arm behind her back, pinning it there. She cried out when he raised her elbow up, jagged bolts of pain shooting from her shoulder.

"Good lass," he praised when she stilled.

Benna whimpered, her free arm dangling at her side. Which is when she felt something hard in her coat pocket.

Her penny knife.

"Now, if you'll just come along wiffout a struggle I won't 'ave to use this twine in me pocket."

"I won't struggle," Benna promised in a defeated voice, her fingers closing around the wooden handle and flicking open the blade.

He chuckled and lowered her elbow. "There, that's a good little—"

Benna swung her free arm back with all her might, the knife blade leading.

Behind her Diggle gave a sharp grunt as the blade struck something warm and soft.

He made a gurgling sound and the hand on her wrist disappeared.

Benna staggered forward, out of reach, before spinning around.

The image of her knife sticking out of Diggle's throat was one that would stay with her for the rest of her life.

His eyes were wide and his mouth moved like a fish's gasping for air. His fingers clenching convulsively at the handle, which he couldn't seem to grab even though it was lodged in his own neck.

At her feet, Tom moaned.

Keeping Diggle in her line of vision, Benna dropped to her knees beside the old man.

"Hard to see," Tom wheezed, blinking his eyes, his pupils huge.

"I need to get you to a doctor." Benna slid her hands beneath his shoulders and tried to lift him. "Help, Tom, I can't lift you without—"

He moaned and Benna saw that blood was leaking out of the ear facing her.

"Oh God." She stared in horror as the ear bled faster. Instead of lifting him the rest of the way, she laid him back down. "Tom? Can you hear me?"

"L-Listen to me, lass." The words were barely audible. "Please …"

"I'm listening."

He swallowed several times, wincing. "Take my coat, hat, purse, and bag. Check Diggle's pockets, too—take anything of value."

"But—"

"*Don't argue!*"

She bit her lip hard enough to taste copper, and nodded.

"Haven't got much ... time." He coughed and gave a piteous cry at the pain it must have caused. "South. Go south. If you need help, write to my broth—*aarrrghhh!*" His back arched in a spasm that gripped his entire body, his face a rictus of agony.

"Tom?" she shrieked, shaking his stiff, unmoving form.

Instead of answering, he sagged limply in her arms.

Benna squeezed his shoulders. "Tom?" She shook him. "*Tom!*"

But the old man didn't move.

Chapter Four

enna was waiting outside Lord Trebolton's study at two minutes before nine-thirty, her hand shaking as she raised it to scratch on the door.

Take a deep breath and calm yourself, Benna. It's only a game of chess—not a romantic trist at Vauxhall Gardens.

Benna scowled, but took a deep breath, held it, and then exhaled. It helped.

"Come." The earl's voice called out from within immediately after her fingers touched the door.

The room looked different at night—less decrepit and gloomy.

The man sitting at the desk robbed her lungs of air, just as he always did.

"Ah, punctual to the minute," Lord Trebolton said, lowering the letter he'd been reading and looking up at her.

It was the first time Benna had seen him dressed for dinner. She had believed him stunning in his buckskins, top boots, and a clawhammer. In his formal blacks he was staggeringly magnificent.

His coat of black superfine was not of the first stare, but it was exquisitely tailored and sheathed his broad shoulders and torso closely enough that he would have needed help to dress himself.

God. What she wouldn't give to see him out of his clothing.

What a doxy I created. Geoffrey's laughter sounded more than a little bitter. *An upstanding, moral gentleman like your darling earl will never give one of his servants what you want, my dear. Even if he didn't believe you to be a lad …*

Benna knew that was all too true.

The earl cocked his head, the candlelight glinting off his spectacles. "Is ought amiss?"

"Er, no. Good evening, my lord." Benna made a hasty bow and dropped her gaze.

Fatuous fool that she was, she'd washed her hair and taken a thorough, if freezing, sponge bath before changing into her only suit of clothing—the same suit she'd been wearing the last night she saw Geoff.

"Thank you for indulging me," he said, rising from behind his desk and offering her a full-body view.

Benna gave a silent prayer of thanks for his cutaway coat, which exposed his slim hips and muscular thighs to her hungry gaze.

"It has been a long time since I've played," she reminded him, not that she was truly worried.

She'd played hundreds of games against Geoff, losing all but the very last one to him. After that, he'd made Benna play for money at the various inns and pubs on their travels. He'd taken whatever money she lost out of her paltry wages as an *incentive not to lose.*

The earl crossed the room to where the chess table had been moved slightly closer to the crackling hearth. The game from earlier was gone, the pieces re-set.

He flipped back his tails and sat, looking expectantly at her.

Benna took the other seat, moving in the jerky, self-conscious way she did whenever she felt herself being observed.

She set her hat on her knees and forced herself to look up at him. He was holding out his fists.

Benna pointed to his right, careful not to touch him.

He opened his hand to expose a white pawn. "First move to you," he said, replacing the pawns and then reaching for something under the table that made a clicking sound. He rotated the top until the white pieces were before her and then she heard the same click.

Benna exhaled slowly and then moved her king's pawn to open.

***

Jago tipped his king onto its side—for the second time that evening—and gave Ben a rueful look. "I believe I shall spare myself some pain and concede now."

He could see by the way that Ben's mouth tightened that the younger man was fighting not to smile.

"Go ahead and gloat," Jago said, chuckling when the Ben's normally serious features shifted into a grin. "Not that much," he chided.

Ben gave a soft, huffing laugh. "I was just lucky, my lord."

"No, you are a better player than I. A far better player." Indeed, Jago had a suspicion that Ben had allowed him to win their second match.

"So, that was two to you and one to me. I'm not sure I'm up for another thrashing tonight," Jago confessed, giving Ben a wry smile. "I'm afraid I'm not accustomed to losing."

Ben's expression, which had been one of intense concentration this past hour and a half, was once again guarded and opaque, that of a servant with his master. "You're a good player, my lord."

"But?" Jago prodded. "Go on, I am not too proud to listen to advice."

Ben dipped his gaze to the board and chewed his lip.

Jago had to laugh. "Fine, just pick *one* thing I do wrong and tell me about it."

Ben peeped up at him, his mouth curving into a shy, taking smile. "You have a tendency to push your pawns without supporting them. My lord," he added.

Jago stared at the board, mentally replaying as much as he could recall; the boy was right.

He glanced up and saw Ben anxiously waiting for his response. "I shall do better next time." The longcase clock chimed eleven and Jago yawned. "I have kept you up late."

"I usually go to bed around now." Ben replaced the game pieces with fingers that were long and slender like his person. Jago noticed the nails had been bitten to the quick and there was a rather nasty cut on the index finger of his right hand.

"That should have had stitches," Jago said, pointing to the cut.

Ben glanced down and looked surprised, as if he'd not even realized that he'd suffered such a deep gash.

"Next time something like that happens, come to me," Jago said, smiling at the lad's startled look. "It's one of the benefits of having a doctor living only across the drive."

Ben inclined his head. "Yes, my lord."

"How did you cut yourself?"

"I was just carving."

"Oh? Carving what?"

Ben hesitated, and then reached into his pocket and brought out a folding penny knife and a small wooden figure, which he handed to Jago.

Jago stared at the tiny, perfect-looking goose in his hand. "Good Lord! You carved this?"

Ben ducked his head. "Yes, my lord."

"It's amazing—and so tiny." He squinted at the boy's grubby glasses. "You must have good vision to be able to carve such details." The miniature goose had its head lowered at a threating angle and Jago could practically hear it hissing.

He handed back the carving. "So, is that what keeps you up so late?" he asked, stifling a yawn. Jago was tired, but it was warm and pleasant by the fire and he was in no hurry to get up. Besides, he decided that he liked the other man's quiet, almost soothing, company—although they'd scarcely exchanged a word over the past hour and a half, so intense had the play been.

"Oh, there is always something to do," Ben said, his answer vague enough to make Jago suspicious.

"I hope you aren't working all night, Ben."

"No, sir. Not working. Sometimes I read."

Jago shouldn't have been surprised by the answer; Ben was exceptionally well-spoken—his speech far more like that of a butler than the postilion he'd been when Jago hired him. "I believe you said you were from outside Bristol?"

"Yes, sir."

"You are a long way from your family."

"My father died a few years ago, so there is nobody left."

"You have no siblings?"

"I had a brother, but he died." The tight way he spoke did not invite more questions on the matter.

"Was your father also a postilion?"

"He was a teacher, my lord."

Ah, that explained his polished speech, the chess, and the reading, among other things. "Where did he teach?"

"Just a small village school."

"I expect you had a good education."

"Yes, sir. My father was quite a stickler about certain things."

"Like your diction?" Jago guessed.

Ben nodded.

"Why do you sometimes try to disguise how well-spoken you are?"

Ben's cheeks darkened and his lips twisted into a wry smile. "If you've noticed then it sounds like my efforts to disguise myself are not too successful."

Jago would not be deterred. "Why, Ben?"

"At my first job one of the other post boys accused me of putting on airs because of the way I talked. I decided it would be easier to fit in if I sounded the same as everyone else."

Jago didn't bother telling him that his accent did not resemble any Bristol accent he'd ever heard. Indeed, the lad had almost no regional accent but spoke more like a gentleman. His father must have indeed been a stickler.

"Where did your father go to school?"

"Oxford, sir."

"Ah, an Oxford man. He must have been clever." Or possessed excellent social connections, but Jago kept that observation to himself.

Ben hesitated, and then said, "He was the youngest son of a baronet—one of seven sons. He, er, lost touch with his family after he married my mother. She was a chambermaid, sir."

Jago took a minute to digest that surprising information. Actually, it *wasn't* so surprising when he thought about it. Ben certainly spoke like the grandson of a baronet.

"You have not considered asking for their help?"

"I wrote my grandfather after my father died, but he wanted nothing to do with me."

Jago was disgusted, but not surprised. He'd had a mate at university—the youngest son of a duke—who eloped with an actress. It had not gone well for him. Or his wife, for that matter.

"You didn't wish to follow in his footsteps and become a teacher?"

"I like working with horses more than people."

Jago chuckled at the blunt response.

"That doesn't sound very kind, does it?"

"Perhaps not, but I like that you're honest. Besides, I think I know what you mean—animals are far easier than people." A yawn slipped out before he could catch it. "Well, I'm for bed, young Piddock." He stood and the boy got up along with him.

"Give me a few days to lick my wounds—and do a bit of practice supporting my pawns—and I shall want a chance for revenge."

Ben stopped, his hand on the doorknob, and looked up at Jago. "Thank you for the games, sir. It was good to play again." He smiled almost wistfully and then let himself out.

As Jago snuffed the candles in the room and replaced the fire screen, he couldn't help thinking that the more he learned about Ben Piddock, the more impressive—and mysterious—the boy seemed to become.

Chapter Five

*B*enna stared at the contents of her pocket and counted nine pence; it would be another evening of 'sleeping rough' tonight—her third since leaving Newcastle.

She sighed and surreptitiously slid the coins back into her pocket. She should have stayed in Newcastle, but after the debacle with the stolen mail bag she'd not wanted to linger.

Although it was well-known that the post boys who delivered expresses—risking their lives for a pittance—were often set upon by robbers while on the road, the postal official who'd questioned her about her empty mail satchel had not been very understanding. Indeed, he'd eyed Benna with so much suspicion that even *she* had begun to think that she might have done something dodgy with the mailbag.

Of course, people often looked at her suspiciously. Or perhaps that was her guilty conscience speaking, although she didn't think so.

Even two months of successfully masquerading as a man had not served to ease her anxiety and boost her confidence.

Although her weeks as a lowly post boy had certainly served to put her new life into perspective.

Benna had always been active, but she had quickly discovered that a day spent hacking or hunting was nothing like a day spent mucking out stalls, riding twelve hours on bone-jarring nags, or—on two dreadful occasions—cleaning out hen houses in exchange for a bit of warm supper and a place to lay her head.

Yes, life had changed so fast that Benna's head spun whenever she thought about it; so she tried not to.

She'd not had a decent night's sleep since she'd fled from that spinney garbed in Tom's coat and hat, her pocket stuffed with stolen money and Diggle's repulsive rings, watch, and fobs.

Too terrified to buy a seat on the stage, Benna had walked for three days, taking only small side roads. Not until she'd reached the town of Otterburn had she risked accepting rides with carters or farmers.

Benna had stumbled into the post boy job on her first evening in Newcastle, even though the city was too close to Scotland for her comfort. But she'd decided to linger in the north to have access to newspapers that might contain some report of what happened that night in the spinney.

Thus far, she'd not read a word about Tom's or Diggle's deaths. And she knew—beyond a doubt—that both men had been dead when she left the spinney that night.

Michael must have covered up the deaths. Or perhaps he'd paid off some official to swear they'd died of natural causes. If he could engineer her brother's *accident*—an accusation that had only gained more traction in her mind the more she'd thought of it—then hiding the deaths of two unimportant persons would present no challenge.

She had also scanned the papers for any mention of her cousin. Only once had she seen his name—in connection with hers. According to the newspaper report, the Earl of Norland had recently accompanied his young ward, the new Duchess of Wake, to an exclusive spa just outside Brighton, where she was expected to spend at least part of the winter, and possibly the spring, recuperating after the tragic death of her elder brother.

What Michael was up to, Benna could not guess.

As for her own situation and future, Benna had, after many nights spent alone cogitating on the matter, come to no conclusion as to what she should do. More and more she suspected that anyone she applied to for help—like Mr. Norris or somebody from his firm of solicitors—would be obliged to hand her over to her guardian.

She was increasingly of the terrifying opinion that she would have to wait until she was of legal age before she could take any action.

Once she was twenty-one she would no longer be at the law's mercy, at least.

That would mean that four long, lonely, cold, and desperate years loomed before her.

Benna would be surprised if she managed to survive the next four days.

She was seized by a sudden urge to crawl under some blankets—although she had none—and hide.

Her current predicament was all her fault. Because she'd been an ignorant looby and spent money too freely during her first weeks in Newcastle she was now pockets-to-let. Diggle's jewelry—which she'd been saving until last to sell—had turned out to be cheap and of little value.

And her efforts at finding work in Durham had been less than—

"Another?"

Benna's head jerked up at the sound of the barkeep's rough voice. "Er, no," she muttered.

He narrowed his eyes at her and then looked at her glass, which she'd been nursing and was still three-quarters full even after half an hour. "Summat wrong?" he demanded.

"No, it's good." She lifted the glass and took a small sip, trying not to grimace; no matter how much she tried, she could not like porter.

"Where you from?"

"Er, up north."

"You sound funny." His eyes, which had already been squinty, narrowed so much that Benna wondered how he could see. "You sound—"

"You drunken no-count lout!" somebody shouted outside the taproom. "This is the end for you. By the time I'm done noisin' your name about you won't be able to get a job muckin' stalls in John o' Groats."

Loud, braying laughter met this threat. "You need me, Courtney," another voice countered none too soberly. "Got a bloke waitin'. You can't—"

"You shut it. I could pluck a lad off the street who'd be of more use to me than you." There was a long pause and then, "Oi! You there! Spider-shanks."

"He's talkin' to you, lad," the barkeep said to Benna, jerking his chin toward the taproom door.

Benna turned to find the innkeeper, whom she'd spoken to an hour earlier, hovering in the doorway.

Good God. What had she done now?

"Me?" she said in a squeaky voice that made the other three patrons at the bar laugh.

"Aye, you. You said you were lookin' for work. I ain't got no stable lad job, but if you can sit a horse without falling off then you're hired."

The same drunken voice, no longer amused, shouted, "Now see here, Courtney, you're not really gonna—"

"Well, boy?" the innkeeper demanded impatiently, ignoring the other man. "Do you want a job, or don't you?"

***

Riding post, it turned out, was far easier than delivering express mail.

It helped that the inn owner, Courtney—or Mr. Courtland— paired Benna with the Stag's most experienced post boy, Jimmy Hutchinson. To call Jimmy a boy was misleading since he was a few years over fifty.

Not only had Jimmy trained more new post boys than most people had forgotten, but he was also a celebrity of sorts, having once ridden five back-to-back stages between Easingwold and York, clocking an impressive one hundred and thirty miles in a day.

Jimmy rode the wheel—the left-handed horse closest to the chaise—and Benna rode the front horse, which meant all she had to do was follow Jimmy's shouted directions and stay on the horse.

The worst part of the trip was wearing a spare postilion boot that Mr. Courtland had flung at her, along with the white leather breeches and red coat that were the Stag's Head's livery.

The breeches were so loose she had to tie them up with some bailing twine, the sleeves of the coat were too short and pinched at her armpits, but it was the right boot that tormented her—the one reinforced with wood to keep her leg from getting crushed between

47

the coach horses. It was so small that her toes were numb by the time they arrived at their destination.

"You've made an enemy in Gary Collins," Jimmy said to Benna as the two of them lounged in the corner of the warm kitchen.

"Who's Gary?" Benna asked, massaging her little toe, which seemed to be permanently blue.

The older man took a few deep puffs, not speaking until the bowl of his pipe had caught. "The lad whose job you took."

"I didn't take—"

An inn wench popped into the kitchen bearing two tankards. "Here ye go, Jimmy."

"Ta, Molly."

Molly winked at Benna and set down her ale with a thump. "And this is for you, pretty lad."

Benna blushed, which made the girl laugh. "Thank you, miss."

"Ooooh, this one's got the manners of a lord." Molly ruffled Benna's hair and disappeared back into the tap room.

"I didn't take Gary's job," Benna repeated, stretching her toes and wincing. "Mr. Courtland discharged him and offered the position to me."

"*Ooh la-la,*" Jimmy mocked, his eyes wide. "Listen to them break-teeth words. You born a nobleman, lad?"

Benna mentally castigated herself for forgetting to disguise her accent. It was rather lowering that, in the time that she'd been on her own, it had been her voice, rather than her person, that had garnered the most suspicion.

Nobody seemed to doubt for a moment that she was a young man, but almost everyone she met raised an eyebrow whenever she opened her mouth.

Fortunately for Benna, Jimmy liked the sound of his own voice too much to require her to talk. He was also great friends with all the inn employees and they didn't spend so much as a penny for their eating and drinking.

Once their horses had been baited and rested, they took another chaise back to the Stag's Head, arriving just after eleven-thirty that night.

Benna was so tired that she could hardly keep her eyes open. And her lower body seemed to have gone the way of the toes on her right foot and become numb.

When she slid off her horse, her legs crumpled beneath her and she fell onto her bottom in the middle of the inn courtyard, much to the amusement of Jimmy and an ostler.

Benna didn't bother trying to get up.

Perhaps they would let me curl up in a corner somewhere and sleep?

But Jimmy held out a hand, still chuckling. He was at least six inches shorter than Benna but he was strong and wiry. Once she was on her feet, he grinned up at her. "You'll get used to it, lad. I'll settle up with Courtland. You go grab a cot and get some kip. We're out again at first light."

Benna was too tired to speak, every bit of energy needed to walk.

Mr. Courtland had showed her the post boy quarters—an abandoned stable block—when he'd given her the inn livery to change into.

Outside the building was a lantern hanging on a hook, but it was dark.

Benna didn't care; she could feel her way by touch to an empty cot and—

"There ye are, ye bastard!"

Something hard—a boot?—slammed into Benna's belly.

"*Oooff!*" For the second time in as many minutes she fell to the ground.

"Think ye can steal my job, eh? Lift 'im up for me, Nigel, you get 'is other arm, Bob."

Hands closed around Benna's shoulders and yanked her to her feet.

'I'll teach ye," a fury-filled voice muttered.

And then her head exploded, lights and pain and a dull ringing sound, like somebody was beating a cowbell with a hammer.

She cowered, trying to lift her arms to guard against more blows, but the men behind her held her immobile.

"Lad's got a head like a rock," the first voice—Gary?—said, causing his mates to laugh.

49

A fist connected with her ribs and Benna doubled over, a yellow light flaring behind her eyelids.

"Now, now, three against one—how unsporting," a new voice drawled.

As much pain as Benna was feeling she was aware enough to notice that the voice was male and undeniably of the higher orders.

"Who the fuck'r you?" Gary demanded.

"That's hardly your concern, my lad."

"Christ, Gary, he's got a pistol."

The hands that had been holding her up disappeared and Benna slid to the ground a third time. She rolled onto her side, tucked her chin to her chest, and curled her arms around her aching ribs and belly.

She was only vaguely aware of the sound of boots retreating, and then nothing.

The light, she realized, wasn't in her head, but from a lantern.

She opened her eyes a crack and looked up into the angelic visage of her rescuer. "Hello, lad."

"Who—who—"

"Name's Morecambe, Geoffrey Morecambe. You're lucky I just happened to be passing this way. Can you stand?"

Benna nodded. "Thank you for your help. But I'm afraid I shall need a bit of assistance." She extended a shaking hand.

Her savior cocked his head and smiled, exposing white, even teeth to add to his perfection. "Listen to you—speaking the king's English just like a bloody duke." His bright blue eyes flickered over Benna's person. "And wearing postilion livery. Intriguing."

Before Benna could formulate a response, he grabbed her hand and pulled her to her feet.

Benna groaned and swayed.

"Here then, don't topple over. Put your arm over my shoulder."

Benna tried to lift her arm but it refused to obey her. She began to list to one side.

"No, no. Don't—Blast and damn," he muttered, catching her in strong arms when she would have slid down yet again. "You've got to help me a bit, lad. Here, let me get my arm under—"

Benna felt a hand brush the side of her breast; the hand froze.

"What in the—" The hand cupped her breast and squeezed. "Bloody hell, you're a girl!"

And that was the last thing Benna heard before everything went blessedly black.

Chapter Six

Cornwall
1817
Present Day

*J*ago had three separate lists along with all the other paperwork he needed for his meetings with solicitors, bankers, and men of business.

"You won't forget, will you, Uncle?" His youngest niece's tentative voice pulled him from his contemplation of the day ahead.

Jago feigned a vague expression. "Forget what, my dear?"

Mariah's sharp chin and cheekbones, more like Jago's side of the family than her mother's, tightened in a comical mask of frustration. "*Uncle.*"

Jago lightly flicked a finger over her clenched jaw; she looked so young and girlish, even though she was seventeen. "No, Mariah, of course I won't forget. You want me to remind Ben to be on the lookout for a black or gray horse with four white socks, is that correct?"

She grinned in a way that melted his heart. How his brother could have been so dismissive of his daughters mystified Jago. Although he'd only gotten to know his nieces since Cadan's death he already appreciated having them in his life and enjoyed spending time with them. He was glad they were his responsibility, even if anxiety for their future kept him awake nights.

Catherine sidled up beside her sister, her large blue eyes beseeching. "And you won't forget my jonquil ribbon or—"

"Girls," their mother chided. "He's your uncle, not your footman."

His nieces flushed.

Jago gave them a reassuring smile. "Don't worry, I shan't forget any of my instructions." He turned to Claire, pleased to see her up and about so early in the day. Although she still was far too pale and thin, he thought the reduction of laudanum was beginning to make a difference.

"I'm sorry that I can't take all of you with me this time," he told his sister-in-law, "but it will be a quick, hectic trip filled with business."

A flicker of anxiety passed over Claire's limpid blue eyes. "I hope you discover good news."

Jago was not so optimistic, but he kept that unhelpful thought to himself.

Instead, he said, "Next time, I promise we'll all go and make a small holiday of it."

The sound of carriage wheels reached his ears.

"I'd better get going." He let himself out of the foyer—which reminded him again that he needed to engage at least one footman—and then froze on the top step, gawking at the coach like a love-struck youth.

"Did you build me a new coach, Ben?" He gazed from the highly polished carriage to his liveried stable master.

The boy grinned and looked down at his boots, his ears bright scarlet beneath his hat.

Jago handed his leather doctor's satchel—now crammed with documents rather than medical implements—to Ben before taking a walk around the coach. He ran his fingers over the slick lacquer. "You are a miracle worker."

"It's nothing, my lord. Just a little beeswax and turpentine."

"It's a damned sight more than that," Jago demurred as he dropped to his haunches to look beneath the coach, which was oiled and free of dirt, dust, cobwebs and even rust, just like a brand-new chassis.

He glanced up at the boy. "Where did you learn to do such work?"

Because Jago had hired the lad directly from Stephen Worth, he'd skipped investigating Ben's background, certain that the American would have already done all that. As a result, he knew little about him.

"Er, my first job was at a smithy in a little village in the North you've probably never heard of, my lord."

"I thought you were from Bristol?"

"Oh, I moved there when I was still quite young."

Jago stood, his knees protesting loudly as he straightened. "Young? You mean as opposed to now when you are so terribly old?'

"I am twenty, my lord."

Twenty? Jago looked at the tall, thin boy, whose eyes were almost on a level with his own. Behind Ben's smudged spectacles were big, round eyes that were an unusual shade of pale blue—almost turquoise. His face, which was deeply tanned from the sun, sported a nose that would have done a Roman senator proud. There was hardly a hint of golden down on Ben's smooth cheeks and his lips were red and bow-shaped, almost girlish.

Jago would have put him closer to seventeen than twenty and he wondered if the boy might be fibbing about his age to help him get work.

Ben flushed under his inspection and lowered his eyes. Eyelashes as thick and pale as freshly made straw brooms swept his tanned cheeks. Sometimes the boy looked downright—

The massive front door swung open.

"You forgot this, Uncle Jago." Catherine ran down the steps, holding out a brown paper package, her eyes on young Piddock rather than Jago.

He took the package, looking from his niece to Ben, who was staring fixedly at his boots.

"Er, thank you, Catherine. Your mother would have been vexed with me if I'd left this behind."

Catherine didn't seem to hear him, her gaze riveted on the young man.

For his part, Ben kept his eyes down, absently spinning his single spur with the toe of his other boot.

Jago looked between the two youngsters and frowned. *Hmmm. This did not look good.*

"Well, I'd better be off," he said.

Catherine's head jerked up and she smiled brightly. "Goodbye, Uncle."

Once Jago was settled inside the coach he watched through the carriage window as Catherine stared at Piddock, adoration writ large over her pretty face.

The boy touched his forelock to her but did not linger.

A moment later the carriage rolled forward and Jago relaxed against the buttery brown leather, which Ben had treated with some miraculous substance to make it glow. He stroked the supple hide absently, pondering his niece's expression. So, Catherine was enamored of his new stable master, was she?

Well, he supposed young women were drawn to handsome young men, even if they were not of the appropriate status. It was an attraction that occurred all too often.

It didn't help that Ben seemed to be a rather singular individual— even Jago found the younger man interesting.

Catherine had lived a sheltered existence and behaved with the fresh openness of a much younger woman. Jago could only hope that she could keep her infatuation in check.

Fortunately, Ben struck him as a solid lad who was too keen to keep his position to meddle with the daughter of the house.

He hoped.

An image of the boy's earnest blue eyes flashed through his mind.

Jago smiled to himself, relief flooding his belly. Yes, he felt sure that he could rely on Ben to be both honorable and truthful.

***

Truro was a bustling town and the economic and social center of Cornwall. While it was nothing to London, Oxford, or even Manchester—where Jago had first practiced medicine—Jago still had a soft spot for it.

The Crown and Dragon was not the most appropriate place for an earl to lodge, but the doctor in him felt more comfortable in the modest hostelry. Not to mention it was far easier on his already over-burdened purse.

Jago was just gathering up the hospital plans he'd been studying when the door opened.

He looked at Ben's eager, earnest face and couldn't help smiling. "You needn't break your neck getting the door for me, Ben. I've been opening my own doors for many years."

S.M. LaViolette

"It is my pleasure, my lord."

"You're heading directly to the auction, I collect?" Jago asked.

"Yes, my lord. I'll have missed the morning lot but there is a second one just after noon."

"Very good. Don't forget to visit the hiring agency, too."

"Yes, my lord."

"Engage a room for me—something with a private parlor for my dinner—and see that this is taken up along with my other luggage." He handed the hospital plans to the lad and then hopped out of the coach. He hesitated, and then said, "I shall want a game tonight—after my meal. I daresay the inn keeps a chess set, see that it is set up in my room."

"Very good, sir."

Jago noticed that Ben's cheeks were more than a little fiery and something occurred to him. "Er, actually, now that I think of it, a young handsome man like yourself might be wishing to go out on the town this evening. If that's the case, you should—"

"I have no such plans, my lord." Ben cleared his throat, eyes downcast. "I would enjoy beating you again this evening."

Jago threw back his head and laughed at the boy's uncharacteristic flare of humor. "You cheeky cockerel," he chided.

"I beg your pardon, my lord," Ben said, a smile tugging at his lips.

"No you don't, you're quite proud of delivering such a leveler. Well," he said, picking up his satchel. "I'd better be off and leave you to it, then."

Ben's amusement slid away and his face took on a pained aspect. "Er, could I not take you to your destination, sir? Or perhaps engage a hack for you?"

"I find that I am missing my exercise these days, Ben. If I don't move around a bit more, I am in danger of becoming portly."

Ben's eyes flickered over him and the younger man's face darkened before he glanced away. "Aye, my lord," he mumbled.

"I shan't be back until near five," Jago said, and then strode in the direction of the street.

It would be a full day; not only did he have several meetings, but he also needed to find time to visit the shops on the high street.

The need for new clothing was both irksome and embarrassing. But, as much as he hated to admit it, he could no longer dress only to please himself. While his servants and family seemed to accept him for what he was—a country doctor who'd unexpectedly inherited an earldom—he owed it to the people who relied on him to show respect for both them and the title he now carried.

It did not matter that it made no sense to spend money he could ill afford. The sad truth was that people expected a man to look the part

Jago turned onto Pydar Street and found himself in the thick of traffic. He hadn't been to Truro since before his brother had banished him and was astonished by how—

"Such a serious expression."

Jago's head jerked up at the sound of the familiar voice.

Directly ahead of him was Ria, who looked to have just stepped out of a milliner's shop. Two liveried footmen waited a short distance away, their arms piled with boxes.

"Ria, what are you doing here?" The question was both rude and foolish; her country house was only a few miles away from Lenshurst Park. Why wouldn't she be shopping in Truro?

"You look as though you were far away, Jago—perhaps back in your quaint village, doing a bit of doctoring?"

He ignored her taunting. "It is true that my mind was elsewhere."

"But you are here, now." Her eyes glinted behind a frothy fall of mint green netting that artistically spilled off her tiny hat. She smiled, exposing a fetching dimple at the corner of her lush mouth. "What are you doing in our provincial little town?" Her gaze flickered over his worn blue coat and best buckskins before pausing on his scuffed, dull top boots. "Clothes shopping?"

Jago smiled. "Is it so obvious?"

It was her turn to ignore a question. "We must have dinner together."

"I'm afraid I am only here tonight."

"Tonight is perfect. "

"I am staying at the Crown, Ria. It is not really an appropriate—"

"Don't be silly. I don't want dinner at your grubby little inn, Jago, but at my town house."

"I was not aware you kept a house here." But then, why would he know anything about her or her houses?

"Henry did not care for the country and often preferred to stay here rather than at Stanford Hall," Ria explained, laying a delicate, kid-sheathed hand on his arm. "*Do* let's be friends again." Her green eyes had turned soft and imploring.

Astoundingly, as he stared at her beautiful face another face rose up in his mind's eye: that of his young stable master, looking so pleased at delivering such a wicked cut to his employer just a few moments earlier.

"I'm sorry, Ria. I've made plans—a business meeting. I'm afraid I can't change things at this point."

Her pleasant expression scarcely flickered. "Of course. I understand. But you do know we must talk—alone—at some point?" She cocked her head, her expression arch and playful, but her eyes as hard as polished jade. "I won't wait for your decision forever, Jago. You might be my most pleasant option, but you are hardly the only one."

Jago met her glittering, expectant gaze and felt more than a little revulsion. Was this really what his future held? Marrying the same woman he'd fled from all those years before?

A woman who made him hate himself for what he'd done.

The thought of being with her for the rest of his life left him feeling hopeless and bleak.

But blaming Ria was hardly fair; after all, it had been Jago who'd agreed to a duel with his best friend, not her—even if she had been the catalyst.

He knew she was right about needing to talk; she held the whip hand when it came to any union between them and he would be a fool to dismiss her offer without due consideration.

But Jago still clung, probably foolishly, to the hope that the earldom could be salvaged without such a sacrifice.

He forced himself to smile at her. "I agree, Ria. We must talk. Soon. But not today."

***

Bester and Lodge auction house was on Bodmin Street, a quarter of an hour walk from the inn.

The area just outside the auction house was noisy, crowded, and even managed to have a few live flies buzzing about this late in the year.

This wasn't Benna's first auction, so at least she wasn't entirely adrift as to how matters proceeded. Tom had once snuck her into an auction when she'd gone to stay in her father's Edinburgh house.

Bester and Lodge was, by contrast, considerably less impressive. Not only were there no liveried attendants to distribute auction pamphlets and wait on buyers, but there was an overall dearth of lackeys, liveried or not, and the auction list wasn't printed, but hand-written in chalk on various slates.

Benna followed the thin crowd toward where one such list was posted. She'd brought her account book with her and jotted down a few notes about today's offerings before making her way to the smaller arena, where the hacking horses would be displayed.

Lord Trebolton had told her the girls' preferences when it came to mounts but had emphasized that the final decisions were Benna's alone.

The afternoon flew by in a blur as she sat through lot after lot.

By the third hour she'd already purchased a liver chestnut—with four socks—for Mariah and an attractive blue roan for Catherine.

As far as carriage horses went, she'd ended up buying some respectable blood bays but had bid rather higher than she'd liked. Still, they were worth it and were head and shoulders above the other offerings. And their coloring would look spectacular with the dignified old coach, which, when buffed, had proven to be a reddish mahogany.

Still remaining on her list was a hack for Lady Trebolton, who apparently did not much care for riding and had requested only that Benna find her a docile mount.

The auctioneer called out the bay mare that Benna had been waiting for and the groom walked the horse around the arena. Benna bit her lip. She was a bit short in the neck but was the best of the three she'd seen. Benna was about to make a bid when a small commotion near the entrance caught her attention.

Two men entered and an auction house attendant hurried over. The men had their backs to Benna but, judging by their multi-caped coats and tall beaver hats, they were rich young bucks.

The taller one turned to survey the auction room.

Time slowed and then stopped.

Benna took a step back, bumping into the man standing off to her side, a white-haired older gentleman who'd also bid on the carriage horses.

He reached out a big, work-scarred hand to steady her. "All right, lad?" he asked, leaning toward her and blocking her view of Lord Richard Fenwick, a nightmare face she'd only seen in her dreams these past six years.

Benna looked down into his concerned gray eyes and smiled. "Yes, sir," she said, not needing to force her voice to be husky this time. "Just a wee bit tired."

The old man's face creased into a grin. "Burning the midnight oil last night, were ye?" He raised his snowy brows waggishly and laughed.

Benna gave a weak chuckle. "I recognize one of those men, but can't recall his name," she said, jerking her chin toward Fenwick. "Is he from around here?"

The man turned to look at the younger men. "I dunno the one in the green coat but the one on the left is from Devoran—about four miles from here. Viss count Fenwick is the name; he's Lord Devoran's heir." He grimaced. "A bad piece o' work by all accounts. You best stay clear a that one, lad."

Benna nodded and then backed in the direction of the north entrance to the auction arena—the opposite side from Lord Fenwick and his friend—hovering at the rear of the small crowd of bidders.

It took everything she had to bid on the hack and not run from the suddenly claustrophobic arena. Thankfully, nobody bid against her and the sale was quick.

As Benna headed to the clerk for the paperwork she kept her eyes on Fenwick and his companion, both of whom were observing the livestock with the condescending smirks of London swells.

Once she was outside in the empty yard she sagged against the nearest wall, her heart pounding so loudly it blocked out the noise around her.

You need to calm yourself. Fenwick didn't see you, and likely would not have recognized you if he had.

Benna knew that was true. Even so, the appearance of somebody who knew who she was—and who knew Michael—sent a chill through her.

It just as easily could have been her cousin here today.

Benna had grown complacent. She needed to remember that no place was safe from Michael, no matter how seemingly remote.

***

After what he'd learned today, all Jago wanted to do was go sit in a gloomy, quiet room and drink himself blind.

Or perhaps board a packet to France and never look back.

His reaction shamed him; he had never been a man to shirk his duty.

But then he'd never found himself in the position he did now: in danger of losing everything his family had built over the last three hundred years.

Jago finished tying his cravat, opting for his usual, humble mail coach rather than the fussier design the tailor had tried to convince him to adopt.

He grimaced at what he saw in the looking glass—more debt.

Well, he'd wanted new clothing and there it was. The tailor, a man named Boone, had been thrilled when Jago walked into his shop today. In fact, Boone had been the only person happy to see Jago that day.

He knew that was only because the unfortunate tailor had no clue that his new aristocratic customer was, in the raw parlance of the street, badly dipped.

Upon learning what Jago needed—almost everything—Boone had immediately brought out several garments that he'd just finished making for another client.

"You're not concerned about angering another customer?" Jago had asked, looking at three reflections of himself wearing a new coat in the triple glass. It was an amazingly close fit; with only a few minor alterations the garment would be perfect.

The tailor smiled as he chalked and pinned several places. "He's not due to pick up his order for two weeks. I'll have something for him by then and he'll never be the wiser, my lord. Now," he'd gestured to the rack of garments he'd brought out. "While one of my seamstresses makes these alterations may I show you this waistcoat …"

Jago frowned at his reflection. It wasn't that the clothing was not tasteful or well-fitting.

No, what bothered him was that he was hardly in a position to pay for it. Oh, he had ample money of his own—not derived from the estate—set aside to cover the expenditures he was making—horses, clothing, more servants—but those funds would not last forever.

And all the money Jago had in his personal accounts wouldn't come close to paying the debt he'd discovered today.

His brother, it appeared, had taken out three loans, using every piece of unentailed property that belonged to the earldom as collateral.

There had been *no* record of any of the loans in the paperwork he'd thus far combed through. All three had been granted within a twenty-four-hour period just before Cadan's death. According to the two bankers he'd spoken to today, his brother had collected the loans in banknotes—which was unusual.

And all three loans would mature less than two months from now.

A knock on the door pulled him away from his nightmarish thoughts.

"Come in."

The door opened and Ben entered bearing Jago's Hessians.

The boy halted and his eyes widened when he saw Jago.

"What? Surprised to see me looking like something other than a down-at-heel country doctor?"

Ben's face flushed. "Oh no, my lord," he mumbled, dropping his gaze to his own highly polished boots.

"These are ready, my lord."

Jago peered down at his reflection in the leather. "Who knew these old fellows could ever look so good."

The boy dropped to his knees and held one of the boots at the ready.

Jago was oddly affected by the sight of his bowed head. "You impress me daily with the addition of new talents, Ben: postilion, groom, stable master, and now batman."

Ben looked up, his blue gaze uncharacteristically direct behind his thick spectacles. "Begging your pardon, my lord, but you need a valet."

Jago blinked.

Ben dropped his head. "Sorry, my lord."

The muttered words were so contrite that Jago smiled as he slipped his foot into the waiting boot. "You needn't apologize, Ben. I know I need to engage a personal servant and quit going about like a ragamuffin."

"I didn't mean—"

"I am only teasing you." He slipped his foot into the second boot and Ben tweaked one of the worn tassels before standing up.

"I can take your coat and breeches with me and see that they are pressed and made ready for the morning, sir."

"Is valeting yet another of your talents?"

"My last master before Mr. Worth trained me up as his batman, my lord."

"I thought Mr. Worth hired you at a posting inn in Bristol?"

"He did, sir. I took that job after I left my previous position."

"How long did you work as a batman?"

Ben cleared his throat and shuffled his feet. "Er, about five years, my lord."

"Goodness—you must be quite skilled. Perhaps I should hire you as my batman and engage a new stable master?"

Ben's expression was so horrified that it surprised a laugh out of Jago.

"I can see you do not find that prospect appealing."

Jago hadn't believed it was possible for the lad to look more embarrassed. "Oh, no sir, not at all. I mean, it would be an honor to valet you, of course. If that is what—"

"Hush, Ben. I am merely roasting you. I recall well what you said several nights ago."

"Sir?"

"About preferring to work with horses rather than people."

Ben opened his mouth—no doubt to demur—but Jago stopped him. "Thank you for offering to see to my clothes for tomorrow—I'll take you up on that. I'd rather trust the task to you than the inn servants."

"Of course, sir." Ben picked up Jago's discarded coat and breeches and draped them over his arm. "Your private parlor is waiting for you, my lord. Shall I tell the innkeeper you are ready for your dinner?"

"Yes, please do so."

Ben turned to go.

Suddenly, the prospect of a meal spent with only the day's thoughts for company seemed too grim to be borne. Jago almost wished that he'd accepted Ria's invitation; even an evening spent enduring incessant baiting would be preferable to eating alone after the day he'd had.

Before he could overthink the matter, he said, "Ben?"

The boy turned, his hand on the doorknob. "My lord?"

"Tell the innkeeper to set another cover."

"You have a guest coming, sir?"

"You are my guest, Ben. It occurs to me that you can tell me how your business went today while eating our supper."

Ben's eyes widened.

Jago ignored his surprise and his own qualms, as well. "Go on, Ben. Tell Mr. Bickford you'll be dining with me. I'll join you after a moment."

The younger man nodded obediently and left the room.

Jago stared at his reflection in the glass.

What the devil was wrong with him? Why in the world would he turn down dinner with Ria—who, after what he'd learned today, he suspected he'd need to start courting—to eat a meal with a servant?

Unfortunately, Jago had no answer for those questions. At least none that didn't generate even more questions.

Chapter Seven

Bath
1813
Five-ish Years Ago

enna set the glass of whiskey on Geoffrey's right side and
then returned to her position against the wall—right next to
the other three manservants who'd accompanied their
masters to the Marquess of Dorking's exclusive town house.

From her vantage point she could only directly see the cards
belonging to the gentleman on Geoffrey's left, Mr. Arthur Nevis.

Placing the drink on Geoff's right meant that her employer
should keep bidding based on what Benna saw in Mr. Nevis's hand.

Benna glanced at the tall longcase clock, the glass front of which,
not coincidentally, showed a blurry reflection of Mr. Nevis's
partner's—Viscount Featherstone—hand.

Even if Featherstone wasn't currently a victim of a world-class
card sharp—Geoff—he still would have lost money tonight. The
viscount wasn't just an unpleasant person, he was also a horrid card
player.

Benna covered her mouth and softly cleared her throat to
indicate that Featherstone had no stoppers in hearts.

Her action—as quiet as it was—earned a displeased look from
the viscount. "I say, Morecambe, send your man away if he's going to
make such a bloody racket."

Geoffrey turned to give Benna a stern look. "Mind yourself,
Piddock."

"Beg pardon, sir." Benna bowed her head in an act of contrition.

The viscount gave an angry sniff and then bid, rather than passed—which is what Mr. Nevin's play had indicated his partner should do.

It would be another lucrative evening for her employer.

***

Benna had just stripped off her linen shirt and tossed it into the bin when she heard an angry shout and the sound of smashing glass. The noises came from the direction of the master chambers.

She smirked; that would be Lady Taunton.

There was a second yell—also female—and then the *thud* of a slamming door and rapidly diminishing footfalls.

So, Geoffrey had finally managed to shed himself of the beautiful, but demanding, countess.

Benna told herself the leaping feeling in her chest was merely relief, but that was a lie.

The truth was that she'd become foolishly infatuated with her savior by her second week working for him. How could she not? After all, Geoff had saved her from a vicious beating—not to mention rescuing her from likely exposure.

Back then, Benna had believed Geoff was perfect.

But a little over a year of working for the Honorable Geoffrey Morecambe had opened her eyes when it came to the gorgeous gamester's less-than-sterling character.

Unfortunately, time had done nothing to diminish Benna's lust for the angelic-looking man's body even though she now knew him to be a self-indulgent, self-absorbed, and self-centered rogue. Basically, if the word had *self* in it, it applied to Geoffrey.

The youngest son of Baron Morecambe, Geoffrey had long ago been cut off by all his relatives. If she had to guess his age, she would have put him somewhere in his mid-to-late-thirties.

As selfish as he was, Benna couldn't really complain about her life with him. After all, before joining up with Geoff she had been alone, hungry, homeless, poor, and vulnerable.

While working for him was not always easy on her conscience, he was not, by and large, a demanding master.

Most importantly, she felt safe with him and no longer lived in constant terror that Michael would swoop down on her in the middle of the night.

She also liked Geoff's itinerant habits, which had brought them to London, a city that Benna had desperately wished to visit since leaving Wake House.

Unfortunately, the call she'd paid on the firm of Norris and Ridgewick had been more than a little disappointing.

Immediately upon reaching London Benna had made the acquaintance of a lowly clerk at the firm. For the inexpensive cost of a few pints of ale the man had told her several things.

First, Mr. Norris the elder, whom Bernna had met, was dead. The new head of the firm was Norris's grandson, a man barely in his twenties, who'd never even met Benna's father.

Second, Mr. Ridgewick the elder had passed on to his final reward almost twenty years earlier.

And third, the firm had once managed Benna's trust, but hadn't done so since a few years before her brother David's death. The clerk had no information about who oversaw the trust now.

Benna's grand plan—such as it was—had been to present herself to the older Norris and hope that he recognized her. After he'd gotten over his shock and anger at learning the Duchess of Wake's guardian had forced her to work as a servant, they would confront Michael and wrest the dukedom from his evil clutches.

Benna now knew that her *plan* was actually more of a child's fantasy, something that kept her going on days when she wanted to just give up.

For several months after her depressing visit to London she'd been … desolate.

It had occurred to her, for the first time ever, that she might never regain her name, her title, or her life.

It had also occurred to her that *this*—what she had now—was her life: she would be a servant until she died.

And finally, it had occurred to her that she should kill Michael. That was the only sure way to stop him and end the nightmare.

The longer she waited, the more he would establish himself. If she waited for her legal age, or until she had enough money to hire somebody, or—God forbid—even longer, until she came into her trust, there might be nothing left.

In the months after London she'd thought of killing him every single day. On some of those days she'd had to fight hard against the impulse, fully aware that it would only end in misery for her.

But a person could only live on the outside of their skin for so long without going mad.

The banalities of daily life had a way of dulling the sharp edges. And so, almost without realizing it, Benna discovered that she'd resigned herself to waiting.

After all, what were her other choices?

Besides, her life with Geoff was, in general, easy enough. There were anxious moments here and there when a card-player questioned Geoffrey's astoundingly good fortune. But her employer had been supporting himself at the gaming table for too long to ever respond to goads or challenges.Instead, when a situation became too unfriendly, they would pack their bags, slip out of town, and pop up in a new city.

It was now Benna who packed their bags, settled their lodging bill, and arranged for transportation to Geoffrey's next destination of choice.

She had, without quite realizing it, become Geoff's only servant since her third month with him, when he'd decided to discharge his expensive—and demanding—valet.

Benna not only learned to valet him and manage his affairs, but Geoff taught her the finer points of fuzzing the cards, to use the vulgar parlance.

In addition to gaming, he also earned his living at the various races scattered around Britain. Wagering on horse races was something Benna was quite good at, given her family's history of breeding more than its fair share of winners on the flat.

Last, but not least, was the income Geoff derived from fleecing the wealthy ladies who fell before his charms like wheat before a scythe.

Rather than diminish over time—as she had hoped—Benna's jealousy of Geoff's lovers seemed to grow with each month that passed. She was rapidly concluding that struggling against physical attraction was a losing battle.

It didn't matter that she knew Geoff was rotten to the core. Nor did it matter that she'd watched him use and then ruthlessly discard dozens of women when he was finished with them.

If there was a God—something Benna was no longer sure of given how much ugliness she'd seen in the world over the past year—he must have spent all his efforts on polishing Geoff's perfect appearance. Because the man had nothing inside him other than a bottomless hunger for money.

The more Benna learned about him, the more amazed she was that he'd ever put himself out to save her that night in Durham.

"Sometimes I stun myself with how wretched I am," Geoff had admitted one evening when Benna had lost her temper and confronted him after he'd sharped a lady so old that she could scarcely see the spots on the playing cards.

His uncharacteristic admission had stopped Benna in mid-scold. "Well," she'd finally managed to say, "You can't be all bad; you *did* save me that night."

Geoff had given her one of his maddeningly mocking smiles. "I only put myself out because I knew, even then, how useful you'd be to me."

Months later—after Geoff had methodically decimated any morals Benna might have still retained—she had understood that he hadn't been speaking in jest.

But as much as she might despise his criminal behavior on occasion, she couldn't deny that it provided them both with a comfortable living.

Indeed, the profits from their gaming were so prodigious that Benna didn't understand why Geoff had to keep bilking women by bedding them and charming expensive gewgaws and gifts of money out of them.

Well, that wasn't true; she knew *exactly* what Geoff got out of the transactions besides money.

Along with the surge of jealousy in her belly, Benna also felt a not unpleasant tingling in her sex. The sensation had become increasingly familiar, assaulting her whenever she thought about Geoffrey and what he got up to in his bedchamber.

The only way to rid herself of the tingling was to rub between her legs until it went away, an agreeable activity that, unfortunately, always managed to leave her feeling guilty.

Benna shoved down both her drawers and the velvet breeches of the expensive livery that Geoff liked her to wear and stepped out of them.

She'd just laid the breeches over a chair when she heard the door open.

Benna spun around, still clutching her drawers, which she raised to her chest while dropping her other hand to cover her mound.

Geoffrey was leaning against the doorway, wearing the blue Chinese silk robe she'd seen often. "Well, well, well, look what you've been hiding under your clothes, Ben."

His robe hung open, exposing a beautiful body that she couldn't seem to see often enough.

Benna's gaze dropped to the most masculine part of him.

She seen him hard before—many times—because it was his habit to strut about naked whenever he pleased.

Like her, Geoff was fair skinned, but his hair was a lovely golden blond rather than Benna's freakish white, which she dyed, even though Geoff often mocked her for it.

"If you're going to try and hide the color, you'll have to do your eyebrows while you're about it," he'd said the first day she worked for him. And so she now carefully darkened her brows, too.

He cocked his head at her, making Benna realize that she was still staring at him. "Why do you look so nervous, Ben? You see me thus daily." Geoff chuckled, the action flexing the tight basketry of muscles that comprised his abdomen. He spread his hands and held his arms out to the sides, as if presenting his person to her like an offering "I can only assume that you are discomposed that I am finally seeing *you* without even a stitch."

He was right; she was discomposed. Actually, *mortified* would be a better word.

It was true that she saw him in various stages of undress ever since she'd taken on the task of valeting him.

But Geoff was the first man to see Benna naked. And he was a connoisseur of beautiful women. And Benna—who was as voluptuous as a stork and easily able to masquerade as a man—was far from beautiful.

"Hmmm." He prowled toward her in the snake-hipped way he had. "Let me look at you, my dear."

Benna took a step back and immediately bumped into the arm of the chair.

Geoffrey didn't stop coming toward her until she could see the magnificent blue of his irises. He was shorter than her—perhaps by two inches—but he was well-developed and muscular, the body of a man in his prime.

He pried the cotton drawers from her clenched fingers and tossed them aside, staring up at her, the nostrils of his aquiline nose flaring slightly. "Just how old are you, Ben? I can't seem to recall."

"That's because you never asked me," she said, her naturally deep voice even deeper.

"I didn't?" He grinned, the expression turning his angelic features into something devilish.

"No."

Indeed, Geoff had never asked Benna a single question about her past since the morning she'd woken up to find herself curled up at his feet on the floor of his hired post chaise.

He had merely smiled down at her, told her they were headed to Leeds, mentioned that he was in need of a groom, and then informed her that she would have to swap places with his valet outside on the box at their next change of horses.

"How remiss of me not to have asked your age," Geoff said in a mocking tone. "You may enlighten me, now."

"Eighteen."

His eyes widened. "*No*, how is that possible? Why, I would have guessed fifteen—sixteen at the outside."

Benna forced down the misery she felt at his admission; he could hardly think her much of a woman if he believed she had the body of an adolescent boy.

"*Tsk, tsk*, don't be hurt, kitten," he said, reading her expression far too easily for her comfort. "I'm delighted to learn of your advanced age."

"You are?"

"Oh, yes. You see, I've been restraining myself for some time, now—not an activity at which I excel, mind." His gaze dropped to her chest. "And now I learn, to my intense joy, that I no longer need to exercise such tiresome self-control."

Benna lifted her hands to hide herself from his piercing stare, but his soft, warm fingers brushed hers aside and he cupped the mortifyingly small mounds.

She sucked in a harsh breath at the feel of another person's skin—Geoff's skin—on a part of her body that only she had ever touched.

Mercifully, he kept his eyes on her breasts rather than her flaming face, his expression oddly pensive.

"I believe it might be time for us to move on soon. Lady Taunton has become quite, er, shrill about the night of cards we recently enjoyed at Mrs. Bergeron's house. It seems she doesn't like the thought of sharing me with another."

Either did Benna.

He smiled faintly, as if she'd spoken the words aloud. "The vixen stayed just long enough tonight to work me into a lather." He demonstrated what he meant by pressing his hot, hard length against Benna's belly.

She made an embarrassing gulping sound.

"Did you know that it is dangerously unhealthy for a man's body to get excited and have no release?"

"N-No."

"It is true. I could suffer permanent damage. You wouldn't want that, would you?" He brushed a thumb over her nipple.

Benna whimpered.

"Ah, such pretty little things—and so sensitive, I see."

Both thumbs moved now, sending spirals of pleasure throughout her body.

"I feared that I'd be reduced to spending in my fist tonight," he continued in a conversational tone. "But then I thought about my faithful servant who probably had her ear pressed to the wall."

Benna opened her mouth to demur.

"I recalled the yearning, burning gaze I feel on my body every single time my valet dresses or undresses me."

Benna had long suspected that she was a failure when it came to hiding her infatuation.

Geoff gently tugged on the pebbled, sensitive nubs.

She groaned; surely she'd go mad from the pleasure?

"You are shaking, Ben." He raised his eyes to hers. "Perhaps I will see if I can make you come by touching only your nipples, hmmm?"

Benna was breathing like a winded coach horse, her entire body trembling. There was too much sensation, she'd fly apart; she needed—

"I've seen the way you look at me when I bring home my lovers." Geoffrey pinched a nipple hard enough to hurt and she flinched. "Shhh," he soothed, caressing the aching peak. "Tell me, do you imagine me in my room, giving them pleasure? Do you slide your fingers between your thighs and pretend that it is you with me, instead?" His eyes glinted with smug amusement at whatever he saw on her face.

Benna hated him in that moment.

"Can you hear my lovers when they cry out my name and beg me for more?"

More than once Benna had dressed and gone out into the night rather than listen to their screaming and moaning.

"I can see by your scowl that you don't care to think about that. Do you want what I give them? Just tell me, and you shall have it." His magical stroking ceased. "Well?" he prodded.

"I want it," she whispered without hesitation, more embarrassed than she'd ever been in her life.

"It?" he teased.

"You," she retorted in a raspy voice.

He laughed. "I know you do, darling." He slid a hand down over her belly, his fingers delving into her private curls, sliding between her lower lips—

She bucked, a mortifying groan bursting out of her mouth before she could catch it.

"Mmmm, so wet and hot." He stroked from just below her core to her entrance, willfully avoiding that most sensitive part of her. "Such a good, eager girl to open yourself up for me."

73

Benna hadn't realized that she'd moved her feet apart to encourage his exploration and was pushing her hips at him, grinding against his fingers.

She knew the memory of her wanton behavior would haunt her for a long time after.

But she couldn't make herself stop.

"Why look at that beautiful blush. Don't be ashamed of your sensual nature." He toyed with a nipple while his questing finger stroked, finally circling and massaging that part of her that felt so very good when she—

Pleasure ambushed her and Benna cried out loudly enough to startle herself, babbling incoherently as her knees buckled.

Geoffrey gave a triumphant laugh and caught her, scooping her up just as he had the first night they'd met.

"Such a wonderfully responsive body," he praised, carrying her to her cot, where he laid her down.

Groggy with pleasure, Benna turned her head to watch through slitted eyes as he shrugged off his banyan, his erection ruddy, slick, and arched against his belly.

He saw her looking and smiled as he climbed onto the small bed, kneeling between her thighs and nudging apart her knees. "You've never had a man inside you before, have you?"

Benna shook her head.

Something primitive and hungry flickered over his handsome features and she knew that he was pleased.

"Mmmm, how delightful. Don't be afraid, my virginal darling, it will only hurt a little this first time," he whispered against her temple, covering her torso with his while pushing a finger against the entrance to her body and sliding deep inside her.

Benna clenched at the sudden invasion.

"Christ, you're so fucking tight. I can't wait to get inside you. But first, let's get you ready, hmmm? Just relax for me." His thumb circled the exquisitely sensitive spot while he worked her with first one and then two fingers, scissoring and stretching her while he drove her toward the precipice. All the while he murmured words of encouragement, his own breathing roughening.

For the second time that night waves of intense pleasure rippled from her sex, flooding every part of her body.

Benna was so dazed with bliss that she was only vaguely aware that he'd removed his fingers and that something far larger pressed against her swollen flesh.

"Be good and stay relaxed for me," he ordered in a strained voice. "Let your legs fall open wider—yes, just so." Without warning he plunged into her, not stopping until they were pelvis to pelvis.

She yelped at the sudden, sharp pain.

He shuddered, holding her still and full. "Good God you feel like heaven."

The eye-watering agony of penetration quickly gave way to an unpleasant sensation of fullness and Benna squirmed as her body clenched, as if to expel him.

Geoff hissed in a breath. "Lord, don't do that, you'll bring me off too bloody quickly." He easily held her pinned while she writhed beneath him. "Shh, now stop that. It'll be fine in a moment. Just hold still like a good girl."

Benna bit her lip hard enough to bleed and obeyed, more than a little amazed when his words turned out to be truthful.

She began to relax as the discomfort dissipated.

"There's my good girl," he whispered in a shaky voice, almost sounding in pain, himself. "You're so bloody tight it's enough to break me in half." He gave a breathless laugh. "Christ, I'll never last—I'll shame myself."

He withdrew until only his tip breeched her.

Benna had just let out a shaky sigh of relief when he plunged in again, harder this time.

She gave a muffled whimper of surprise.

"Hush now, I know it doesn't hurt," he muttered, withdrawing more quickly than before.

Benna grit her teeth to keep from making any more noises; he was right: it didn't hurt like it had the first time he'd entered her, but it was still far from comfortable.

Somewhere around the tenth stroke Geoffrey changed, becoming somebody else—a wild, primitive man—cursing and grunting and ramming deeply over and over and over again, shaking the bed so violently with his thrusts that Benna feared it would shatter to pieces.

She squeezed her eyes shut and willed her body to relax and accept what was happened.

After a long moment, she felt something begin to build inside her—something … delicious. Benna tilted her hips to chase the feeling, the action bringing him slightly deeper.

"Oh, Christ yes—just like that," he praised, his hips picking up speed.

The sensation was similar to that from earlier, but more elusive … more—

Benna wrapped her legs around his hips, flexing a muscle inside herself in the process.

He cried out hoarsely, "Fuck!" His thrusts becoming jerky and uncontrolled. "Yes!" he shouted, and then he buried himself ballocks-deep and froze, his hard length jerking inside her passage as he spent, flooding her with warmth.

"Bloody hell," he mumbled, collapsing on top of her and crushing her with his weight.

She tasted salt on her lip and quickly wiped her cheeks dry, not wanting him to see her tears.

It turned out that she needn't have worried. Not even thirty seconds passed before she heard soft snore.

He'd fallen asleep.

Benna snorted in disbelief. So, that was what all the fuss was about. She had to admit that she had quite enjoyed herself before he'd shoved inside her. And even that had not been unpleasant toward the end.

She shifted so that his hip bone wasn't digging into her. It was difficult to breathe, but she liked his weight and the feel of his bare skin. He was warm and solid and smelled enticingly of the expensive cologne that he favored.

Tentatively, she raised her hands to stroke the taut, silky skin of his waist, reveling in this opportunity to explore his body.

He muttered something in his sleep and shifted but didn't wake.

Benna wrapped her arms around his body and held him, smiling to herself. It took her a moment to identify her feelings: it was happiness. For the first time since before her brother died, she was happy.

She must have dozed, because she was startled when he moved off her, his feet hitting the wood floor with a soft thud.

Benna watched without speaking as he bent and picked up his robe, his cock now soft and his balls pendulous between his slightly hairy thighs.

He shook out the fine blue silk before slipping it over his shoulders. Only then did he look down at her.

Her stomach clenched at the cool detachment in his eyes and the faint curl of disgust on his lips. "You need to clean yourself up." He gestured to her legs, which she realized were still splayed.

Not only that, but there were smears of blood on her thighs and pelvis.

Benna pushed up onto her elbows and gasped. She wasn't due for her courses for two weeks and was always regular to the day. "What happened? Am I—"

Geoffrey gave a sharp, unamused laugh. "You poor ninny," he said, tying the sash around his waist. "A maiden's cunny bleeds her first time—didn't anyone ever tell you that?" Before she could answer he said, "Unless you want a babe, you need to cleanse yourself thoroughly of my seed."

When Benna merely gaped, irritation flickered across his handsome features and he heaved a sigh of annoyance. "Christ. How is it that you can be so bloody ignorant at your age?" He shoved a hand through his hair. "Don't worry, you can't get with child your first time. But tomorrow go see the apothecary on Hall Road. Tell him you are bedding a servant girl and don't want to put a brat in her belly. He will sell you what you need for the next time."

He turned and strode toward the door without another word.

Benna lay motionless, staring unseeingly at the ceiling in her grim little room.

She felt … strange: dizzy—almost woozy. In fact, she felt remarkably like she had the night she'd been ambushed and pummeled by Gary and his mates.

Geoffrey's words echoed in her head, two of them especially standing out: next time.

Chapter Eight

Cornwall
1817
Present Day

t's just a meal, Benna told herself as she dropped off Lord Trebolton's clothing in her tiny room in the attic and scurried back to the parlor she'd engaged for him earlier in the day.

You know where meals lead, my dear Benna.

Benna had not needed to listen to Geoff's annoying voice all day today. She should have known his silence would never last.

She scratched softly on the parlor door before opening it.

Lord Trebolton was standing before a merry fire, a glass in his hand. He raised it in Benna's direction. "Would you care for a brandy?"

Benna could murder one. But it was never a good idea to muddle her wits with alcohol.

"No thank you, sir. I believe Mr. Bickford has selected an excellent bottle of wine to accompany dinner."

The earl nodded, his gaze on the window, which was dark and steadily pelted by rain. "A good night to stay in." His mouth pulled into a strange little smile, and then he turned to Benna.

"So, tell me about the horses you bought today."

They briefly discussed Benna's purchases at the auction and also her plans to call on the saddler tomorrow and arrange for him to come out to Lenshurst.

"And the employment agency?" Lord Trebolton asked.

"I'd thought to go first thing in the morning."

"While you're there, have them send out some prospects for the positions of valet, footman, gardener, and kitchen and chambermaid. Tell them I'll interview people beginning next week."

"Very good, sir."

The earl must have had good financial news today if he could afford to hire so many new servants.

Benna was surprised by how relieved that made her feel. She liked working at Lenshurst Park and would be happy to make it her last place of employment before she could finally seize control of her home and fortune.

The door opened and Mr. Bickford and two young serving maids laden with trays entered the room.

Benna and the earl took their seats while the servants laid out the food and poured the wine

"Thank you, Mr. Bickford, this looks excellent," the earl said to innkeeper.

"So," Lord Trebolton said, once they'd both served themselves from the impressive bounty arrayed before them. "Tell me about this gentleman you valeted for several years. You must have been very young. Didn't you say you were just recently turned what was it—twenty?"

"That's correct, sir. I started working for Mr. Fenton when I was fourteen. I assisted his valet and groom. Over time, Mr. Fenton fell on hard times and could no longer afford to employ three servants, so I took on both tasks."

"Ah, so he retained you because you were the most efficient."

"Rather because I was so inexpensive."

The earl smiled. "Where did you live during this time?"

"Mr. Fenton liked to travel, so we often moved about."

"A traveling gentleman?"

"Er, yes, sir. He earned his living by his wits."

"I see." The earl nodded and Benna saw the understanding in his eyes. "You say *was*—did he suddenly inherit a competence and was able to give his wits a holiday?"

"No, sir." She hesitated and then added mendaciously, "He was quite an older gentleman and took ill last winter and died."

Very droll, Geoff's voice sounded less than amused.

They ate in silence for a few minutes, nothing but the clinking of cutlery, the crackling of the fire, and wind rattling the windowpanes.

"That's an interesting change you made—going from a batman to a postilion."

"I discovered that I'd developed a taste for traveling," Benna was able to answer without hesitation, having already told this part of her story to Stephen Worth when the American hired her.

"But then you took a job with Mr. Worth after a short time, it would seem. Are you tired of traveling?"

"Mr. Worth made an offer that was difficult to refuse." That was true enough. The man paid more than anyone she'd ever heard of. "It also turned out that the life of a post boy was far more grueling than that of an itinerant gentleman's servant." Not to mention a hell of a lot more dangerous, in more ways than one.

"Who taught you to play chess?" One of the earl's jet-black brows arched. "Please tell me that playing chess was not how your *itinerant* gentleman made his living?"

"My father taught me the game but Mr. Fenton, er, honed my skills."

"I've fallen in with a sort of chess sharp, haven't I?"

Benna couldn't deny it. "Let's just say that I'd advise you against wagering any money on our games, sir."

The earl laughed. "Duly noted."

***

"Well damn and blast," Jago muttered, staring at the board in some surprise. "How the devil did that happen so quickly?" he asked, looking up at his youthful opponent.

"I would argue it was a steady downward progression right from your first move, sir."

Jago laughed at the understated taunt. Ben strongly reminded him of his erstwhile best mate, Brian St. John. They, too, had mocked each other's prowess at various activities, although they'd been rather better matched at chess. Like Ben, Brian had normally been quiet and shy—until they were in competition over something.

Ria's face rose in his mind's eye.

"Do you wish for another game, my lord?"

Jago shook off his old memories. "I'm determined that we shall sit here until I've won at least one game."

Ben's lips twitched.

"Ah, I can see by your almost-smirk that you believe that might be a very long time."

"You *did* mention that you have a meeting to attend at nine tomorrow morning, my lord."

Once again the lad's sly humor made him chuckle. "Impudent rascal."

Ben allowed himself a brief smile as he went about setting up the pieces.

It occurred to Jago that he'd laughed more often in his young stable master's company than he had in ages.

Ben held out his fists for Jago to choose.

"No, you play white—you won the last game," he insisted at Ben's hesitation.

Ben moved his pawn to king four and they played in silence for a few moments, until Jago began to get a familiar feeling—that of being trapped.

"I think I recognize your moves from an earlier game," he said.

Ben merely smiled and advanced his king's bishop.

Jago frowned and deliberated, his hand hovering over his queen's knight. Perhaps it was time to try something different? He lifted the piece.

"I shouldn't do that, my lord, or it will be over in four."

Jago squinted at the board, playing out the moves until he saw what Ben meant. "Dammit," he muttered. "What would you do?"

Ben bent low, squinting over the top of his spectacles, rather than looking through them.

"Lord, Ben. How the devil can you even see through those filthy lenses?" Jago demanded, frowning at the other man's grubby glasses. "Here, give them to me."

Ben sat back in his chair. "Oh, you needn't—"

Jago held out his hand and wiggled his fingers.

"You needn't sir. I can—"

"I can't bear to look at them—I'm not sure how you can. Don't worry; I won't break them," he assured him, "I've worn spectacles since before I was breeched and I know how to handle them properly."

Ben hesitated and Jago swore it was actual fear that flickered across his normally impassive face. What the devil was that all about?

"Ben, what is—"

Ben yanked off the glasses and handed them over.

Jago pulled out one of the small squares of cotton he always kept in his pocket and held it up. "I'll give you this cloth when I'm done," he said, fogging the lens and then drying it. "It's especially soft cotton and I have at least a dozen of them."

When the boy didn't answer, he glanced up. "Lord, are you feeling ill, Ben? You suddenly look quite peaked. Perhaps something you ate didn't agree with you." Jago raised the glasses and glanced through the lens he had just cleaned.

And then he glanced through it again.

He frowned.

"I'm sure that is good, my lord. May I have them back, now?"

Jago ignored the boy's outstretched hand and raised the spectacles higher, until he could look though them at Ben's tense, pale face.

"These are glass," he said, after checking the second, still-grubby lens and finding the same unmagnified image.

Ben reached out and snatched them from his hands.

"Careful—you'll break them," Jago cautioned. "Not that you appear to need them."

Jago stared at the boy as he replaced spectacles, his face now flushed rather than pale.

"Why would you wear clear glass spectacles, Ben?"

Ben's mouth opened, and then closed. Finally, he shrugged. "They make me look older."

Jago studied his face, trying to decide if that were true.

No, Ben still looked young, just young with glasses.

The boy was lying—Jago could see that in his guarded eyes. Besides, nobody wore spectacles if they didn't have to. Not only were they a nuisance, but they were damned expensive.

He stared at Ben; just what was it about him that—

The truth hit him with all the subtlety of a mallet.

"Bloody hell," Jago muttered. His gaze froze on Ben's brow—the little bit he could see that wasn't covered with a sheaf of light brown hair. "Your supraorbital ridge—how is it that I didn't notice?"

"I'm s-sorry sir, my super what?"

"Your brow, Ben—" Jago gave an abrupt bark of unamused laughter. "Ben? I think not. What's your real name?"

"I don't know what you mean, my lord?"

Jago looked into eyes he'd once thought honest and true. "Please, don't make the mistake of believing me a fool, even if you *have* been fooling me," he said, coldly. "Now, who the devil are you and why the hell are you working as my bloody stable master?"

Chapter Nine

Ascot
1814
Three Years Ago

*B*enna pulled out her pocket watch and scowled.

Bloody Geoff. At this rate he'd be late. And this after he'd been so insistent on coming to Ascot and working the swells who flocked to the races.

If he thought that dragging his heels was somehow going to force Benna into changing her mind and helping him tonight, he was delusional.

She glared at the door to his bedchamber; she would give him five more minutes and then she would march into that room—regardless of who he was with and what they were doing—and drag him out like a beagle hauling a rabbit from its burrow.

Benna smiled at the imagery, but her amusement was short lived.

Thanks to Geoff's inability to plan any further than the length of his cock all the decent hotels in town had been packed to the gunnels by the time they arrived. That meant they'd needed to hire this shoddy little cottage, which came with *no* servants, leaving only Benna to wait on her extremely demanding employer.

Six days of serving as Geoff's footman, valet, maid, boot boy, and all-around dogsbody were taking their toll. Usually they stayed in hotels—or, when fortunate, at various country estates—which left her with only Geoff's person to tend.

Since arriving in Ascot she'd been responsible for everything from drawing his bloody baths—he took one every damned day—to emptying his goddamned chamber pot and making his breakfast.

Yesterday, after Geoff—shaved, bathed, and dressed by her—had wandered off for an early afternoon liaison with his current lover, Benna had stood staring down at the mess he'd left in his dressing room.

It had struck her—with considerable force—just how far she had fallen during her short life.

Benna had discovered early on—perhaps her second month away from Wake House—that she had to forget who she used to be if she was to survive. The whole point of hiding was so that nobody knew she was a duchess. If she *behaved* like a duchess, or expected to be treated like one, then she had taken this extremely uncomfortable fork in the road for no reason.

Whenever she became despondent—which she allowed to happen more often than was safe or wise—she allowed herself to think about Michael, and what he had done to her brother and wanted to do to her. That led, logically, to pondering the way she was living now. Which led to the realization that she would be forced to live this way until she could hire a solicitor and *demand* access to her trust.

If she thought about all the years—and all the obstacles—laid out before her she became frantic and insane with despair.

And then she did foolish, dangerous things.

For example: one night, perhaps two months after she'd started working for Geoffrey, she had been engaged in some grim, domestic drudgery when she'd suddenly realized—with blinding clarity—that she would likely spend her life working as a servant until she turned twenty-five.

She had wracked her brain for ways to stop Michael—to seize control of what was legally hers—but there was nothing and nobody that she could turn to or trust. Only herself. And to be of any use to herself, she needed to have the legal authority to act on her own behalf.

Before that could happen, she had to wait.

And wait.

And wait.

Years of waiting stared her in the face that night.

And, for the first time since overhearing Michael in the priest hole that night, Benna had felt despair.

Despair had led her to the decision that her life, the way it was, was simply too much to bear; she couldn't do it. Death would be better.

Benna had been alone that night as Geoff had been out with one of his lovers. She had taken his pistols, gathered up her few possessions and the small amount of money she'd saved, and booked a seat on the next stage headed for Scotland.

Her plan was simple: she would kill Michael before he could kill her. That was the only way to put a stop to the nightmare that was her life.

She hadn't given any thought to the where or the how, all she'd thought about was ending the interminable waiting and stopping the fear.

She had not come back to her senses until late in the morning on the following day, somewhere around Bradford.

By the time Benna had purchased a seat on a southbound coach—which ate up most of the rest of her paltry savings—and returned to whatever town they'd been staying in, it had been late in the evening.

Benna had expected to get a thorough bollocking from Geoffrey—perhaps he might even sack her if he noticed that she'd taken his guns.

As it turned out, he'd stayed with his lover and hadn't come back to their hotel. He never even knew that Benna had been gone for a day and a half.

That was the last time she'd given in to such bleak despair.

Today she was angry—furious, even—at all the work she was shouldering, but she had not fallen into despair.

Life with Geoffrey might not be the life she wanted, but it was tolerable. As demanding as he could be in some ways, she had plenty of time to herself. She also had enough money that she could keep herself in books, and also rent the occasional hack to ride. She'd even purchased a book about the law of trusts and wills. It was cluttered with words and phrases that were incomprehensible, but she had nothing but time to learn what it all meant.

Benna stopped her pacing and looked again at her watch; sometime over the last five minutes her temper had cooled. That was just as well because being abrupt with Geoffrey only amused him.

She rapped softly on the door and waited.

Just when she was about to knock again, he called out, "What the hell do you want?"

Benna opened the door a crack. Even though heavy drapes covered the windows enough light shone through the gaps to illuminate the huge four-poster bed.

Geoffrey was lying against the headboard, naked from the waist up—and doubtless naked below, too—holding his temple in a way that didn't bode well for his card-playing acumen tonight. "What in God's name is it, Ben?"

"You've got an engagement in an hour, sir."

"An hour?" He stared blankly.

"It's with Lord Philpot, sir."

Benna watched as comprehension dawned. Geoff grunted and then raised a hand and swatted a lump beneath the covers. "Come along, my lady. It's past time we were off." His lips curled into a smirk. "Your husband will be expecting both of us, but it's better that we don't arrive together."

He threw back the covers and slid out of bed, striding naked toward the adjoining chamber, where he kept all his personal possessions, even though it was much smaller than the master suite.

It was his habit to use two adjoining rooms whenever he knew he'd be entertaining in his bedchamber and didn't wish to vie with a woman for space at the looking glass.

Indeed, Geoffrey spent more time in front of his mirror than any woman Benna had ever met.

He stopped and glared at Benna when she wasn't quick enough to trot after him. "Well?"

She sighed and strode through the bedchamber just as Lady Philpot began to emerge from the tangle of bedding, like a rumpled butterfly from a cocoon.

Benna had just shut the door between the rooms when Geoff yawned and stretched languidly, the muscles of his magnificent body rippling. "Fetch my robe and shave me. And then you can bring me the newspaper and I shall read it while you ready my bath," he added, as if lugging buckets of water up two flights of stairs would be a treat for her.

He narrowed his eyes her. "And make sure the water is hot today. Yesterday you dallied so much it was tepid." He poured himself a glass of the expensive brandy he favored and then paused to examine himself in the cheval glass.

Benna swallowed the urge to hurl a candlestick at his head, instead looking inside the small dressing room; there was no robe. "You must have left it in the other room," she told him.

"Then go and get it." He turned to the side and was rubbing a hand over his flat midriff. "Do you think I've put on weight?"

"Yes," she said, untruthfully.

Geoffrey barked a laugh. "Insolent upstart."

Benna didn't bother knocking on the adjoining door before entering the room Geoff had just left.

Lady Philpot already had her dress on, which didn't surprise Benna since she knew for a fact that the woman went without stays or underclothes on these visits.

"Ah, Ben," Lady Philpot greeted him with a coy smile while she reached behind her to do up her buttons, the action not-so-coincidentally thrusting out her impressive bosom. "Will you get these last two for me?"

"Of course, madam."

It wasn't the first time the other woman had asked for help dressing.

Benna quickly did up the remaining buttons, which Lady Philpot could have easily reached.

"Thank you, you darling boy," she murmured, trying to catch Benna's gaze in the glass.

"My pleasure, my lady." Benna turned to fetch the robe, which she saw was tangled up in the blankets, but Lady Philpot caught her wrist.

For a small woman, her grasp was remarkably strong.

"Yes, my lady?" Benna hoped the other woman didn't hear the annoyance in her voice; they were not done with Lady Philpot and her husband just yet. It would be better not to offend her.

Lady Philpot, who was perhaps six years Benna's senior, but decades older in sin, looked up at Benna through her lashes, stroking her trapped hand. "Such manly, strong hands," she murmured.

Before Benna knew what the other woman meant to do, Lady Philpot lifted her hand and took her thumb between her full lips, sucking hard enough to hollow her cheeks.

Benna goggled, a choked sound slipping from her open mouth.

"Now, now, Lucinda, you know it's never a good idea to fuck one's servant—especially when I have only one."

Lady Philpot's eyes moved to the doorway, where Geoff was now leaning, still naked but with an amused smirk on his handsome face.

Benna couldn't help noticing that his cock, which had been flaccid only a moment earlier, had begun to thicken with interest as he watched Lady Philpot fellate Benna's finger.

She wasn't surprised by his arousal; Geoff had taken two women to his bed on more than one occasion.

Benna narrowed her eyes at him in a way she hoped communicated that she would never be one of those women.

Geoff snapped his fingers. "Come along, Ben," he ordered, as if it were Benna who was dragging her heels. "We shall be late."

Lady Philpot released Benna's thumb with a vulgar pop, her gaze on Geoff. "Why, Geoffrey, I believe you're enjoying watching me suck Ben's … finger. What else would you like to watch me suck?"

Geoffrey laughed.

Benna amused herself by imagining the other woman's surprise—and Geoff's anger—if Benna were to drop her breeches right then.

"Perhaps later, darling," Geoff said. "Right now Ben has an appointment with my face and a razor. He also needs to fill my tub." He fixed Benna with a stern look. "Sharpish."

"Mmm, later, then," Lady Philpot murmured, not releasing Benna's hand until she tugged it free.

Geoffrey waited until the door was closed to pat Benna on the shoulder. "You look fit to be tied, my dear Ben. Come, it was just a bit of funning." He turned his back to her and Benna held up his robe for him to slide in his arms, clenching her jaws to keep from giving vent to her anger.

And her hurt.

You'd think that she would no longer care what he did or said after the night she'd given him her maidenhood and he'd behaved like a callous, unmitigated arse.

What had been a singular event for Benna had meant less than nothing to Geoff.

He'd proven that by bringing home another woman the very next evening.

When Benna had refused to wait on him and his lover while they were in bed together, Geoff had been furious.

"Lord, Ben, what we shared was just a fuck—it doesn't make us man and wife. If I'd have known that you'd become so bloody gothic about it I never would have come near you to begin with. Don't worry, darling—it wasn't so great that I'll ever bother touching you again."

And he had been as good as his word.

Benna honestly couldn't blame him for despising her. She was a fool—a weak, pitiful, needy fool. Only a fool would expect anything out of Geoffrey Morecambe, a man so selfish there should be a monument to him.

It was seven months since that night. Seven months of watching him *fuck* women in every city, town, and posting inn they passed through. Seven months of being ordered around and treated like Ben-the-obedient-servant-boy. Seven months of bathing and shaving and tending to Geoff's body, preparing him for other women's arms and beds.

The infatuation—adoration, actually—that she had once felt for him was long gone, not even a shadow of that earlier feeling remained.

But that did not mean that Geoff didn't still have his hooks in her.

It *infuriated* her that he'd used and then so easily discarded her.

"Don't worry about her," Geoffrey said, his words pulling her out of her rapidly spiraling rage. He gave Benna what was—for him—a kind smile and then jerked her toward him and gave her a smacking kiss on the lips. "I won't let her touch you, Ben."

Benna thrust him away and scowled. "The next time you touch me I'll cut you, Geoffrey."

He laughed.

But when he saw she wasn't laughing with him, he compressed his lips and said, with unconvincing meekness, "I won't do it again."

Benna turned away from him and poured a bit of water into the cup with his shaving soap.

Geoff must have realized that he'd pushed her far enough because he pulled his robe modestly closed and sat down on the bench in front of the dressing table.

"After tonight I think we'd best be off. Have our bags packed and be ready to leave tomorrow morning."

Benna grunted at Geoff's version of a peace offering. "Where are we going?"

"I'm not sure, yet. I'll know more when I return this evening. I'm hoping that Mr. Ravenscar invites us to his country house as he did last year."

Benna went about the business of shaving him in silence.

It wasn't unusual for Geoffrey to choose their destination based on the whim of the moment. She wished that he'd give her more time to arrange for their transportation, but he didn't care about her wishes.

Not until she was finished and had wrapped a steaming towel around his face did he speak.

"I hope you've changed your mind about accompanying me tonight. I could really use you there," he said.

"I have not changed my mind."

Geoffrey flung down the towel in a rare display of anger. "Goddammit, Ben. You are my servant; that means you *serve* me. How the hell can you serve me if you refuse to join me tonight?"

"You can always give me the sack if you don't like my *service*, sir."

Geoffrey's blue eyes glittered dangerously. "I should bloody fire you—just to watch you flounder about and expose yourself. Just as you were about to do the night I *saved* you."

Geoff knew as well as Benna that she was no longer the same ignorant, scared girl that he'd encountered that night all those months ago; she would survive just fine without him. Geoff also knew that

91

he'd never be able to find somebody who served him so well—and so cheaply—as groom, footman, secretary, valet, and occasional card sharp partner.

Benna wasn't budging on this issue. He could bloody well fire her. With the skills she'd picked up working for him she could write her own recommendation and get another job.

Besides, he'd been sharping others at cards for years before she came along; he could do without her help for one day.

"What is it about Ascot and Epsom that you dislike so much?" Geoff demanded, his gorgeous blue eyes narrowed. "Was your family connected to racing—is that why you know so much about horses and are so good with them? Just who or what are you afraid of, Ben?"

Never before had Geoffrey asked her such a personal—and frightening—question.

The reason she'd put her foot down was because she'd seen that Viscount Fenwick owned a share in one of the horses that would be running later today. The last thing she wanted was to run into her cousin's bosom friend at Lord Philpot's card party, not that Benna thought the young drunk would recognize her looking so different and after so much time.

"What makes you think I'm afraid of anybody?" she retorted when she saw Geoff was still glaring.

"I don't think you masquerade as a man for the sheer joy of it."

"It just so happens that working as a man—even working for a clutch-fist like you—is a lot more lucrative than any job I could get as a woman, Geoff."

"What other employer would allow you to speak to me the way you do?" he demanded.

"I promise to keep my mouth shut if you pay me a more substantial salary."

"Don't bother; I find your carping and moralizing amusing."

Benna briefly wished that she had let the razor slip a little when she was shaving his throat.

Instead, she cleaned off the blade and gave it a few strops before sliding it back into its case.

She took her penny knife from her pocket and Geoff held out his left hand.

Benna inspected his already immaculate nails, waiting for him to resume his nagging.

"With your help we could really clean up tonight. You know that one of the men coming to play is the Earl of Selwin; the man bets more recklessly than anyone since Charles Fox."

Benna took his right hand, frowned, and then trimmed back a nail that was a hair longer than the others.

"Did you ever play cards with Fox?" she asked, genuinely interested.

She could tell that her rare personal question startled—and pleased—him. If there was one thing Geoffrey liked—aside from money, women, and cards—it was talking about himself.

"I did," he said, smiling fondly. "I won a packet that night, too. Unfortunately, it was not long before his death and I was stuck with a fistful of vowels." He paused, smirking. "However, I was later able to sell them to a silly gudgeon who wanted them for their *historical* value." Geoff barked a laugh.

"What was he like?" Benna asked. If she could keep him talking long enough maybe he'd stop badgering her about tonight.

"He was too concerned about his gallstones to be particularly amusing," Geoffrey said. "And he was quite the ugliest man I've ever met."

Benna lowered his hand and folded her knife before dropping it in her pocket.

"If you'll excuse me, sir, the water will be ready by now. I'd better fetch it up quickly." She gave him a sour smile. "We wouldn't want it to get tepid."

Geoff nodded his dismissal, but the way his gaze burnt into her told Benna that he'd not forgotten his questions from earlier—the one about Benna's background.

As Benna left the room she felt his gaze on her back and shivered.

In the future she'd have to do better about quelling Geoff's interest in her past. Because if there was one man in Britain whom she trusted less than Michael, it would be her greedy, immoral, and unscrupulous employer.

Chapter Ten

Cornwall
1817
Present Day

*B*enna stared across the table at the cold-eyed stranger across from her. The earl didn't even look like the same man as a moment earlier.

His full lips twisted into an unpleasant smile. "Since you appear to be at a loss for where to start, let me assist you. What is your name?"

She said her real name out loud for the first time in years. "Benna."

"Benna," he repeated flatly, the word dripping with disbelief. "What kind of name is that?"

She almost laughed. She lied all the time and people believed her without blinking; here she was telling the truth, and—

"Fine. It hardly matters." He pushed away from the table and strode over to the fire, staring out the window into the blackness.

Benna got to her feet and turned toward the door.

"Where the devil do you think you're going?"

She stopped and turned. "I assumed you wanted me to leave, sir."

"You assumed wrong. Sit," he ordered sharply.

Benna sat.

"I trusted you—brought you into my home and exposed my family to you—I think I deserve some answers, don't you?"

Benna flinched at his accusatory tone. "What do you want to know?"

"How much of what you've told me about yourself is true?"

"Most of it." That was true enough when it came to her past work history. But the personal information? Well ...

"Why?" he demanded.

"Because it was the only way I could get work."

"A smart woman like you? I don't believe you."

Benna didn't blame him. "It might help if I could go back a way, sir."

"I am in no hurry," he said, the words heavy with sarcasm. "Do you want a drink?"

The offer surprised her. She bloody well would. "Please, sir."

He went to the tray with the brandy on it. "Ring the bell and have them clear dinner away."

Benna was grateful for the ten-minute distraction.

By the time the servants had removed the crockery and fed the fire, she'd regained her composure. He only knew her gender, not her identity. He was right: she was intelligent. She could—somehow—make this situation work in her favor.

He took the chair across from her. "I'm listening."

"What I told you before about my father was true—he was a schoolteacher. I lived with him until I was not quite fifteen. After he died our landlord offered to marry me—"

"At fourteen?" he interrupted, revulsion on his handsome features.

Nice touch, my dear—build some sympathy. It seems I taught you some guile, after all.

Oh yes, Benna knew how to lie well enough. Indeed, she hardly knew what the truth was anymore.

"When I refused to marry him, things became unpleasant."

I learned that from you, too, Geoffrey.

But there was no answer from her phantom companion on *that* subject.

"Not only did our landlord make me leave our house, he also made the situation in our village, er, untenable. I had little money and even less time to decide what to do. My father hadn't managed to save much and most of what he had went for the burial expenses and various debts."

To her surprise, there was sympathy in his gaze. "As a doctor I have, unfortunately, witnessed similar scenarios—sans the unscrupulous pedophile landlord—more than once after a male provider died." He looked slightly less severe. "I know it is not easy to be an orphan, far less to be a female orphan."

Shame flooded her at how quickly he believed her.

"Go on," the earl prodded.

"My father believed in, er, self-sufficiency, my lord. We didn't have enough money to employ either cook maids or other servants, so we did for ourselves. We took care of our cottage for a reduction in rent. As for my experience with horses, we kept a cob and dogcart and I learned early on that I had a way with livestock."

"I still don't see how all this led you to impersonate a man."

"It just seemed safer to pretend to be a boy, especially after what I'd experienced with our landlord." She shrugged. "I often wore my father's castoffs to do heavier work and when I tucked my hair under my hat I was frequently mistaken for a boy. My height seemed to be the only thing people noticed about me."

Benna could see by the faint flush on the earl's normally pale cheeks that he was thinking that he'd been fooled by the same thing.

"Good Lord," he said, his beautiful brown eyes widening as something occurred to him. "Did Stephen Worth find out about you? Is that why you left his employ?"

"No, my lord. It was Mr. Fielding."

He gave an unamused snort. "I guess that shouldn't surprise me. He's a man who has his wits about him—unlike me, apparently. When did that happen?"

"It was the day after the Redruth Mine cave-in."

"Tell me what happened."

Benna was grateful to put the rest of her story aside for the moment.

"Do you know Mr. Fielding well?" she asked, genuinely curious.

"No. I get the feeling that nobody does, not even Worth."

Benna could well believe it.

The enigmatic John Fielding worked for Stephen Worth, although Benna thought he was something more than just a servant to the wealthy American.

Fielding was built like a stone wall with a personality to match. His face was hideously scarred with violent cuts that extended out from the corners of his mouth, as if his assailants had wanted to slice his head in half. What kind of man could not only survive such horrific punishment, but thrive afterward?

John Fielding had not just survived the pain of his past, he had been forged by it: forged into something hard and inhuman and implacable.

It wasn't just Fielding's huge body and disfigured face that were terrifying, it was his eyes: dark, pitiless pools of black that bored through everything in their path like augers. Eyes that had made Benna's blood turn cold whenever they'd landed on her.

Benna saw the earl was waiting. "The day of the cave-in had been chaos in the stables—you remember I came to fetch you?"

"Yes—Fielding sent you, didn't he?"

She nodded. "Well, earlier that day I, er, ran into Mr. Fielding and he caught me before I fell."

Benna could see from the earl's expression that he knew where this was going.

"I didn't think anything of it until the next day. Fielding came to me while I was grooming one of Mr. Worth's horses."

"*Piddock!*" Benna could still recall how her body had frozen in mid-curry at the sound of Fielding's bellow.

When he'd stalked into the stall Benna had tried not to stare at his scars, not an easy thing to do when they covered most of his face.

"Yes, Mr. Fielding?"

"Come with me." The huge man had turned smoothly; he moved like a cat for a man well over six feet.

Benna had followed him to Fielding's horse's stall, her legs wobbly with fear, her mind shrieking to run in the opposite direction.

Fielding jabbed a finger at his horse. "Did you do this?"

Benna glanced from the horse's mane to the grim giant. "You mean did I groom him, sir?"

Fielding jerked out a nod.

"Uh, yes, sir. I just thought I'd give him a bit of care when I brought him his oats."

"How many times have I told you not to come near him?"

Benna's face got hot and she looked down at her feet. "A few, sir."

"You need to find yourself another place."

Her head whipped up. "But, Mr. Fielding, I promise that won't happen again, please, I won't—"

"Shut it." The words were a low rumble, like the sound of boulders bouncing down a rocky cliff. Fielding's harsh features had then twitched into an even more horrifying expression: a smile. He took a long stride toward Ben and it was all she could do not to step back. Instead, she craned her neck until it hurt.

Eyes like tar pits held her mesmerized. "I know what you are, *boy.*"

"Wha-What I am, sir?"

"It took me longer than it should have. I must be dicked in the nob to have been fooled for so long. But even a thick-witted bastard like me could guess what you are when you ran into me yesterday."

Benna's breath froze in her chest.

Hell-black eyes drifted down Ben's body in a manner calculated to insult. "You're not much of a girl, but a girl you are. And you've no place in Worth's household with whatever joukery-pawkery you're up to."

For one horrible moment she'd thought that he'd somehow found out *who* she was, not just what.

Benna had opened her mouth to protest any trickery but he held up a big hand. A big *six-fingered* hand.

"Whatever it is you want to say? Don't bother. I don't care why you're here or what you're doing. But I know trouble when I see it. Mr. Worth is my responsibility and he doesn't need any more trouble." He added under his breath, "He makes enough for himself. So, find yourself other employment. Understood?"

How could Ben have possibly *mis*understood?

"*Go ask Trebolton for work,* is what he told me," Benna said, leaving out the insulting part of Fielding's suggestion.

But the earl snorted. "I think you left out the part where he mentioned that I was too skint to be choosy."

Benna didn't bother to deny it.

"I wonder why Fielding never told Worth?"

"I'm still perplexed by that," Benna admitted. "All he would say is that he did not want Mr. Worth drawn into the matter or made a fool."

The earl snorted. "Imagine that."

Benna's face, already hot, became even warmer under his sardonic gaze.

Thankfully, the earl moved on from the matter. "You say your father was a teacher. Why didn't you consider teaching—at least once you'd eluded your landlord and had time to think. Surely that would be easier than masquerading as a man?"

"I did consider teaching," Benna said, honestly, this time. She'd given a great deal of thought to applying for a governess position. "But finding a decent post takes time and connections and I had neither. And even if I'd had the time, I did not possess the credentials or recommendations."

"Why not write your own recommendation. I daresay you had to have some sort of reference to get your first job? Or, barring that, why not seek a position as a maid or even a serving lass?"

"Anyone hiring a domestic would almost certainly check my references. As for working as a serving wench?" She gave him a pointed look.

He nodded. "Fair enough; that was a foolish suggestion on my part."

Benna knew that not all serving wenches sold their wares, but many customers treated them as if they did.

"Besides," she added, "I could earn more than twice as much as a post boy than I could as a maid or tavern wench—or even a governess." All three positions required much harder work than postilions but reaped neither the money nor respect.

Once again the earl nodded. "So, the rest of your tale—the part about working for the same master for several years—that's all twaddle? You've really been working as a postilion until Worth hired you?"

Benna hesitated. "Er, actually, my lord I did work for Mr. Fenton in the capacity I previously described to you."

"As a groom?"

Benna swallowed. "And all the rest."

S.M. LaViolette

The earl's eyes grew huge. "Good Lord. I cannot believe you are serious. You actually valeted a man?"

She nodded.

Tell him you were also my lover, darling—and a most inventive and energetic one, at that, I might add. Let's see what the good, upstanding doctor you so adore has to say about that. *Perhaps he'll offer you a similar position.* Geoff chortled at that.

Benna's face heated; she was ashamed by the sudden tightening in her sex at the far-too-enticing thought.

"Did the man *know* that you were a woman?" the earl finally asked.

"Yes."

The earl sat back in his chair as if Benna had punched him. "When did he find out?"

"Right from the first. He saved me when I was getting a thrashing at my first postilion job. He, er, cared for me while I was unconscious and discovered the truth then."

He looked nauseated. "My God. Were they beating you because they learned you were a woman?"

"No, they were beating me because I took a man's job when he was too intoxicated to work."

He looked down and seemed startled to find a drink in his hand. He raised the brandy to his mouth and emptied the glass.

And then he stared at her, as if she were a tangled ball of yarn that he had no idea how to begin unraveling.

Benna had already finished her brandy and was pondering the wisdom of asking for another when he finally spoke.

"Is it your plan to live out the remainder of your life as a man?"

Benna's shoulders sagged in relief at the change of subject. She opened her mouth and told her second-biggest lie of the evening. "My plans are to work until I have enough money saved up to hire a cottage in a small village, somewhere I could teach and live a simple life—as a woman."

Well, that last part was true. At this point in her life, she had forgotten why she'd once hated dressing in women's clothing. In fact, she got positively giddy at the thought of wearing stays, petticoats, and gowns.

"*Six* years you have lived this way. It is positively … staggering."

Benna decided to take that as a compliment.

When he seemed disposed to merely stare at her, Benna felt compelled to ask, "I know I deceived you. I understand if you want me to leave, my lord."

"Why would you understand that?" he demanded, suddenly sounding irritable.

At her? Or at himself?

"Well," she said, after a moment. "I suppose because you might believe I made a fool of you, sir."

"I *am* angry," he said, "but mainly at myself for being such an unobservant lump. Aside from my wounded pride, I can't deny that you are one of the hardest workers I employ, so it isn't as if I didn't get good value while I was being a fool."

Benna wasn't quite sure what to say to that.

He snorted and shook his head. "I suppose I should look on the bright side."

"Er, the bright side, my lord?"

"I saw how Lady Catherine was mooning over you; at least I don't have to worry about you being alone with either of my nieces, now."

Benna couldn't help smiling. "Yes sir, she is safe as houses with me." She lifted her empty glass to place it on the end table but somehow misjudged the distance and gave it a good crack against the edge of the marble top. When she tried to catch it, a shard of glass stabbed into her palm.

"Blast and damn," she muttered.

The earl was up and across the room in an instant and dropped to his haunches. "Let me see."

"It's nothing, my lord."

He gave her an exasperated look. "As I am a doctor, why don't you let me be the judge of whether it is nothing. Or is medicine something else you've been trained in?"

Benna's face heated under his glare and she held out her hand.

He gently cradled her hand while he examined it. "You've jammed it in there good and deep. Hold still, this will smart."

Benna gritted her teeth, not making a sound.

He put the shard inside the broken glass and cut her a wry look. "Tough, aren't you? Now, let me make sure there isn't anything smaller still in there." He bent his head, gently prodding at her palm. "Just as I suspected," he murmured, and then finished his digging and dropped a second piece into the glass with a soft *clink*. "It will need to be properly cleaned to avoid infection." He looked up, the action bringing his handsome face only an inch or two from hers.

His smooth brow was wrinkled with concern—for her—his eyes once again soft, gorgeous, and velvety.

Don't do it, Geoffrey warned her.

But Benna didn't listen.

Instead, she did what she'd been wanting to do for weeks; she leaned forward and pressed her mouth against the Earl of Trebolton's.

Chapter Eleven

Leeds
1815
Two Years Ago

I won't go," Benna said, and then tugged off Geoffrey's boot hard enough to almost jerk him from the chair.

Geoff clutched at the armrests, glaring down at her. "This will be an *exceedingly* profitable endeavor, Ben—you know how downy Lord Jevington is. Surely you recall last year, in Bristol?"

Benna recalled the four-day massacre very well. She must still possess an iota of conscience because she squirmed to remember the thorough plucking Geoff had given the witless young nobleman.

"You didn't leave him a feather to fly with," Benna, retorted, reaching for his other boot. "I find it hard to believe that he is so lacking in sense as to sit across a table from you again. Even if he is that stupid, I doubt he'll have the blunt."

Geoff scoffed. "Listen to you! Haven't I taught you anything? The silly gudgeon is panting to give me his money. I'd insult him if I *didn't* take it from him." His eyes narrowed accusingly. "And why do you care, anyway? Did you fancy the idiotic young lordling? Is that why you're refusing to go?"

Benna opened her mouth to deny it, but Geoff wasn't interested.

"Don't waste your sympathy on him, Ben, his father is Lord Stonehaven. The only Scottish family more well-larded than the Jevingtons are the de Montforts."

Benna jolted at the familiar name, but Geoff didn't notice.

His expression shifted from sharp annoyance to fondly nostalgic. "I won quite a packet off the last Duke of Wake. Bloody shame about his passing. I hear that his cousin, Norland, is a different kettle of fish."

At the sound of Michael's name Benna clenched Geoffrey's foot so hard he yelped.

"Good God, Ben! *Must* you maul me so savagely with those brutish paws of yours?"

She muttered an apology and carefully pulled off the boot, placing it beside its partner before removing Geoffrey's stockings.

"Get over your foolishness and prepare yourself to leave first thing in the morning."

"I'm not going."

"You bloody well *will*, Ben." Geoff shoved the words through clenched teeth, his expression murderous.

Benna had caviled about fleecing certain punters in the past, but she'd never refused to accompany him on any of his trips before. Still, she could hardly tell him the real reason she had no intention of going to Edinburgh.

She began to stand and he grabbed her shoulder.

"Ow!" Her yelp was more from surprise than pain.

Benna tried to jerk away, but he held her fast with one hand. For a man who did little other than gamble, drink, and fuck, he was remarkably strong.

"You listen to me, you arrogant ingrate; *I'm* the one who earns the money that feeds you, houses you, and keeps you in those bloody books you so enjoy reading. That means *I'm* the one who says where we go and when. Understood?"

Benna clamped her mouth shut and stared at him; it drove him mad when she refused to argue.

His nostrils flared and he shoved her hard enough that she fell back hard on her tailbone. "Fine, you scrawny, ungrateful pillock," he said, eying her in an odiously snubbing way that normally reduced people to stammering dunces. "I don't need you, anyway. All you do is scowl at me like a rejected, jealous mooncalf whenever I bring home any woman better looking than you."

Benna ignored his cruel jab, her heart pounding in her ears. "Is this—are you giving me the sack, Geoff?" she asked, annoyed by the warble in her voice.

He scoffed. "Not this time—darling, although I should. But no, that would only inconvenience *me*. You'll pack our things and remove yourself to Newcastle after you've made arrangements for my trip. You can wait for me there at the Royal York." He smiled unpleasantly. "I shall take those extra nights out of your wages."

Benna didn't care. He only ever paid for a servant's room for her when they stayed at hotels; while that wasn't exactly cheap at the Royal York, avoiding Scotland was worth the expense.

"I shall only be a week in Edinburgh." He sneered. "You're not so bloody important that I can't survive without you—you'd better remember that."

"Thank you. I'm grateful," she said, meaning it. And then got to her feet.

He leveled a finger at her. "The next time you defy me you will find yourself standing on the side of the road while I wave goodbye."

Newcastle
Six Days Later

Benna smiled at the handsome lad who delivered the steaming mug and plate of biscuits to her table. "Thank you."

She had discovered Dirty Nelly's Coffeehouse her second day in Newcastle and had gone there for coffee and biscuits every day since.

She'd found it while searching for a newspaper office after a servant at the last house party they'd attended had told her that she might, for a fee, look at older issues of the paper.

Now that Benna had the leisure to do so, she'd decided to go back to the date of her departure from Scotland and see if there was anything more in the Newcastle paper about her, Michael, or anything else related to Wake House.

Even though Newcastle was a good day's ride from her old home, it was still the closest city of any size, and the Dukes of Wake had once been well-known figures in the northern metropolis.

In fact, her father had purchased a life membership in the races held at the Newcastle Town Moor and used to attend every year. He took David with him, but not Benna. For once, her father had steadfastly rejected all Benna's—loud and emotional—entreaties.

"It is not the sort of place I wish to bring my daughter," the duke had said when she'd resorted to using tears—usually an effective last resort—to accompany him and David. His expression had been so uncharacteristically forbidding that Benna had known there was no chance that he'd capitulate.

Tom, on the other hand—after enduring intense nagging and whining—had risked the wrath of his master and sneaked her down south one magical day in September.

Benna pushed aside the fond memory and took a sip of the strong brew the old coffeehouse was famous for. She had passed an exceedingly pleasurable—if not especially productive—six days by herself.

She'd found nothing of any note in the back issues of the Newcastle paper—no mention at all of either Michael or the elusive Duchess of Wake.

Benna still had no idea whether that was a good or bad thing. What was Michael up to?

She had also spent some of her hard-earned money to speak to a solicitor about wills, trusts, guardianship, and other legal matters.

It had been a singularly unhelpful, and expensive, hour. Without the trust document the man could tell her very little that was of any use. Not only that, but he'd become increasingly suspicious even with the vague details Benna *had* decided to share.

Still, as little as she'd actually learned, the time without Geoffrey had been glorious.

But all that would soon come to an end.

She laid aside today's paper and enjoyed her coffee and the shortbread the little shop baked fresh every day.

She had received a message yesterday that Geoffrey would be returning late tonight, which meant she still had several hours to prepare things the way he liked for his return. He'd not written much, only that his trip had been successful.

Benna tossed a few coins onto the table, picked up her paper, and nodded to the waiter as she left.

The Royal Hotel was only a block away. The January wind was brisk and the streets were thin of pedestrian traffic at this time of day.

When she approached the foyer of the Royal a lackey scurried out to open the door for her thanks to Benna's propensity for keeping the hotel staff's fists well-greased.

"Evenin', Mr. Piddock."

"Good evening, Earnest."

"I see Mr. Morecambe has returned."

Well, drat. Benna had not expected him until much later. She smiled at Earnest. "Thanks for the warning."

He chuckled and she pressed a coin into his palm before heading up to the second floor of the enormous hotel.

Even if she'd not been told that Geoff had returned, she could have guessed by the luggage, clothing, and other detritus strewn all over the sitting room.

The master, himself, was sprawled across the settee nearest the fire, wrapped in a shocking new robe of red silk with gold dragons embroidered up the front.

"Well, if it isn't young Master Piddock, gent about town," Geoff mocked, quickly plucking off the glasses he needed for reading. It amused Benna that the spectacles offended his vanity.

"Welcome back, Geoffrey," she said, tossing her paper and room key onto the console table before pulling off her gloves and hat.

Geoffrey grunted at her greeting, his shrewd eyes taking in the new suit she was wearing. "Fetch me a brandy," he ordered.

Benna sighed; the holiday was over.

As she poured him a drink she wondered what had happened to put him into one of his *moods*.

"Here you are, sir."

Geoff looked up, but didn't immediately take the glass, instead making her stand there, holding it. "I hope you don't think I'll permit you to strut about town dressed in such finery."

"Afraid I'm more handsome than you?" she taunted.

"Ha!" He snatched the glass.

She couldn't help noticing that he had dark smudges under his eyes, which told her that he'd been burning the candle at both ends. The grooves that bracketed his sensual lips also seemed deeper. And there was a petulant twist to his mouth that told her he'd not had the pampering he'd come to believe he deserved.

107

"I shall go change into my livery directly." Benna began to turn.

"Don't be a fool. Sit down, I wish to talk to you."

Benna took the chair nearest him, crossed one leg over the other, and absently pinched the crease of her trouser leg.

"Don't you want to hear how things went?" Geoff demanded peevishly.

Benna suspected that he'd not had his desired number of bedpartners.

"Nothing would delight me more, sir."

Geoff's eyes narrowed. "You're developing quite a mouth, aren't you?"

She prudently ignored the rhetorical question.

"It was an excessively lucrative journey. Indeed, I did so well that I ended up not only with a good deal of money, but also my own chaise."

That made Benna sit up. "Somebody put up their carriage?"

"And a good deal more besides—you remember Crawford? The prosy old bore who made his fortune in India?"

"He put up his *carriage*? I thought he was full of juice?"

"Not anymore."

"Good Lord," she murmured, thinking, not for the first time, that it must be dreadful to be seized by the gambling fever.

"He not only put up his carriage, he also threw in a great pile of jewelry." Geoff pulled a face. "All of it hideous, I'm afraid. But I daresay you'll know how to make some money for it." He sighed. "You might as well sell the carriage, too. It's too much of a bother to keep one, I've decided."

Visiting pawn shops was one of Benna's many duties. Selling a carriage would be a new experience.

Geoff rattled on about the various games he'd played, the houses he'd played in, and the players he'd fleeced, for a good half-hour.

The clock on the mantle chimed and Benna saw it was time to ring for his shaving water and lay out his evening clothing.

But when Benna stood, he shook his head.

"I'm staying in tonight," he said, struggling and failing to contain a yawn. At her astounded look—she couldn't recall Geoff *ever* staying in of an evening—he gave her a weary smile. "I'm bloody knackered. I burned the midnight oil this past week."

"I'll call up a bath and a meal for you," Benna said.

"Call up enough food for both of us."

Benna turned around and stared.

"What?" he demanded.

"Nothing," she lied.

Geoffrey condescending to eat with his *scrawny* servant? Unheard of!

Well, well, he *was* exhausted if he was going to sit across a table from her.

While circumstances sometimes forced them to share their board, never had Geoff actually invited Benna to sit down at a table with him.

There was a time, even as little as nine or ten months ago, when Benna would have been overjoyed by his offer.

Now she was only suspicious of his motives.

Chapter Twelve

Cornwall
1817
Present Day

*J*ago had the oddest feeling that he was hovering outside his body, watching himself.

He was kissing his stable master.

Actually, he was frozen with shock and his stable master was doing a bloody good job of kissing him, even without his participation.

Her tongue took advantage of his gaping mouth and slick heat teased between his lips, exploring his teeth, gums, and even the roof of his mouth.

Her hands slid around his neck, the skin on her fingers work-roughened and calloused, but her lips so very, very soft and warm.

His own hands twitched to touch her, to hold her.

Jago, this is madness. Madness.

It was the voice of reason, usually his guiding light—especially in sexual matters. Tonight it was as faint as the rain gently pattering against the parlor window.

Fortunately—or unfortunately, as he would later feel—it was just loud enough.

Jago steeled himself to pull away from her—the activity as arduous as stopping a runaway carriage—but then she made a noise, a barely perceptible, wholly feminine, whimper of pleasure, and gently bit his lower lip.

The groan that tore out of his chest at her erotic gesture startled a jolt out of her, which was enough to bring him back to his senses.

Jago jerked away and pushed to his feet, staggering back a step before staring down at her.

Her pale turquoise eyes were dark, almost navy, and her parted lips looked far fuller than usual.

Jago saw the exact moment that she came back to herself and realized what she'd done. Her tanned cheeks turned the dull, dark red of a brick. She raised her hands to her hot face, the gesture oddly girlish.

"Oh, no. I'm so—"

Jago shook his head. "Don't." She recoiled at the sharp word and Jago grimaced. "I only meant you needn't bother with an apology—it hardly matters."

Well done, Jago. Do you think you could bungle the moment any more thoroughly?

He tried again. "I think it might be better if we spoke about this issue later—when we both have cooler heads. After we return to Lenshurst."

"You mean you don't wish me to leave?"

"No, no, that's not, er, necessary." He shoved a hand through his hair and gave it a good tug, hoping the pain would focus his scattered wits.

"Thank you, sir."

She stood and Jago realized, for the first time, that he barely needed to look down an inch to meet her eyes.

"I've got your breeches and coat in my room, sir. Should I bring them to your room once I've cared for them?"

Visions of her handling his clothing—putting garments on his body—or, God help him, taking clothing *off* his body—assaulted him like a hail of erotic arrows.

His cock, which had just begun to soften, sprang back to life.

"Er, no." He cleared his throat, trying to get the fist-sized obstruction out of it. "I think we should both just go to bed."

Her brows rose.

"In our respective rooms." *Christ.*

Jago turned away before he said anything else stupid. "Have a servant run the clothing down to my room in the morning," he said over his shoulder, heading for the brandy. "I shall want the coach ready to leave at noon."

"Very good, my lord. Good night, sir."

111

Jago grunted something suitable and she left without making a sound.

He expelled a gusty lungful of air and sank into the chair she'd just vacated. "Bloody hell," he murmured. "Bloody hell."

***

Benna blamed Lord Trebolton's intoxicating scent for making her behave so boldly.

Or perhaps living with me for so long has just turned you into a randy tart.

That, too, was a possibility.

The earl smelled of shaving soap and a hint of brandy mingled with the heat of his body and the wool of his coat and it had been … irresistible.

Yes, that was the word: irresistible. Benna had had no choice in the matter.

Unlike Benna, he had cleaned himself after the day's exertions, even going so far as to shave again for dinner. His angular jaw and firm chin had looked smooth and soft and her hands had itched to touch him.

When he'd looked up from treating her cut hand, his face had been so close that she had seen the fine lines etched into his pale skin. Tiny striations from squinting against the sun, or frowning in deep thought, or simply earned by living.

Added to all that had been the fact that his beautiful eyes had been creased in sympathy—for her, for her pain—and, well …

Not even the fear of rejection could exercise any control over her actions.

Besides, she'd believed that he was going to give her the sack. Why not kiss him before he tossed her out?

His lips, which she'd stared at so often that she could have drawn them from memory, were *right there*, only inches away.

And so Benna had taken what she wanted and damn the consequences.

For a moment, she had thought he might kiss her back.

But then he'd pulled away and stood, removing himself from her reach, as if he feared she might grab him again.

The thought had definitely crossed her mind.

Benna was scarcely a virginal miss, but never had she grabbed a man and kissed him.

While she was mortified by her behavior—and his reaction—she wasn't *that* mortified.

No, what mortified her more was the knowledge that she would grab him and do the same thing all over again if another opportunity presented itself.

Chapter Thirteen

Brighton
1815
Two Years Ago

*B*en?"

Benna jolted upright in her bed. "Is he here?" she demanded, her eyes darting around in the darkness.

"Shhh, Ben—everything is fine." Geoffrey's voice was soothing. "There is nobody here but me. I didn't mean to startle you." The bed beside her moved as Geoff sat on the mattress.

"What's the matter?" she asked, her heart still pounding. The only light in her small, windowless servant's room came from the candle he must have left on the hallway table. She could hardly see more than his shadow in the near darkness.

"Nothing is wrong."

Benna frowned; his voice sounded ... different. Softer.

Geoff stood and she heard the soft susurration of silk sliding to the floor.

"What—"

"Oh, hush," he chided, this time lifting the blanket before slipping in beside her.

Benna's pulse, which had already been elevated from fear thundered in her ears. And her body, cool under the thin bedding only a moment before, was suddenly sweaty.

"What do you want, Geoff?"

She felt the ghostly touch of a hand in the darkness and then Geoffrey's fingers slid around her neck and his mouth descended over hers.

For the briefest of moments, Benna kissed him back.

Then she stiffened, outraged at his audacity; did he just think he could come to her whenever there was nobody else?

She was even more outraged by her body's traitorous response to the smallest touch from him.

He chuckled softly against her unyielding mouth and body, trailing soft, teasing kisses over her lips, down her chin, and then hovering over her pulse at the base of her throat.

"You try to act as if you're unaffected by me," he murmured, his hands sliding down her sides until they reached the bottom of the man's nightshirt she slept in, "but your body betrays you." He lifted the hem. "Rise up a bit, so that I might take this off," he ordered, in between kissing the fine material covering her already hard nipples.

"No," she said, pushing him away.

But not very hard.

"Just let me touch you—give you pleasure with my lips, tongue, and fingers. I don't need to put my cock inside you to make you come." His instincts for prey were well-honed and Benna hesitated as his words acted on both her mind and body.

He wanted to put his mouth on her sex?

Benna had walked in on Geoff and his lovers enough to know that human mouths were useful in several ways she'd never imagined. But she had not had a lover's mouth on her own body.

She wanted to experience the feeling. Fiercely.

He's not your lover; he's a manipulative, horny, selfish beast. Boot him out of bed. Now.

Geoff's hands tugged on her nightgown. "Lift up, Ben. I'll make you scream with pleasure, I promise."

Benna was on the verge of giving in when she suddenly saw herself—as if from a distance.

She was the Duchess of Wake, for pity's sake! She'd been cheated out of her house, home, and position by a scheming degenerate male relative.

And here she was, working for yet another scheming degenerate—a man who had the morality and conscience of a rotted log.

And now he wanted *this* from her? After rejecting her so coldly that she had cried herself to sleep for a week?

Not. Bloody. Likely. No matter how much she might want it or how good it would feel.

"No." Benna shoved him back, this time with some force.

For a moment, she felt him resist and icy panic skittered down her spine.

If he were to force her, she would not be strong enough to resist him.

But he heaved an exasperated sigh and flung himself onto his back, shaking her rickety bed.

"Hell, Ben. I can't believe you cling to such puritanical scruples after all this time with me," he groused. "Or is it that you are still mad at me over the last time?

Benna gave a humorless laugh. "Oh, you mean the *only* time? The time when you took my maidenhead and then treated me like a diseased doxy five minutes later?"

"It wasn't like that," he insisted.

"You're right," she said, "It was more like ten minutes—after you *fell asleep* on me."

He groaned, sounding like a whiney schoolboy. "So? I never promised you anything or lied to you, did I? All I did was—"

"Bed me and behave like a callous spalpeen ten minutes after."

He snorted. "Spalpeen?" When she didn't respond, he sighed. "Fine, you have me there. I was a bit harsh—"

It was Benna's turn to snort.

"I was *exceedingly* harsh."

Benna suspected that was the best apology that she would ever get from a man who never apologized.

"What do you want from me, Geoffrey? We have a good arrangement, don't we? Why wreck it?" Indeed, ever since Geoff had come back from Edinburgh he'd been almost enjoyable to work for.

Well, she amended, maybe not enjoyable. But at least not unbearable.

"But … would becoming lovers really wreck things?" he asked, sounding tentative for the first time since she'd met him.

"Probably. Besides, why risk what we have?" *Just because you're bored and have nobody else to bed?*

"Because … dammit, Ben! Because I missed you, all right?"

116

"Missed me? But I haven't gone anywhere."

"I meant that I missed you when I went to Edinburgh without you."

Even though it was dark, Benna turned her head to stare at him.

"What?" he demanded, turning on his side to face her, the light illuminating just one of his eyes and part of his forehead.

"That was months ago, Geoff. Why are you suddenly—" Benna felt his hand on her side and flinched.

"Please, don't," he said

"Don't what? Deny you the fleeting pleasure of my body tonight?"

He reached out to stroke her again. "Don't pull away from me, Ben—" He gave a growl of frustration. "Lord, I can't call you that. What's your real name?"

"I cannot believe you, Geoffrey" she said, not bothering to hide her exasperation and stupefaction. "You've known me for *years* and this is the first time you thought to ask me my real name."

He groaned. "I know, I know. I'm a selfish clod."

"Go on," she said.

"And I'm heartless, unprincipled, self-centered, capricious—is that enough? My vocabulary isn't that extensive."

"That'll do for now," she said, amused but disconcerted by this unprecedented version of her normally vapid, selfish, conscienceless employer. "So tell me, why do you think I don't trust you, Geoffrey?"

"Oh, hell, Ben. I know. And I don't blame you—it's probably wise not to trust me. I daresay I'll revert to being my arsehole self tomorrow."

"Or even before you leave my bed."

He gave a choked laugh. "So, you won't tell me your name?"

"Ben has worked well enough up until now."

"I'm so sorry—you can't know how much I regret so much of my behavior toward you." For once, there was no trace of mockery in his voice.

Benna was stunned speechless.

"Even though I can't see you I can feel your astonishment," he said drily. "Trust me, you can't be more astonished by my ... *feelings*"—he said the word as if it were the pox—"than I am. It's

117

just—well, I didn't realize myself how important you'd become until I had to do without you."

"Didn't like polishing your own boots, tossing your lovers out of your bed when you're finished with them, and making all your own travel arrangements?" Rather than the dismissive insouciance she'd been hoping for, she sounded nervous and confused.

Once again, he caressed her hip with his hand, but in a soothing, comforting way, rather than a sexual fashion. The same way a man would touch a woman he loved and cherished.

Or so Benna imagined.

He leaned close and spoke against her shoulder, his breath hot and his lips sinfully soft. "God, I missed you so bloody much. It scared the hell out of me, Ben. I've never needed anyone before. And—and, well, I didn't like it."

Benna's breathing froze at the ache in his voice.

"I don't expect you to believe me," he went on, his voice muffled by the thin material of her nightshirt. "Especially not after all this time and how rotten I've been. Lord, I never expected to feel like this, myself—ever. I kept waiting for it to go away, but it hasn't. I—I'd just like a chance to prove I'm not a lost cause. Just … give me a chance, Ben." His lips landed on her temple so softly that she might have imagined the kiss.

He rose from the bed, taking the heat of his body and his intoxicating scent with him.

She had to bite her tongue not to give in to weakness and call him back.

"I swear to you that I'm still worth something, Ben. I know I don't deserve you—yet. But I'll prove to you that I can be a man you can trust and rely on."

Benna heard the squeak of a floorboard, and the soft click of the door closing, leaving her completely in the dark; in more ways than one.

Chapter Fourteen

Cornwall
1817
Present Day

The morning was a frosty one and Benna could see her breath in the air.

She'd just finished bringing hay to the horses when a throat cleared behind her.

Benna yelped and spun around.

"I apologize for startling you," Lord Trebolton said coolly, a faint smile on his lips.

"Oh, your lordship. Er, was there something you needed?" she asked, when he just looked at her, his dark eyes inscrutable.

He'd barely said a word to her yesterday when they'd left Truro. When they got back to Lenshurst he thanked her, instructed her to see that all the packages were delivered to the appropriate persons, and took his leave.

And now here he was, dressed in a dark green claw hammer she'd never seen before and leather breeches so formfitting that she thought they must be lambskin.

Her hands twitched to feel the soft leather on his warm, hard body.

Benna swallowed. Lord; he was a masterpiece. As awe-inspiring as a holy relic.

And you want to drop to your knees and worship at his altar.

God help her; she did.

Lord Trebolton tapped his whip against his top boot—the only thing he was wearing that she recognized—and her head jerked up.

"Saddle Asclepius for me, please."

She bobbed her head. "Right away, sir."

Benna was worried that he would stand there and watch her work, but, to her relief, he strolled through the stable block and disappeared into the smithy.

Befitting his status as the master's horse Asclepius's stall was the biggest and airiest in that block of the stables. "Come along, lad," she murmured to the powerful gelding, who looked haughtily annoyed to be interrupted in the middle of his breakfast.

Benna clucked her tongue at him. "Don't look daggers at me— your master is here. You'll love a good, hard ride, won't you?"

He's not the only one ...

Benna sighed, her face burning in the frosty air.

Asclepius's ears perked up and Benna swore the gelding knew the word *ride*.

The earl hadn't ridden much in these past few weeks, certainly not for pleasure. Not that she knew where he was going this morning. She was just happy that he was getting out and not hunched over a desk.

She'd be even happier if he told her what he planned to do with her.

"Well, if wishes were horses, eh?" she whispered, scratching that spot beneath Asclepius's chin that made him her drooling slave. If only that worked as well on men.

As she saddled and bridled the restive horse she couldn't help noticing that his lordship's saddle, while soft and supple from her sedulous care, was worn with age.

The earl was a clipping rider and Asclepius a top shelf mount, they both deserved far better and she hoped he would order a new saddle when the man came to fit the girls and Lady Trebolton.

When Benna led the horse out to the courtyard, she found his lordship waiting, his gaze on a section of rock wall that she'd been working on.

"Here you are, my lord. He's got the fidgets," she warned.

"Thank you, er, Ben," he said, his hesitation and slight flush the only indication that the evening in Truro had actually happened.

He mounted smoothly, gave her a nod, and cantered from the yard. He had an excellent seat; in more ways than one.

Benna took off her hat and watched him ride away, scratching her head. The only dye she'd found that didn't run when she perspired was harsh and left her scalp dry and itchy.

She watched until she couldn't see him any longer, put on her cap, and turned back to her chores.

What had that been all about? Was he going to pretend that he'd never learned that she was a woman?

Was he going to act as though she'd never kissed him?

***

Six days later Benna decided that, indeed, his lordship seemed determined to go along as though nothing had changed between them.

Every morning he appeared a half-hour after dawn.

After that first morning, she had Asclepius saddled and ready for him when he arrived.

He would bid her a polite—but cool—good morning and then go for an hour-long ride.

When he returned—deliciously damp and sweaty—he let Benna tend to his mount while he roamed the stable blocks and environs.

After she finished caring for Asclepius, the earl might spend a few minutes discussing what projects she was working on and what he wanted done next.

The whole time he spoke to her pleasantly, but without the spark of humor and friendliness that she only now realized—after it was gone—he'd employed especially with her. Gone were the smiles, the little jests, the requests for her opinion on various matters.

Gone was any suggestion of intimate games of chess up in his study.

Now he treated her with the same aloofness that he did every other female. Well, everyone except his friend Mrs. Elinor Worth. With her he was always as warm and affectionate as he had once been with Benna.

Benna didn't know if his change in behavior was because she was a woman or because she was a liar, or perhaps both.

Or perhaps it was because he didn't want her to fling herself at him like some sort of demented heroine in a gothic romance?

Had Benna become yet another one of many women who'd repelled him with their amorous advances?

She feared it was so.

Just recalling her behavior that night was enough to make her want to crawl under a rock and stay there. Forever.

But there was no time for hiding under rocks or anywhere else. Today, for the first time, she was accompanying her new charges out on their first *refresher* ride.

Benna kept trying to fall behind the two girls, as was proper for a male servant accompanying his mistresses, but they kept thwarting her, until she ended up riding between them.

"What do you think, Ben? Am I an accomplished rider?"

"You appear very comfortable in the saddle, Lady Mariah." *Accomplished* would take a little longer.

"I was seven when Papa sold my pony. He said Blossom was too small for me and that he would find me a proper mount."

Catherine snorted. "He never had any intention of replacing either of our ponies, Mariah. He sold them because he needed the money."

"I think Father was just looking for the perfect horses for us," the younger girl insisted.

"You are such a ninny, Mariah. Sometimes I think you are *still* seven. Do you really think it takes *ten years* to find two horses? Ben managed it in one day."

Benna wished that she'd managed to drop back behind the bickering siblings before this conversation began. She knew that the last earl had had money problems, but it was hardly the kind of information the two sisters should be discussing in front of a servant.

Mariah bit her lip and stared down at her too-tightly clenched hands.

Benna opened her mouth, but Lady Catherine wasn't done.

"It doesn't matter what Papa did or said anymore. Uncle Jago promised we shall have all the things we've been lacking." Catherine turned her navy-blue eyes on Benna. "He said we will go to London in the spring. I shall have a *Season*." Her eyes sparkled and her voice was hushed, as though she were passing along a juicy tidbit of gossip.

"That sounds very nice, my lady," Benna murmured.

It actually sounded like hell, but Benna knew she was in the minority with that opinion.

"It will be divine. I shall have dozens of gowns and dance until the early hours and meet wonderful—"

Benna let her ramble, pleased not to have to speak. She had wondered why the younger woman had stopped haunting the stables recently. It seemed that the lure of a London Season would be Benna's savior.

Benna had always done her best to avoid London like the plague. It was worse than the plague, actually. She'd rather have buboes and gangrene than be forced to wear some dreadful gown while men four inches shorter than she wagered with each other to see who would be the first to ask her to dance.

"Who do you think that is?" Mariah's voice broke into Benna's musings.

Two riders approached from the main road.

"That looks like Mrs. Valera's lovely auburn hair." Catherine raised her hand to shield her eyes. "But I don't recognize the gentleman. Mrs. Valera always wears the most beautiful clothes to church." Catherine's voice throbbed with envy.

Benna knew both sisters were wearing habits that had once belonged to their mother. Catherine—who was apparently very skilled with a needle—had altered them.

That information had made Benna realize just how short of money the earl's family must be.

It also made her realize the list of items she'd been compiling for the stables should probably wait. How could she ask for a flat of roof slates, three score fence posts, and a sledge mallet when the earl's nieces were having to make their own clothing?

"Did you know Uncle Jago used be in love with her?" Mariah asked, the words jarring Benna from her musing.

Catherine's head whipped around. "Who told you that, Mariah?"

"I heard Nana telling Miss Kemp."

"You heard? You mean you were eavesdropping, Mariah. That is a disgusting habit."

"I didn't," Mariah protested.

"You did." Catherine turned to Benna. "Mariah has dozens of places where she hides and listens to people's private conversations."

Mariah looked to be on the verge of weeping.

123

The thought of Jago being in love with another woman made Benna feel like weeping.

Listen to you—*Jago, now, is it?*

Benna ignored Geoffrey's taunting, more interested in the subject under discussion.

"*Everyone* was in love with Mrs. Valera, Mariah. Not just Uncle Jago. I doubt he would appreciate you *eavesdropping* or spreading tales about such a private matter," Catherine added.

Benna possessed a self-destructive urge to hear more about the earl and the woman he had loved—or still did—and who was apparently approaching them.

But Lady Catherine switched back to the subject of dresses.

Benna listened to the girls' chatter with one ear, her gaze fixed on the approaching riders. The closer the pair got, the sicker she felt.

Having seen him only days earlier, she recognized the man even from a distance: it was Viscount Fenwick.

Hysteria bubbled up inside her; it was just her bloody luck.

Calm down, Benna. You can hardly bolt off right now without drawing attention, can you? Besides, you look nothing like you did almost six years ago.

For a change, Geoff's voice calmed her.

And he was right; she couldn't bolt, all she could do was brazen it out.

As the riders came closer, she saw that Fenwick—who'd aged far more than six years, his skin yellowish and pouchy—was riding beside the most beautiful woman Benna had ever seen.

Of course Jago would have been in love with her; what a magnificent couple they must have made.

"That's Mrs. Valera," Mariah whispered in a stage whisper.

"Why, look at these two fabulous equestriennes," the fiery-haired beauty called out as the pair approached.

"Hallo, Mrs. Valera," the girls chimed.

The widow gave them a mocking glare. "I thought I told you two to call me Ria. You shall make me feel positively ancient otherwise. Let me introduce a dear friend of mine, Viscount Fenwick, this is Lady Catherine and Lady Mariah."

Fenwick bowed, his smile reptilian as he took in Catherine's innocent, pretty face.

124

Benna watched from beneath lowered lashes, grateful for the low brim of her hat.

As horrified as she was to be face to face with a man who knew her, it was difficult to pull her gaze away from Mrs. Valera, who looked like something out of a painting. Everything about her was jewel-toned. Her habit was the same emerald as her eyes and she wore gold epaulettes and a jaunty military-style hat, neither of which made her look anything like a soldier.

She glanced from girl to girl, her green eyes glinting with interest. "I see your uncle wasted no time in mounting you. What a lovely steed you have, Mariah. I do love a horse with socks."

"Thank you Mrs. Va—er Ria. His name is Shadow. Ben picked him out for me."

"Ben?" The woman's expressive auburn eyebrows arched.

"Ben is our stable master." Catherine shifted slightly in her seat to face Benna.

Benna doffed her cap but kept her chin and eyes down. "Good afternoon, ma'am, my lord."

Fenwick's gaze remained fastened on Catherine and Mrs. Valera didn't even glance in Benna's direction; acknowledging servants was beneath her.

Neither of them had even registered her existence; Benna wanted to jump and cheer, but that would probably get her noticed.

"Lord Fenwick and I were just going to Lenshurst Park to deliver an invitation to a ball."

"A ball?" Catherine could not have sounded more stunned if Mrs. Valera had said she was inviting her on a five-year expedition to China.

The siren chuckled, a low, earthy sound at odds with her fragile beauty. "A *masquerade* ball."

Catherine's horse skittered sideways into her sister's mount and she scrambled to bring the gelding under control. She glanced at Benna, who pretended not to notice her equestrian mishap.

"But that's marvelous, er, Ria. I've always wanted to—" Catherine broke off, biting her lip. "Oh, your invitation is for my mother and Uncle Jago."

"Of course you are invited, my dear."

"But I'm not out yet—neither of us are."

"It doesn't matter out here in the wilds of Cornwall whether you've been presented or attended some stuffy Drawing Room. Both you and Mariah must join in at least part of the evening."

By the grudging way the other woman said the words *stuffy* and *Drawing Room* Benna guessed that she'd not been invited to meet the queen.

Benna couldn't have said exactly why, but she suspected Mrs. Valera was not what her father would have called *good ton*.

"If you are heading back then we shall accompany you," Mrs. Valera declared.

Benna fell in behind the foursome, grateful to be out of Fenwick's line of vision. Not that he'd even glanced at her. But still she could not rest easy—not as long as he remained in the area and was liable to pop up at any moment.

It didn't matter that he'd been drunk to near insensibility on most of the occasions that she'd seen him. The man *had* looked at her those two mornings when she'd argued with Michael in the breakfast room; he'd even joined in the baiting.

Every time she encountered him was just another opportunity to rouse his slumbering memory. If it happened often enough, he just might remember.

***

Jago was returning from Redruth when he encountered Ria, Viscount Fenwick, his nieces, and Benna in the cobbled courtyard.

"Look who we met while out on our very first ride," Catherine called out as he rode up.

It had been years since he'd last seen Fenwick, a man he'd never cared for. Jago knew the viscount had once been a close associate of Cadan's and lived in the area, but he was more than a little disturbed to find Ria sharing the company of such a scoundrel and fortune-hunter.

He forced a smile. "Good morning, Ria, Fenwick, how kind of you to call,"

Ria gave him one of her carnivorous smirks, her unsubtle message clear in her bright green gaze: *You see, Jago, how quickly I can have a substitute ready and waiting if you do not come up to scratch.*

126

"Hello, Jago," she said. "I'm so delighted we were able to catch you at home."

"Trebolton," Fenwick acknowledged with a slight incline of his head, his face a supercilious mask.

Jago dismounted and handed his reins to Gordon, the new groom. "Would you care to come in for tea?"

"We can't stay long, Jago, we've just come to deliver a delightful surprise."

He was afraid to ask. As it was, he didn't have to.

"Mrs. Valera is having a masquerade ball," Catherine blurted, clambering ungracefully off her mount. Jago saw Benna wince at her pupil's clumsy dismount.

"A masquerade ball," he repeated, turning from his niece to his guests. "Indeed, that is delightful, Ria," he lied. "When is the happy event?"

Again, it was Catherine who answered. "It will be the week before Christmas, and Ria has invited both me and Mariah. May we go, Uncle?"

Jago frowned at the girl's use of the older woman's pet name. "You will have to ask your mother, Catherine." He looked up at Ria. "Are you sure you won't come inside and deliver the happy news to Lady Trebolton?"

Ria made a moue of regret. "I am afraid I simply don't have a moment to spare today. I shall let Catherine have the joy of surprising the countess."

Irritation surged in his chest. Claire was the highest-ranking woman in their neighborhood and it was disrespectful of Ria to treat her so dismissively.

He happened to glance at Fenwick and saw that the other man was eying Catherine in a way that he could not like.

For her part, Catherine was prettily flushed and breathless at her first hint of attention from a male under the age of fifty who was not a servant.

Jago sighed; the girl would require close observation with this rake lurking about the area.

"You'll be attending the masquerade ball, Fenwick?" Jago asked.

Fenwick pulled his eyes from Catherine with obvious reluctance. "I wouldn't miss it for anything."

Ria gave one of her throaty chuckles, which Jago found grating rather than appealing. "Lord Fenwick is the advance guard of a large house party that I shall host two weeks before the ball."

Fenwick's family seat was less than an hour away and yet he was staying at Ria's house?

Knowing Ria the house party would be the sort that seethed with nocturnal adventures.

"The ball will be held at the end of the party—a grand finale of sorts."

Jago's gaze drifted to Benna, who'd helped Mariah dismount and was examining the point straps on her new saddle. Now that he knew she was a woman he couldn't believe that he'd ever been fooled. Indeed, her rough clothing made her look even more feminine.

"Jago?"

Ria's voice shook him from his musing. "I beg your pardon?"

She gave him an arch look and turned in her saddle, her eyes flickering over Benna, the horse, and Mariah. Jago could see she was befuddled at what could have pulled his attention away from *her*.

"I asked what costume you would choose for my party," Ria said.

"I already know what I will be," Catherine piped up.

Jago smiled at his niece's childlike excitement. "And what is that?"

"I can't tell you; it is a secret." She pursed her lips, her eyes dancing. He couldn't recall her looking so happy in ages—if ever. So, at least Ria was good for something.

"Thank you, Ben," Mariah said when Benna had finished adjusting her saddle.

Fenwick glanced absently at Jago's stable master and then did a double take. "You look familiar. Do I know you from somewhere?" he asked, his tone imperious.

"I don't think so, my lord." Her expression was unreadable but Jago could see that she'd paled beneath her tan.

Fenwick stared, his eyes narrow and his expression no longer lazy.

"Benna used to be a groom for a gentleman called Mr. Fenton—perhaps you knew him?" Mariah volunteered.

Benna shot the girl a look of surprise and Mariah blushed. Jago knew what that meant: his youngest niece must have been eavesdropping again.

Jago stepped into the awkward silence. "Ben worked for Mr. Stephen Worth before coming to Lenshurst. Perhaps that is where you saw him before," Jago said.

Fenwick grunted, and turned back to Catherine, already bored with the subject.

"We'd best be on our way if we are to deliver the rest of our invitations." Ria cast Jago an openly chiding look that said more clearly than words that she would much rather be somewhere people didn't waste time discussing a mere servant's work history. "We are on our way to hand-deliver our invitation at Oakland Manor. Shall I pass along your regards to Mrs. Worth, Jago?"

"I dined with them last night, Ria. But thank you for your kind offer."

She frowned. "Didn't they arrive only yesterday?"

"Yes." Jago could see that his one-word answer did not provide the information she'd wished for—such as why Jago would be invited over to their wealthy neighbors' house before they'd hardly had time to unpack and settle in.

"Well," Ria said coolly, shifting in her saddle. "I look forward to seeing you girls at the ball, if not before."

Fenwick nodded to Catherine and Mariah, and they were off.

Catherine waited just until Ria and Fenwick were out of earshot to say, "I'm going to tell Mama." She left the courtyard at a near run, Mariah on her heels.

Jago turned to where Ben had been standing with the horses, but his mysterious employee was already gone.

Why did Fenwick think he recognized his stable master?

Why had Benna looked so terrified at the possibility?

And why did Jago suspect that there was a great deal of her story that Benna had not shared with him?

Chapter Fifteen

Bath
December 1816
One Year Ago

Benna stared at the contents of the black velvet box that Geoffrey had just handed her.

"Well? Do you like it?"

She looked up at him, unable to close her mouth. "Er, it's a ring."

"Very good, Ben!" He gave a bark of laugher. "Of course it's a bloody ring."

"But—"

"But what?"

"It's a woman's ring."

Geoff raised his eyebrows, as if to say: *And?*

"How can I wear this without getting strange looks?"

"Well," he said with exaggerated slowness, "if you were to go about as a woman, nobody would give you strange looks."

Benna closed the box and set it on the table. "You'd better explain what you mean."

"Do you know what day it is?" he demanded.

She blinked. "Er, Wednesday?"

"What day of the month?" he asked, his smile beginning to look strained.

"December fifth," she said.

"We met each other four years ago on this very day." He crossed his arms and gave her a look of triumph.

"No, we didn't."

"Yes, we did."

"No, we didn't. We met in mid-February 1812. I don't recall the day, but that was certainly the month."

"Oh." His eyebrows knitted, his expression confused.

"Is that what this is?" She gestured to the box, suddenly feeling churlish for taking the wind from his sails. "An anniversary gift? If so, then I'm grate—"

"I want you to marry me."

"*What?*"

Geoff frowned. "Why the devil do you look so bloody stunned?"

Benna could only sputter.

"Haven't we been getting along well since, er—"

"Since you returned from your Edinburgh trip?" As if Benna could forget the day when he'd invited her to eat with him and began to behave more like a decent, thoughtful human being.

Well, not entirely decent, of course, since he still made his money by cheating flats. But in most other matters he'd been almost … pleasant.

"Yes, it has been quite pleasant," she admitted.

"Pleasant," he said flatly. "You call what happened last night—at least three times—*pleasant?* Based on the way you were *screaming* my name when I had you bent over the back of the settee an hour ago I would have—"

"Good God, Geoffrey!" Benna's face heated; she could only be grateful that they were in Geoff's sitting room rather than down in the hotel dining room.

He calmed down enough to give a genuine-sounding chuckle. "Lord. What a little prude you still are."

While she might retain some vestiges of restraint when it came to the sorts of things they did to one another—although less with every day that passed—Benna was well-aware that Geoff had positively no shame when it came to sexual activity. And he *especially* liked talking about the things he was going to do to her and the things he wanted done. At length and in excruciating detail.

"Tell me it was more than pleasant," he ordered. "If you don't, I won't do that thing with my tongue and your tight little—"

"Fine, Geoff," she shouted. "Last night—and an hour ago—was, er, *extremely* pleasant."

Benna had lasted barely a month after Geoff's nighttime visit to her bedroom in Brighton. Yes, she was a weak, despicable person and she knew it.

She had wanted to make him wait—to make him suffer and beg—but then she'd realized that she was only depriving herself and making herself suffer in the process. She was tired of her own hand and she recalled, far too well, how much pleasure Geoff had given her that night—before he'd turned into an offensive, obnoxious cad.

And then there was the fact that Geoff could have any woman he wanted in his bed but had not taken a single lover since his return from Edinburgh. Yes, that had been very persuasive.

Benna rationalized her weakness with the argument that she couldn't exactly enjoy intimate relations with somebody new. At least not without explaining why she was masquerading as a man.

So that left her with Geoff for a partner if she wanted to enjoy any carnal pleasure at all.

Other than Geoff's personality, it wasn't exactly a hardship to take him as her lover. Not only was he exceedingly attractive, but when it came to bed sport, it seemed to be a matter of honor for him to give his partner physical pleasure. Even that first time—before he'd behaved like such a boor—he'd made her climax more than once.

Not only that, but he was extremely open-minded and adventurous when it came to amorous activities. While Benna wasn't quite prepared to accept every suggestion he'd made, she'd found herself doing things she never would have believed. And enjoying herself immensely.

And so, one night—after he'd been especially charming and given her a book she'd been wanting—Benna had opened her bedroom door to him when he'd knocked.

Since then, they had scarcely spent an evening apart.

Not only had Benna learned more about the wonderful ways that men and women could entertain each other with their bodies than she'd ever thought possible, but she'd also discovered that sexual pleasure was not something she liked going without.

"Now that you're my only lover you're going to have to learn to keep me satisfied," Geoff had instructed her that first week. "I shall have to give you lessons and bring you up to scratch," he'd said, speaking in a hilariously pompous way that had left her choking with laughter.

Benna had also been secretly pleased by the news that she was to be his only lover, but she'd hidden that fact by laughing at him and asking if there would be an exam after his lessons.

"Absolutely. And girls who fail will be punished. Severely."

That, she'd learned, had been rather enjoyable, too.

Although Benna had indulged most of Geoff's desires and demands there was one area where she refused to budge.

"I do wish you'd swallow your stubbornness and spend evenings in my far more luxurious chambers, you obstinate little shrew. Or at least allow me to hire adjoining chambers."

But Benna had refused to relent on that matter. She liked keeping some distance between them—even though Geoff ended up staying overnight in her room more often than not. But it was important to her that she was not living in his pocket.

Besides, she was by no means convinced that this new and improved Geoffrey was permanent. Even if it was, she had other plans in her future, and they didn't involve marrying Geoffrey—not even after her twenty-fifth birthday.

Of course, she could hardly tell him that.

Benna wasn't convinced that Geoffrey really wanted to get married—or whether he was just afraid that he'd lose her services— both in and out of bed—if he didn't secure her.

She glanced at the ring box. "Why do you want to get married?"

"For one thing, I want you in my bed, with me, every night."

"That hardly seems like a reason to marry. I can visit your rooms any time I please without marrying you."

"But you won't. Not that I can understand *why*. Especially when my rooms are much more spacious and commodious. Why must we creep around in your pokey servant room?"

"You never had any problem with me occupying my *pokey servant room* before you were visiting me nightly."

He ignored that dig. "Not only are servant beds more uncomfortable, but yours is invariably full of bloody wood shavings from your infernal whittling."

Benna grinned at him, her eyes flickering to her nightstand, where she'd set out her little Noah's ark of carved creatures, albeit only one of everything so far.

Only a month ago, to her intense delight, she'd actually sold three carvings to a man who'd seen her working on a ground squirrel and wanted three different animals for his daughters.

When Geoff had learned that she'd only charged six shillings for them he'd hooted. "It took you weeks to carve each one, yet you've sold them for an amount that will scarcely buy a firkin of beer."

But right now, Geoff wasn't laughing. Instead, he was settling in for a sulk.

Benna gave him a friendly nudge with her elbow. "See, you should look on the bright side of things, Geoffrey."

"What bright side?"

"You should be grateful that I won't come to your bed since I'd likely just leave it all full of shavings."

He grunted. It didn't matter that Geoff was almost twenty years her senior; he behaved like a child of seven.

Benna realized he would not be jollied out of his snit. "Fine. What would happen if I married you? Would we go on the same way?" she prodded, curious.

"What? You mean with you acting as my servant?"

Benna nodded.

"Good God, no! You'd be my wife. We'd engage a servant—or servants, rather. A maid for you—proper clothing."

"Perhaps settle down somewhere?"

His eyebrows knitted. "I suppose we could do less traveling."

"Have a few brats?" she suggested.

The corners of his mouth turned down. "I don't care for your tone."

"See, that is a good thing to consider."

"What? Your tone?"

She nodded. "As your servant, you can always sack me if you don't like my tone. Conversely, I can always leave your employ if I don't care to amend my tone. As your wife, one of us would have to conform. And I know who that would be."

"Ha! Since when have you ever conformed, Ben?" He stopped abruptly and fixed her with a darkling look. "Ben." He gave a rude snort of laughter. "Christ! I don't even know your real bloody name. Trust me, sweetheart, if either of us has conformed, it has been *me*." He raised a hand and ticked off one long, elegant finger. "First, I no longer take lovers—even though that has certainly hurt our bottom line."

That was true; Geoff had earned a sizeable chunk of money from the gifts—both monetary and otherwise—his wealthy lovers had showered on him.

"Second, we've given up most of the race meets because *you* don't care for them."

Also true.

"Third, I'm not allowed to play cards with anyone who has a mere *competence*—an amount which *you* decide, by the way."

Yes, Benna refused to aid Geoff in plucking old lady pensioners or sending feckless young bucks to the sponging house.

Geoff flung up his hands. "Good God!" he said, looking and sounding genuinely amazed. "When I lay it all out like that I realize that it's as if I'm *already* married."

Benna couldn't resist laughing.

He narrowed his eyes at her and, quick as an adder strike, he grabbed and pulled her onto his lap, forcing her to straddle his thighs, holding her waist in an unbreakable grip. "I think I love you, you scrawny, bossy harpy. Won't you make me the happiest man alive and marry me?"

Benna looked down into his eyes, which had darkened as he stared up at her. She recognized his dilated pupils as signs of his desire and her own body was already responding: her pulse pounding, her sex swelling, and her inner muscles clenching as she imagined him filling her. She wanted him, that was true enough. But did she love him?

As she stared down at his handsome face she considered her feelings for him—those aside from lust. Even now, after months of his best behavior—albeit interspersed with periodic lapses—she did not trust him not to hurt her.

Maybe once she might have been able to love him—back before she'd seen the worst of him: his selfishness, his willingness to manipulate anyone for his own reasons, and his callous treatment of far too many women—more than a few of whom had lost not only their dignity but also their hearts to him.

Benna could not forget those parts of him existed, even though he no longer showed that side of himself to her.

"Well?" he said, his charming smile reminding her of the night that he'd rescued her from that beating. "What do you say, love?"

"I'm honored, Geoff—really. But I—"

Some emotion flickered behind his dark blue gaze—disappointment? Anger? "Shh, never mind, love. What a cow-handed clod I am to be rushing my fences. Let me make up for my clumsiness."

He yanked her head down, crushing her mouth with his.

Benna gave as good as she got, the desire she felt for him mingling with guilt that she could not give him what he wanted.

They consumed each other, their kiss turning into a battle of wills.

She felt the hard, throbbing ridge of him beneath the silk robe he wore and ground against him, making him shudder.

Well, maybe she couldn't give him love and marriage, but she could give him the next best thing: pleasure.

Benna slid off his lap, shoved his thighs wide, and dropped to her knees.

He gave a low, throaty chuckle. "Mmm, I like the way your mind works, darling."

Benna pushed open his robe and exposed his thick, hard shaft. She took him in her hand and pumped him slowly, marveling at his beautiful body, just as she always did.

"Oh God, Ben." He sucked in a harsh breath, his lids lowering, hips pulsing as he thrust into her tight fist. "I want you so badly," he said, his voice more of a groan. "I need to be inside you. Now."

Benna shook her head as she lowered her mouth. "Let me give you pleasure, Geoff."

He stilled only for a heartbeat, and Benna wondered if he heard the second part of that thought—the part she left unspoken: *because I cannot give you love.*

But she must have imagined his hesitation because he gave a low, wicked chuckle, threading his fingers into her hair and pushing down her head while raising his hips. "Yes. Take me deep, my darling Ben, just the way I like it."

Chapter Sixteen

Cornwall
1817
Present Day

A few days after the shock of discovering that Fenwick was haunting the area Benna suffered another surprise.

She had just sent the two new lads she'd hired in Truro—Gordon and Jem—off to the south close to work on the fence and was preparing to start repairing some stonework when Kenneth Pike arrived.

Pike had shown up an hour ago, arriving with several other servants the earl had apparently hired last week. He was in his mid-thirties and had the shrewd, knowing eyes of a man who missed little.

Benna knew within five minutes of meeting Pike that he was going to cause her problems.

But what could she do about it, other than quit?

So, instead, she put him to work.

Stonework was a slow, careful task that required strength but very little thought.

That was just as well because Benna's mind was racing: why had the earl hired this man? Was he *trying* to get her to quit? Did he—

"Mr. Piddock?"

Benna looked up to find Nance in the doorway. "Aye?" she asked, her arms screaming as she and Pike carefully wiggled the block of gray stone until it fit into the gap that Pike had chiseled out.

"His lordship wants to see you."

Once the stone had been shimmied into its space—Pike had done an excellent job, she grudgingly admitted—Benna stood up slowly, her lower back on fire.

She took off her cap, shoved her damp hair off her forehead, and glanced down at her filthy breeches. "He wants me like this?"

"He said *immediately.*"

Benna snatched her coat off its peg, her heart thudding at the terse summons.

She turned to Pike, who was staring at her with a fish-eyed stare. Not that he could help it, since his gray-green eyes naturally bulged out like those of a fish.

"Go measure the block for the next one. I doubt I'll be long. Don't try to lift it until I come back," she added.

He nodded. "Aye, *sir.*"

Benna ignored the emphasis he put on the word "sir." The man had reason to be irritable; at thirty-five, he was more than a decade her senior.

Following the old butler back to the house was a process more painful than undergoing a tooth extraction. Not only was Nance's snaillike pace maddening, but it gave her far too much time to wonder what this was about.

Had Jago finally made up his mind to send her away?

She shuddered at the thought. *Oh please, God. Don't let him send me away.*

Somehow I think that God won't be on your side in this issue, darling.

Geoff was right. She'd lied to the man—and continued to do so—and had made a fool of him. Doubtless the earl was reminded of that fact every time he saw her face.

Benna crept behind Nance while, in her head, she covered the same ground she'd gone over and over and over since that night in Truro, like a desperate farmer who worked an arid plot of land he already knew would yield no harvest.

After things had ended with Geoff, Benna had lost all the money she'd so carefully scrimped and saved.

All she had now was what she'd been able to save these past ten months or so; it simply wasn't enough money to allow her to go somewhere and hide until she turned twenty-five. She had to keep working.

If the earl discharged her, she would most likely have to go someplace else. Someplace away from Redruth—away from *him*.

Yes, it was irrational, foolish, and not a little bit pitiful that the thought of never again seeing the Earl of Trebolton left her feeling nauseated. Especially now, when he could hardly stand to be around her. She should be grateful to get away from him and quit rubbing salt on an open wound.

At least that's what she tried to tell herself.

By the time they reached the top step of the servant entrance Benna felt like an exhausted hound that had lost the scent of the fox.

She deftly skirted the old man and opened the door for him.

Nance sniffed at the small courtesy and headed toward the kitchen. "You don't need me to lead you up there," he threw over his shoulder.

Feeling as if she were walking a gang plank, Benna used the back stairs, trudging up as slowly as Nance. She encountered a new maid on her way to the second floor—so, that was at least seven new employees that she'd seen.

That did not seem to be the actions of a man who was skint.

Then again, his increased spending might mean that he had expectations from some other quarter, rather than the estate, itself.

And what other source of money could an unmarried male aristocrat count on?

Benna couldn't think about that right now.

She scratched on the door to his study.

It was the same room and the same man yet nothing felt the same.

Lord Trebolton's quill was flying across the parchment, his dark head bent over the desk.

"I'll be just a moment." He did not look up. Nor did he sound happy.

Things had changed.

He wrote something with a flourish—a signature?— and then sanded the sheet before looking up.

His mouth was pressed into a stern line, but there was an odd gleam in his eyes. "Good afternoon, Ben. Have a seat." The earl gestured to the chair in front of his desk. *Right* in front of his desk, almost as if it had been put there for some sort of interrogation.

Benna sat, clutching her hat with both hands and staring at the cluttered surface of his desk rather than the man behind it.

The earl came out from behind the piles of paper, leaned against the front of his desk, and crossed his arms, his face an unreadable mask as he looked down at her. "What do you think of your new assistant?"

"Is he my replacement, sir?"

"I engaged him to help you with the heavier work."

Benna chewed her lip to keep from speaking her mind.

"What? Out with it." He dropped his hands to the desk's beveled edge and leaned back.

"He's already suspicious of me."

"Why? What have you done?"

"I haven't done anything. It's just—"

"Yes?"

"He's older than me and believes he has more experience."

"Do you think he has more experience?"

"He does," she said, her tone grudging to her own ears.

"And he is physically stronger than you?"

Benna chewed the inside of her cheek. Why was he doing this to her? Why did he not simply discharge her?

The earl didn't wait for her answer. "He *does* have more experience and he *is* stronger."

"Very well, my lord." Benna stood.

"I am not finished yet, *Ben*."

Benna glared at him and he stared coolly back.

She dropped into her chair.

"What I was going to say, is that I believe Pike would do an adequate job of running my stables. However, I do have a position available that is not so easy to fill." He eyed her with something that looked suspiciously like amusement.

For one mad, intoxicating moment she thought he was going to ask her to be his valet.

But then she recalled that a valet was among the new servants who'd arrived with Pike.

"What position would that be, sir?"

"It would be a combination of secretary and steward."

The word *secretary* was almost as surprising as *valet* would have been. "You want me to be your *secretary*?"

"Why not?"

She could only stare; the man must have rats in his garret.

"Why not?" he repeated.

"Because hiring your groom to become your secretary will raise even more eyebrows than hiring a postilion to be your stable master."

His lips curled into an expression of haughty disdain. "One of the few benefits of being an earl rather than a humble country doctor is that I don't need to give a rap about other people's eyebrows."

He was right. Who in this area would call an earl to account for his behavior? Aristocrats were known to pursue any and all whims, no matter who such whims might horrify.

And as far as aristocratic fancies went, hiring one's groom to be one's secretary was hardly on the level of debauching one's tenant's daughters.

Still ….

"You appear skeptical, Ben."

"It won't be you who attracts unwanted attention, my lord, but me."

"There will probably be some speculation below stairs about your change in status," he admitted. "Would that bother you enough that you would not want the position?"

Would it?

Benna had been so ready to be offended at being pushed out of her stable job that she had given no thought to his offer.

The truth was, her body hurt most days from work that was too strenuous for her frame, the skin on her hands was cracked and bleeding, she'd burnt herself repeatedly mending items on the forge, and—

If you worked as his secretary you could see him every day. All day. Just think what a fool you could make of yourself in such circumstances.

Yes, there was that.

Benna caught her lower lip and bit hard to keep from grinning like a loon.

Oh, Benna—you should run. As fast and as far as you can. That wasn't Geoff's voice, but Benna's own.

And she knew it was correct.

Once she'd composed herself, she looked up and asked, "Could you tell me what you would expect of me, sir?"

"I'm still going through several years' worth of paperwork that is, quite frankly, in a disastrous state of disorganization. I would require your help putting that in order. I also need assistance with things that would be more in keeping with a steward's duties. I'm leasing two tenant properties as they are, but I've committed to completing maintenance on twelve others which are currently leased but in dire need of work. I cannot direct all the repairs myself, there just aren't enough hours in the day. And then there is the dairy, the home farm, and the house." He waved at the room around them, a small chamber more suited to a servant's room than the master of the house. "All the rooms are in need of—Well, *something*. Again, it is too much for me to manage and I'm afraid the countess is simply not well enough to handle the day-to-day running of the house. Those are a few of the tasks."

Those tasks all sounded far more pleasant than digging fence post holes, hauling stone, or replacing missing roof slates.

"How would you explain such a transition to Pike?"

"I'm not in the habit of explaining my decisions to my servants." He frowned and Benna knew that he'd just realized that was exactly what he *was* doing. "You will retain some of your duties, such as assessing the buildings and conducting the girls' riding lessons. That would allow you to keep some oversight of Pike until we are certain he is suited to the position."

"Will I continue living in my current quarters?"

"I'll leave that up to you. There is, however, a small suite connected to this study; it used to be part of the steward's quarters." He pointed to a door behind the large trestle table. "The chambers are separated from this room by a sort of butler's pantry. This office will be yours whether or not you choose to occupy the adjacent chambers, since I'm planning to move back to the library."

Benna thought about the tub that she had gone to so much effort to move and restore, which she had only bathed in once, But, in all truthfulness, she could not see herself bathing with Pike roaming the property.

"Well?" the earl prodded.

Really, the choice was no choice at all. "Thank you for the offer. I should like the position and I would also like the steward's quarters, my lord."

He didn't look surprised. "Good. You may start immediately."

Benna opened her mouth, and then closed it.

"What is it, Ben?"

"Why are you doing this, my lord?"

He gave her a cool smile. "To salve my conscience."

It was pretty much the answer she'd expected.

"Any other questions?"

"I know you do not need to explain yourself to your servants, my lord, but I will have to justify the rather surprising move from the stables to the house."

"Tell them the truth."

His words surprised a laugh out of her.

"Not the entire truth," he amended. "Just tell them that you are the child of a teacher who was raised to follow in your father's footsteps. You will say that because of your youth and lack of teaching experience, you took a position as a postilion because it was the only job you could find. In the course of working for me I learned of your background and decided to benefit from your education." He shrugged. "It is, in the important ways, the truth."

If only he knew how far from the truth it really was.

***

"Come, I'll show you your new quarters so that you might settle in." Jago strode to the door that led to the strange little cupboard-closet-hallway. "This was last used as a linen closet, but I've coopted it for storage." He pointed at the precarious ledgers and account books that filled most of the shelves. "These are what I have already examined."

"My goodness," she said.

"That is a polite way of putting it," he said wryly. "My brother's record-keeping was non-existent. Those ledgers might look like distinct bound collections, but they are often incomplete and even out of chronological order. The reason it is taking me so long to sort through everything is two-fold. One, my brother stopped organizing anything twelve years ago.

"And two, I am stretched rather thin since my return. I need to get the tenant farms up to snuff before the spring, but I also need to know the extent of my finances before I can commit to having more work done."

His new secretary quietly scrutinized the small sitting area that contained only a few pieces of furniture.

That gave Jago an opportunity to scrutinize *her*, something he couldn't get enough of.

Her bone structure was delicate and her features finely drawn and feminine. Her skin was flawless and smooth with no hint of facial hair.

She was tall—taller than any woman he'd ever met. He would not be surprised if she stood five feet eleven inches.

He liked to think that he would have noticed her deception sooner if he'd not been so consumed with sorting out the disastrous estate, but he suspected that was wishful thinking.

There was no point thinking about it; he knew the truth about her now, and that was what mattered.

Well, there was also the issue of *that kiss*, which stood in the room with them like a third presence.

Yes, that kiss most certainly mattered. For something that had barely lasted a minute its effect on Jago's mental processes was prodigious.

He was both fascinated and unnerved by the attraction that had sprouted from it—and grown quickly, like a weed given a bit of water and daylight.

A dozen times a day Jago forcibly thrust the brief but startling interlude from his brain, and yet the enticing memory came slithering back again and again. At night, it settled into his brain and kept both his mind and body awake, spawning other, far less innocent, thoughts.

Bringing her into the house as his secretary—while salving his conscience—was unwise, not to mention dangerous.

Still, it was a far safer position than the one he really wanted to offer her—that of valet.

Why not? the devil on his shoulder had demanded; Jago needed a valet and she had valeted a man for years. What could be more logical?

Oh, he had entertained the notion—he blushed to think of just how often he'd entertained it—but he had never seriously considered it.

Even so, thoughts of her dressing and undressing his body, shaving him, and drawing his bath consumed, incited, and shamed him.

Jago had not been so hard, so often—and so inconveniently— since he'd been a lad. Even nightly sessions with his fist couldn't seem to dull the edge of his desire for her.

The last time he'd wanted a woman so badly—so *fervently*—had been eighteen years ago with Ria.

And look how that had ended.

Jago realized Benna had turned to him and was patiently waiting.

He cleared his throat. "As my secretary, you will soon know the financial condition of the earldom."

"I will be discreet, my lord."

"I'm sure you won't be surprised, given the condition of my stables and house. I am, quite bluntly, in a pickle." Jago hesitated; he really didn't want to spell out exactly what he was doing—trying to discover why his brother had needed all those loans—but he had to trust her if he was turning her loose with his family's secrets.

"Your priority is to look for anything regarding my brother's investments—especially anything in the last year." There, that was vague and yet still to the purpose.

Jago crossed the dusty wood floor to the two doors on the opposite wall. He opened the one on the left. "This is your bedchamber."

The room beyond was cluttered with a few sticks of furniture and a heavy bedstead that had been shoved to the side. The floor was without rugs, the walls without pictures. Just like so many rooms in this once lovely house, the space was bare and depressing.

Jago closed the door, walked to the second door, and opened it. "You might find suitable furnishings in *this* room."

The room beyond was filled, floor to ceiling, with piled-up furniture, stacked wooden crates, giant dusty bundles that looked to be

146

drapes, rugs, and bedding, brass-bound chests, and other, less immediately identifiable items.

Benna's jaw dropped as she eyed the chaotic mess. "Oh," was all she said.

Standing this close Jago could smell her: a blend of horse, leather, and the outdoors.

Beneath those typically masculine aromas were the biting tang of lye soap and an earthy whiff of wool.

And more subtle, still, was the sweet, musky smell of sweat.

Jago inhaled deeply, filling his lungs greedily and holding the scent of her inside his body.

Good God. What the hell was wrong with him?

"Lord Trebolton?"

"Hmmm?" he said, turning to look at her.

Crystalline turquoise eyes met his. "I asked if you wished to dispose of the items in this room. Is that why they are all in here?"

"I have no idea why they are all in here. There are at least two dozen rooms piled full like this, all over the house."

She looked even more confused.

Jago knew the feeling. He suspected that his brother had assembled all the items to sell, hoping to raise money for ... well, for what, Jago did not know.

Benna did not need to know all that.

Instead, he said, "I've been waiting until I have a few extra hands to help sort and return all these items to their appropriate locations."

"You say there are *dozens* of rooms like this?"

"Yes. I hope that wild look around your eyes does not mean that you will run screaming."

Her lips—the bottom one, so sensual and full—curved up slightly at his words. "No. I will view it as a challenge."

Jago barked a laugh. "You are fearless." He turned away. "As you see more of the house, you will be able to discern what goes where. And I'm sure Nance and Mrs. Gates will be able to help. Go room to room and make a list of whatever else might be lacking, especially in the public rooms. My nieces will shortly be out of mourning, so one of your duties, as my secretary, shall be to plan a few dinners and a ball for after the New Year."

Only because he was looking at her did he see her face fall.

"You do not look particularly excited about that, Ben."

"I know nothing of such matters, my lord."

"You said you managed all aspects of your, er, Mr. Fenton's household."

He experienced an unpleasant frisson in his belly at the thought of her handling *all* facets of some stranger's life. He was pathetic; how was it possible to be jealous of an old dead man whom he'd never met?

Jago shook off the demoralizing thought and turned back to Benna. "Surely you must have arranged dinners and so forth for him?"

"I can't imagine you want me to organize the same sort of parties Mr. Fenton preferred."

Jago laughed at her tart rejoinder. "No, probably not card parties, but no doubt the precepts are similar."

She did not look optimistic.

"In any event," he said, "you can't know less than I do."

"I will be pleased to help wherever I can, my lord."

Jago paused, and then said, "I'm going to call you Ben even in private. I believe using the name at all times will keep me from slipping up." It was too bad that calling her by a male name could not make him think of her as a man.

"Tomorrow your first official act should be to supervise the moving of my desk and the trestle table back into the library. Then the study can function as your office."

"Yes, my lord."

"I assume you own no dinner dress?"

Her eyebrows, which he suddenly noticed were far darker than her hair, arched. "Sir?"

"It is common practice for a secretary or steward to dine with the family. Besides, you will hardly be comfortable below stairs once you begin to work in such an elevated capacity." Jago continued without waiting for an answer. "There is a tailor in Redruth, you needn't go all the way to Truro to purchase appropriate clothing. Until he can make you something appropriate you may wear the suit you wore in Truro. My sister-in-law rarely joins us for meals and my nieces and I are not sticklers when it comes to proper dress."

"Yes, sir."

Jago turned away from the unspoken questions in her eyes and opened the door to the corridor. "Dinner is served at seven o'clock sharp."

Chapter Seventeen

*H*appy birthday, darling!"

Geoff topped up both their glasses and then raised his in yet another a toast—the dozent of the evening, or so it seemed. "Here is to the five happiest years of my life. Bottoms up, my dear."

Benna threw back the contents of her glass in a couple of gulps, burped, wiped her mouth with the back of her hand, and set the empty vessel down with a thump, looking up when Geoff laughed.

She had to blink rapidly to focus her blurry gaze. "Huh?"

"Such delightful manners, my love," he teased. His heavy-lidded gaze told Benna that she wasn't the only one who was more than a trifle disguised.

Geoff had insisted on celebrating her twenty-second birthday by first dragging her out to a vulgar little theater—where they'd stood in the pit along with all the other young bucks—and afterward taking her to the grubbiest gambling hell Benna had ever seen.

She wasn't sure why they'd come to Carlisle as Geoff hadn't been invited to stay at any of his usual haunts. Although the town was bustling, it was gray with smoke from all the industrial endeavors, not to mention painfully provincial.

She'd just caught her breath from the last round when Geoff poured the remains of the bottle into both their glasses and once again raised his.

Benna groaned. "Ugh, Geoff, I'm not sure—"

"This is the last one, my love. And I'm sure enough for both of us." His charming grin stretched from ear to ear. "This last toast is to you." He cocked his head, his eyes glittering. "The only woman who can make me a happy man. What say you, Ben? Will you do me the honor of becoming my wife."

Benna's glass shook, some of the wine he'd poured sloshing over the rim. "Oh, Geoff." She wanted to say more, but her wits were too fuddled, her tongue too thick.

He chuckled. "Oh, you needn't look so tragic, darling. You can't blame a man for trying—*again*—can you?" His eyes seemed especially blue as he gazed across at her. "I didn't mean to distress you. Instead, let's drink to whatever the future holds." He raised his glass again. "May we each get what we desire, rather than what we deserve." He gave an odd-sounding laugh and threw back his head.

Benna raised the glass and drained it in four laborious swallows.

This time, when she lowered the glass, the room spun around her. She put down her glass and missed the table entirely.

"Whoops," Geoff said. "Look who's finished celebrating. Come on, lass." He stood and reached out a hand for her, the gesture so achingly familiar that Benna felt something warm trickle down her cheek.

A sob slipped out of her. "I'm sho—I mean I'm *so* shorry, Geoffy."

"Shhh, hush now. No tears. Who would have pegged you for a blubbering drunk?"

Benna gave a watery, choked laugh. "Shorry," she whispered. She gazed up at him, seeing three Geoffs, hoping he knew what she was trying to say.

"I know you are, love." He pulled her to her feet and deftly slid his arms beneath her, cradling her to his chest. "You seem so … substantial but you're just a slip of a thing, aren't you?" he asked, his voice subdued.

Benna's head lolled back. "Urgh, shhkinny," she mumbled.

"Let's put you to bed—mine tonight, I think." The door to his chambers was already open, the room still toasty warm from the fire Benna had fed when they'd returned from their carousing.

For somebody who'd just consumed the better part of two bottles of claret Geoff worked with remarkable deftness to undress her.

"Shank you," she muttered when he unbuttoned her fall and pushed down her breeches and drawers.

"It's always a pleasure to undress you, Benna."

She smiled woozily as he pulled the blankets up to her chin and then kissed her temple.

"Get some sleep, love," he whispered. "Tomorrow's going to be a long, difficult day."

***

Benna didn't know what it was that woke her, but she knew immediately that she was alone in the bed.

The room was so dark that it took her a moment to remember where she was—Geoff's bedchamber.

Her head was pounding like a war drum. But behind the pain something niggled, something that had been swimming just at the edge of her consciousness, around and around and around like a circling shark.

God, her head *hurt*. What had she been thinking to drink so much? She rarely drank at all, knowing how poorly she tolerated it.

But Geoff had been pouring the wine down her throat.

Geoff.

Her lips curved into a smile as she recalled how tenderly he'd undressed her before tucking her into—

Benna. He called me Benna.

She jolted upright, or, at least she tried to. That's when she noticed that her wrists were tied together, as were her ankles.

"Geoff!" Her voice was shrill with terror.

"Shhh, don't be frightened, love. I'm right here. Sorry I had to tie you. But I know how strong you are, for all that you don't look it. I couldn't risk you getting the upper hand and kicking my arse, now could I?" Geoff chuckled, his voice eerie and disembodied in the darkness.

Benna shifted clumsily, until she was on her side. She could barely see the outline of his head; he was sitting in a chair by the fire.

"What's going on, Geoff?" she asked, her voice froggy.

152

She saw his hand lift and realized he was drinking.

"Are you drunk?" she demanded.

"No, I wish I were—Lord knows I've been trying hard enough. I've not stopped drinking all night, but I'm as sober as a bloody judge."

Every hair on Benna's body stood up at the chilling deadness in his voice.

"Tell me why you are doing this?"

"Don't you want to ask how I know your name, Benna?"

Benna squeezed her eyes shut; so, she'd not dreamed it.

Her drink-addled mind struggled to make sense of it, but she came up with nothing. "I don't understand, how—"

"Come now, Benna. I taught you better than that. Think, my dear."

So Benna thought. It turned out to be a good exercise as it cleared her mind of both alcoholic haze and debilitating fear.

"You found out in Edinburgh, didn't you?"

"Very good, Benna. You were quite right to refuse to go with me. Of course that, in itself, told me there was something there you very much wanted to avoid."

"How?"

"It was young Lord Jevington—whom you were so anxious to protect—who inadvertently led to your undoing. The third night I was there he told me that he'd met a gentleman who was eager to play— somebody who'd heard about my skills. He took me to a rather unusual house on the Royal Mile—an ancient old place with overhanging gables. The house had belonged to the Dukes of Wake since 1477. That's what the current master, the Earl of Norland, told me."

Benna clenched her teeth against her rising gorge. It took a long moment before she could force herself to ask, "How did Michael find out I was with you?"

"Oh no, darling, that's not how it happened. I had met Norland in the past—I played against him. But that was years ago, before he'd acceded to his title and become the guardian to the current duchess, a young woman nobody has ever seen. She's barking mad, by all accounts, and Norland keeps her under lock and key in a sanitorium somewhere down south." Geoff made a humming sound in the darkness. "*That* in itself was odd—why keep her so far away, I wondered."

"How did you hear about that?" The only story Benna had ever found mentioned a spa, not an insane asylum. She couldn't believe how stupid she'd been not to guess they were one and the same.

"It's exactly the sort of gossip one hears once the evening is over and men relax and talk. Jevington cautioned me against bringing up the matter before we arrived—told me the current duchess's condition was a touchy matter, one which Norland was notorious for not wishing to discuss I could understand that; who wants to have their family's unpleasant secrets aired in public?

"I'd met your brother, too—played against him several years before I met you. He was a charming young man, but I quite cleaned him out. Not too clever and not much of a head for cards. Nothing like you in that department, Benna. Norland is a far better player, but he, too, lost a packet. He didn't become churlish about his losses."

Geoff paused, as if waiting for her to speak.

When she said nothing, he continued, "I stayed in your family home for three days. Norland is quite the most generous host I've ever met. Top shelf food, liquor … whores. Not only did he have his own mistress in attendance—a lovely, pricy bit of muslin—but he brought in beautiful, willing ladies for the rest of us." He snorted. "That was an effective distraction for a man like Jevington, of course—the fool."

Benna clamped her jaws shut, fury—at herself—churning in her belly. What a witless idiot she'd been.

Geoff made a low noise of contentment. "Yes, I enjoyed myself to the fullest. The man spends money like water. Tell me, Benna, is that Norland's money that he's losing at the tables and spending on high-fliers? Or is it yours?"

Benna was awake now, her mind frighteningly sharp, rage pumping through her body. "The one thing you can be certain of, *darling*, is that it will never be *your* money."

There was a moment of silence and then Geoff's laughter filled the room. "You speak the truth—and a somewhat demoralizing truth, at that. I've tried my damnedest, but you are the first and only woman I've ever failed to charm."

"As far as you know."

"Ah, still able to deliver a killing blow even with your hands tied, I see," he said. "Yes, that is true: as far as I know."

"If Michael didn't tell you who I was then how did you figure it out?"

"First off, I saw that portrait of your father—all six bloody feet of it—in the library of your Edinburgh house. You could be the man's twin; you look far more like him than you do your poor dead brother.

"The painter—Reynolds, I think your cousin said—did a bang-up job capturing the unusual turquoise color of your eyes. Of course, your father's striking hair was quite different than your mousy brown, but I'd seen your cunny—recall—and knew what your natural color was. Added to that was his bone structure, height, and that great beak of a nose. It was almost like looking at *you*, Benna."

"Congratulations," she mocked in a derisive voice. "You've seen a picture of my father. My mother, on the other hand, was not a duchess but a parlor maid at the duke's country estate." Benna prayed as she waited.

There was a long pause and then Geoffrey chuckled again. "My God, but you are clever and quick. And, indeed that was the first thing I thought, too. After all, who in the world would ever believe an actual duchess was emptying my chamber pot?" He laughed. "But if that were the case, why were you masquerading as a man? And why were you so bloody terrified to go to Scotland? No, a valiant effort, Benna, but you are no bastard."

Benna had to bite her tongue to keep from screaming. Why had she been such a fool these past months? How could she not have recognized his mawkish courtship for what it was: clever, cold-blooded manipulation? And she'd wandered into his snare like an innocent little bunny.

"Once I caught the scent there was no way I could give up the chase," Geoff said, his tone musing. "I nosed about a bit and found a disgruntled employee of your cousin's—a man willing to talk and talk and talk."

"And you believe the words of a bitter servant?" she scoffed.

"Oh, no. The servant didn't say a word about you, specifically. But he did tell me about your loving cousin's quarterly journeys to a particular establishment in Sussex. It was easy enough to find out just who dear Michael was visiting there."

"Well, who was it?" she demanded when he remained irksomely quiet.

"A slender, pale young woman who is—allegedly—so lost to reason that she is kept in a solitary environment, fed a constant diet of laudanum, and restrained hand and foot so that she is not a danger to herself or others."

"Y-You saw this woman?" Who in the name of all that was unholy had Michael locked away?

"Oh yes, I saw her. I made a special two-day trip from Brighton when you and I were last there."

Benna recalled the journey in question; she'd been surprised, but grateful, that he'd not needed her and gave her a holiday.

"I threw around a great deal of brass and was finally allowed to see her. She's got the same silvery hair but her nose is not as prominent and she is only of middling height. But the resemblance is strong and I daresay it would fool most people."

Benna's stomach pitched, and not just from too much wine. That could be *her* locked up in that place.

She had to ask, "Did you talk to her?"

"Oh no, my dear. She doesn't do much talking, I'm afraid."

"Good God." She squeezed her eyes shut, horror threatening to choke her.

"Indeed," Geoff agreed, not sounding particularly bothered by this poor woman's suffering.

"Who is she?"

"She has been there since the end of 1811—several months after your brother's demise. Norland must be very secure in himself because he made little effort to cover the girl's tracks. It was easy for me to find the shack where she lived her first sixteen years with her grandmother, an old woman who loves gin a great deal more than she loves her unfortunate granddaughter."

"A shack where?" Benna asked.

"Why, on the extensive properties that are attached to Wake House, my dear."

Benna had no words.

"In any event," Geoff went on, "the old lady sold the simple-minded girl to Norland for a few bob. She consoles herself with the fiction that poor little Gillyflower went someplace better."

"Gillyflower."

"Yes, quite a whimsical name, isn't it? Apparently, your esteemed father managed to impregnate Gillyflower's seventeen-year-old mother while he was mourning the death of your own mother. The young woman was a parlor maid—just as you so presciently mentioned earlier—no doubt innocently grateful for her master's amorous attentions. At least according to her mother."

Benna refused to be angered by the crude picture of the duke that Geoff was painting. She had loved her father dearly—and always would—but several years out in the cold, cruel world had taught her plenty about men and their feet of clay.

"Quite a local beauty your father's young mistress was, according to her fond mama. But the unfortunate girl died in the straw shortly after naming her squalling offspring." He clucked his tongue. "A tragic tale."

She ignored his cruel mockery. "It must have taken you months to find all this out."

"Oh, it did. I wasn't quite sure of all the details until only a month ago."

"But then—"

"But then why did I begin courting you before I could be certain that you really were the golden goose? Come, come, Benna—you should know me better than to ask that. If you *weren't* the duchess, I thought you might be amendable to earning a bit of the ready by giving your cousin a scare at some point in the future. And if you were? Well, let's just say there was enough hanging in the balance that I was persuaded to proceed with caution. When the situation demands it, I can be patience itself."

That was true; when it came to money, Geoff bore more than a passing resemblance to a tom cat waiting at a mouse hole.

"And Good God did you try my patience, dear Benna. Not to mention delivering a blow to my pride."

"What if I were to say that I'd changed my mind? That I'd be willing to marry you?"

157

Geoff laughed. "Lord," he said, once he'd stopped chortling. "How I will miss you, Benna."

"You don't believe that I'd rather marry you than go back to my cousin—because I assume that is where you're taking me. Trust me, Geoffrey, if my choices are you or Michael, you are by far the more appealing option."

"Well, thank you, Benna. I'm quite flattered. But I'm guessing that I would instantly become a decidedly *un*appealing choice the moment I freed you. No, I've watched you handle that sharp little penny knife of yours for years. I daresay I'd end up with it between my eyes before I could ever get you in front of a vicar."

"So, what now?" she asked. "Are you planning to stuff me into a post chaise and drive me all the way to Scotland in the hope that my cousin will reward you?"

"No, although that idea did occur to me. Instead, I decided to contact your cousin."

"And you plan on keeping me tied up until he gets your message?" Benna taunted. "Because if you sent it last night, it might be days before he comes. If he even believes you."

"I sent the message a week ago."

Benna gasped. "You've been planning to sell me to my cousin even while you've spent every night in my bed?"

He hesitated, and then said, "Yes."

Even for Geoff that was mercenary behavior.

"What would you have done in the highly unlikely event I'd accepted your offer last night?"

"I had a chaise and four ready to take us up to Gretna Green, my love. I daresay we would have passed the earl's man on our way up north."

Benna opened her mouth, but then closed it. There was no point in begging; once Geoff made up his mind, he never went back on a decision.

"How long do I have until he gets here?"

"We don't have much time together, Benna. I'm expecting—"

A sharp rap on the door interrupted his words.

Geoff let out a gusty sigh. "It looks like we have no time at all, love," he said, his voice empty of all emotion. "I'm—I'm sorry, Benna."

The thing of it was, Benna really believed that he meant it.

Chapter Eighteen

Benna put the seven-year-old bill for window glazing in the appropriate stack and turned back to the towering pile. The job of organizing what she referred to as the *Mountain* was simple but tedious work.

"Only spend a few hours each day on that," the earl had told her on the first morning of her new position. "I also want you to work on the house inventory with Mrs. Gates and Nance. And on Wednesdays you can come with me to inspect the work on the various cottages."

Each morning they met in the library and discussed her progress the prior day and his lordship's plans for the next few days.

In the eight days that she'd worked as his secretary Benna had been alone with him only during those brief morning meetings. She saw him at dinner each night, but of course they were not alone.

Benna had foolishly believed that being closer to him would be more pleasurable. Instead, it was agony.

She lived in hope that he'd invite her to another intimate evening of chess. This time, she swore, she would ask questions about *him*, no matter how aloof he became when confronted with anything personal.

Thus far, however, he'd given no sign of wanting to spend a few hours pitting his wits across a board.

Indeed, Benna got the distinct impression that he was avoiding her.

Or, more likely, she had inflated her importance in his mind. He'd probably forgotten all about her and was consumed by estate business and his frequent meetings with Mr. and Mrs. Worth and the new hospital in Redruth.

Benna had met Mrs. Worth on several occasions, most recently when she came to help Lady Trebolton with plans for the girls' first Season—apparently both would be launched together.

The Worths came to dinner the fifth night of Benna's new position.

Benna had not seen Stephen Worth since she had tried to return the expensive livery Worth had purchased when he'd hired her.

"Good Lord," he'd said, lounging in his chair while Benna had stood in front of his enormous desk. "Where in the hell would I ever find another beanpole like you to wear it?" He'd laughed good-naturedly at Benna's reddened face. "Don't worry, boy, you'll grow into your height eventually, same thing with your whiskers. I was a beardless, gangly youth myself until I was almost five-and-twenty." He'd paused, his smile teasing but not unkind, "As for growing into that beak of yours? Well, that might take a bit longer."

Benna had merely smiled. Her years with Geoffrey had inured her to insults or ribbing of any kind.

"Keep the clothing, lad. Consider it a parting gift." Worth had glanced up from the money box he'd pulled out of his desk, his handsome face suddenly serious. "You're damned good with my horses and I shall miss you. But I'm glad you're taking a job with Trebolton. He's a good man and will treat you well. And if things don't work out you are always welcome back here."

Despite his kind parting words Benna had been a bit concerned about the reception she'd get when Mr. and Mrs. Worth discovered that they'd be dining with their former postilion.

But Stephen Worth had grinned at her as if they were old friends and extended his hand.

Luckily Benna knew how to respond to the American custom of handshaking, but only because of her first encounter with Worth.

"It's good to see you here tonight, Ben. Now I won't be the only commoner at the table."

Benna knew Worth had purposely said those words within the servants' hearing.

He was the wealthiest man in this part of England, so if he did not have a problem sitting across from a postilion turned secretary it would be difficult for anyone else to demur. At least in Cornwall.

The dinner had been enjoyable and lively, with much laughter. It was difficult not to like the flamboyant American, who was not a respecter of *ton* etiquette and clearly believed in broad-ranging topics of conversation.

Mrs. Worth, was, in her quiet way, every bit as fascinating as her husband.

Even before Benna had met her she'd heard plenty about the English lady doctor who treated local people even when they didn't have the money to pay for it.

Back then she had been known as Elinor Atwood. Not until after she married Worth did everyone learn that she'd once been the Countess of Trentham.

The fact that Mrs. Worth had been masquerading as somebody else when she came to Redruth—albeit not as a man—made Benna feel an unspoken kinship with her.

As if thinking about Mrs. Worth had summoned her, Charles, one of the new footmen, opened Benna's door and announced, "Mrs. Worth here to see you, Mr. Piddock."

Benna set down her quill and crossed the room to greet the small and quite pregnant woman.

"Thank you so much for helping me plan his lordship's first dinner and ball next month, ma'am," Benna said.

"It is my pleasure, Mr. Piddock." Just like her husband, Mrs. Worth hadn't expressed any surprise at Benna's meteoric rise from postilion to stable master to secretary.

"Would you care for tea?" Benna asked as she led Mrs. Worth to a comfortable chair.

"Thank you, but I've only got a few minutes." She reached into her reticule and extracted several sheets of folded paper. "I have taken the liberty of bringing you a copy of the guest list I compiled for our last dinner party."

"Thank you so much, Mrs. Worth, I was, er, floundering."

At the earl's direction Benna had asked Lady Trebolton who they should invite to the function, but the countess—while unfailingly kind—had been less than helpful.

"At the bottom of the list is information for the stationers and several other local tradespeople you might find helpful," she added.

Benna wanted to kiss the woman.

Mrs. Worth smiled. "I take it this is your first experience planning a large function?"

"Yes, it is," Benna admitted. "I'm afraid Lord Trebolton might place more faith in my abilities than they merit."

"I doubt that very much, Ben. My husband esteems you most highly and he is a difficult man to impress." Mrs. Worth stood, her slight form showing her condition as more advanced than a woman who'd only been married a few months should be.

Benna wouldn't be the only person to have noticed, but there wasn't a person in the area foolish enough to say anything negative to or about the wife of Stephen Worth. His generosity was legendary, but so was his temper.

Mrs. Worth's unusual silvery-gray eyes twinkled up at her. "I shall leave you to your slaving, Ben. I am scheduled to meet with the girls on the critical subject of new gowns. It will likely take most of the afternoon since a dressmaker has come from Redruth." She laughed at Benna's expression. "See, you could be in charge of matters far more objectionable than flowers and guest lists."

After seeing the older woman out Benna returned to her desk and put Mrs. Worth's list in a safe place where she could find it easily.

One of today's goals was to finish working on the spare room in her chambers, which she had ransacked for furniture, but had not come close to emptying.

Benna took off her coat and donned the huge apron she'd begged from Cook when she'd realized just what filthy work inventorying the earl's house would be.

As she began the arduous, dirty task of digging through the room's contents she recalled what the earl had said the day he'd hired her—that there were dozens of other rooms just as full, and the attics held even more.

She groaned. There simply were not enough hours in the day.

***

It was late afternoon and Jago was looking over the competing roofing bids he'd received for his tenant cottages when there was a knock on the door.

"Yes?" he called absently.

"Hello, Jago."

His head jerked up at the sound of Elinor's voice and he got to his feet. "Elinor." He glanced at the window; it was dusk.

"Yes," she said, reading his look correctly, "it *is* quite late."

Jago gestured to the settee in front of the gargantuan fireplace. There was a chill in the air and he had taken to keeping a fire going now that he spent much of his day in the draughty room.

Elinor lowered herself onto the couch with a heavy sigh.

"Are you going to get me in trouble with your husband for working you too hard?" He studied her face for signs of fatigue, but, thankfully, found none.

"Stephen is more likely to thank you, Jago. He knows I would go mad from inactivity and would soon set up a surgery in his stables. Besides"—she grinned at him—"it wasn't very strenuous to look through pattern books and help the girls choose gowns all afternoon. By the way, I met with Ben before our dress-shopping orgy and helped him get started with your upcoming party." She smiled. "I love planning parties and balls and dinners. It was an activity I rarely engaged in … before."

She was alluding to her first marriage, which Jago knew had not been a happy one, even though they'd never spoken of it.

"Well, I, for one, am deeply grateful that you adore planning parties."

She waved away his gratitude. "I just wanted to apprise you of our progress. I've set about acquiring an adequate wardrobe for both girls. At first I wondered if it was wise to launch them together, but I believe they will be a comfort to each other."

"I don't see the point of keeping one back to launch the other. That approach has always mystified me. It's insulting, as if young women were identical bolts of fabric that should not be put out for sale at the same time."

164

Elinor laughed. "Spoken like the true social subversive you are, Jago. I agree; the girls *are* very different and shall attract and be attracted to completely different men." Elinor glanced around the room. "This room looks much nicer than when I last saw it."

"It is all thanks to Ben," Jago admitted.

"You have your plate full, my friend. You must be happy to have Ben's help."

"Yes, he has turned out to be quite skilled at many things."

"Stephen and I were both impressed with Ben's conversation at dinner the other night. Any previous shyness seems to have dissipated."

"Yes, he is blossoming." *And becoming more attractive to me with every bloody day that passes.*

Elinor cocked her head at him, her lips curving into a slight, but knowing, smile. For one terrifying moment Jago thought he'd spoken that last thought aloud.

"What?" he asked rudely.

"Jago," she said, her tone slightly reproving. "How long are you going to keep me in the dark about what is going on?"

"Er, I don't know what you mean?"

"Ben—who is she?"

He goggled. "Good God, Elinor. You know? For how long?"

"Since the first day I saw her—when you were using Stephen's coach and stopped by my cottage. She'd just begun working for him, I believe."

Jago groaned. "You put me to shame. I only found out a few weeks ago."

"Don't feel bad; Stephen *still* hasn't guessed, even though he talked to her for hours when we were here the other night—not to mention he partnered her in whist."

Benna and Stephen had been a formidable and bloodthirsty team, thrashing Jago and Elinor twice that night.

"Well, I guess that makes me feel a little better—although Stephen isn't a doctor and shouldn't have been expected to notice the obvious physical signs."

"Do you know why she left Oakland Manor?" Elinor asked, apparently deciding not to tease him about his ignorance.

"She said Fielding found out and cautioned her to find another position before she caused Stephen any trouble."

"Ah, I should have suspected as much. Fielding is always concerned with Stephen's welfare first and foremost. I would have taken action on her behalf if it had not been you that she'd gone to." She hesitated. "I take it this move from the stables to the house was a compromise with your conscience."

"You know me so well," he said drily. As usual, he thought about the position he'd really wanted to give her and his face heated. Thank God Elinor couldn't see the contents of his head.

Jago looked at his friend and smiled. "I should have known you'd guess. I actually wanted to tell you and ask your opinion, but it never seemed like the right moment."

"Do you know why she is doing this?" Elinor asked.

"I don't know much," he hesitated, and then said, "I might as well tell you the little I know."

A few minutes later, after Jago was finished, Elinor shook her head in wonder. "It is an extreme—and daring—reaction to a problem," she said, a rueful smile on her lips. "I am envious of her audacity. I wish—" She bit her lip and then shook her head. "I was going to say I wish that I'd had the courage to do such a thing when I was fifteen, but then I realized that would have changed my whole life and I wouldn't be where I am, today."

Jago smiled. "A wise philosophy."

"Is it your plan to keep her employed as your secretary … indefinitely?"

"I don't know. I thought I might help her find a new position—something less, er, dangerous—when I take her to London with us in the spring."

"As what? A governess?"

"If that is what she would like." He shrugged. "I'd just like to see her working for a master who would take care of—rather than prey on—her."

Her forehead furrowed. "I don't understand. Is that what you think you are doing, Jago—preying on her?"

Jago suspected that his face was as red as a poppy.

"Oh, goodness," she said softly. "It's that way, is it?"

He gave a choked laugh of mortification and squeezed his temples between his thumb and forefinger. "Not yet. But I'm ashamed to admit that I don't know how much longer I can behave myself."

"Why?"

His head swung up. "What?"

"Why are you so ashamed that you are attracted to her?"

"I can't believe you have to ask me such a question, Elinor."

"And I can't believe that you've forgotten you are talking to a woman who married her father's footman."

Jago blinked. "I suppose it is true that Worth was a footman when you first met," he conceded, "but when you married him, he was a wealthy banker."

"And is that all that stands between you and the first woman I've ever seen you show any interest in? Money?"

Jago gave a helpless-sounding laugh. "Surely not the first woman?" Before she could answer he gave a dismissive wave. "Fine, I won't argue. But that doesn't matter. And, no, money is not the only matter that stands between us." He cut her a hard look. "Although I'm sure you must realize that I no longer have the leisure to ignore such mercenary considerations."

"I understand that you have inherited a situation which is less than desirable."

He snorted.

"I hope you know that marriage is not the only way out of such a quandary. Indeed, speaking as somebody who was once married for her money, I am the last person to recommend it."

Jago decided to leave the question of money alone for the moment. "She is only twenty—a mere child."

"Putting aside the fact that I was married at sixteen and that Lady Trebolton married your brother at seventeen *and* that most girls of our class are considered to be on the shelf by twenty—"

"Fine, she is not a child," he conceded. "But what *is* undeniable is the fact that she is my servant."

"By circumstance, yes. But her speech, countenance, and behavior indicate that she was raised to be a gentlewoman—before matters beyond her control made living as a woman undesirable—if not necessarily impossible. I recall you telling me that Ben had admitted to being the grandchild of a baronet. Is that still true—or was it part of her disguise? And didn't she say her father was educated at Oxford? Isn't that where you went?"

Jago couldn't help laughing. "Are you studying to be a barrister next, Elinor?"

"All I am saying, Jago, is that I've known you for years and have never seen you look at a woman with anything other than courtesy. It is clear to me that you find this young woman—as unconventional as she is—appealing."

No, Elinor, I find her damned near irresistible.

Fortunately, Jago didn't say that. Instead, he said, "I hope my interest in her isn't as clear to everyone else as it is to you."

"Don't be silly, I noticed because I know you. What I am trying to say is this: we neither of us chose a normal path in life—at least not compared to our peers. I know the circumstances are less than ideal, but sometimes you need to look outside of what is comfortable to find what you need."

Jago thought about the fascinating, clever, and mysterious woman who'd kissed him in Truro that night. Indeed, he'd done little but think of her ever since. He knew almost nothing about her, but what he did know, he liked.

He admired her dry wit and humor, he enjoyed pitting his— admittedly inferior—wits against her at a chess table, and he found her inherent dignity and attractive person eminently desirable.

But surely what Elinor was suggesting was not only madness, but impossible?

He saw that his friend was studying him. "You say that you've never seen me evince interest in a woman. You forget that I offered to marry you, Elinor—twice."

"I know you did. But you offered out of friendship, not love. I've watched for years as women—young, old, pretty, plain, rich, and poor—flung themselves at your feet and not once have you so much as blinked. Yet now, my dear, dear friend, I believe you are blinking very hard, indeed."

Jago chewed the inside of his cheek and thought about what she was saying rather than simply refuting it on principle. Elinor was one of the smartest people he knew and he respected her.

He sighed at the knowing look in her eyes. "Lord."

She laughed.

"That's not nice, Elinor."

"Oh, it's not mocking laughter—I'm happy for you. You are such a magnificent person, Jago. You deserve happiness."

"You are putting me to the blush."

"I don't know why, for it is only the truth. As for your Ben—" She frowned. "Did she tell you her name?"

"She claims her name is Benna."

"Hmm, interesting."

"Yes, very."

"You say *claims*, does that mean you don't believe her?"

"I'm hesitant to believe anything she says, at this point."

Elinor gave him a sympathetic look. "I daresay you are feeling, er—"

"Like an idiot?" he suggested.

She chuckled. "Well, if it's any consolation, you are not alone in being taken in. My husband prides himself on being up to all the tricks and he hasn't guessed. Would you consider keeping her as your secretary? She seems to do well at it."

"I think she would do well at anything. But, no, I shall do the wise thing and find her work elsewhere."

"Is that what she wants?"

"I haven't mentioned it to her," he admitted. "But surely she will appreciate the opportunity to make a fresh start in the city?"

"Oh, Jago. We women like to make our own plans. Or haven't you learned that?"

He smiled wryly. "I daresay you are right and she'll tell me to go to the devil. For all that she appears so compliant she possesses a strong will."

"A woman after my own heart."

Jago snorted. "Indeed."

"Well, my friend," she said, pushing herself to her feet with a groan. "I had better return home before Stephen sends out the hounds. You are still coming to dinner tonight?"

169

"Yes, tell Mr. Worth I'll bring my updated plans. You and I will then gang up on him and convince him of the necessity of adding a separate natal wing."

Chapter Nineteen

Carlisle
February 1817
Nine Months Ago

Not much to look at, is she?" Willy Karp asked Geoff, having to force the words around a huge mouthful of ham.

"I could say the same about you, mate," Benna retorted.

Rather than be offended, Benna's massive captor—Michael's errand boy—let out a snort of laughter, forgetting that he still had food in his mouth.

Geoff grimaced with distaste and flicked a piece of half-chewed pork off his cuff. "I still do not understand why the bloody hell you are traveling at night." He'd been edgy all day, anxious to be shed of both of them.

"Ye don't need to understand," Willy said, not for the first time.

The first thing the huge ruffian had done after arriving that morning was hand Geoff the blunt for selling Benna.

He'd then informed Geoff that he and Benna would be spending the day in his company as the post chaise he'd hired would not be arriving until dusk.

"I got me orders," was all he would say when Geoff questioned him on the matter.

He'd then frog-marched them both down to the kitchen—to keep his *oggles* on them, he'd said—and then proceeded to eat Geoff out of house and home for the next ten hours.

Now, half an hour after sunset, Geoff's nerves were visibly ragged.

If Benna hadn't had her own concerns to occupy her she might have enjoyed watching Geoff kick his heels in the kitchen of their rented townhouse for hours—a room she knew he had never entered before today.

"How much longer?" Geoff asked; it was the same question he'd been asking every ten minutes for the last hour.

Willy glanced at the clock on the mantle. "I told ye ten minutes ago: it'll be 'ere in under an hour." He shoved more food into his mouth.

Geoff turned to Benna. "You'll want to finish getting dressed and I'm sure you need to use the necessary before you go?"

"Yes," Benna lied, all but leaping to her feet and taking a step toward the kitchen door.

"Oi!"

Benna stopped and turned at the muffled syllable. "Wouldn't you rather I go now than in the carriage," she asked Willy.

A rumbling chuckle shook his chest while he stolidly chewed, this time swallowing before speaking. "I don't give a tinker's toss where ye piss, lass. If ye piss in your breeches, ye can bloody well sit in yer filf all the ways to—" he broke off.

"All the way to where? Surely you can tell me where you're taking me?" Benna was impressed that she didn't sound nearly as terrified as she felt.

"I'll tell ye, but I ain't sayin' anyfing in front of 'im." He jerked his chin at Geoff.

"Why? Think he'll have a change of heart and rescue me?" Benna sneered at Geoff, pleased—and more than a little surprised—when a tinge of red stained the pale skin over his sharp cheekbones. Who would have guessed the man had even a scrap of conscience left to shame?

"If ye wan' te piss ye can do it right 'ere." He pointed a thick finger at Geoff. "Go an' fetch the pot."

Geoff, who was exceeding fussy and squeamish about bodily functions—all except his own—recoiled at the suggestion. "Good Lord! Surely you don't expect her to do *that* in front of us?"

"She ain't to go out of my sight. *That's* what I'm paid for. You"—he pointed his fork at Geoff—"'ave already been paid, so shut yer gob."

The last four words were uttered in a tone of such menace that Geoff blenched. "All right, all right, keep your drawers on," he muttered, turning to Benna, "Do you still want—"

"No, I don't need the pot. But can I have a waistcoat, coat, cravat, and my overcoat?" She cut Willy a look of intense loathing. "Or are your *orders* that I must travel half-naked?"

"Ain't got no orders about that. Bring out 'er togs and dress 'er. You can untie 'er hands." He showed Benna his teeth, several of which were black stumps. "You try to run, girlie, and I'll make you sorry. Hear?"

"I hear."

"And you"—he glared at Geoff—"don't fink about nippin' off nowheres. You stay 'ere until we're gone."

"Since this is my bloody house, I shan't be *nipping off* anywhere," Geoff retorted, scowling at Willy.

Willy didn't seem to hear him and Geoff flounced out, returning ten minutes later with various articles of clothing slung over his arm.

Geoff untied her and Benna massaged her sore wrists while he held out her vest.

Benna curled her lip and slid her arms into the garment. "This will be a novel experience for you—dressing somebody else for a change."

"Consider it my parting gift to you, darling."

"What a prince," she muttered, buttoning up the double-breasted waistcoat with numb, clumsy fingers.

Thankfully, Geoff had already helped her into drawers, breeches, and a shirt before handing her over to Willy, so at least she'd not needed to lounge about naked all day long.

Once she was dressed, Willy nodded. "Go on, tie up 'er 'ands again."

"Can he tie them in front, at least?" she asked.

Willy shrugged. "Makes no odds to me."

"And does the rope have to be so tight that my fingers turn blue?" she demanded.

Again he nodded at Geoff. "Tie it looser. But I'll be checkin' it, lass, so don't get no ideas."

Benna stared at Geoff as he tied the rope, willing him to meet her gaze.

"You bloody Judas. You can't even look at me."

His cheeks flushed and his eyes jumped to meet hers. "The game is up, Ben. Complaining after you lost is a flat's way."

"My life isn't a bloody card game, you bastard."

He pursed his mouth and finished his task in silence.

Willy, who'd been picking his teeth with a butter knife in between putting away the better part of a pitcher of porter and an entire ham, sat up, his head tilted in the manner of a spaniel listening for something. "There. That'll be the carriage now." He heaved his bulk up from the table and began to roll his shirtsleeves down over forearms that were as ropey and thick as hawsers. "Ye sure ye don't want the pot, lass? Now's yer last chance."

Benna ignored his question. "Let's get on with it, already."

Geoffrey patted her awkwardly on the hip. "Best of luck to—"

Benna whirled on him. "Keep your hands off me, you tosser."

Willy hooted. "Better step back, lad, she's got claws!"

Geoff swallowed, as pale as a ghost. Good. She hoped that what he'd done to her would haunt him for the rest of his miserable life.

His lips twisted, but instead of his usual insouciant grin, his smile was a rictus. "No hard feelings, Benna."

"Go sod yourself, Geoff."

Willy threw back his head and roared. "Mebbe I can see why 'is lordship fancies ye now," he said, once he could catch his breath. "Yer a right feisty 'un, ain't ye?" He tossed a rag over her bound hands to cover the rope and then jerked her toward him. "You try any of your tricks with me, lass, and I'll put ye to sleep for the journey. Ye ken?"

Benna jerked out a nod.

"Good. Now, it's time to go."

Willy shoved her through the doorway and she brushed up against the frame; something in the pocket of her overcoat— something hard—dug into her hip.

It took her brain a moment to figure out what it was. *Her penny knife.*

But the knife hadn't been in her coat, it had been on her nightstand, along with her most recent—and unfinished—carving of an owl.

Benna tried to control the wild fluttering in her chest; it was no reason to get excited. It was just one small knife and Willy was a giant, cruel bloke at least three and a half times her size. She had as much chance getting away from him as a rabbit had escaping a snare.

But it was a chance.

And Geoff had given it to her.

A post chaise and four prime-looking coach horses waited outside; wherever they were going, Willy clearly planned to get there in a hurry.

"Up you go, lass," he murmured, pushing her up the steps.

Benna cast a last glance up at the townhouse. Geoff was standing in the window of the study, staring down at her. He raised a hand in farewell when he saw her looking.

Benna deliberately turned her back on him and stepped into the carriage.

Chapter Twenty

*D*inner that night was only Ben, Catherine, and Mariah since Lady Trebolton didn't feel well and ate in her room and Lord Trebolton had gone to dine with the Worths at Oakland Manor.

The sisters bickered through the entire meal—about anything and everything—which had left Benna too agitated to return to her room and read or carve.

Instead, she decided to take advantage of the earl's absence in the library to begin re-shelving the hundreds of books she'd found.

"Get Thomas and Charles to assist you with the lifting and actual re-shelving," the earl had told her when she had shown him the exciting bounty: trunks and crates full of books.

Benna would rather manage the entire process herself, no matter that it entailed frequent trips up the ladders or a good deal of dusting. She fetched her work apron before making her way to the library.

The shelf-lined room had once been grand, but, like the rest of the house, it had suffered from decades of neglect, not to mention all the pillaging it had endured. Already the addition of more furniture and two enormous oil landscapes that she'd found tucked away in the room next to her bedchamber had made the room more inviting.

She had also found lovely bottle-green velvet drapes, which she'd given to Mrs. Gates to clean and rehang. The curtains had obviously come from the library but had, inexplicably, been filled with silver serving dishes and rolled into bundles and piled on top of the chests in the storage room.

Benna lighted three candelabras and placed them strategically in cavernous room so they illuminated the greatest number of shelves.

She dusted the books as she removed them from the trunks and stacked them in piles according to subject. While the books covered a vast array of subjects, they had one thing in common: they were all old.

It seemed as if somebody had gone through the library and plucked out volumes based on age alone. In many instances the gaps on the shelves where the books had once sat were still visible.

Benna had worked her way through four of the ten chests when she encountered a locked trunk.

She fetched a letter opener from the earl's desk and was gently probing the lock when she heard the library door open.

"Good evening, Ben," Lord Trebolton said.

One glance at the longcase clock showed it was close to midnight; she had been working for almost two hours. Benna clambered to her feet. She'd taken off her fake spectacles earlier to read book spines without interference. As a result, she could see the earl more clearly than usual. He was gorgeous in his form-hugging black tailcoat, antique gold waistcoat, and skin-tight black pantaloons.

His new valet, a grim-looking Londoner named Toomey, had cut and styled his hair in a way that swept it forward, which meant it had the tendency to tumble attractively over his forehead.

Benna guessed that he did not much care for the flattering style as she'd seen him brush the thick locks back, his eyebrows knitted in irritation. Every morning she expected him to appear without the charming curls, the victim of scissors which he'd employed himself, or ordered his man to use.

"Ben?"

She'd been staring at him. Again.

"Good evening, my lord." She took a step toward the door. "I shall leave you in private."

"No need to go haring off." He pointed to her hand. "What have you got there?"

Benna glanced down at the letter opener. "One of the trunks is locked and I was trying to open it."

"I think I have something more effective."

She watched from beneath lowered lashes as he went to the desk that had been moved back to its place in the library.

The earl lifted a heavy ring of keys from one of the drawers and handed over the unwieldy bundle. "I admit to knowing only what two or three of these are. I suppose that is another project to add to the list—going through the house and seeing which key fits what lock."

Benna sat cross legged in front of the chest. "Nance and Mrs. Gates both have keys but none of theirs fit the chest." She picked a key with a distinctive shape to start, so she could tell when she had tested them all.

The earl had taken a seat not far from her and Benna looked up at the sound of his soft snort. "You managed to get the pair to cooperate with one another in such an activity?"

Benna tried the next key. "I told Nance that Mrs. Gates did not think he had the complete set and then I told Mrs. Gates the same thing."

He chuckled but Benna was wise enough not to glance up. Just hearing him laugh was enough to make her stomach flutter. If she looked at him she'd probably launch herself at him again.

"It sounds as if you are very skillful at managing my staff."

"They're not difficult to understand. Each has been guarding their turf for almost forty years."

"Yes, only Cook is new to the battle, which is a triangle now. When I was a boy, Gates and Nance conducted a two-front war."

Benna smirked at the apt description as she dismissed the next two keys as too small without even testing them. "That was the same case as the stable master and head groom at my—" She caught herself barely in time before blurting *father's house*.

"—at my first job," she finished awkwardly.

"You mean at the posting inn or when you worked for Mr. Fenton?"

Benna deliberately hesitated, examining a key, as if to check the configuration of its bit more closely. She waited a few seconds before looking up.

"I beg your pardon, my lord?"

His eyes were obscured by the candlelight, his lenses two small gold reflections. "Tell me a little about your life with your father. Did you move often?"

Benna breathed a quiet sigh of relief that he'd left the other matter alone. As she looked down at the lock, her mind spun to recall what she'd told him about her father thus far.

I always told you that the best lie was the simplest one. I'm very disappointed in you, Benna.

Well, so was she; why the devil was her tale getting so tangled? She had always been so good about sticking with her story in the past. Something about the earl just ...

Scrambles your wits?

Benna discarded another key and tried the next before speaking. "Before we moved to Bristol my father taught at a village school in Yorkshire," she said, purposely trying to keep her answers vague. "The local lord died and the new lord no longer believed the school was a priority. He reduced my father's pay by half."

"It is criminal that the education of the many is contingent on the caprices of a few," he said, his words making Benna love him even more.

"My father had kept in touch with friends from his university days and was able to secure another position in a village not far from Bristol."

"You mentioned that your father attended Oxford—which college?"

"Balliol." That was true enough.

"Ah, my alma mater." He cocked his head. "What years was he there? I don't recall anybody named Piddock."

Benna ignored the sound of Geoff's mocking laughter.

"Er, I daresay he was a bit older than you, sir. He was fifty-two when he died."

"Yes, a *bit* older. Just how old do you think I am, Ben?"

She looked up, surprised by his irritable tone.

Benna had given plenty of thought to his age. He was younger than Geoff, of that she was sure.

Why you obnoxious little—

"I'd say thirty-five, sir."

179

His lips curved slightly—up rather than down—so at least she'd not insulted him. "I'm thirty-seven. You mentioned once that your grandfather was a baronet—I looked in my copy of the peerage and couldn't find a Piddock."

He is checking up on you, my dear. Your lies will catch you up.

Benna didn't doubt that for a minute. But at least she wasn't surprised by the question. Indeed, she'd been expecting it since she'd been so witless as to tell him such a stupid bouncer as a way to explain her elevated manners and speech.

Tsk, tsk—don't lie to yourself, darling. You told him that because you couldn't bear that he would think you just another couthless yokel.

Benna ground her teeth.

"Er, Piddock is actually my mother's maiden name, sir. I didn't want to use my grandfather's surname. It is Hazelton; Baron Hazleton of Percy Hall in Northumberland."

Benna had looked at the earl's outdated peerage, too, and picked a family with seven male offspring, one of whom was named John and about whom there was no information recorded.

She risked a glance at him but could not guess what he was thinking.

A long silence ensued, broken by only the clinking of keys and ticking of the longcase clock.

***

Jago let her work in silence, content to watch her.

There was just something about her that drew his eye like a magnet and made him burn with curiosity.

He knew that she was lying to him—at least about some things.

He also knew that it was tempting fate to be here alone with her. He should go to bed. Now.

But was far too restless to sleep.

He had returned from Elinor and Stephen Worth's house invigorated with excitement over the hospital Worth was financing.

The three of them had enjoyed a lively, argument-filled dinner, with Elinor and Jago defending their crumbling social system against Worth's new world order built on business, an enlarged franchise, and republican governance.

After dinner, while they'd enjoyed their port, Worth had made him a generous offer, inviting Jago to join an investment project involving a colliery and canal that he'd begun the prior year and then placed on hold.

Jago did not doubt for a minute that he had Elinor to thank for such an offer. He could not afford to be offended that it was his penury that motivated Worth's generosity—not when the American's scheme might well rescue him from financial disaster.

On the ride home, he considered Worth's proposition, questions roiling furiously in his mind like fish trapped in a bucket.

Jago had decided to confide in the American, telling him about Cadan's three loans. Worth had suggested that he negotiate an extension. "It is done all the time, Jago."

He knew that sort of thing was done—gaining credit on one's expectations. Would an investment with Worth, a well-known man of business and banker, qualify as an expectation?

Or would the bankers require something more certain—like Jago's impending marriage to a wealthy woman?

When he'd returned from Truro, Jago had asked Claire about the loans, hoping that she might have some idea about his brother's business dealings at the time of his death—some information that might help him decide what to do next.

"Oh, goodness! I had no idea, Jago. How could he use the same collateral for all three loans?"

Her use of the word *collateral* had jolted Jago. But then he recalled that her father had been a successful businessman and Claire had grown up in a household where discussions about money probably hadn't been hidden like dirty secrets. In fact, he wouldn't be surprised to learn that Claire knew a great deal more about finance than Jago did.

"I don't know how he did it—or why," Jago had admitted. "According to all three bankers, Cadan took the money in bank notes—which is apparently unusual. I don't understand what he could have done with it all such a short time before his death."

Claire's expression had been distant. "Cadan and I did not speak about much, Jago—and never about his business." She chewed her lip.

"I have to admit I thought he was a bit … odd in the weeks before his accident."

"How do you mean *odd*?"

"He seemed frenetic, almost. I knew he was worried about money, but that was hardly new. He looked exhausted after that trip to Plymouth." Claire raised a lacy handkerchief to her face. "I daresay you think I should have noticed something was amiss and insisted that he not go out that day—"

"Lord, Claire, if Cadan wished to take out his curricle in such vile weather there was nothing you could have said or done to stop him from acting like a cabbage head."

She'd given him a faint, but grateful nod.

Jago hadn't been just placating her; his brother had been a fool to take such a light carriage out in a storm. The only one responsible for the accident which took his life was Cadan.

After making his sister-in-law cry—and getting nothing of value for his efforts—Jago had decided to let the matter of the missing money drop.

If he was to commit money to Worth's investment scheme, he would need to tap into the small pool of capital that he'd managed to save over the last two decades. He was naturally hesitant to do so as it was all that stood between his small family and insolvency.

Thanks to Jago's untouched quarterly allowance—which had grown steadily in the low percents over almost twenty years—and the money he'd inherited upon his mother's death, Jago had an annual income of approximately £5000. That would provide a lavish lifestyle for one man, but it was hardly enough to get Lenshurst Park in shape—not to mention give his two nieces a London Season.

And it was not nearly enough to pay off those three loans.

Jago's mind had still been in a whirl when he'd ridden up the driveway and seen the lights in the library windows.

Because he was a selfish swine, he'd hoped that Benna was the one working so late.

Benna.

Jago had stayed away from her since she'd moved to the house, but it had not been easy.

Every night he saw her at dinner and learned more and more about the quiet but clever woman who hid behind short brown hair and glasses.

He was pleased and impressed by the sheer volume of work she got through and the competent efficiency with which she approached any task. Whether it was sorting through piles of documents or organizing the contents of the enormous ramshackle house, she tackled each job with a cool determination that was awe-inspiring.

It certainly inspired him.

And there were many days when he dearly needed inspiration.

Jago had loved being a doctor. He'd loved not just the sense of purpose helping others gave to his life, but also the simplicity of his existence.

He had employed one servant and owned very few possessions. His needs had been few and he'd had ample time to pursue the things he enjoyed; things like furthering his medical knowledge or corresponding with his many colleagues, or, most recently, sharing his medical skills with others, as he'd done with Elinor.

There is no use yearning for that which you cannot have.

That was true; self-pity was worse than useless.

Jago looked across at the woman in front of the old trunk. She was not wearing her faux spectacles and the feminine curve of her face was more evident without the obstruction.

She was patiently trying the keys, her façade as cool and undisturbed as the untouched surface of a lake.

Memories of that ridiculously tame kiss assaulted him and the dull ache in his groin he'd been feeling from the moment he'd seen the lights in the library window sharpened.

"This one wants to fit, but it is catching on something." She looked up at him, her blue eyes questioning. "I'm afraid to twist too hard and damage the lock."

"Here." He held out his hand. "Let me have a try."

He studied the key she gave him. "There are scratch marks on the bottom of the bit, where it has stuck before."

Jago dropped to his haunches beside her and re-inserted the key, steadying himself on the trunk with one hand while he gently jiggled

183

the lock to and fro a few times. There was an almost inaudible *click* and the lock popped.

"You did it." She looked up, a smile on her normally serious face, as though he'd done something marvelous.

Their eyes locked and her smile slowly faded, her warm blue irises shrinking, her pupils dark and bottomless.

Jago felt like a man gazing over a precipice; there was still time for him to make the right decision and step back.

Instead, he swayed toward her like a tree bowed by an irresistible wind.

"Dammit," Jago muttered, and then claimed her mouth with his.

Chapter Twenty-One

Wherever they were going, it wasn't to Scotland.

It seemed to Benna that they were heading west.

All that was west of Carlisle were tiny villages and hamlets and miles and miles of desolate coastland.

Willy, who was crammed onto the seat beside her, had fallen asleep almost instantly upon sitting down.

But any hope that he was a sound sleeper was dashed when she shifted slightly and the eye that was on her side popped open.

"What? I'm not doing anything," she said before he could speak.

"See that ye don't."

"Can't we at least open the shades so that I might look out the window? Or do you *have orders* about that, too?"

"It's dark; there's nothin' to see." He'd then crossed his huge arms over his chest and slept.

That had been about four hours ago and he'd scarcely moved since.

There was a gap in one of the louvers and Benna could see a thin slice of the night. Only scattered beams of moonlight made their way through the cloud-strewn sky. The chaise had its lamps lighted but the postilions were observing a sober pace and creeping along. Benna doubted they were traveling more than five or six miles an hour.

It had occurred to her, more than once, that she might open the door and leap out of the carriage before Willy could grab her. But she had no idea what the roadway and verge were like. She knew there was a canal being built somewhere to the west of Carlisle; it would be her luck that the road ran along it and she'd fling herself into a deep, narrow ditch.

So, she waited. For what, she didn't know.

What would Michael do to her? If he had some other woman locked up already, did he even need her? After so many years would anyone remember what she looked like?

After what Geoff had told her, Benna feared that Michael had already prepared the way to claiming her trust by using the faux Benna he kept locked up in Sussex.

She could just imagine what the trustees in charge of her inheritance would do if they were forced to choose between a scruffy, shorn-headed servant dressed in men's clothing or the powerful, confident Earl of Norland.

Not that any of that would be an issue as things stood right now.

Whether Michael planned to marry her, lock her up, or kill her, she needed to escape.

The carriage slowed and the road became rutted and bumpy.

Beside her, Willy stirred. He leaned forward and flicked open one of the blinds.

Benna saw a flat expanse of beach, tufted with sparse clumps of grass, stretched out as far as the eye could see, which was quite a distance given the reflection of moonlight on the ocean.

Willy grunted. "Were 'ere."

"Where is here?"

"At the cottage," he answered unhelpfully.

When the carriage shuddered to a halt a few minutes later, he opened the door and flicked down the steps.

Benna saw he'd not been lying: there was indeed a cottage; it looked to be no more than four or five rooms. There were no bars on the windows, which made her think her stay there would be of short duration.

"On you go, lass," Willy said, not rushing her when it was clear her legs had fallen asleep.

Once they were outside the carriage he ignored the postilions, who simply spurred their leaders and turned the chaise in a wide circle before rolling back down the same road.

Willy led her to the cottage, opened the door, and gave her a gentle push inside.

"What are we doing here?" she asked as he fumbled with a flint to light the branch of candles on a table beside the door.

"Waitin'."

"For what?"

"Never you mind."

The candles flared to life, illuminating her new prison. They were standing in a small parlor that had two doors that must lead to bedrooms. Directly across from them was a doorless entryway that led to a kitchen.

"You 'ungry?"

"No. But I need to use the pot."

He led her to one of the doors and opened it, exposing a small bedchamber with nothing but a rustic bureau, metal bedstead, and a plain ceramic chamber pot in one corner. Once he'd lighted the three candles on the dresser he gestured to the pot. "Go on."

"Can you at least untie my hands?"

He hesitated and then gave his characteristic shrug. "You try anyfing and I'll—"

"Make me sorry. Yes, I know."

As thick as his fingers were, he still managed to make quick work of the rope.

Benna rubbed her wrists and flexed her fingers; at least they weren't numb like before. "Surely you don't need to stay and watch? We're all the way out here, where could I go?"

He grinned, and the dark glint in his eyes made her breath freeze in her chest. "I'm thinkin' mebbe I *want* to watch—get a gander at that cunny 'is lordship is so des-puh-rate for." He jerked his chin toward the chamber pot. "Go on, drop your breeches and show us what you got. I ain't all niffy-naffy like yon fine gen'elman you was wiff, I don't mind watching a lass 'ave a piss."

This is your chance, Benna.

Geoff's voice was so loud that she startled and glanced around her.

But no, it was just the two of them. And the unwanted voice was right; this was her chance.

She forced herself to smile—the sort of sultry expression she'd seen but never attempted to emulate—and then she brazenly inspected his body, allowing her eyes to linger on the terrifying bulge in his grubby breeches.

Swallowing down her bile, she deliberately licked her lips.

Willy's big body stiffened, all of it. He chuckled, his chest moving faster. "Pantin' for it, ain'tcha?"

"From what I can see of you, I'm guessing you strip to advantage, Willy," she said, shuddering at the hunger in his gaze. "Why don't you drop *your* breeches and show me Big Willy?" She grinned. "And I'll give you a taste of why the earl is so eager to get me back."

Willy threw back his head and roared, his hands at his placket before she'd even finished speaking.

"You're a one, you!" he said when he brought his head back down. "I like that—Big Willy," he chuckled, not taking his eyes from her as he shoved down his breeches.

Willy wasn't wearing any drawers and the monster he freed made even his big hand look small. He gave himself a brutal pump. "I could see what ye wanted the minnit I first saw ye," he said, his voice even lower and raspier than normal. "A real man, not a weakling toff."

Benna was unable to tear her eyes off the beast in his fist. Good. God. It was like a fence post.

"Come 'ere," he ordered gruffly.

That first step toward him was the hardest she'd ever taken.

He was only two strides away, but before Benna could drop to her knees he grabbed her hair with his free hand and jerked her head back hard enough to make her eyes water.

"Don't try nuffink on me, girlie," he growled, his breath hot and fetid on her skin. "'Is lordship never said you needed to 'ave all yer teef."

Benna gave him a confident, smirking look that she was far from feeling and sank to her knees, her right hand already fumbling in her pocket.

"Go on," he said, holding his cock around the base and pushing out his hips, making himself look twice as long and utterly terrifying.

Benna swallowed, said a prayer that she didn't vomit, and opened her mouth as wide as she could, flicking open her knife.

Willy grabbed her hair again. This time, instead of jerking her head back, he forced himself deep.

Benna gagged, her eyes streaming tears.

He gave a grunt of pleasure, holding her still.

Quit struggling and stay calm; you can hold your breath far longer than this—we both know that for a fact. And for God's sake don't bite him.

Yet.

Benna willed herself to quit fighting. It would be pointless in any case as his grip was like iron.

Above her, he chuckled and slowly withdrew. "Big Willy's roight, eh?"

The next time he plunged, she was expecting it.

She gagged and jolted, her shaking fingers slipping on the handle of the knife before she could get a good grip on it.

"Rub me bollocks," he demanded, unwittingly playing right into her hands. Both literally and figuratively.

Willy spread his feet wider to accommodate her shaking left hand and he pulled out just long enough for her to fill her lungs.

When he jammed himself back in, Benna jammed the two-inch blade into the spot just behind his balls, which she squeezed hard with her left hand, biting down at the same time.

Willy's high-pitched scream was probably audible in Carlisle.

"Get offa me! Get off! Get off!" He frantically buffeted her head with fists the size of shovels, trying to push her off. One of his punches slammed into Benna's temple, tripling her vision, and she released him.

He flung himself backward to get away.

For a long moment time seemed to stretch and slow. Willy's hard bootheels skidded and scraped for purchase on the rough wooden floor, the sound of his animal-like keening filling the room.

But Willy was hobbled by the breeches around his knees and couldn't stop his fall.

He went down like a felled tree, and even with her ears ringing from his savage blow Benna heard the crack of his skull against the iron bed frame.

She scooted backward on her knees, not stopping to push to her feet until she was well beyond his reach. Even then she didn't stop to look. Instead, she ran to the hearth in the front room, grabbed the iron poker, and then crept back to the eerily silent bedroom.

Willy lay where he'd fallen, his body bent at an awkward angle, half on the bed and half on the floor.

She raised the poker like a cricket bat. "Willy?"

He didn't twitch.

"*Willy.*"

Benna crept closer, holding the poker higher, ready to bring it down with all her might if he was trying to trick her.

But when she saw Willy's face, the poker fell from her nerveless fingers and hit the floor with a dull *thud*.

She clamped a hand over her mouth to keep from screaming. Willy's left eye was open and staring, but the pointy metal rod on the bed's footboard jutted out of his right eye socket.

Benna held back her scream but couldn't stop the contents of her stomach from coming back up.

She retched until there was nothing left, unable to tear her eyes from Willy's face.

And then a noise penetrated her horror and Benna swung around, her gaze jumping wildly around the parlor beyond. But nobody was in the cottage.

The sound was coming from outside; the familiar racket made by horses.

Michael had arrived.

Chapter Twenty-Two

Cornwall
1817
Present Day

*T*his kiss was nothing like the last.

Rather than shocked acceptance—which had been Jago's response when Benna kissed him that night in Truro—this time Jago claimed her with raw, demanding passion, his firm mouth crushing hers, his slick, hot tongue teasing her lips apart and plunging into her.

It felt like forever since Benna had kissed a man, but her lips had a memory of their own—which was just as well as her brain had gone foggier than a London pea souper.

Jago was kissing her.

The thought clanged around inside her skull like the flapper of a bell.

He was kissing *her.* Not like the last time, when she'd ambushed him.

A noise of pure joy rose up in her throat and Benna pushed up onto her knees to get closer to him.

Jago stood, gently but firmly pulling Benna up along with him, his mouth never leaving hers.

Once they were standing, he slid an arm around her, his splayed fingers at the base of her spine, pressing her close to his warm, hard torso.

He cradled her head with his other hand, holding her steady for his erotic invasion.

Benna cradled his face with both hands, reveling in the feel of hot skin, scratchy bristles, and his hard, angular jaw.

He gave an encouraging growl as she explored, caressing his throat and massaging his shoulders.

"Yes," he murmured, exerting a subtle, exquisite pressure and molding their bodies together.

And all the while his mouth continued to obliterate what remained of her wits.

I'm kissing the Earl of Trebolton.

Mercifully, that voice was hers, and not Geoffrey's. Right now it was only Benna and the man she'd been dreaming about for weeks.

She opened her eyes to find his swollen black pupils looking back at her.

For an instant they both froze.

If he pulled away and offered some vague excuse about her being his servant or too young—or anything else—Benna would brain him with a book.

Maybe he saw the threat in her gaze.

Or maybe he just wanted her as badly as she wanted him.

Whatever the reason, he tightened his hold on her rather than pushing her away.

"Your hands feel so good, Benna," he murmured, feathering kisses over her jaw and nibbling the lobe of her ear.

The sound of her name on his lips was almost as devastating as his kisses.

Benna allowed her fingers to roam lower, across his chest, her hands moving inexorably toward a part of his body that she'd fantasized about touching an embarrassing number of times.

His rock-hard hips were a delicious counterpoint to the smooth, silky material that sheathed his lower body. Her fingertips twitched to grab his buttocks, but at the last moment she turned shy, instead smoothing her palms up over his taut belly and digging her fingers into the tight, narrow column of his waist.

Benna closed her eyes and visualized what she was touching—corded, ridged muscles beneath pale skin—her fingers drifting dangerously south, getting ever closer to the stiff ridge that was thrusting against the placket of his pantaloons.

Jago pressed closer, his growl encouraging, the erection grinding against her belly unmistakable proof of his desire for her.

He wants me as badly as I want him.

The thought sent bolts of lust arrowing throughout her body and need pooled in her belly, sex, and breasts.

She felt a touch on her side and realized, with a shock, that his hand was no longer on her back, but he'd somehow managed to pull her shirttails from the waist of her trousers without her noticing.

Warm fingers skimmed over her belly, and then up over the strips of cotton that bound her breasts. He pressed his palm over her heart and stilled, the *thud thud thud* of her pulse deafening in her ears.

Benna's neck became boneless and her head fell back like a flower tilting on its stem.

"Unbutton your coat and waistcoat, Benna," he murmured against her mouth before nipping her lower lip.

She hissed in a breath, her fingers fumbling at the buttons on her clothing.

He didn't let her vest deter his questing fingers, his hand stroking between the layers of wool and cotton, not stopping until he cupped an imprisoned breast.

"You bind them," he whispered against her throat, nuzzling her neckcloth aside to kiss her throat.

Once Benna's vest and coat both hung open he speedily located the end of the cotton strip and plucked it loose, insinuating his hand beneath the fabric.

When his finger grazed her nipple, she whimpered and arched against him.

"Oh, God, Benna."

Benna thrilled at the raw need in his voice.

He tugged and pulled and sloughed away the bindings until he could settle a bare hand over each breast.

"You feel so beautiful," he murmured, looking into her eyes as his thumbs caressed her already stiff peaks. "I have spent far too much time imagining what you look like beneath your clothing."

His words were more erotic than anything she'd ever heard. Benna threaded her hands into his soft hair and pulled him toward her, plundering his mouth. The kiss was wild and wet and robbed her of breath.

When she came up for air his lust-swollen lips curved into a wicked smile and he gently pinched one of her nipples.

Benna groaned and pushed against him. "Please," she whispered.

"Like this?" He smiled wickedly and stroked her again, his fingers alternating pinching and stroking until her nipples were as hard as diamonds and she was shuddering and thrusting against him.

"You have bewitched me, Benna," he whispered, his mouth hot on her throat, his hands relentless.

Benna ground her pelvis against his and then slid a hand over the front of his snug pantaloons and squeezed his thick, hard shaft. "I need you inside me, my lord."

Her harsh, raspy words were like sharp bits of metal that pierced the fog of desire that enveloped them.

Jago's body jolted and his clever fingers ceased their magic.

Benna wanted to weep with frustration; it had been those two small words, *my lord.*

She grabbed his waist, digging her fingers into the warm, compact flesh—to keep him near—and opened her mouth to beg.

But he pulled back far enough to look at her, his eyes hooded and dark. "Bloody hell. What am I doing?" His hands slid from her breasts to her hips. "I'm not the sort of man who molests his servants." His words were soft and almost questioning, as if he were asking himself, testing his resolve.

He released her entirely and stepped back. "This is wrong."

It was like having a part of her body ripped away.

***

"I'm sorry for losing control, Benna."

Her usually pale pink lips were a dark rose from the savagery of their kisses and the twin slashes of color on her cheeks were vivid.

Her blue eyes narrowed dangerously. "I don't need your apology, my lord. I wanted—"

Jago raised a hand in an uncharacteristically imperious gesture that made him cringe. But he had to stop her; one of them needed to show some sense. "You are my servant," he said in a flat tone. "I am supposed to put your welfare first. Not use you to slake my—"

"I may be a servant, but that does not mean I lack sentience, like some inanimate *thing.*" Her mouth twisted and her eyes glittered.

Jago briefly closed his eyes. "I apologize if I implied that," he said, meaning it. "What I mean to say is that—" He scrubbed a hand over his forehead. "We are not in any way—other than physically—well-suited."

That sounded even worse.

Jago grimaced, annoyed at his own inability to articulate. "Let us put aside, for the moment, our difference in status. You are twenty—not even legally—"

"I am almost twenty-three."

Jago gave a humorless laugh. "Ah, another lie, I see."

Her mouth tightened.

"Twenty or twenty-three, it scarcely matters. You could be my daughter and—"

"But I'm not your daughter, sir, neither am I a child. Women my age are usually married with a child or two." She cut him a sharp look. "Nor am I an innocent maiden." The expression that accompanied her disclosure was challenging and, for a moment, Jago wondered whether she expected him to chide her for a lack of virtue or resume ravaging her person.

Jago held her furious gaze and admired the way her startling blue eyes sparked.

No, she was not a child and what she said was true; women younger than her were the staple of the London Marriage Mart.

Fine, he would have to spell out what he meant in bluntly. "What do you expect will happen between us after I take what I want from you?"

Her flush deepened at his brusque question.

Good. He wanted to shock her, to make her consider the gravity of what almost happened. And what must never happen again.

"What you fail to understand, my lord, is that you were not *taking* anything. What I was giving is mine alone to give."

Her words froze him and their eyes locked.

"As for what I expect to happen?" Her gaze flickered over him in an angry, but hungry, examination. "I am not such a pea goose as to expect anything from you but sexual pleasure."

Jago's erection, which had dissipated in the face of his shocking behavior, came roaring back at her words.

He realized that his hand was still raised, as if to touch her, to comfort her—

Or perhaps to pull her back into his embrace.

He dropped his arm and took another step back before he did something that made matters worse.

Her eyes, which had been so dark and heavy moments before, were blank and her shoulders had slumped beneath her loose coats and billowing, untucked shirt.

"I will leave you now, my lord."

Jago had an almost overwhelming desire to grab her and finish what they'd started.

Instead, he watched her go. "Good night—Ben."

She didn't answer and the door clicked shut behind her.

He stood in the middle of the room for a long moment, his thoughts churning.

It had been a mistake to bring her from the stables into the house, a terrible mistake. But he had been selfish and he'd wanted her near—all under the guise of saying it was for her own good.

Having her so close all day was driving him to distraction. Before, when she'd lived outside, he'd paced the house thinking of her out there. And now, she was only mere rooms away—

"Enough," he ground out, striding to the small table that held several decanters and pouring himself a good three fingers of brandy.

Jago hissed as the rough, fiery liquid burned its way down his throat. Stephen Worth was spoiling him; Jago's spirits were far inferior to those served at Oakland Manor.

Even so, he finished the glass in a second swallow and then dropped into the nearest chair.

He was a conscienceless hound. He'd known what he wanted from her tonight before he'd even stepped foot inside the library and found her working late.

Working late for him.

What a way to repay her loyalty and diligence—by molesting her.

His gaze snagged on the trunk she'd been working on; the lock was hanging open with the key still inserted.

He put down his empty glass and absently leaned down to flip open the lid; it didn't contain books, but more papers.

Just what he needed: more bloody bills and dunning letters.

Jago was about to close the lid again—and perhaps hurl the trunk out the window—when a piece of pale lavender paper snagged his attention. He pulled that letter, and a couple others like it, from the jumble of documents.

There was no address, just Cadan's name.

He turned it over in his hands but did not open it.

Jago had come across a fair number of personal letters tossed in among the dunning notices. Although it went against the grain, he'd read everything he found, hoping to solve the mystery of what had deviled his brother's final days.

This letter, more than anything he'd thus far encountered, shrieked mystery and smacked, oddly, of menace.

Indeed, it seemed to coil and hiss in his hands.

He should throw it back into the trunk before it bared its fangs. Better yet, he should burn it.

Instead, his fingers began to unfold the paper, working as slowly and carefully as they did when he performed a delicate surgery.

His gaze dropped to the bottom of the letter; there was no signature.

"Cadan:

I'm tired of waiting. You got what you wanted and you still look like a knight in shining armor while I look like a duplicitous whore. I didn't take care of Fenwick and Brian for nothing.

I want two-thirds, not half. I earned it and you know it. I expect you to live up to your part of the bargain before the end of the month. If you keep dragging your heels, I'll visit the squire and his grieving wife and tell them the real reason their son is dead. And then I'll send a letter to Jago. We both know how honorable your brother is—it will kill him to do so, but he'll do the right thing when he learns the truth.

Give me my money and I'll be gone."

There was no name or date, but Jago didn't really need one. The context—although obscure—meant the sender could only have been Ria. As for the date—there was none—he hazarded a guess Cadan would have received it in late 1799, not long after Brian had committed suicide and Jago had been banished from Lenshurst.

What money was she talking about? And Fenwick? He must have been only a lad back then. No, wait—his elder brother would have been Fenwick back then, wouldn't he?

Christ, Jago couldn't recall; it was all so long ago.

But the most burning question of all was what in the hell she meant about the *real* reason behind Brian's death? His friend had hanged himself after Jago had humiliated him—at least that is what the brief, but succinct, letter Brian had left said.

Jago stared blindly at the paper in his hands.

What the devil did this mean?

Burn it. Burn the others, too.

That was exactly what he should do. Jago looked at the pieces of lavender paper.

They were just lifeless bits of parchment, but they beckoned and coaxed and demanded.

He would never be able to burn them.

Not until he'd read them.

He poured himself another brandy and lighted more candles.

And then he sat down to read.

Chapter Twenty-Three

Cornwall
1817
Present Day

*B*enna watched Jago ride Asclepius down the front drive not long after ten.

Ooooh, Jago now, is it?

Shut up, Geoffrey.

After what had happened last night in the library, Benna hadn't possessed the fortitude to go to the earl's office this morning for their usual meeting.

When he hadn't sent a servant to fetch her—which she couldn't decide if she was grateful for or annoyed about—she'd hidden in her study working all morning.

It was cowardly to dodge him, but she had plenty to do and busied herself with the most recent set of bills from the two cottages, which she was supposed to inspect with Jago this afternoon.

She had been looking forward to going on a ride with him but she somehow doubted that he'd want her to accompany him after what happened last night.

Benna squeezed her eyes shut, but then shook the unproductive worry away. She'd already spent a restless night dwelling on the matter.

Not an entirely restless night, if I remember correctly.

Her face heated at the memory of the only *restful* part of last night.

Benna sometimes had to remind herself that it wasn't *really* Geoff taunting her, but her own mischievous mind.

And right now, her mind—her conscience, probably—was attempting to shame her for taking satisfaction from her body.

What a wanton monster I created. Geoffrey chortled.

Fury sparked inside her as she considered society's hypocrisy when it came to such matters. Men could visit brothels, entice widows into their beds, and mount expensive mistresses to satiate their sexual hunger, but women were made to feel shame for even having the audacity to admit they had any desire—not to mention an ability—to experience physical pleasure.

She snatched another infernal bill out of the trunk—this one for the cost of a new shaft for a curricle that was no longer in the earl's carriage house—and put it in chronological order in the pile she had created for 1815.

Fueled by anger and a sense of injustice she worked her way through the chest of documents.

Eventually, she reached out to grab another bill and saw the trunk was empty. Benna glanced at the clock; it was almost noon.

Two hours had flown by in a flash.

She sighed, stretched, and stood. There was *that* loathsome task done—at least for today.

Next, she gathered up the most recent bills for the cottages.

It was her duty to check them against the blueprints Jago kept in the library, since their carpenter wasn't above adding additional work to his bills.

It was safe to go to the library since Jago hadn't yet returned.

The big room felt oddly empty this morning and Benna couldn't help glancing at the spot where they'd embraced each other last night.

Lord, but his body had felt delicious. She could only imagine what—

A sharp knock on the door cut off her erotic reverie.

It was Nance. "Ah, *here* you are, Mr. Piddock," he said, as if Benna had been hiding. "Mrs. Valera wishes to speak to you."

That must have been the magnificent carriage Benna had seen rolling up the drive not long ago.

"Did you tell her the earl is gone out this morning?"

"Were you not listening?" The old man gave her a testy look. "She wishes to speak with *you*, Mr. Piddock. "

"Me?"

Nance sighed like a person pushed beyond human endurance.

"Ben?" The female voice came from behind the butler, making the old man jump. A rich, bawdy laugh floated through the air. "I'm terribly sorry, Nance, I'm afraid I followed you. I *thought* Mr. Piddock might be beavering away in the library." She appeared in the doorway and laid a hand on Nance's shoulder, the action earning her a venomous glare. "You needn't stand on ceremony with me, we're old friends, after all."

Nance gave her a look that could freeze water and then turned to Benna. "Tea?" He made the word sound more than a little ominous.

Mrs. Valera answered him, "Goodness no, Nance, I'm only here to ask a quick favor of Mr. Piddock."

"Very good, ma'am." He turned stiffly, his posture broadcasting his opinion of women who did not stay where he put them.

Once they were alone, the red-haired beauty gave Benna a smile that could launch a thousand ships. She held out a dainty hand sheathed in lemon-yellow kid, which perfectly matched her form-fitting carriage gown.

Benna had to admit—grudgingly—that if she had looked even half as magnificent in a dress as Mrs. Valera she wouldn't have minded wearing them so much.

"Good afternoon, ma'am. How may I serve you?"

The other woman's lips curled in a way that made Benna feel like she was engaged in something wicked.

Her vivid green eyes flickered to the trestle table. "Are those the drawings for the famous hospital we are all hearing so much about?" She didn't wait for an answer before strolling over to the trestle table.

Benna followed. *What the devil did the woman want?* "Yes, these are the plans for Mr. Worth's hospital. Oh, not those," she said when Mrs. Valera began flicking through the plans that Benna had just been checking. "Those are for two of the earl's cottages."

A vee of annoyance formed between Mrs. Valera's delicate brows. "The earl is building new cottages?"

"He's not building new ones, but several are in need of a great deal of work."

"That must cost a pretty penny—doing such extensive repairs."

The comment puzzled her. Did she expect Benna to divulge the costs? "Er, I suppose so, ma'am."

"How much has he spent getting them ready?"

Benna stared. Not only was her question intrusive, but Benna found the other woman's reference to money vulgar.

What a little snob you still are, even after all these years.

She knew that was true.

No doubt Mrs. Valera—the widow of a man who'd made his fortune in trade—probably believed that speaking about one's finances with complete strangers was acceptable behavior.

"I couldn't say," Benna lied. She refused to discuss his lordship's business with the odiously nosey woman.

My, my, so angry! Or is that jealousy?

How could she *not* be jealous of this woman? She was gorgeous and wealthy and held Jago's interest—or at least she had done many years ago.

Mrs. Valera strolled around the table toward Benna, not stopping until she was almost standing on the toes of her boots.

Benna was just about to step back when Mrs. Valera looked up from the plans on the table, her eyelids heavy. "You are quite an all-around man, aren't you, Ben? First a groom—or was it a postilion?—and now a secretary. What next? Nobleman in disguise?" She chuckled, dragging a finger across the back of Benna's bare hand.

Benna's heart lurched at the woman's bizarre words and she snatched her hand back as if she'd been burnt.

Mrs. Valera laughed. "Such a nervous young gentleman." She fluttered her lashes and then turned away with a swish of her skirts, her hips swaying seductively as she strolled across the room, casually inspecting the row of trunks in front of the desk.

"Is the earl moving somewhere?"

"I b-beg your pardon?" Benna stammered, her mind still reeling from the other woman's terrifyingly accurate comment. Did she know something? After all, she was a friend of Viscount Fenwick's. Had he recognized Benna? But that had been days ago. Surely if—

"I asked if he was moving; what are all these for?" Mrs. Valera gestured to the trunks that were lined up on the floor.

"Er, they were filled with books and his lordship is having them re-shelved."

Mrs. Valera's auburn eyebrows arched. "These don't look like books." She nudged one of the open trunks with the toe of a lemon-yellow ankle boot.

Benna pushed up her glasses and squinted through a thumbprint at what the other woman was pointing at. It looked like the trunk they'd unlocked last night.

"No, those are just some old documents."

"Old documents? How tedious that must be. Why would you go through such things? Why not just burn them?"

Benna frowned. "Because Lord Trebolton has requested that I look through them all." Just what was the woman after? And what favor did she want from Benna?

As if she'd spoken aloud, Mrs. Valera said, "I daresay you're wondering why I wanted—"

The door opened and Benna turned at the sound.

The earl stood on the threshold, his eyes flickering between Benna and Mrs. Valera.

"Ria, how are you? Nance told me you were in here." His expression was strangely ... tight as he came toward the redhead and took her hand in both of his, raising it to his mouth in a courtly, almost romantic, gesture.

Benna turned away, absently straightening a stack of papers that were on the corner of the trestle table. She saw that her fingers were shaking and clasped her hands behind her back.

"Nance told me you wished to speak to Ben," Jago said.

"Oh, I just wanted to make sure that Ben knew he was invited to my costume ball."

Benna looked up, more than a little surprised.

She couldn't have been more surprised than Jago, who was briefly wide-eyed before his polite mask slipped back into place. "How thoughtful of you, Ria." He glanced at Benna. "I'm sure Ben would love to attend, provided he has time to cobble together a costume on such short notice."

"Oh pooh. A costume for a man is hardly the work of a moment and Ben is such a clever young gentleman." Mrs. Valera gave Benna a dismissive smile and turned to the earl. "Now that you are here, Jago, there *was* something I wished to speak to you about. In private."

That was Benna's cue. "If you would excuse me, my lord, Mrs. Valera."

Jago nodded but didn't look at her, seemingly unable to pull his gaze from Mrs. Valera as he led her toward the couch, still holding her hand.

Benna closed the door and leaned back against it, briefly closing her eyes, as if that could erase the vision of the two beautiful people burnt into her brain.

It was as clear as the very prominent nose on her face; Lord Trebolton was in love with the gorgeous—and wealthy—woman.

Chapter Twenty-Four

Cornwall
1817
Present Day

*J*ago relaxed slightly once Benna had left the room.

He couldn't have said why, but something about seeing Ria alone with the younger woman had left him feeling disturbed—like leaving a kitten unattended with a cobra.

"I am so glad you returned before I left," Ria said as they settled down on the settee. She did not release his hand and Jago did not push the issue. Ria would play her games and Jago would go along with her. Any illusions that he'd clung to—such as the foolishly persistent belief that she might actually care for him a little—had been shattered by the letters he'd read last night.

"It is always a pleasure to see you, Ria."

She smiled, visibly gratified by his words. "I had begun to believe that you no longer liked me very much, Jago."

He didn't like her. Indeed, it was now safe to say that he actively disliked and mistrusted her. But the way to get bees was not with vinegar.

"Nonsense, my dear. I'm afraid I've been distracted since my return."

"Ah, yes. I take it the estate is in some disrepair." Her lips tightened and Jago fancied it was to keep a smile from forming.

"I am slowly getting matters under control."

"That is what Ben said. What an exceptional young man he must be—such a broad array of talents for such a youthful ... boy."

Jago studied her beautiful face for any sign that she might have guessed Benna's secret—not that he had much faith in being able to read something in Ria's expression if she wished to conceal it. He was no fool; when it came to deception, she was far more adept at obfuscation than he would ever be.

"Ben has indeed been helpful." He paused and then added, "It was kind of you to add him to your guest list."

"I wouldn't have dreamed of inviting him *before*. But I am given to understand that, as your secretary, such an invitation is unexceptionable. After all, he takes dinner with your family and guests."

Jago smiled. "How well-informed you are about what goes on in my household, Ria."

Her face creased into an expression of displeasure at his obvious amusement. "I haven't been gossiping with servants, dear Jago, if that is what you are thinking."

"I would never think such a thing."

She colored at whatever she saw on his face—likely disbelief, which is what he was feeling—and her full lips thinned. "Mariah mentioned it when I encountered your nieces with Mrs. Worth at the modiste's in Redruth."

"I see."

"I actually came here on another matter and extending an invitation to Ben was merely an excuse to wait for your return."

"How may I be of service, Ria?"

"It's about Lord Fenwick."

"What about him?"

"I know I've been a bit naughty to tease you with him." She paused, as if waiting for Jago to confirm her words.

"Yes, you've been wicked," he agreed, sure that statement would cover a variety of sins, not only the one she was unsubtly hinting at.

"He is not—that is to say, I view him in the manner of a younger sibling. A brother I never had," she added.

"Ah." Jago waited for the rest of it.

"Perhaps you did not know it as you've been away, but his older brother died perhaps six or seven years ago. Poor Fenwick is like you in that he has unexpectedly had the mantle of heir thrust upon him." She hesitated and added. "And his elder brother and father certainly played ducks and drakes with their estate."

"I see," Jago said, hoping that was the only characteristic that he shared with Fenwick, whom he'd found more than a little odious from his brief exposure to the man. Hearing that the viscount's family fortune was much diminished explained why Fenwick was dangling after a woman that his father—the profligate, but notoriously high in the instep, Marquess of Devoran—was unlikely to approve of.

"How is it that you became acquainted with Fenwick?" he asked.

"My husband and I first met him at one of the Earl of Trentham's parties in London."

Even as removed as Jago was from *ton* gossip he'd heard about the infamous parties. He wasn't sure what Elinor knew about her dead husband's London bashes, but her current husband, Stephen, had told Jago enough about Trentham's proclivities for buying virgins, engaging in orgies, and experimenting with illicit substances to leave him with a deep disgust of the deceased earl.

And Ria had attended such parties? And enjoyed them?

"I've heard those affairs were rather … unusual," he said.

"Oh yes, quite unusual. And delicious." She moistened her full lips and smiled fondly, the concupiscent gleam in her eyes making his stomach churn. "I didn't dare hope that you held such sophisticated tastes, Jago."

"And that is where you met Fenwick?" he asked, ignoring her subtle probing.

"Yes. This was some time ago, before he became the heir. He was far too young to be a part of Trentham's set, but he came as the guest of the Earl of Norland. Of course, Norland was plain Michael de Montfort back then."

"I'm not acquainted with the man." And he had no wish to be if he ran with Fenwick and the last Earl of Trentham.

"The parties stopped after Trentham's death and I didn't see Fenwick for some time. We encountered each other quite by accident in Truro several months after Henry died."

"And you knew his older brother as well?"

Her eyes widened slightly. "Er, no. I shouldn't say that. I knew *of* him, of course."

Jago had no patience for such verbal fencing. "I found some letters that you wrote to Cadan, Ria."

Her lips parted and Jago saw a flash of fear in her eyes. For a moment he thought she'd deny authorship of the unsigned missives.

She bit her lower lip. "I was hoping that he'd destroyed them."

"He didn't—at least not these four. Are there more?"

"Did you—that is, er, you won't have read them, of course."

Jago noticed that she didn't answer his question. "Actually, I did. That is why I'm asking about Fenwick. The letters are old, so I gather you were referring to the current viscount's elder brother."

The look on her face was the first genuine expression he could recall seeing: shock, with no small amount of fury. "How dare you read private correspondence?"

"There was nothing to indicate that it *was* private, Ria; the letters were in with the rest of Cadan's business correspondence. Besides," he added, "there was no signature."

"Then how can you be sure they are from me?"

"I could guess based on the content." He smiled. "And now I know because you confirmed it."

"I should like to see what you are talking about. In fact, if they are mine, I want them back."

"I have a few questions, Ria."

He could see that she was struggling to hold her temper. "About what?"

"About the content of those letters."

"It was all a long time ago. I don't recall what—"

"What deal did you make with Cadan?"

"I don't remember."

Jago stared.

She scowled. "If you've read the letters then I'm sure you can guess."

"He gave you money to what—discourage my suit? Or perhaps to encourage others?"

"Why should that surprise you? You know how proud Cadan was—how little he liked the thought of you marrying me."

Those might have been the first truthful words that she'd spoken.

Jago gave a mirthless chuckle. "To be honest, I'm fairly sure— with the clarity of hindsight—that you were merely toying with me and

208

never had any notion of marrying me. You wanted money and status and I could give you neither."

"Cadan should have been able to see as much, but he wanted to be *certain*," she retorted, not bothering to deny his accusation. "Had he not been so obsessed with the notion of marrying you to—what was that wretched girl's name, again?"

He ignored the question. "So, Cadan paid you to do something that you'd already planned to do—jilt me."

She shrugged.

"And what about Brian? Because it struck me there was something else in those letters aside from Cadan paying you to keep away. Just what were you two up to?"

"I threatened to tell Brian's parents about Cadan's part in the duel."

"His part? What do you mean *his part*? Cadan ordered me to stand down that day."

She glanced down at her hands, which were clenched in her lap. "Oh, that was all just an act. Cadan encouraged Brian—it didn't take much; you know what a short temper he had." She raised her face to him, her expression defiant, but Jago saw shame beneath it. "Neither of us imagined that he'd be so humiliated as to take his own life."

Jago could only stare in amazement. "You expect me to believe that Cadan stirred the coals so that we would fight?"

"Think what you like, but you asked me for the truth."

Jago gave a bitter laugh; Ria and the truth, he suspected, had always been strangers.

She was lying—or at least not giving him the whole story.

"Don't you recall how you were back then—I daresay how you *still* are, Jago?"

"What do you mean, *how I was*?"

"Oh come," she scoffed. "You have always been such a pattern card of honor and nobility."

He flinched at the scathing disdain in her voice. "I wasn't aware that behaving honorably was so contemptible, Ria."

"Oh, I daresay you weren't—honorable people never realize just how difficult it is for the rest of us mortal beings to measure up to their standards. But Cadan knew it well enough—he knew that giving me up must derive from your own elevated notions of honor or you would turn marriage to me into a holy crusade. Poor Cadan." She gave a bitter laugh. "His ham-fistedness left him worse off than he'd been before his meddling. Not only did you *not* marry the heiress, but you abandoned him to deal with the mess he'd created."

The shame he felt at her accusation was ancient, but it was still as sharp and cruel as a razor.

He *had* left his brother to deal with a mess—true, one of his own making—while he'd gone off to lick his wounds.

Jago shook away the old guilt, unwilling to be distracted from the point by Ria's diversion. "So, between the two of you—with me as your ignorant dupe—you drove Brian to kill himself."

"We could hardly imagine that he would do such a thing," she insisted. "You can never know how heavily what happened weighed on the two of us."

"Oh, can't I? You had no problem allowing me to shoulder the guilt, did you? Did Brian even *write* that letter, Ria?"

"How dare you?" she demanded, but her outrage lacked any real heat. "Besides, you would have reacted the same without a letter. You were *eager* to martyr yourself for the cause, Jago, don't try to deny it."

Jago didn't deny it; he happened to agree with her. He'd been an arrogant self-important pup back then. Hell, perhaps she was right and he still was.

Whether or not that was true, he knew one thing for certain: this farrago that she'd just spun for his consumption made no sense. She was lying; whatever it was that she'd gotten up to with Cadan, it had nothing to do with paying her to reject Jago.

Her lower lip trembled as he stared at her, trying to see beyond her beautiful façade to the untruths beneath.

But there was no point; her mask was a thick carapace of lies accumulated over decades.

"I can see that you will never forgive me, Jago."

She was right about that, at least.

"I deeply regret what happened. We were just foolish children—it was so long ago." Ria grabbed his hand. "Please, I implore you, Jago. Can't we put all that behind? I know we could if only you would give us a chance." When he didn't answer she squeezed his hand painfully hard. "I can help you, Jago."

He didn't pretend to be ignorant of what she meant. "I am flattered and tempted by your offer, Ria." Both statements were blatant lies but there was no reason to be offensive.

The corners of her lush mouth pulled down. "You're flattered but your answer is a gentlemanly but unequivocal *no*, isn't it?"

"I am no bargain, Ria. You can do far better."

Her hand tightened. "We were once so good together. That summer, before Cadan interfered, there *was* something between us, wasn't there?"

For the first time, Jago noticed the web of fine lines around her eyes.

She was right; it was a lifetime ago and they had been different people then.

When Jago tried to recall that long ago summer and recapture his feelings for her the image that formed in his mind's eye wasn't Ria's face, but a different woman entirely: Benna.

Even a man who was infatuated with Benna—as Jago clearly was—could not objectively call her beautiful.

And yet there was something so taking—so loveable—in the character, intelligence, and strength in her face that she had speedily become the most attractive woman of Jago's acquaintance.

He met Ria's pleading green gaze and gave her hand a gentle squeeze. "You may always count me among your friends, Ria."

It wasn't until after Jago had escorted Ria to her grand coach and watched it disappear down the driveway that he remembered that she had never answered his question about her connection to the prior Viscount Fenwick.

Chapter Twenty-Five

Cornwall
1817
Present Day

After being dismissed from the library Benna was far too abstracted to do anything that required concentration.

Instead, she'd tied on her apron and went to tackle an enormous suite of rooms in the long-disused east wing of the house. Not only were the rooms in question cold and musty, but they were positively stuffed with trunks and crates.

She'd only been working half an hour when the heavy oak door creaked open.

"Ah, there you are," Nance said for the second time that day.

"You need me?"

"His lordship wanted to remind you to meet him down at the stables at four o'clock."

As if Benna were likely to forget a ride with Lord Trebolton.

"Thank you, Nance," she said, wondering why he was delivering messages today instead of a footman.

Rather than turn and leave, Nance glanced up at the coffered ceiling of the magnificent room. "Our current king's grandfather once slept in this room."

"Oh?"

"It's a disgrace that it is in this state," he mumbled.

Benna just grunted.

Nance shoved a bundle of drapes off a wingchair covered in rotting yellow silk and then carefully lowered his ancient bones onto the seat, groaning as he did so.

Once he'd shifted his narrow carcass around and made himself comfortable, he looked up at Benna, who was staring.

His face, already deeply grooved with wrinkles, puckered into a disdainful frown. "*She* has finally left."

Benna didn't need to ask which *she* he meant.

Besides, she'd seen Mrs. Valera's carriage depart a scant quarter of an hour after she'd left the library. But even the knowledge that the two weren't still alone together hadn't wiped the memory of the earl's besotted expression from her mind.

Benna turned back to the crate she'd just opened.

The dishes inside it were old and costly. It was Maiolica, a form of Italianate plate from the early fifteenth century. There were similar serving pieces at Wake House, but she'd never seen such an extensive collection. It looked like somebody had just tossed the pieces into a crate full of wood shavings.

"What do you have there?" Nance asked.

She held up a piece. "I do hope none of it is broken." She set it on a nearby settee. It would better to haul it all back in small batches rather than risk dropping a full crate.

"Ah, yes. Maiolica." Nance appeared unsurprised by the fact that valuable dishes were sitting in one of the state guest bedchambers.

In fact, neither he nor the housekeeper, Mrs. Gates, had raised an eyebrow at any of the oddities she'd found at Lenshurst, which told her that it had likely been going on for some time.

Benna went about her work, waiting for the old servant to get to the point of his visit.

Several minutes passed in silence, only the soft clinking of ceramic filling the big room. Benna had just moved on to the next crate when the old man finally spoke.

"Mrs. Valera's mother, Margaret, was a tweeny over at Oakland Manor."

Ah, here it was. Nance—usually so proper—wished to gossip.

"Margaret was a pretty little thing—although nothing to her daughter—and caught the eye of the vicar's younger brother. This was the last vicar—John Bennett—not the one now." He clucked his tongue. "The vicar and his brother were poor sons of a gentleman

213

farmer somewhere in the north." He waved a boney hand in a direction Benna believed was westerly.

Benna set aside the jemmy bar she'd been using to open the crate and lifted off the lid: more books. She replaced the lid and moved on.

"The younger son was a wild boy who'd been sent to the vicar to be tamed. Ha! He wasn't here a month before he got a babe on Meg and then scarpered. Meg went into the straw and then took her own life not long after the child was born. Her family was strict and would have made her days a hell on earth. As it was, they sent the babe to Meg's spinster sister, Tilly."

He glanced at Benna, who'd paused in the middle of emptying yet another crate full of dishes to listen to the tragic but all too common tale.

Nance's gaze dropped to the pewter pitcher he held. "We've been searching for that for months," he said.

Benna put the pitcher aside and Nance resumed his story.

"When Tilly died suddenly, the girl was brought back. Not to Meg's family—they wouldn't have her—but to live with the vicar and his wife. 'Course they put the story about that Gloria was an orphaned niece." He shrugged. "They were well-liked and so people played along."

"What happened to Mrs. Valera's father?" Benna asked.

"Oh, well, he'd died in the war." Nance sighed, as if the tale were exhausting him. "The vicar and his wife loved that girl like she was their own—they never did have children—and they gave her everything. Some think the vicar beggared himself to make sure she always had the very best."

Benna closed the crate of books and went to check the contents of the three large armoires that were stacked like soldiers along one long wall.

The first armoire was stuffed with clothing. Old clothing. Must and dust billowed around Benna when she shifted the piles to see what they were.

The garments had been wadded up with no care and expensive silks and satins were jumbled in with cheap muslin. A flash of salmon pink attracted her attention and she pulled out a man's skirted frockcoat.

"That was his lordship's," Nance said. "I recall when he wore it."

"Lord Cadan wore *this*?"

Nance cut her a look of amusement. "No, you daft boy, his *father*."

Benna held up the garment, which was made from the most beautiful satin she had ever seen. It was embroidered with pagodas and trees. The earl must have purchased it around the same time as the silver epergne she'd found a few days ago.

"I recall that night. The countess had a dress to match and they looked like a king and queen," Nance said, his voice wistful.

Benna shook out the coat and held it up to herself in front of the mirror.

"Why, you're just about the same height as the old master," Nance said. "He was also a slender man when he was younger."

Benna stared at her reflection. "Do you think I might borrow this?" she asked.

The old man's eyes bulged. "Where in the world would you wear such a thing?"

"Mrs. Valera invited me to her masquerade," she said, sniffing the garment and recoiling at the camphor smell.

Nance clucked his tongue and shook his head.

Benna frowned. "What? Mayn't I borrow it?"

Nance waved a dismissive, bony hand. "Of course you can use the coat—there are breeches, too. I'm talking about Mrs. Valera—you stay away from her, lad. She's like one of those things that sings to men."

Benna chuckled and turned away from the mirror. "A siren?"

"Aye, don't laugh. That woman has brought more men to their end than some wreckers."

Benna set the garment on the settee, rather than back in the armoire. She didn't believe the other woman had been serious about her invitation, but she had given it. Although Benna hadn't decided yet to accept the offer, it couldn't hurt to have a costume at the ready.

The next two armoires contained more garments. Benna sighed and began to unload them, just in case there were valuables wrapped up in with the clothes.

"We were all stunned when Master Jago left." The name *Jago* acted like a string and yanked up Benna's head.

The old man's eyes became vague. "I thought for sure that girl would catch one of them and Master Jago loved her fiercely, that was plain for all to see. He was wild back then—not at all like he is now." He saw Benna's look of disbelief and shrugged. "He was. But young men are allowed to sow their oats." Nance shot her a tolerant look, as if to let Benna know that he would excuse whatever antics she might get up to. "Lord Jago and yon squire's lad—young Brian Paisley—were like as two peas. Oh, the things those two got tangled up in." His eyes brightened. "I'll never forget the time they got it into their heads to become the next Kings of Prussia."

"Kings of Prussia?" Benna asked.

"Aye—those were what they called the gentlemen." At Benna's continued confusion he explained, "smugglers."

"Oh."

"They couldn't have been more than eleven or twelve. They'd hauled their skiff all the way to Penryn. They were almost out of the harbor, headed to France to take prisoners for ransom, when a strong current caught them." He grinned at Benna. "You should have seen Lord Trebolton's face when *real* gentlemen brought young Master Jago home."

"You mean real smugglers rescued them?"

"Aye, poor Master Jago couldn't sit for a week such a caning he got." The smile drained from his face. "I think all the heart went out of him after young Brian St. John's death." He pursed his lips and went quiet, lost in the past.

Benna wanted to grab him and squeeze more gossip out of him, but she kept her mouth shut. She knew from experience that people talked more freely when they were under no pressure.

"Master Cadan now …" he trailed off and shook his head.

"What about him?" she finally prodded when she could stand it no longer.

"He never did like Mrs. Valera. Leastways it seemed that way. But she did come around a bit—even after Master Jago had left."

"Oh?" Benna said, to keep him talking.

"Mmm-hmm. But then she married old Valera and we didn't see her more than once or twice a year, until after he died. Then she started to come around more—to flaunt herself and her money. Couldn't think of no other reason since her and the master always did seem to fall crossways with one another. Why, even this past year they—"

Benna lost interest in the old man's musings. She didn't care how often Mrs. Valera had visited the last master of Lenshurst or what they'd been to each other. It was Jago she wanted to know about.

She found two silver serving platters sandwiched between a motheaten gown and velvet cloak trimmed in fur that must have once been white.

She closed the armoire, put the trays with the other dishes and made a mental note to ask Mrs. Gates where all the old garments should be stored. Perhaps some of the materials could be reused or—

"—once Lord Jago had gone Miss Ria disappeared for a few months and when she returned it was with the news that she was to wed old Valera. He was a dried-up old stick." Nance—something of a dried-up old stick himself—laughed. "It wasn't hard to see why she'd agreed to marry him. Plenty of brass there."

Benna had paused at the sound of the word *Jago* but turned to another crate when it seemed the old man was done talking.

The wood screeched beneath her small pry bar and she pushed aside wood shavings to find ornate pistols. Not just one or two, but dozens—a veritable fortune in antique firearms—all jumbled in together.

Benna took one of the beautiful old guns from the box. The stock was made from a wood that was almost black, and intricately chased with silver.

"Ah, from the gun room," Nance said, nodding his head as if she'd asked him a question.

She waited for him to say more—perhaps tell her *why* the guns were not in the gun room—but he didn't appear to find the matter of interest.

Benna replaced the gun and slowly lowered the lid, her gaze flickering over all the crates she hadn't yet opened.

217

Why were all these valuables packed in crates like this? Did Jago know why?

Somehow, Benna didn't think so; she got the impression that he was just as much in the dark about it as she was.

What the devil was going on at Lenshurst?

***

The sky was menacingly dark by the time Benna and the earl left Lenshurst Park to go inspect the two cottages.

Benna gritted her teeth as she waited for him to mention last night, but when he finally spoke, it was about something else, entirely.

"So, do you like working as a secretary as well as working in the stables?"

If he wanted to pretend last night had not happened, that was fine with Benna.

"I like it better, my lord. My hands and back thank you."

"But not your eyes, I'll wager. We did not meet this morning," he said. When she remained quiet, he went on, "How goes the work on the various rooms?"

"I've finished up the rooms in the family wing and have moved to the east wing. I'm afraid the task is taking more time than I expected." She couldn't help wondering how long it had taken the last earl to strip all the rooms so thoroughly.

"Have you come across any other trunks filled with papers?" he asked.

"Everything I've found of that sort I've sent to the library."

"Well, that's one bit of good news," he said. "There are over one hundred rooms at Lenshurst Park, I guess we can be grateful that only a few dozen are a mess. The last time I was in most of them was when I was a boy. Even when I was younger the east and south wings weren't safe to use. My brother and I were forbidden to venture onto the second floor of the east wing." He cut her a grin. "Although of course we played there, anyway."

So had Benna and David, back before he grew too old to play with his little sister. Wake House was even larger than Lenshurst and far older. It was a rabbit warren and an ideal playground for imaginative children. Every king and queen from the Plantagenet era forward had stayed in one bedroom or another.

Unlike Lenshurst, however, there were no badly decayed areas at Wake House. Being in rooms like the one she'd visited today made her realize just what good caretakers her ancestors had been.

What was Michael doing after she'd run away and left him in control of the vast estate and its coffers—

Benna yanked her mind back from heading down that path; no good could come from fretting about that now.

"That last trunk you delivered to the library," the earl asked, distracting her from her unwanted thoughts, "the one that was locked?"

She looked across at him. Their eyes met and bolts of heat shot through her body; was he remembering their embrace?

"Yes, my lord?"

"Where did you find it?"

"It was the last of the trunks from my chambers."

"Oh." He sounded disappointed. "I'd like you to make it a priority to search for any remaining correspondence."

"Yes, my lord." That was interesting; what had been in that trunk?

"I have another question for you."

"Yes, my lord?"

"What did Mrs. Valera want from you today? I know it wasn't just an invitation to her party she came to deliver, was it?"

"I don't know, sir. She was still working up to asking me for a favor—as she termed it—when you entered the library."

"I see," he said, sounding abstracted.

They rode without speaking for a while.

"Tell me more about your time as a postilion, Ben," he suddenly asked.

"What do you wish to know, my lord?"

"Many people see them as romantic figures—was it a romantic life?"

"I thought only tavern wenches viewed them as such."

He smiled. "It sounds like there's a story behind that observation."

"Not an interesting one."

"You have extensive knowledge of tavern wenches?"

219

"Not by choice, but they seemed to be drawn to me.

"You *do* have a mysterious and brooding air about you," he teased.

She scoffed. "As far as I could tell my attraction sprang from the fact that I actively avoided socializing and scarcely opened my mouth when I couldn't escape it. Who would have guessed such traits were attractive?"

"You came across a tortured, poetic soul. I believe that is how Catherine views you."

Benna couldn't help smiling. "Yes, well, her interest in me has greatly diminished now that she has the appeal of a London Season ahead of her."

"Tell me about a day in the life of a post boy. It only seems fair since you know what a day in the life of an impoverished peer is like."

Benna spoke before she could stop herself, "I'd like to hear about a day in the life of a country doctor."

He gave her an unreadable look. "Very well," he finally said. "We shall trade stories; ladies first."

Benna felt like she'd just won at cards. "Seniority plays a big part in what stages a boy gets, as do good relations with the owner of the posting house. There's no pay for sitting around waiting at inns so competition is often fierce to pick up jobs."

Benna decided not to tell him that more than once she'd had to back down from physical confrontations with other postilions who'd wanted to fight her.

"And did you find the work itself difficult?"

"It was far easier on the road than at the inns."

"Really? I would have thought it would be the opposite."

"It's physically more demanding on the road, but it's not a difficult job when it comes down to it. Especially not if you are the lead-boy, which is what I always was." She hesitated, and then added, "Except for one time, when the wheel-boy I was paired with got cup-shot and was unfit to ride."

"What happened?" he asked.

"I was the only post boy they had, so I rode wheel on a four-horse team. I made it to the next inn without running the bounder into a ditch, but I did so at a less than courageous pace."

The earl laughed. "Sometimes caution is wise."

"Not that time. The worst part of that job was the gentleman in the chaise, who raged at me every ten minutes to step up the pace. He was positively irate that I wouldn't give the horses their heads." She could laugh now, but it had been terrifying at the time. Before that journey she'd only ever ridden lead-boy. Riding wheel meant making all the decisions.

"Did you never have trouble with highwaymen?"

"I was robbed twice." The words were out of Benna mouth before she could stop them. Ah well, she'd just have to tweak her story a bit.

"Good God!" He turned his body toward her. "What happened?"

"The first time was actually during my very first post boy job—not as a postilion but delivering the mail—an express."

"Ah, I've heard that can be dangerous."

"I was petrified at the time," she admitted. "But the two robbers had no interest in violence, all they wanted was the mail bag. I gave it to them without a struggle."

"A wise move. But I daresay your postmaster wasn't happy."

"No, he was furious and also suspicious. Anyhow, that was my first and last express."

"And the second time you were robbed?"

"Er, well, I was actually bringing a horse back to the inn where I was working. I was by myself." That much was true. "Anyhow, I was in a hurry and out after dusk." Again, the truth. "There were three of them and they took the horse, my boots, my coat, my hat, watch, and all the money in my pockets." Benna had been terrified they'd take her shirt and pants, too.

"Good lord! Robbing a post boy," he said, getting to the weak point in her story quickly.

"Yes, not too wise. They weren't too happy with such a measly haul." And *that* was the lie in the story. Her robbers had been elated by what they'd found in Benna's valise.

"A dangerous job," he said, shaking his head.

"To be honest, living closely with other post boys was far more dangerous than any highwayman."

"You are quite an impressive young woman."

221

Benna snorted. "Because I can ride a coach horse, once *almost* delivered the mail, and have been robbed twice?" She turned to meet his gaze. "What I've done—the dangers I've navigated—are nothing to the perils that serving wenches and female servants have to face daily."

"Yes, there is some truth to what you say," the earl agreed. "Life is not easy for women of any order, but most certainly not the servant class. But, no, I didn't say you were impressive because of your equestrian skills—although you have a better seat than anyone I've ever met—male or female."

His words warmed her, and she had to look away from his appreciative gaze.

"What I meant was that I admire your stoicism. You have not chosen an easy path in life and yet you do not appear bitter or unhappy."

She was glad that was how he viewed her, but the truth was far less impressive. How often, especially during those early months, had the enormity of what lay before her threatened to crush her? How many times, in the depths of despair, had she considered taking an easier way out of her troubles?

Especially the weeks after Geoff had turned traitor on her?

No, those days were better forgotten.

And yet even with all the pain, fear, and hardship there was no denying that her life had been filled with fascinating experiences, most of which she never would have had if she'd remained sequestered at Wake House.

"I suppose if I'd wanted a more, er, traditional life, I might be less content with my lot," Benna finally said.

"And here I have dragooned you into working with mountains of tedious paperwork—not exactly exciting."

"I liked working outside but you were right, my lord—it was simply too physically grueling. Besides, there is so much that needs to be done in the house that even a single day's work yields progress, which is satisfying in its own way."

"I'm glad you can find some fulfillment. I've always been dreadful with accounts and business matters, myself."

"Did you not have a great deal of such work as a doctor?"

"I kept detailed records on patients, of course, but that wasn't unpleasant like the management of a vast estate." He snorted. "Listen to me—whining about my lot in life. As bad as this situation is, there are thousands of people who would trade places with me in an instant."

"That might be true, but the fact that others might envy you doesn't make an unpleasant situation any more palatable."

He grinned at her, the sight so rare and stunning it almost knocked her off her horse. "I appreciate your outlook—no doubt because it excuses my sniveling."

"I believe it is your turn, my lord," she reminded him.

He heaved an exaggerated sigh. "Very well. But I warn you, the life of a country doctor is not particularly interesting, although it *is* very busy. I was the only doctor for miles around Trentham so in that way our jobs were similar because I spent a good deal of time on horseback."

"And that is where you met Mrs. Worth—at Trentham?"

"Yes. She was Countess of Trentham."

"Did you live there a long time?"

"A little over five years. I moved there from Manchester." He smiled faintly, his profile to her. "It was … quite a change," he said, almost to himself.

"I heard Mr. Fielding once call you Doctor Venable."

"That was my courtesy title—Viscount Venable. My brother asked that I not disgrace the family name of Crewe, so I used Venable."

They rode for a moment in silence, and Benna wondered if he regretted having spoken so candidly to a mere servant. Certainly those few words had told her a great deal about his relationship with his dead brother.

He turned and caught her staring. It didn't seem to matter how much she saw him, she never tired of looking at him.

"Tell me, er, Ben, I know you said your father's landlord wished to marry you, but did you leave behind no particular beau?"

"No, my lord, there was nobody. There has not been a great rush of men eager to court a woman who can successfully masquerade as a man for years."

223

His eyebrows rose at her hostile tone. "Come now, Ben. Not *so* successfully, I think. At least three men have noticed."

Benna opened her mouth, but then closed it. She was his servant; it was not her place to bicker with him.

"You resent my prying questions."

"Of course not, my lord."

"What a bouncer."

She couldn't help smiling. "Well, perhaps just a little."

"There, that's better. You are far too serious for one so young."

"Can one be too serious, my lord?"

"Yes, if left unchecked it can become a life-threatening medical condition."

She laughed.

A distant rumbling made them both glance up at the darkening sky. A drop of moisture hit Benna's nose.

The storm was arriving far sooner than they'd expected.

***

"I'm afraid we're going to get wet," Jago said, even as rain began to pelt down. "I think it might be wiser to take shelter until this passes.

"Shelter? Where?"

"There is a hunting cottage just ahead through the trees. Let's take this path."

He preceded her down an overgrown, ancient trail that hadn't received much use as of late.

It began to rain in earnest once they were a few minutes into the small wood. He glanced over his shoulder. She had pulled up the collar on her serviceable, but not especially heavy coat. Jago wanted to offer her his greatcoat but knew the gesture would be viewed as strange by anyone they encountered—not that that was very likely. But it would not be good to get into the habit of treating her like a woman to be cherished.

The trees shielded them from a good deal of wind, but the rain still found its way through the canopy.

Directly ahead of them a bolt of lightning pierced the woods.

Asclepius reared up. "Easy boy," Jago murmured into the gelding's twitching ear, just before the accompanying crack of thunder caused both his horse and Benna's mare to whinny.

224

The rain started to bucket down and Jago was beginning to wonder if he'd somehow gone wide of the cottage when he saw it ahead. Next to the one-room cabin was a little outbuilding large enough to hold a few horses. Jago dismounted and turned to help Benna but she was already down and leading her mount toward the shack, murmuring something in the animal's ear.

The shed had only three walls and a roof, but at least it was dry. Benna began to unsaddle her horse.

"I'll manage the horses," Jago said. "Go inside and take off your wet coat." He could see she wanted to argue. "That was not a request, Benna." Her eyes flickered at his slip with her name. "Start the fire, I shall be right behind you."

An old wooden bucket hung from a peg and Jago knew he would find water in the small rill that ran just behind the cabin, no doubt the reason this location had been selected. He pulled down his hat before heading back into the now horizontal rain.

The horses vied for control of the full bucket and managed to drain it in a matter of minutes so Jago made one more trip before picking up their saddles and carrying them toward the cabin's only entrance.

He discovered a veritable domestic heaven when he opened the door.

Benna turned from the hearth, where she'd started a fire and was already boiling water.

"The fire was set and waiting," she said.

"It's always been kept ready. I've not been here for years but I daresay my brother used it whenever he hunted gamecock." Jago placed the saddles near the hearth so they might dry, before shrugging off his greatcoat. He'd believed the new overcoat a ridiculous waste of money when purchasing it in Truro, but now realized the multi-caped, floor-length garment was better than a blanket in such weather.

Unfortunately, it was also half-soaked and heavier than a blanket.

He hung it from a peg, one of several placed near the hearth for just that purpose. Beneath the coat he was dry, except his boots. Benna had also removed her overcoat but her woolen breeches and coat looked damp

"You'll catch your death in those clothes."

225

"It's warm enough that I don't notice." She ruined that claim by shivering.

Jago unbuttoned his coat. "Here, take this." He glanced around the small cabin. A table with two chairs, a cupboard with a basin, and a bed were the only items immediately visible. The bed had a woolen blanket folded at the foot end.

"Wrap this around yourself."

She took it in her free hand, holding his coat away from her person as if it were some sort of contagion.

"Change into it."

"I don't want to ruin it—this is one of your new coats."

It amused him that she knew his clothing so well. "Change into it," he repeated, using his doctor's voice.

Once she took the blanket Jago turned his back, trying not to think about the fact that she was stripping behind him.

The last time the cabin had been stocked was when his brother was alive, so at least a year ago. There was a canister of tea that, while not exactly fresh, was better than nothing. There were also several ceramic pots that had been sealed with wax, and he recognized them as Cook's handiwork. His stomach growled with anticipation at the thought of their contents.

A moment later he felt movement beside him and turned.

She had wrapped the blanket around her waist and put his coat over her shirt and vest. For all that she was so tall, his coat swamped her delicate form.

How she managed to appear so bloody alluring damp, disheveled, and wearing a man's clawhammer was a mystery.

"Hold out your arm," he ordered, reaching for her sleeve.

"You'll wrinkle it," she said, when he began to roll up the cuff.

"Then Toomey will have something to do." As he turned up the sleeves his gaze lingered on her work-scarred hands. The nails were chewed to the quick and the calluses on her palms spoke of hard work. When he glanced up, she was staring at him with an unreadable expression, although her pale eyes had gone as dark as the storm clouds currently blotting out the sun.

Jago could imagine what expression was on his face; he was so hard that his prick actually hurt. It had not escaped him that he was alone in a cottage with the object of his desire.

A bolt of lightning illuminated the room and they both turned to stare out the cottage's only window.

"One … two …"

They spoke at the time.

She met his gaze as they continued the count. "Three … four …"

A deafening boom rocked the small building.

"A little over half a mile, I'd guess," he said.

"But moving this way."

"I'm afraid so. Are you bothered by storms?"

"I find them less than soothing."

While she made tea, Jago moved the table and chairs closer to the fire. The storm was indeed coming their way and the windowpane rattled as if it were being pummeled by pebbles.

"I'm going to quickly check on the horses." Jago pulled on his wet overcoat and ventured into the tempest, hoping the beasts had not spooked and ran.

But they were crowded together in the corner, Penny Bright's eyes showing white as she cowered against Asclepius; the big gelding looked anxious, but not terrified.

The rotted wood of the enclosure would offer no resistance if the horses decided to bolt, but there was nothing Jago could do about that.

He soothed them as best he could, taking the time to calm his own over-active body while he was at it.

If he were truly a gentleman he would have insisted they return to Lenshurst. But he suspected that he was far from decent because he hoped—to his shame—that the storm raged all night.

He stood out in the wind and cold until he was no longer hard.

When he finally returned to the cottage it was to find two mugs, a steaming pot, and three little tubs of preserves on the table.

"Strawberry, brambleberry, and apricot," she said.

He took the spoon she offered and waited until she sat before taking the chair across from her. She should have looked comical with the loose coat hanging off her shoulders and the rough handspun blanket about her hips. Instead, she was the most arousing sight he'd ever seen.

She poured the fragrant-smelling liquid into the mugs. "In Russia they take their tea with jam in it."

"I didn't know that. Where did you learn such an interesting fact?"

"I like to read."

She'd lighted a few tallow candles but the room was dim as the storm raged. The glow cast by the firelight illuminated her, turning her face and throat a sensual golden-red.

Jago didn't usually take sugar with his tea but put a spoonful of apricot into his steaming mug and smiled at her. "Today we shall be Russians."

She spooned a glob of strawberry jam into her mug, stirred, and then sipped. She then reached for a spoonful of apricot. "I have a sweet tooth," she admitted, her spoon clinking softly against the stoneware.

"It does not look as if you overdo it."

She dropped her gaze at his reference to her body.

Her body.

His cock roused instantly at the thought of what she concealed beneath the coat and blanket.

Jago floundered for something harmless to talk about. "You mentioned that your father was responsible for your diction. Did you attend school where he taught?"

She sipped her tea before answering and Jago couldn't help thinking that she displayed far too much caution each time he asked about her past. What was she hiding? Or was she merely private?

"Until I was twelve."

"What happened then?"

"Most of his students only attended school until they were twelve so it made more sense for me to continue my studies at home."

They drank their tea in silence, the air between them crackling so loudly it rivaled the noise from the fire and storm.

"Your knowledge of horses and equestrian matters is impressive—especially your aptitude with the forge and my family's old coach. Who taught you such things?"

"When I was younger my father employed a couple to care for the house and me. It was when we lived in Yorkshire and his salary was more generous. The husband of the couple taught me about horses and their care." Her lips quirked into a genuine smile. "His name was Tom and he'd been a stable master in a great house before he was pensioned off. They had no children and I believe he greatly regretted not having a son. His wife did not think it proper that I spent so much time on mannish pursuits but my father was of the mindset that all learning was valuable. I learned to ride astride because we had no money for a side-saddle."

She stirred her tea absently. "Tom and his wife could not go with us when we moved away."

A bolt of lightning struck just outside the kitchen window, turning everything inside an eerie silvery-blue. The bolt disappeared in a heartbeat but the image of her face—taut and stark—was burnt into his mind's eye.

Jago could see that she was unnerved by the storm even though she mastered her anxiety. There was a certain tension around her eyes that gave away her fear as she gazed out the window, her mouth tight. He knew she was counting when she closed her eyes just as his own count brought him to the number *four*.

Thunder shook the little cottage and the mugs and tubs of jam jiggled on the table. Her lips compressed into thin line and Jago laid a hand over her white-knuckled fist. Her eyes remained closed at his touch but her hand turned palm up and she laced her fingers with his.

They sat in the near darkness of the storm and waited. For what, Jago was afraid to ask.

Chapter Twenty-Six

Cornwall
1817
Present Day

*B*enna wasn't usually so bothered by thunder and lightning, but never had she been in such a small, insubstantial building during a raging tempest.

And never had she been all alone with a man she desired so intensely, either.

Whatever she'd felt with Geoff—lust or curiosity or loneliness—was a pale imitation of the emotions surging through her at that moment.

She looked at their clasped hands. Benna had always thought her hands mannish, but now she saw that her fingers looked slim and delicate when compared with his.

"I do not have the hands of a gentleman."

She looked up at the sound of his voice.

"I suppose, in time, and with a lack of any meaningful labor, they will become soft and smooth. But even so, they will never be without scars or marks." He opened her hand palm up and spread her fingers. "The same will be true for you, Benna."

A shudder went through her at the sound of her name on his lips.

"Are you cold?"

Benna shook her head, unable to speak from the sheer joy of touching him.

"In a way we are alike," he said, his dark gaze holding hers.

"How so, my lord?" Her voice was scratchy and breathless.

"I, too, left my life behind when I decided to become a doctor. It was not as great a masquerade as yours, but for many years I lived as somebody else and was able to hide from who I am. But now I've been brought back to myself." His lips twitched. "Not quite kicking and screaming, but not happily, either."

"I don't believe you left your old self—the doctor part—behind you; I saw what you did during the mine cave-in."

"Ah, I know that look."

Benna pulled her hand away and he let her. "What look?"

He sat back in his chair, his smile turning wry. "It is the look a doctor gets from patients—or their patients' loved ones—when he does his job and cures them of their illness or sets a broken bone. It is akin to hero worship."

His comment stung. "Is that so wrong? You *are* a hero; you didn't have to go into the mine to treat those men; you risked your life to go into that collapsing tunnel. And everyone knows that you did it all without pay."

"I only did what I was trained to do, Benna. I took an oath to help. That is not the same as being a hero. I am certainly not thinking heroic thoughts at the moment."

The comment caught her off guard. "Oh?" was all she could manage.

He leaned closer, his pupils and irises dark and indistinguishable, adding a satanic cast to his sculptured face "I want to touch you, even though I know it would be wrong." His voice was so low she shouldn't have been able to hear it over the howling wind and pounding rain. "I want to explore every part of your body and make you cry out my name."

Benna throbbed at the desire she saw in his eyes. But she knew, from the restraint that shadowed his gaze, that he would not allow his passion to dictate his actions.

It would have to be Benna who crossed the line between them. She slid her hand beneath his jaw, her touch light but firm.

He swallowed, his jaws flexing, as if he were fighting to keep something in check. A bolt of lightning illuminated the room, throwing his handsome features into relief.

"I want you," she said.

His chest expanded as he filled his lungs, doubtless to argue.

"You are not taking something from me; I am willingly offering. I am no virginal miss, my lord." Benna waited for his disgust at her bold disclosure.

Instead, he smiled. "I am grateful for that—since I am no virginal mister." He laid a hand over hers and then moved her palm to his mouth. His lips were soft, warm, and firm. He kissed her not once, but over and over, the hot, wet tip of his tongue licking the stunningly sensitive flesh.

Benna could only stare as he made gentle, cherishing love to her work-ravaged hand.

"Say my name, Benna," he murmured against her skin.

"Jago."

"Why do I like the sound of that so much?"

It seemed like an honest question, but Benna had no answer for him; she knew what he meant. Her name on his tongue made her feel like she was being wrapped in warm, sweet honey.

He lowered her hand to the table, his expression growing somber. "I am not my own master—I have …"—his mouth twisted into an unhappy smile—"responsibilities. What I want no longer matters." He held her gaze. "You know how things are with the estate?"

The question caught her off guard, but she understood his meaning.

Benna chose her words carefully. "I know there are … problems."

"The house and some portion of the land are entailed, but the outer farms—properties that have supported the earldom for generations—have been used to secure an extremely large debt that is coming due in less than two months. I'm running out of time to find the necessary funds. If I cannot—"

"I know," Benna said, not wanting to hear him say the words out loud. She stared into his weary, hopeless eyes, her heart aching to soothe him—to save him.

But she couldn't save him—not now, not for almost two years.

And he could not wait even two months.

Benna wanted him fiercely, but she could not take even this fleeting pleasure if he were already promised to another. "Are you trying to tell me that you're going to marry Mrs. Valera?"

"No, I'm not marrying Mrs. Valera. But it is likely that I will have to—very soon—marry with the earldom, rather than personal preference, in mind." His jaw flexed. "I will be faithful to my wife, Benna. So, anything between us would be—"

"Short-lived. I understand; I want you."

"Benna—"

"I want you," she repeated more firmly.

"Twice I've had you in my arms and both times I found the strength to do the decent thing." His dark eyes burned into hers. "I'm not sure I can—"

"I want you," she said a third time, like a heroine in a fairytale speaking magical talisman words.

His full mouth firmed and his eyes became hooded. "Come here," he ordered softly.

Benna stood, her legs remarkably steady for all that her heart was threatening to beat its way out of her chest.

He pushed his chair back from the table and held out a hand.

When she took it, he spread his thighs and drew her closer, until her legs touched the front edge of his chair. His thumb rubbed circles in her calloused palm as he stared up at her.

He opened his mouth—no doubt to give her one last chance to save herself—but Benna placed the fingers of her free hand over his lips.

"You are my employer—not my father or my conscience."

"I *am* your employer. Seducing a servant has n—"

"You aren't seducing me, my lord. I am seducing you."

His lips parted, but no words came out.

I taught you well, my girl.

Go away, Geoffrey. You're not welcome here.

"I have been my own mistress and made my own decisions for years. You pay my wages, my lord, but you do not own me. Nobody does." Her voice was calm and clear and gave no indication of the storm raging inside her—a furor as wild and uncontrolled as that battering the cottage. "I would only ask you for one thing—" she broke off, suddenly hesitant at how to phrase what she wanted.

He lifted her hand to his mouth and brushed his lips across her clenched fingers. "Tell me what you would ask of me."

233

"I have no expectations, but I would ask that you tell me if—when—you want no more from me—rather than simply ignoring me."

Benna didn't want to live through the same thing she had with Geoffrey—as if what they'd done had never happened.

It had hurt enough with a man she didn't love. It would crush her with Jago.

He nodded. "I would ask the same of you." He smiled briefly, "I know that is easier said than done, given our differing stations, but if—after tonight—you don't want me to touch you again, you must tell me so."

Benna knew that would never happen, but she nodded.

He kissed the tips of her fingers, the intimate touch sending spirals of anticipation through her body. "You are eloquent. And most persuasive." One corner of his mouth pulled up. "Of course I am most eager to be persuaded—and seduced." He took her index finger into his mouth.

Benna hissed in a breath at the unspeakably soft, wet heat, closing her eyes as he sucked and tongued and nibbled.

The pounding in her ears drowned out the howling wind that lashed the house and rattled the window.

Enjoy this moment—savor it, she told herself, even though her body ached to be filled by him.

He removed her finger with a damp *pop* and Benna opened her eyes; his smile was wolfish and his hands slid around her wrists like warm, unbreakable manacles. He stood, keeping her so close that she had to tilt her head slightly to meet his intense stare.

Looking up at a lover was unique and heady and his broad shoulders made her feel feminine and vulnerable.

He had the elegant build of a gentleman, but Benna knew from experience that his body was hard and muscular, honed and strengthened by years of physical activity.

His eyes glinted with lights that were both hungry and challenging as he bent his head to claim her mouth.

His lips teased and played, but Benna leaned into him, wanting more.

He laughed softly. "So impatient." He flicked the seam of her mouth with his tongue, but didn't enter her, kissing her as if he had the rest of their lives to explore her, instead of only tonight.

When he released her wrists, Benna thrust her hands into his hair and pulled his head down, holding him immobile for her invasion, which was anything but gentle or patient.

Instead, she slanted her mouth over his and speared into hot, apricot sweetness.

He opened to her, his hand sliding slowly, deliberately, up the knobs of her spine while he pulled her ever closer.

"Mmmmm, I think I like being seduced," he said when she released him to come up for air. He trailed hot kisses over her mouth, cheek, and stopped beneath her ear. "Benna," he whispered before lightly nipping the sensitive lobe. "An unusual name for an unusual woman."

She tilted her head back, exposing her throat to him. His eager mouth took up her invitation, caressing the sensitive skin with soft lips and sharp teeth.

"You taste and feel so good," he murmured, kissing her fluttering pulse and then taking a mouthful of fragile skin, sucking hard enough to mark her.

Benna shivered with animal pleasure; she would have a bruise to remember this night by.

She carded her fingers through the soft waves of his hair, stroking and petting and tugging on his silky locks until he rumbled against her with a purring sound that made her chuckle.

"I like the sound of your laughter, Benna," he said against her throat, alternating his words with kisses.

"I want to see you ... Jago. All of you."

His big body stiffened and he sucked in a rough breath, his hands gripping her waist almost painfully hard. "That's right," he said, sounding darkly amused, "This is *your* seduction." He bit her chin before meeting her gaze. "Tell me what you want."

Benna spread her fingers over his broad chest, and then pushed him down into his chair. "I want to strip you, slowly."

***

235

Jago gazed up at her like a wide-eyed yokel, aroused by both her physical strength and sexual aggression. He'd never had a lover who took the upper hand when it came to bed sport.

Nor had a woman demanded to undress him.

"I feel like you're reading my mind," he murmured.

She smirked, the expression wicked—and one he'd never seen on her face before—and took a damp top boot in both hands, tugging with the perfect amount of force to remove it.

She set the boot aside and made short work of the second one before rolling down his stockings.

When Jago would have stood, to make removing his waistcoat easier, she shook her head and straddled his thighs, her fingers dropping to the buttons.

"I think you've been imagining me ... servicing you, my lord."

Jago swallowed. Noisily. "Yes."

She flicked open another two buttons. "I think you've been wishing that you'd engaged me to valet you instead of Mr. Toomey, *my lord.*"

Jago's belly flooded with lust at her words. He shifted uncomfortably in his chair to ease the effects of such thoughts on his cock. "I suppose that makes me a bit of a—"

"Lecher?" she suggested teasingly.

He gave a startled laugh. "Well, it is an obvious fantasy, isn't it?"

When she nudged his waistcoat over his shoulders Jago leaned forward in the chair.

She gracefully flowed to her feet and stepped behind him.

Rather than lift the garment from his shoulders she leaned close, massaging his shoulders, her breath hot on his neck. "Have you been imagining me undressing you? Shaving you? Tending to your every ... need, my lord?"

"All those things, Benna," he said, his voice raspy.

She removed his waistcoat and laid it over the back of the other chair before coming back to straddle his thighs.

"I have imagined you, too, Jago."

"Have you?" The two words harsh with raw need.

"Mmm-hmm." Her hands moved to his buckskins, her fingers deftly opening the catches before moving to the row of four buttons.

Jago hissed in a breath as her knuckles grazed his erection. When his cock sprang free of the tight, constricting leather, he gave a soft grunt of relief.

She dropped her gaze to his obscenely tented drawers, her lips curving into a smile at what she saw.

He'd been leaking copiously and was fully erect, his sensitive glans exposed and pressed against the damp, almost transparent muslin.

"Beautiful," she whispered, and then she dragged her thumb over his tiny slit.

Jago's hips bucked, lifting them both off the chair, his breath soughing between his clenched jaws. "Bloody. Hell."

She met his gaze, her eyes heavy-lidded and hot. "You're wet for me, Jago."

He throbbed at her erotic words.

She abruptly stood and Jago lifted his hips as she yanked down both his drawers and buckskins, becoming rough in her haste. Once she'd tossed the garments aside, she stared at his erection.

"Tell me what you've imagined, Benna?"

"Why don't I show you instead, Jago?"

And then she sank to her knees.

Chapter Twenty-Seven

Cornwall
1817
Present Day

*B*enna could tell by Jago's wide-eyed stare and gasp that she was shocking him with her behavior.

A decent woman didn't do the things she was doing or say the things she'd said.

She didn't care.

This might be the only time they were together. She wanted to feel and taste and caress every part of him.

Once she'd sunk to her knees he slid a hand beneath her chin, tilting her face until she met his dark gaze. His chest was rising and falling quickly, his nostrils flared. "You don't need to—"

Benna slid her hand around his thick, hot shaft; he was beautiful, just as she'd known he'd be.

He gave an explosive groan of pent-up desire and slumped back in his chair. "Benna—"

His body tightened as she pumped him, the diamond of moisture on the tip of his crown as telling as the harsh rasp of his breathing. She felt the struggle in his body as he fought against the animal urge to thrust into her fist.

Benna would have him every way she could before the night was over, but this—pleasuring him with her mouth—she had been imagining this for weeks.

She met his needy gaze and smiled. "Watch," she whispered, opening her mouth and taking him between her lips.

"Oh God." His hips bucked once before he mastered his urge to plunder and thrust.

She tongued him playfully—the way he'd kissed her earlier—teasing his shaft with long, languid strokes.

"Urgh."

Benna smiled around his cock at the desperate sound, drinking in the sight of him, from the smooth planes of his face to the ridged muscles of his belly, which quivered and flexed as he fought to hold his need in check.

"So good," he murmured softly, his eyes mere slits as he traced a finger lightly over her stretched lips, his own curving into a possessive smile. "Beautiful." He brushed the hair from her brow and then cupped her face lightly with both hands, his gaze hungry and heavy with passion.

Benna worked him with ruthless efficiency, determined to smash his façade—to watch him come apart; to *make* this glorious, self-contained man shatter into a thousand pieces.

His breathing grew ragged and his shaft began to thicken.

"No." His hands firmed on her face and he stilled her, his gaze burning into her as he wrestled with his desire, slowly, but surely, regaining control.

"No," he repeated.

He slid from her mouth with a tortured moan and then took her hands and helped her to her feet.

His expression was almost crazed as he claimed her mouth with a ravaging kiss.

When he finally pulled away, he held her gaze, his own eyes unreadable.

Did he think her a doxy? A whore?

"I adored your mouth on me," he said, his words shattering her worries. "But I don't want our evening to be over so quickly. Besides," he added, his lips twitching into a wicked smile. "You are still clothed. Will you strip for me, Benna?"

As many experiences as she'd had in the bedchamber, stripping for a lover was not among them.

While she was no longer shy about her body, neither was she especially proud of it.

But then Geoff had never looked at her the way Jago was looking at her—his eyes blazing with an intoxicating blend of desire, awe, and adoration that warmed not just her skin, but her starved soul.

He wanted *her*, not just any woman. But her.

Benna nodded and took a step back; she would strip for him in a way that he'd never forget.

***

Benna stepped back and gracefully sank into the chair Jago had been occupying.

She didn't sit like any lady he'd ever seen. Instead, she hooked an arm over the wooden back and lounged, her long, elegant legs splayed enough that the blanket she'd wrapped around her waist split, exposing smooth, white flesh to midthigh.

Her lips curved into a faint smile and she slid a hand up her leg, lightly caressing herself and pushing aside the blanket until it was open all the way up to her hip. She teased the ragged woolen edge until it just barely covered her sex, and then her hand stilled.

Jago's head jerked up and he closed his mouth, distractedly wondering if there was drool on his chin.

She smirked at him as her fingers worked the buttons of his clawhammer.

"You've been thinking about me?" she asked, one of her legs moving in a way that shifted the blanket.

He nodded dumbly, not trusting his voice.

She cocked her head. "Did you touch yourself, my lord?"

His jaw sagged and his eyes threatened to roll out of his head.

She chuckled and Jago felt his face burn.

"Well?" Her voice brimmed with laughter and Jago suddenly felt like *he* was the twenty-two-year-old.

No, he mentally amended, *I've not felt this gauche since I was fifteen.*

"I did," he admitted gruffly.

"Show me."

Jago's cock jumped with mindless joy at her quiet command but the rest of his body was momentarily frozen in shock.

He swallowed the surplus of moisture in his mouth. "You want me to, er—"

"Yes, I want you to er."

Her words surprised a laugh out of him, but the way she was looking at him—*consuming* him—made him wildly aroused at the thought of stroking himself for her pleasure.

"As you wish, Benna." Jago closed his fist around his shaft and hissed with pleasure.

Now it was *her* lips that parted and *her* breathing that roughened.

Jago gave himself a slow, thorough pump, smirking when she swallowed hard enough for him to hear it.

She cut him a quick glance when he stopped. "Go on," she ordered, standing and shrugging his coat from her shoulders, never taking her gaze from his stroking hand.

"What a demanding taskmaster you are." Jago forced the words through his gritted teeth, determined not to embarrass himself. Who would have imagined that pleasuring himself in front of a woman could be so bloody arousing?

With the coat gone she wore only her loose working man's shirt and a blanket. As calm as she appeared, the throbbing pulse at the base of her throat gave away the tumult inside her.

She took the hem of her shirt, lifted it over her head, and tossed it aside. Strips of fabric covered her from her waist to just below her collar bones. She tugged out the end, which was tucked under at her waist.

"Let me." Jago released himself and stepped forward, taking the strip from her fingers. He passed the fabric behind her, his arms encircling her body, but not touching her.

As cool as the room was her skin was sheened and she smelled of sweat, and horse, and rain. No perfume had ever smelled so erotic.

There were three layers and the last was thin, her body limned beneath the flimsy cloth.

He could see the half-moon shadows beneath her small, firm breasts and the dark circles of her areolae. His hand shook as he pulled away the remaining muslin and let it flutter to the floor.

"Good God," he muttered.

He slid his hands around her narrow waist and felt her shudder. Her pink nipples were already tight, like the bud of a rose.

She whimpered when Jago lowered his mouth over her breast, her hands clutching his shoulders in a punishing grasp. Something

241

about the unexpected strength in her elegant limbs made him smile as he teased first one peak and then the other, until her breathing was ragged and raw.

He pushed his fingers beneath the blanket encircling her waist and felt the muscles of her stomach flutter as he gave a slight tug and the blanket joined the bindings on the floor.

Jago stood back to admire her. She was tall and sleek with only the slightest curve to her narrow hips. Her pubic hair, he couldn't help noticing, was lighter than the hair on her head.

When he looked up, he saw that she was watching him with an expression that was both aloof and challenging.

Jago slid his arms around her again and squeezed her tight. Already her lithe, slender body felt familiar and beloved.

"You're magnificent," he whispered against her temple. "I know you promised me a seduction, but I need to be inside you, Benna."

She nodded. "There's just one more thing."

"Oh?"

Her hands glided over his shoulders, down his back, and came to rest on his buttocks. And then she squeezed both his cheeks, her fingers digging into the muscle.

Jago laughed and pulled away so he could see her face.

She gave him an uncharacteristically shy smile. "I needed to do that."

"I think it needed doing," he said, no doubt grinning like a fool. He kissed the tip of her nose and then scooped up the discarded blanket and spread it out in front of the fire.

He took her hand. "Lie down with me."

Once they were side by side and hip to hip he kissed her. "Touch me, Benna," he whispered against her mouth. "Everywhere."

Her hand, calloused and strong, caressed from his waist to his chest, dropping lower with each stroke, until her palm again rested on one of his buttocks.

When she squeezed him again, he groaned. "That feels delicious. Do it harder."

She chuckled and dug her fingers into the hard globes of flesh while Jago trailed kisses down her throat and chest, pausing to suck a nipple into his mouth. He teased both her breasts until the tips were hard and pebbled.

"Benna," he whispered against the thin, sensitive skin before resuming his journey, nipping and licking and kissing his way down to the source of her pleasure.

***

The muscular globes of his bottom slipped away from Benna's greedy hand.

"Roll over," Jago muttered against her belly, giving her a gentle push.

Once she was on her back, he nudged her thighs apart and settled between them, his hair silky soft as it slid over the quivering muscles of her stomach.

Warm slightly rough fingers brushed against her lower lips and she shivered as he parted her folds.

"So pretty," he praised.

Benna watched through slitted eyes as he lowered himself between her spread thighs. His lips were parted in an expression of anticipation, the light from the fire reflected on his spectacles.

His spectacles.

"You are still wearing your glasses," she said.

He looked up at her, a wicked smile curling his lips. "I actually need mine, darling."

Her sex, already overstimulated, clenched at the word *darling*, the contraction sending exquisite ripples of pleasure through her body. Unlike Geoff, Jago was not the sort of man who threw such endearments around indiscriminately.

"Besides," he said, his eyes dropping to where she was open and exposed to his hungry gaze. "I want to see every part of you."

And then he lowered his mouth over her, bathing her in wet, soft, heat.

Benna groaned and spread her legs wider.

He chuckled against her sensitive skin and proceeded to make love to her with his tongue, teeth, and lips.

As he'd done with his earlier kisses, he teased and played and maddened her, pushing her slowly but inexorably toward the peak of pleasure. Only when she was shaking and begging did he shove her over the edge.

He thrust two fingers into her convulsing passage. "I can feel your pleasure," he said, his lips slick and swollen, his expression wondrous.

Wave after wave of bliss washed over her, leaving her boneless and wrecked.

Benna was beginning to come back to herself when he whispered, "Just once more, for me, darling." And then he lowered his mouth over her again.

After that, Benna briefly lost track of time, vaguely aware that she was babbling—her voice hoarse and desperate—her pleas filling the small room.

The last of the tremors had not yet died away when he kissed her sensitive peak and raised himself over her.

"Will you take me, Benna?"

She tilted her hips in answer and he lowered his body over hers, guiding himself to her entrance.

He entered her with a single, long thrust, his thick shaft filling and stretching her. "So good," he whispered as her body accommodated his. He kissed her temple and then propped himself up on his forearms, smiling down at her, his eyes glowing with something more than lust. Affection? Joy?

"Are you ready?" he asked, flexing inside her.

"Please, Jago."

He pulled out slowly, and then plunged back in, working her with deep, thorough thrusts, rubbing against her core with every stroke, taking his time and shoving her slowly, but inexorably, toward bliss.

Sweat beaded on his brow as he pounded into her, his eyes locked with hers. "Need to feel you come," he said, his voice harsh with the effort of holding back, his hips drumming a brutal, relentless rhythm.

Benna tilted her pelvis and dug her heels into the bed, urging him deeper.

His control frayed a bit with each thrust, until his lips were curled into a feral snarl as he stared down at her, "Can't—hold—much— *aaargh!*" His last word was a muffled roar and he slammed into her, hilting himself exquisitely deep. His body froze as his shaft thickened and swelled inside her, flooding her with warmth.

Benna's mind exploded and her climax swallowed her whole. "Jago," she gasped, holding him tightly enough to hurt, tears squeezing out of the corners of her eyes.

How had she ever believed that having him once was better than never having him at all?

Chapter Twenty-Eight

Cornwall
1817
Present Day

*B*enna woke to the feel of a warm body beside her.

Lost between sleep and wakefulness, it took her a long moment to recall where she was. But then she turned and saw the dark head on the mattress beside her.

Jago had carried her to the narrow bed after he'd woken from their lovemaking. The last thing Benna remembered was him kissing her and asking her if she was warm enough and comfortable. She must have been both because she'd instantly dropped into a deep, dreamless sleep.

Outside it was full dark and the rain had slowed to a gentle patter. The wind had died and the storm appeared to have blown itself out.

Jago slept on, his beautiful face even more gorgeous in repose.

She considered waking him.

No doubt he would be eager to head back—back to the material world and away from this intimate fantasy for two.

Whatever decision he might make, Benna decided to let it wait a while longer.

Instead of waking him, she took the opportunity to gorge on his masculine beauty.

Like most people, his face was more relaxed and youthful looking in sleep. His full lips were slack and slightly parted and his night beard was dark against his pale skin.

As Benna looked at him it took her a moment to identify the emotion swelling inside her; she felt safe.

But it wasn't only that. She'd felt safe with Geoff—at least at first, after he'd rescued her from a beating.

No, this was something more complex. Not only did she trust Jago, but, for the first time since she'd run away from Wake House she felt tempted to let somebody else help shoulder her burden.

Even before this disastrous mess with Michael—long before she'd had to survive on her own—she had possessed what her brother David called an unfeminine tendency toward self-sufficiency.

"Men want a woman they can cherish and care for, Benna. Not an Amazon who can best them at everything." David had flung the words at her after they'd raced their new hunters and she had—not for the first time—beaten him.

He might have spoken in anger, but she'd known that his words were the truth.

Unlike David, who'd been intensely social, Benna had always liked her own company and preferred to keep other people at a distance. Never before had she yearned to know another person's inner workings and private thoughts.

Like she now did with Jago.

Based on what Benna knew about him—which was, albeit, limited—Jago was one of the most honest and honorable people she'd ever met. Honesty and honor were two rare characteristics that she'd come to value highly after five years with Geoff.

The little bit of his doctoring that she'd been privileged to observe had demonstrated a man who was kind without being mawkish, competent without sliding into arrogance, and gentle but willing to do whatever was necessary, even if it was unpleasant.

It wasn't a wonder that she'd fallen in love; it was a wonder that *every* woman in his orbit wasn't hopelessly besotted.

In the flickering light of the fire, she could see the deep lines fanning from his eyelids, something she had never noticed when looking into his magnificent eyes.

Benna ran a finger over the same place on her own face and felt only smooth, unlined skin. She felt unformed compared to him. He'd lived a full life while she'd spent her first seventeen years hiding from the world on her father's estate and the last six pretending to be somebody else entirely.

Tonight had been the single most wonderful night of her life. Benna had wanted him sexually, of course, but even more than that, she had craved closeness and intimacy.

Before Jago she'd never been tempted to confide who she really was to anyone. She was no fool; in a world where people had to scrape and struggle to survive, a wealthy renegade duchess on the run from her guardian would always be a temptation—just as she had been to Geoffrey.

As much as she wanted to wake Jago up and pour out the truth to him, it chilled her to recall just how easily Geoff could have convinced her of his love if he'd known her identity those first few months, back before she'd really known him.

What if she was making a similar mistake now?

Benna shook her head; she refused to believe it was the same thing.

Geoff and Jago were cut from two entirely different types of cloth. It would no more occur to Jago to exploit her for his own gain than he would think to leave a stranger broken and bleeding if they couldn't afford to pay for treatment.

She didn't have to take her own word for his sterling character; his actions at the mine that day spoke far louder than words.

Benna looked down at the beautiful, loving man beside her. Even though he had denied it earlier, he was a hero of the sort she'd come to believe were only found in fairytales.

But she could not confide in him.

He'd been difficult enough to seduce when he believed her an independent woman of experience. If he ever discovered that he'd bedded a peeress of the realm he would feel honor bound to marry her, no matter what the consequences.

If she were twenty-five, she might tell him the truth, even knowing that to do so would trap him into marriage. But at least he would get something from the union.

But if she were to tell him now? He would be throwing away his chance to save his estate.

He denied wanting to marry Mrs. Valera, but Benna had seen the determination in the other woman's eyes; it was the look of a person who was accustomed to getting what she wanted.

If Jago married the wealthy widow he could save Lenshurst Park and his family's legacy. He could provide for his nieces and ensure they had promising futures. He could care for Lady Trebolton, a fragile, needy woman who would never survive without somebody to look after her. He could pay off his crushing debts and improve the lives of the hundreds of people who depended on the earldom for their survival.

Benna had been raised on a great estate; duty and responsibility had been bred into her. She knew that was the same thing Jago would be feeling.

She stared down at him, drinking him in—storing him up like a desert dromedary caching water for the dry time ahead. And that time would come far too soon.

Jago had less than two months to find enough money to pay off the debt he'd mentioned. There was only one way for the people of their class to increase their fortune: they had to marry it.

Benna needed to leave before that happened.

She would leave on Boxing Day; it would be easier to slip away when there were other matters to keep him distracted.

That meant she had him for ten more days.

***

Jago was having the sort of dream where he knew that he was dreaming.

He also knew that the moment he woke up, the exquisite pleasure would recede.

He couldn't allow that to happen; he was so hard that it would take only a few strokes to ease the ache.

But when he reached for himself, he found a hand already there.

"Wake up, Jago." The words were hot and damp against this temple.

He opened his eyes and blinked; the blurry room around him seemed to have been painted from a palette containing only shades of gray.

It was just before dawn.

He recalled where he was: in the hunting cottage.

With Benna. And it was Benna's strong fingers that were stroking him.

249

His lips curled into a smile and he turned to her. "What a lovely way to wake up," he said, his voice scratchy with sleep.

She was on her side, wedged between his body and the wall, her head propped up by her palm, her other arm beneath the woolen blanket. In the gray light her features were bleached of color and even starker, her eyes dark with desire.

Jago placed his hand over hers beneath the blanket and stilled her. "You'll make me spend like a callow youth." He brought her hand to his mouth and kissed her palm. "Mmm," he hummed, tonguing the damp, musky skin. "You taste like us." He kissed her one last time and reluctantly lowered her hand. "I want to talk about—"

"No talking."

His brows shot up at her soft but emphatic words.

She shook her head, as if he'd spoken. "No talking … Jago." She tugged her hand away and stroked his belly, her hand already moving south.

Because he was weak—and because he was as eager as she to avoid whatever the future held—he gave in.

Her hand slid around his shaft with a confidence he found wildly arousing; she was as comfortable with his body as he was.

Jago held her gaze while she worked him, thumbing the small slit and then slicking his crown and shaft. Her eyelids became heavy as she pumped him from root to tip, her grip just on the edge of painful. His breathing quickened and his hips snapped with each stroke of her fist.

"Are you too sore to take me again?" he asked in a breathless voice, stilling her hand before she brought him much further.

She shook her head.

"Mount me, Benna."

Her nostrils flared and she didn't hesitate to obey.

Once she was astride him Jago reveled in the sight of her. She was lean-hipped and sinuous, her shoulders, while delicate, were as broad as a man's. And her legs—

"I adore your thighs," Jago muttered, worshipfully stroking said appendages with both hands.

She rose high on her knees, the action sending muscles flexing in her legs, hips, and belly.

Jago stared like a love-struck boy as she placed him at her entrance and proceeded to take him into her body inch by inch with a deliberation that caused them both to hiss.

She didn't stop until he was buried as deeply as he could go, and then she tightened around him like a silken vise.

"Benna!" The word was a hoarse shout and Jago's hips bucked off the bed.

A wicked grin transformed her from stern seductress into gleeful ingenue.

"You *devil*," he said through clenched teeth, grabbing her hips and holding her still. "You brought me too close while I was sleeping, I need a moment to—"

She laughed and ground her pelvis against him, massaging him with her inner muscles.

Jago lifted her bodily, his biceps burning as he raised her up until only his crown breached her.

And then he pulsed his hips in teasing thrusts.

It was her turn to groan. She squirmed in his grasp and it was all he could do to hold her, his arms shaking from the effort. She might look fragile and frail, but she was surprisingly substantial.

"Please, Jago … *more*," she whined, straining to take him deeper.

"I like hearing you beg," he said through gritted teeth, and then brought her down hard while thrusting at the same time.

She made a needy whimpering sound that drove him half mad and he drummed into her with vigorous thrusts, pumping wildly until his body refused to obey his commands.

He gave a breathless laugh. "The old man is tired now," he gasped as he lowered her, the muscles in his arms jumping and shaking.

Her body was in motion before the last word left his mouth.

Jago groaned. "Yes—ride me, Benna."

She rolled her hips sinuously, posting him with controlled, undulating strokes that soon sheened her lithe torso with sweat. She made it look effortless, but he saw the elegant, powerful musculature at play beneath her pale skin.

The sight was almost painfully erotic and, yet again, he raced far too quickly toward his climax.

251

Jago slid a hand between her thighs and circled her bud with his thumb, working her as relentlessly as she did him.

"Yes, that's right, darling," he praised when she began to shake. "Come for me."

"Jago!" she rasped, her rhythm becoming erratic as her first contraction closed around him.

He grabbed her hips and pulled her down, his back arching off the bed as he spent in violent, body-wracking spasms.

"Jago," she whispered, shuddering once before slumping down on top of him.

I love you, Benna.

Jago wasn't sure if he'd said that out loud, or only thought it.

I hope I said it.

And that was the last semi-coherent thought he had before his arms closed around her damp, slender body and he sank into blissful oblivion.

Chapter Twenty-Nine

Corwall
1817
Present Day

*L*enshurst Park was already bustling with activity when Jago and Benna rode into the stables an hour after first light.

To Jago's surprise their absence the night before hadn't raised any eyebrows.

And why should it? he realized with something of a shock. After all, they were merely a master and his male servant taking shelter in the middle of the storm.

Nance met him in the foyer and helped Jago out of his overcoat. "I told Mr. Toomey that was what you would have done. Also, John Dixon sent his oldest son by this morning, it seems one of the old oaks around his barn was struck by lightning and he asked for your permission to cut it down."

"Of course, send Gordon over with a message and tell him to help Dixon if needed."

"Very good, my lord."

When Jago reached his chambers Toomey regarded his rumpled, ruined clothing with a longsuffering look that made him laugh. "You see," he teased as the valet helped him out of his coats. "This is why I should not be allowed to have nice things. You'd better lay out my oldest leathers and coat as I'll be tearing about most of the day inspecting the damage from last night's storm."

Once he was shaved, bathed, and dressed he went down to breakfast. By the time he entered the breakfast room it was still only nine and he was surprised to see Mariah eating so early.

"Oh, Uncle—I'd heard you were back. Did you stay in the hunting cottage near the Collingsworth farm?" she asked, heaping marmalade on her toast.

"Yes," he said, frowning slightly. "How did you—" His frown deepened and his niece's face flushed.

Mariah chewed her lip. "I really wasn't *trying* to listen but Mama summoned Nance when you didn't come for dinner. It was he who thought you might have sat out the storm with Ben."

He tried not to be annoyed at Mariah—after all, it was no great secret where he'd spent the evening—but she really needed to learn to respect private conversations.

He decided he was not in the mood for fighting that battle today.

Before he could ask her why she was awake so early the door opened and Benna entered. She hesitated upon seeing Jago and inclined her head. "Good morning, my lord, Lady Mariah."

"Ben." Jago's body tensed as erotic images from only a few hours ago assaulted him, when the cool, reserved-looking woman across from him had been wild and demanding in her passion, riding him to a lather.

Her tanned skin flushed, as if she could see what he was thinking.

"Hallo, Ben," Mariah said around a mouthful of toast. "Are we still taking out the gig today?"

"If it's not too mucky, my lady."

"Cat won't be joining us," Mariah said, "She's going to Ria's house later this afternoon. In fact, she's coming here to pick her up."

Jago frowned at this unwanted news. "Why is Catherine going to *Mrs. Valera's* house?"

Mariah's brow furrowed at either his tone or the emphasis he'd put on Ria's name. "I don't know. Something about her costume for the masquerade." She turned from Jago to Benna. "Will you have time to take me up to those trunks you mentioned, Ben?"

"Yes, of course," Benna said.

Jago couldn't help noticing that Benna sat down as far from him as the table allowed.

"Why don't we go after breakfast, say in half an hour?"

Mariah nodded eagerly.

"What trunks are these, Ben?" Jago asked.

"I found another half dozen not far from the section of attic where the roofers replaced the lead. They look as they've been there for a long time—years," she added. "They're mainly filled with clothes."

"I need to change my costume," Mariah volunteered.

"Oh?" Jago said, buttering a slice of bread. "You've not got much time."

"I know," she said, her expression anxious. "But it turns out that Mrs. Valera will be going as Cleopatra, so …"

"Ah, I see. Not a good idea to wear the same costume as one's hostess," Jago said. Especially not when one's hostess could have doubled for the real Egyptian queen.

Benna and Mariah chatted about possible costumes while Jago tried not to gaze at his secretary in calf-eyed adoration.

***

Jago was working in the library some hours later when there was a light knock on the door.

"Yes?" he called, removing his glasses and rubbing at his eyes; as delightful as last night had been, he was rather sleep-deprived today.

Nance entered. "You've got visitors, my lord."

Jago could tell by his butler's pursed lips who at least one of the visitors was.

"It's Mrs. Valera and several of her houseguests, sir. I've taken the liberty of showing them into the Yellow Salon and ordering tea."

Jago glanced at the longcase clock. Well, it was teatime, anyhow. He nodded at his butler. "Very good. I shall join them directly. Er, did you tell Lady Trebolton?"

"I'm afraid she is not feeling well, my lord."

Jago knew what that meant. He watched absently as Nance left the room, his mind on his sister-in-law. Today must be one of her bad days; Jago had a sneaking suspicion that her mood had something to do with Ria's wretched masquerade ball, which Claire was insisting on attending.

While Jago certainly could use the help supervising his gregarious nieces, he didn't like exposing Claire to such exertion. Still, he was pleased that she was finally taking an interest in her daughters.

He sighed, pushed to his feet, and strode to the large mirror that hung above the mantlepiece.

As he'd suspected, he had a smudge of ink on one cheek. He wet his finger and rubbed at the stain, his mind still on Claire. He had diminished her laudanum dose gradually, until she was taking only about one-third of what she used to consume every day.

While she had looked more robust lately, he'd noticed a disturbing tendency toward extreme vivacity that was often followed by worrisome lows.

Jago didn't understand; she should have begun to feel more emotionally level by now. He hoped she wasn't somehow managing to sneak more of the drug into the house.

Or perhaps it had just been a difficult few weeks what with all the excitement about the wretched ball and upcoming holidays. He knew the process of weaning oneself from opium—even a derivative—was long and exhausting.

He'd go check on her after dispensing with Ria and her guests.

As Jago strode down the corridor toward the newer part of the house he couldn't stop thinking of his sister-in-law and the rather lurching nature of her treatment. He wondered, not for the first time, if he shouldn't bring in outside help.

He wasn't comfortable treating a member of his own family for such a condition, it just seemed too fraught with emotions to impose the proper distance. Perhaps he might ask Elinor for her opinion, although that felt like a betrayal of Claire's confidence.

When he reached the sitting room, he pushed the matter of Claire from his mind, pasted a smile on his face, and prepared to deal with whatever foolishness Ria and her guests were likely to have brought with them.

***

"I love it!" Lady Mariah cried, her grin lighting up the dim, cobweb-ridden attic.

Benna couldn't help returning the younger woman's smile; the gown they'd found in one of the trunks was truly spectacular.

"Do you think Newton will be able to get this—what is this called?" Mariah held up a gorgeously jeweled garment.

"Um, I believe that is called a stomacher, my lady."

"Do you think she can have it ready in time for the ball?"

"It mainly needs airing and pressing. I don't see why not."

"It's badly bent," Mariah said, trying to straighten the boning.

"I think you should let Miss Newton fix it," Benna said, before the other girl damaged the brittle old garment.

Mariah nodded and lowered the garment. "Yes, she knows everything about clothing. This was probably something ladies wore when she was young."

Benna had to bite her lower lip to keep from laughing. Unless Newton—the countess's lady's maid—had been born in the early part of the last century, she wouldn't have dealt with such a garment before.

"What are you going to wear, Ben?" Mariah asked as they scooped up the various parts and pieces of the huge dress Mariah had chosen.

"It's a surprise," Benna said.

"That's no fair—I told you."

Benna just smiled and turned back to the trunk. "Do you want these shoes, too?"

Mariah frowned at the wood and velvet shoes, which looked to be motheaten. "No, I'd never fit my foot into those."

Benna closed the trunk and they carried the dress down to Newton—who looked skeptical but promised she would do her best—before heading down to the stables.

They were on the second-floor landing when they heard voices below.

Mariah caught at Benna's arm and held her back.

When she turned, the girl held a finger up to her lips. "Shhh," she whispered, pulling Benna toward a recessed doorway, clearly intent on spying on whoever was down in the huge foyer below.

Benna shook her head. "*No*, Lady Mariah." She headed down the hall in the opposite direction of the grand staircase toward the smaller set of stairs that came out near the solarium. Benna didn't wait to see if Mariah followed. She could eavesdrop and spy if she wanted, but Benna would have no part in it.

She heard Mariah's footsteps behind her. "You're no fun," she grumbled as they descended the stairs. "That was Ria and some of her fancy guests from London. We could have sneaked a look at them."

"You'll see them all at the party, my lady."

"Pfft! I'll get to go for two hours after dinner and then Uncle Jago will send me home early. He said I'm too young to stay until the unmasking." She scowled. "I don't know why *Catherine* gets to stay."

"I daresay because she's two years older than you."

"Oh, fiddle."

Based on what she'd seen of Mrs. Valera's guests so far—which, granted, was only Fenwick—Benna didn't think either girl should go to the party. But then that wasn't her decision.

"Where do you want to take the gig today?" she asked, turning the subject.

They ended up driving into the village and Benna decided to have the wainwright, Mr. Jeffers, look over the little cart while they went to the Jolly Taxpayer Inn.

"You must try their scones with cream," Mariah assured her. "They are even better than Cook's—but you mustn't tell her I said that or she'll never let me have another."

Benna wasn't sure it was entirely proper for the daughter of the house to take tea at an inn with her uncle's secretary, but there was little enough to do while they waited the hour Mr. Jeffers said would be needed to grease the axels and inspect the undercarriage.

Mariah ate not one but three scones and chattered happily about the ball, leaving Benna free to go over and over the prior evening.

She'd hardly seen Jago today, but then what had she been expecting? That he'd corner her in her office for another torrid encounter?

"—don't you think, Ben?"

Benna looked up from her half-eaten scone. "I'm sorry, my lady?"

"Don't you think Ria is in love with my uncle?"

Benna blinked at the unexpected question. "Er, I'm sure I don't know, my lady." She hesitated, and then did something despicable. "Why? Have you heard something?"

Mariah leaned across the table, even though they were the only two eating in the tiny coffee room. "I heard her talking to Mama on Saturday."

"Mrs. Valera called on the countess?"

Mariah nodded. "She brought over the most beautiful hand-painted shawl that she is loaning Catherine." She paused, frowning. "She didn't offer to loan anything like that to *me*."

"That was nice of her—to make a special trip just for a shawl," Benna prodded shamelessly.

"No, it wasn't just that. She also came by to drop off something Mama had asked her to pick up in Redruth—something from the chemists."

"What makes you think she was in love with your uncle?"

Oh Benna, you will roast in Hell.

Benna didn't doubt it for an instant.

"Oh, well she told Mama that matters would change for the better at Lenshurst Park once the house had a proper mistress again."

Jealousy, hopelessness, and anger roiled in her belly at the girl's words. "She said that to Lady Trebolton?" Benna asked, startled to hear the two women liked each other well enough to discuss such personal matters.

Just last week Lady Trebolton had asked Benna to keep Mrs. Valera out of the library when nobody was with her.

"That woman snoops," the countess had said.

At Benna's surprised look the older woman's pasty skin had darkened. "I know that is a very rude thing to say, but it is true. She has always been, er, inquisitive. If you leave anything sitting out, she won't be able to resist taking a peek. I saw her coming out of the library several weeks ago; she claimed she was looking for the earl."

Benna believed the countess. After all, Mrs. Valera had behaved very shiftily in the library yesterday. Still, she'd not expected to hear such an astute, bitter comment coming from her ladyship, who was usually so vague and gentle—not that she'd looked either of those things at that moment. Indeed, Benna had been nonplussed by the countess's vicious expression.

259

She'd wondered more than once if Lady Trebolton didn't use too much laudanum. Just last week she'd asked Benna to pick up two bottles for her.

Was that what Mrs. Valera had brought her from the chemists—more laudanum?

But who was Benna to judge? She was as healthy as a horse while the poor countess was in constant pain.

"Ben?"

She looked up from the scone she'd crumbled on her plate. "Yes, my lady?"

"Do you think what Ria said means that she and my uncle might marry?"

Benna was grateful that she'd not eaten more of the scone. "I don't know, my lady."

"She is said to be monstrously wealthy and Mama and Papa used to fight over money—or the lack of it—all the time. The last time they argued—just before Papa left in his curricle—Mama shouted at him. She said we would all end up in an almshouse thanks to his foolishness." The look she gave Benna was both ashamed and afraid. "Do you think that is what will happen if my uncle does not marry an heiress, Ben?"

"You won't end up in an almshouse," Benna said with more certainty than she felt. She had no idea what would happen if Jago couldn't pay off the loan that he'd mentioned.

Mariah didn't look especially comforted. "Although—"

"Although?" Benna prodded, once again feeling like a louse. Especially when Mariah's cheeks flushed and she cut Benna a guilty look.

"Oh, nothing," she said, popping the rest of her scone in her mouth. "Do you think the gig is ready yet? Or might we have time to go to Cooper's Mercantile to pick up a length of blue ribbon for my hat?"

That was the last they spoke about Jago and Mrs. Valera, but the bitter seed had been planted. Already Benna felt jealousy and frustration growing within her. And it would grow and grow and grow, until it choked her.

Benna had to get away from him, and she couldn't wait ten more days to do so.

Chapter Thirty

*J*ago?"

Jago looked up into the pale gray eyes of his friend and blinked. "I'm sorry, Elinor, I'm afraid I didn't catch what you said," he admitted, his face heating at his rudeness. "I can't seem to keep my mind on business today."

He hadn't done too well yesterday. Or the day before.

In fact, in the three days since that night in the cottage with Benna he'd scarcely had a thought that wasn't about her.

He was … obsessed. And it was a feeling he hadn't had for eighteen years.

It was also a feeling that was making him avoid her, not an easy task given that they lived in the same house.

But he knew what he'd do if he were in a room alone with her.

Jago wanted her with an ache that was more than just physical.

And so he'd finally given up trying to concentrate on Lenshurst Park business and had come over to Oakland to see Elinor and work on the new hospital, a subject that was normally very close to his heart.

But not today.

"Are you distracted because you're so excited about tonight's ball?" she teased.

Jago rolled his eyes. "Lord, it is tonight—I'd almost forgotten the wretched affair. Thank you *so much* for reminding me."

She grinned.

"I wish you and Stephen were coming, but I can understand why you're avoiding it."

"I think Stephen would find a reason to avoid it even if I were not *in an interesting condition*." She gave him a wry smile. "But enough about the ball. Tell me what is bothering you, Jago."

As he'd done a hundred times already, Jago considered that night in the cottage—the selfish, disastrous, and delicious evening with Benna. How was it possible to be so ashamed and yet so unrepentant about one's behavior?

When he didn't immediately answer, Elinor said, "You know a good deal about me, Jago—some things that even Stephen does not know. When I needed a friend, you were the person I went to."

"And I was honored by your trust," Jago said without hesitation. "But I'm afraid that what is bothering me is … well, it is something I'm not proud of."

"Do you think that I was proud of what I'd done when I came to you for help in the dead of night?"

The night she was referring to was months ago, before she was married to Worth. Indeed, Worth had been the cause of her trouble.

"You are right, as usual, Elinor."

"Is this about Ben?"

He gave a bark of laughter. "Are you a mind reader?"

"No, but I flatter myself that I know you quite well. You have always had a certain … serenity that I have envied."

He snorted. "Whatever serenity I might have once cultivated fled when I moved back to Lenshurst. But yes, you are correct, my current dilemma is about Ben."

She waited patiently.

"I'm—It's—" Jago laughed, but there was no amusement in it.

"I have never seen your peace so cut up, Jago."

"That is because I have not been such an impulsive, emotional fool for almost two decades." He met Elinor's direct gaze. "I'm afraid I have become, er, enamored of my secretary."

Elinor did not look surprised.

"How can you look so calm at such an announcement? Lord, Elinor. The girl is almost fifteen years my junior—not to mention my servant."

"I married my father's servant, Jago."

It took Jago a moment to recall what she meant. "Well, that is true—in a sense. But Stephen was a footman fifteen years ago and is now a wealthy man."

"Is that all that stands in your way—a lack of wealth?"

"I hate to sound like pillock, but that's certainly part of it. At least it was at first."

"At first?"

"Before I decided—"

Elinor remained quiet.

"Oh why not?" Jago asked himself, and then said to Elinor, "I find myself going over and over every interaction I've ever had with her—even before I knew she was a woman. I liked Ben Piddock—a great deal. I enjoyed his quiet company, his intelligence, his humor. Ever since I learned the truth about her I can't stop thinking of *before*.

"I mine my brain for memories, images, things she said. I remember her smiles, her every expression, no matter how slight—and everything I find is a diamond, everything is … precious."

Jago couldn't tell Elinor about the rest of it, about the way Benna *looked* at him when she thought he didn't notice. He'd been the focus of female attention all his life, but never had a woman watched him with such thoughtful intensity—almost as if she wanted to … *ravish* him.

Yes, that was it, exactly: she wanted to ravish him.

Her cool blue eyes became hot, the expression speculative, as if she were imagining shoving him up against the nearest hard surface and—

"Jago?"

His head whipped up. "Er, yes?"

"You were talking about Benna—about—"

"Yes, yes," he muttered, his face heating as he recalled the way he'd been raving, not to mention what he'd been thinking.

He shoved a hand through his hair, pulling painfully. "I cannot believe I am actually going to say this, but I think I might be in love with her."

"And why would that be so horrid?"

"You mean aside from the obvious?" Jago gave a mirthless laugh, not waiting for an answer. "Besides, how can I be sure of what I'm really feeling? The last time I thought I was in love it turned out to be nothing but lust and obsession." *And it killed my friend.* Jago couldn't admit that shame, not even to Elinor. "How the devil can I be sure this isn't the same thing, just with slightly different symptoms?"

"Oh, Jago—love is not like an influenza or infection." She chuckled. "Listen to me, speaking as though I am an expert on the matter."

"You know more than I do—you love your husband."

Her humor slid away, leaving an almost fervid glint in her silvery-gray eyes. "I do, deeply and irrevocably."

"When did you know that? Because I feel like a bloody ninny; I've scarcely spent any time with Benna since discovering that she was a woman. How can a person fall in love so fast? Wouldn't that indicate this is infatuation?"

"But you liked, respected, and admired the person you knew *before* you found out her gender?"

"Very much so, but—"

"How would you feel tomorrow morning if you woke up and discovered that she was gone? Forever."

Jago opened his mouth, but the sorrow, hopelessness, and desolation he experienced at the thought of her disappearing from his life choked him.

She nodded. "You don't have to speak; I can see it on your face. Sexual attraction is delightful, Jago." Her cheeks pinkened. "But love is everything. When I believed Stephen was out of my life forever, I knew that I would go on living—for the child I was carrying, as well as for myself—but I also knew that I would miss him every single day of my life. I would miss the things I already knew about him and I would miss all the things I hadn't had a chance to discover."

Jago closed his eyes; she had described the way he was feeling perfectly.

"Is it really so bad—to be in love with a woman who is not of our station?" she asked him.

He opened his eyes and sighed. "If it were just me that I had to worry about then the difficulties this situation presented would be manageable. But, Lord, Elinor, you know the earldom is all to pieces. I need money. A great deal of it and quickly. And there is only one way for a man such as me to acquire it."

"Please tell me you are not considering Mrs. Valera?"

Jago smiled faintly at Elinor's uncharacteristically arch tone. "I take it you don't care for her?"

"I cannot like her for you, Jago."

He sighed. "I'm not marrying Mrs. Valera." Elinor didn't need to know that Ria had already offered him such a solution and he'd rejected her.

"I'm relieved to hear it," she said. "You might think that paying your debts and fixing Lenshurst Park are worth it, but no amount of money is worth being shackled to somebody you don't love, and who doesn't love you. Find some other way, Jago."

"I could not bring myself to marry for money eighteen years ago and—it seems—I cannot make myself do it today—even though the need is far greater." His face heated under her serious gaze. "It appears I am a romantic fool. When and if I marry, it will be for love."

The smile she gave him was dazzling.

Jago laughed. "I can see you will do nothing to check my headlong run to disaster."

"Would marrying for love really be so disastrous?"

"Lord, Elinor—how in the world can I ever marry somebody who is not only my servant, but whom everyone believes to be a man? Even if I were still just Doctor Venable the matter would present difficulties."

"But does it follow that those difficulties must be insurmountable?"

"No." He sighed. "But I'll be damned if I can think of a way around this. Er, begging your pardon."

"Anything can be contrived, Jago, if you put your mind to it. Have you talked to her?"

"No," he said, absently, rubbing a hand over his jaw. He snorted. "I am acting as if all the reservations are on my side," he said, giving her a wry smile. "As if she will be thrilled to shackle herself to an impoverished man old enough to be her father. Perhaps I will declare myself and she will tell me to go to the devil." Just thinking about such an eventuality made his stomach churn.

"Somehow I doubt that, my friend."

Jago wasn't quite so sure, especially given his idiotic behavior these past few days. It shamed him that he had done the exact opposite of what he'd promised her: to deal honestly with her. Instead, he'd gone out of his way to avoid her.

Suddenly, Jago burned to get back to Lenshurst Park and talk to her. Good God! What if she decided to leave him for being such an idiot? He needed to apologize—to try and explain—to—

He got to his feet so quickly his chair almost tipped. "I'm sorry, but I should—"

"Go," she said, chuckling.

"Don't get up, Elinor," he said, taking her hands and pressing them gently. "Thank you so much not only for listening, but also for your excellent advice."

She smiled up at him. "Good luck, Jago."

"Thank you. I suspect I'm going to need it."

***

Jago had no memory of the ride back from Oakland Park.

In fact, the last thing he recalled was taking his leave of Elinor and when he looked up, Pike was holding Asclepius's bridle, waiting for him to dismount.

Because it was already five o'clock, he hesitated to have this particular conversation with Benna right now.

But the thought of waiting through what was likely to be an interminable night until he could get her alone tomorrow was simply not to be borne.

"Have you seen Mr. Piddock?" he asked Nance as he handed his hat and gloves to the footman while the old butler relieved him of his coat.

"He just summoned two footmen to the east wing, my lord."

Jago pulled a face as he tried to fix his wrecked hair in the looking glass; he looked like a bloody rooster. "More crates or trunks?" he guessed, shoving back the stupid lock of hair that insisted on flopping onto his forehead.

"That is what Charles and James brought back to the library, sir."

267

S.M. LaViolette

Jago scowled; he was just making his already messy hair messier. "Ah, to hell with it," he muttered, drawing a surprised look from Nance.

"I need a haircut," he explained, his face heating at the blatant untruth.

Nance's rheumy eyes flickered over Jago's hair, which Toomey had just cut two days before. "Yes, my lord."

Lord, he was acting like a bloody idiot at his first assembly. Benna didn't give a rap about his hair.

Jago felt his butler's gaze burning into his back as he strode with immoderate haste toward the decrepit east wing of the house.

As always, walking through the dank, musty-smelling corridors made him even more aware of the pressures of the earldom.

And yet, in a few moments, he was going to do something that would irrevocably ensure that he would never be able to restore these grand old rooms to their former glory.

Indeed, by the time he lost the outlying farms he'd be lucky if he could keep a roof over the entire structure.

That was usually an argument that motivated him to do what needed to be done. But, today, he had little room in his mind for anything other than Benna.

He immediately saw which room she was working in because it was the only one with the door open.

Jago paused for a moment in the doorway.

Her back was to him and she was kneeling in front of yet another infernal trunk.

Her head was bowed and she was rummaging through it.

At the sight of her slender, vulnerable nape an unexpected wave of tenderness slammed into him so violently that, for a moment, it was if somebody had knocked the wind from his chest.

He clutched at the doorframe, gazing at the ill-fitting coat stretched across her shoulders as if it were the most beautiful sight he had ever seen.

Elinor was right; there was no question of giving her up. Ever. How had he been so blind?

He knocked softly on the doorframe. "Benna?"

She gave a startled yelp and spun around on her knees, clutching her chest.

"I'm sorry," he said, hastening toward her. "I didn't want to give you a fright." He dropped to his haunches beside her and took her hand.

As he watched, her expression went from alarmed to displeased to the blank, obedient stare of a well-trained servant.

She tried to pull away her hand, but Jago held it firm. "I am sorry."

She did him the courtesy of not asking him what he meant. Neither did her expression soften one iota. The haughty look she gave him would have done a duchess proud.

"I've been acting like a confused boy rather than a man of thirty-seven. I won't ask you to forgive me, but I do have some things I must say."

The ice showed no sign of melting. "Here?"

"If you wouldn't mind."

She hesitated and then nodded.

Jago stood, drawing her up with him. He gestured to a spindly settee, hoping it would hold their combined weight.

She glanced at the door, which was still open. "Should I—"

"I will close it."

When he returned, she was seated all the way at one end of the small sofa.

Jago sat so that there was distance between them, which is clearly what she wanted.

"I'd like to explain why I've, er—"

"Been avoiding me?" she supplied.

He gave a pained smile. "Yes. I have been avoiding you. That evening—and morning—was the most enjoyable that I can remember." He saw a flicker of something in her eyes, but her features did not relax.

"I have already thought of it *many* times since and daresay I will continue to do so often in the years to come."

The only sign that his words touched her was a slight darkening of the skin over her cheekbones.

269

"To explain my reaction these past few days I will have to bore you a bit with some ancient history."

She nodded.

"The other night, you mentioned my behavior at the Redruth mine the day of the cave-in."

Jago could see by her raised eyebrows that his choice of topic had surprised her.

"My immediate response was to disabuse you of any fantasies you might hold where I am concerned." His mouth twisted into a self-deprecating smile. "You see, I am not a *good* man by design—as I believe some people are, like Elinor Worth, for example. My natural impulses are … well, let's just say they are selfish and less than pure and noble. I flatter myself that struggling against my natural inclinations these past eighteen years might have done something to wipe away the stain on my soul from the first eighteen."

Jago smiled at the look of disbelief on her face. "It's true. When I was a young man, I was arrogant, willful, and careless. I acted on every impulse that fluttered into my head. I was my mother's favorite and she spoiled me atrociously. I was raised knowing that all the responsibility for the family fell on Cadan's shoulders. Cadan would have to make the sacrifices, not me. Cadan would have to marry an heiress to save the family fortunes, not me. Cadan would have to devote his life to resuscitating a crumbling estate, not me." He shrugged. "I never saw anything wrong with that. It seemed my natural birthright to have exactly what I wanted."

Jago hesitated and considered what he was about to confess. It had been many years, but the pain was still surprisingly sharp. But she needed to know the truth; she deserved to know.

He looked up from unhappy thoughts of his distant past and found the woman he hoped to share his future with, watching him. "My best friend since I could toddle was a neighboring squire's son—Brian St. John. We were the same age, grew up together, and ended up going to Eton together. He lived closer to the village than I and spent more time with the neighboring children than I ever did. It was Brian who first met the vicar's enchanting niece—Gloria Bennett, who came to live with her uncle and aunt when she was an adolescent.

"Brian fell in love with her at first sight—I could see it, so could everyone else. Including Ria. I could also see, even back then, that she would never have him. Ria had—well, let's just say that I don't think her childhood had been easy. She was an orphan who'd been passed from family member to family member. Even at that age it was clear that she'd set her sights on something grander than the wife of a country squire." He snorted softly. "For a while I fancied that something was me."

He looked into Benna's cool blue eyes, his face heating at what he was about to say. "It would be false modesty to say that I'm unaware of my appearance, or that I don't realize that some women find me attractive."

For the first time, she wore an expression he recognized: amusement.

"What?" he asked.

She just shook her head. "Go on," she ordered.

He narrowed his eyes at her but continued, "At eighteen I was fully aware of the power my looks afforded me; it was a power I enjoyed greatly and exercised often. In my limited experience there had been no woman who did not fall before my handsome face and easy manners. To be honest, I had not paid much mind to Gloria before that summer, believing her to be beneath me. Yes," he said when she pursed her lips with disappointment. "I was quite the puffed-up little toad.

"In any case, I saw her at one of the local assemblies and it was as if I'd been struck between the eyes with a mallet. I knew in that moment that I was the man for her—even though I couldn't give her a fortune and the title she so dearly—and unabashedly—desired. I was sure that I could give her something better than mere money or an earldom: I could give her my love."

Jago paused, dreading this next part. "It's such a common story: a woman coming between two friends—not that it was Ria's fault. No, I was the one who pursued her. I behaved like an arrogant young fool, making life unbearable for both Brian and Ria. Finally, when he could bear it no longer, Brian challenged me to a duel."

He saw disappointment on her face, but not surprise. So, somebody had already told her the tale—or at least a version of it.

271

"Instead of understanding his anger at feeling cut out and apologizing to him—which I certainly should have done—I was eager to have a chance to show Ria that I was the better, worthier, man."

Jago could see the day so clearly in his mind's eye.

"As foolish as I was, I was at least wise enough to choose swords—practice swords, at that—and insist that the duel would end when one of us got three touches. I'd been a fencing champion at Eton for three years running and knew that I could make short work of the matter." He swallowed, a memory of Brian's face that day— after half an hour at the end of Jago's rapier—rising up in his mind's eye. "Instead, I decided to … teach him a lesson."

He looked up and met her steady gaze. "I shamed him. Not only that, but word of this epic sword battle—a rarity in our tiny community—had spread far and wide and people came to watch. One of them was Ria."

Benna made a muffled sound of distress but didn't speak.

If she could have seen Brian that day, as Jago systematically stripped him of his dignity, she would have fled the room in disgust by now.

"I had always been the leader of our little band of friends here in Redruth; I was also a popular boy at school. Brian, on the other hand, was undersized for his age and almost cripplingly shy. I was furious that my humble acolyte had the audacity to challenge me. Not only that, but he'd done so in a maddeningly public manner—at the harvest ball that my parents gave every fall. And so I humiliated my best friend." He gave a bitter snort of laughter. "I only came back to myself—and sanity—after I'd made him cry."

Jago couldn't look at her. "He flung down his rapier and ran. And then he hanged himself that night."

She gasped softly. "Oh, Jago. I'm so sorry."

Jago could hear the truth in her voice; she was sympathetic and kind, she would know how he felt—what such a thing would do to anyone other than an inhuman monster.

"I told you that horribly unedifying story because for eighteen years I curbed my natural instincts—my selfish and willful and prideful nature—and I turned my prodigious energy to something positive. Before Brian's death my greatest wish was to be a Corinthian and to

272

enjoy myself to the fullest." He gave a weary laugh. "Instead, I decided to devote my life to a good cause—as though the Almighty would be personally interested in how I managed my guilt. I was fortunate and came to love—rather than loathe—the penance I'd chosen to punish myself."

Jago forced himself to look at her. "And then I came back here. To the place of my greatest disappointment. All the self-control and decency that I believed I had learned over almost two decades went up in flames as quickly as brittle twigs when I decided I wanted you. Once again I've behaved selfishly and willfully."

She started shaking her head before he'd finished speaking. "The decision was one we both made, my lord. You are not respons—"

"I know that I did not take advantage of you, Benna. You are a grown woman. But I *did* take advantage of my position." He laughed, but it contained no amusement. "Trust me, I am no saint. These past few days I have wrestled with my conscience. At first I told myself that you had seduced me and it had been beyond my control." He snorted. "That argument did not last even half an hour.

"Next, I was angry with you for cutting up my peace. I was furious with you for effortlessly destroying the fortification that I'd been building stone by stone since that summer when I killed my friend."

Jago scooted a bit closer to her, encouraged by the fact that she didn't flinch away.

He took her hand. "The demolition of my defenses began before I was even aware it had begun. All those weeks I watched you going about your work with a quiet assurance that inspired me to persevere." He smiled. "And then there were those few—*tragically* few—games of chess, which demonstrated your razor-sharp intellect. An intellect I had already suspected, but which left me awed, all the same."

She turned away; her cheeks fiery.

But Jago wasn't done. "And then there was our night together. I'm not a fool—I've experienced passion in the past. But not once have I ever experienced the deep, oppressive sense of loss I felt when I contemplated never seeing you again." He raised her hand to his mouth, lightly kissing the back of it. "I know so little of you Benna, but I love—yes, *love*—the little I know. You have captured my heart, darling. If you would take me as your husband, you would make me far happier than I deserve."

Jago was rewarded by an open-mouthed look of shock.

After a long moment, during which she only stared, Jago squeezed her hand. "Benna? I am beginning to worry."

"Are you saying you love me?"

He pulled a wry face. "Lord, did I leave out that important bit? Yes, that is exactly what I am saying. I love you."

The muscles beneath the skin of her face shifted, and the result was an expression he couldn't quite identify. "And you want to marry me?"

Jago frowned at her tone, which was unmistakably ... hostile. "Well, yes."

She yanked her hand away and surged to her feet, her expression one of such deep loathing that it felt as if she'd thrown acid on his face.

"Good Lord, what is wrong?" he demanded, getting to his feet. "What did I say?"

"Don't touch me," she hissed, the expression so ugly that he almost didn't recognize her. She slid her hand into her coat pocket and came out with a penny knife. A *big* penny knife.

Jago raised both his hands. "I won't touch you if you don't wish me to."

She sneered at him, her eyes suddenly a wintry blue, her pupils pinpricks. "How long do I have?"

He blinked. "Er—"

She flicked opened the blade and Jago's eyes widened. "You had better warn whoever is waiting out there that I won't go without a struggle."

Jago gaped at the knife in her hand. "Bloody hell, Benna. Be careful with that. It has to be—"

"It is four inches long, and I am not afraid to use it. Now, tell me how long I have before they come for me," she repeated.

Jago felt as if he'd been catapulted into the middle of an intensely melodramatic—and bizarre—stage play.

"Good God, Benna, what in the world are you talking about? How long do you have before *who* comes for you?"

Chapter Thirty-One

Cornwall
1817
Present Day

The air in front of Benna rippled, as if she were looking through steam.

Rage vied with disbelief; why did this keep happening to her? Was she truly such a fool that she could not see when a man was using her?

Across from her, Jago's brow furrowed, his expression one of deep concern.

He was an even better liar than Geoff.

"Benna?"

She could see his mouth move, but his voice was tinny and faint, barely audible beneath the roaring and crashing of her fury.

When you can spare a moment from your insane rage, you might want to recall this isn't me you're talking to, darling. I personally find your Jago far too honorable and noble—nauseatingly so, in fact—but what has he ever done to make you think that he is lying?

The question worked as effectively as a footbrake on her violently spiraling temper.

"Benna?" A deep vee of apprehension had formed between Jago's coffee-brown eyes, which flickered from the knife in her hand back to her face. "Do you not feel well?"

"That night in the cottage you couldn't have made it clearer that there was no future for us," she accused, her voice as sharp as the blade in her hand.

"Yes, that is true."

"What made you change your mind and decide that you loved me—that you should marry me?"

He blinked at the contempt in her voice but did not back away. "I wish I could say I was smart enough to work through it all on my own, but I wasn't. Today, after no sleep for the past few nights, I went to see Elinor Worth." His cheeks darkened at the admission. "She is somebody whose opinion I respect. Also, her situation was not so very different than ours."

"What situation?"

"Her marriage."

Benna squinted and shook her head. "What are you saying? I don't understand."

"You never heard how she first met Worth?"

"No."

"Her father is Viscount Yarmouth."

Benna actually knew that. "Why is that relevant?" she asked abruptly, her gaze drifting toward the door. Was he wasting time while he waited for somebody—another Willy Karp? Or would it be Michael, himself, this time?

"Stephen Worth was a footman in Yarmouth's house."

Her head jerked around at his words. "Stephen Worth the rich banker?"

His lips twitched. "He is the only Stephen Worth I know. It was fifteen years between the time they first met and married. The point I'm trying to make—rather clumsily—is that Elinor has some experience when it comes to defying convention."

"And so you told her—what, exactly?" Benna sneered. That we'd *fucked*?"

He flinched as if she'd slapped him. "Is that all it was to you?" he asked softly.

Shame flooded her, making her head hot; she was treating him the way Geoff had treated her. "Just answer the question; what did you tell her?"

He hesitated for so long that Benna feared he might tell her to go to the devil.

Finally, he nodded—as if to himself—and said, "Truth be told, I maundered on like a lovelorn boy—not much differently than I did

276

with you earlier. But I'll spare you all that and just give you the truncated version. I told her that I loved you and didn't want to face a future without you."

Benna could only stare.

He held her gaze for a moment and then glanced at her hand. "Would you mind terribly putting that away. Just for now? I'd like to come nearer, but I don't wish to get stabbed."

"You told her that?"

"Yes."

"When?"

"Today."

"If I asked her right now, what would she say?"

He blinked, visibly confused. "Er, I'm guessing she'd tell you that I'm an idiot but to be kind to me because I am her friend."

Benna could only stare. Did he—was it possible that—

Lord, the poor fool loves you. Put down the damned knife.

Reeling, Benna folded the blade and dropped it into her coat pocket.

"Thank you." Jago came close enough to take her hand and lift it to his mouth, lightly kissing her rough, dusty knuckles.

"My hands are dirty," she said in an abstracted tone, her mind clinging to his words like a dog with a bone.

"I don't care." His eyes never left hers while his lips drifted over her fingers "Won't you please tell me what is going on, darling? Why did you pull a penny knife on me? Is that a sign of affection up north—or perhaps a form of courtship?"

She gave a slightly hysterical snort of laughter. "I can't marry you."

He frowned. "Do you mean you can't because you don't wish to? Or you can't because you ... can't?" His eyes opened wide. "Good Lord—are you telling me that you're already married?"

In a heartbeat his normally pleasant features shifted into a dangerous mask. "Did your husband mistreat you?" he demanded, his tone coldly menacing. "Is that why you are hiding? If so, you needn't worry; I would never allow anyone to take you away against your will. You are safe here—whether you want to marry me or not. But if you wish to get away—if being around me makes you uncomfortable—

Elinor has already said she would give you a safe place to stay for as long as you need. Just say the word."

The gudgeon really doesn't know who you are, Benna. The bloody fool has actually offered marriage to a stable master. It is beyond price.

Benna ignored Geoff's howling laughter.

Instead, she met Jago's fierce, yet worried gaze. "You really don't know who I am."

"You're Benna Piddock—or, Hazleton, rather."

She stared into his eyes harder than she'd ever stared at anything in her life, looking for the truth.

The skin at the outer edges of his eyes crinkled.

"Why are you smiling?" she demanded.

"Because I suddenly understand the true meaning of the word *scrutinize*. Just what are you looking for, Benna? What do you think I am hiding?"

Benna just shook her head; he really didn't know.

He wasn't using her or manipulating her or lying to her to get her money.

He didn't know.

Which meant …

Which means the pathetic pillock really loves you. Congratulations, you two bloody deserve each other.

Benna flung herself at Jago so hard that he staggered back.

He gave a startled laugh, but his arms closed around her. "Steady, my love," he soothed, holding her tightly.

Benna hugged him until it felt like her arms might pull out of the sockets.

A shudder wracked her body and she squeezed her eyes shut, but still the tears—years' worth of them—came flooding out.

His hands, gentle and loving, stroked her back in soothing circles. "Shhh, sweetheart. It's all right. Whatever it is—it will be all right. I promise you. Please don't cry, darling."

He sounded so piteous that a watery laugh gurgled out of her.

For the first time since that night in the spinney there was somebody she could trust. Why had she doubted him?

A hand with a handkerchief came between her wet face and his chest.

She took it and wiped her eyes, but the tears just came faster.

"Benna, darling—why are you crying? Please tell me what I've done to upset you."

A sob tore out of her at his anguished, loving tone.

She clutched him even harder, squeezing him to her so tightly that her fingers burned. "I'm so sorry." The words were choked and muffled.

"Sorry for what?"

"That I doubted you. I love you so much, Jago. I've loved you almost from the first moment I saw you."

And then Benna proceeded to soak the lapel of his new coat.

Five minutes later ...

Jago was beginning to wonder if she'd fallen asleep. She had certainly earned a rest after that bout of weeping. He felt more than a little wrung out, himself.

"Sweetheart?"

She shifted beside him. "Hmm?"

"I don't want to rush you, but we've only got a few hours before this horrid ball. I would gladly stay home, but you know how my nieces—"

"No, no—" Although it sounded more like, *dough, dough.*

She sat up and Jago reluctantly removed his arm from around her shoulders.

"Won't you look at me, Benna?"

"I look awful when I cry."

Jago put a finger beneath her chin and tilted her face toward him.

"Oh don't," she begged.

He smiled. "Well, your nose is a bit red, but you look lovely to me."

She groaned but didn't try to turn away.

"You can stay home tonight," he told her, releasing her chin, even though he didn't want to stop touching her. Ever.

"No, I'll go," she insisted.

"Are you sure?" he asked. "Because you needn't."

"I want to go." She smiled shyly. "I have a wonderful costume."

Swine that he was, he didn't argue; he wanted her there with him. So, instead of insisting, he nodded. "Now that that's settled, will you please tell me what is going on?"

A guarded look crept into her beautiful eyes.

He cupped her cheek, caressing her with his thumb. "Whatever it is, you should know I'll stand by you, Benna."

She gave a slight nod and swallowed. "My name is Benedicta Elizabeth Norah Winslow de Montfort. I'm—I'm the tenth Duchess of Wake."

Chapter Thirty-Two

Cornwall
1817
Present Day

The laugh slipped out before Jago could catch it.

But Benna didn't laugh with him.

Jago stared. And stared some more.

But still she didn't break into a smile or tell him she was joking. Instead, she fixed him with a coolly level gaze.

"My God," he breathed, shaking his head. "You're telling the truth."

She nodded.

"But—" Jago had no idea where to go from there.

"There is a great deal I have to tell you. Perhaps we should wait until—"

"No waiting." Jago shook his head. Emphatically. "We can make time for this right now. I don't care if we miss the entire blasted ball. I need to know what this means."

"Perhaps the truncated version?" she said, echoing his words from earlier.

"That'll do for now."

She took a deep breath, and the words began to tumble out, "My brother died in a hunting accident and I—thanks to my family's royal patent—acceded to the title. Because I was underage, my cousin was my guardian. I have good reason to believe that he—the Earl of Norland—killed my brother."

"Good God," he breathed. Jago had heard that name—and recently. Before he could recall where, she went on.

"I know he planned to force me to marry him and then have me locked up—and likely kill me at some point—because I overheard him say so. I've since learned that he has a woman he claims to be me locked up in a sanitorium. I honestly don't know what his plan is."

"So you … ran away?"

She nodded.

Jago made a noise of strangled fury. "There is nobody who could help you?" he demanded.

She shook her head.

"Good God, Benna. You've been forced to live like this for how long?"

Her mouth opened, but no words came out.

"What is it, darling?"

"You—you *believe* me?"

It was his turn to gawk. "Of course I believe you. Why in the world would you lie about something like that?"

She closed her eyes, squeezing them shut.

Oh Lord, he'd made her cry again.

"Please, sweetheart, I didn't mean—"

She shook her head almost violently before looking at him, her eyes glassy with unshed tears. "I just never thought anyone would believe me." Her voice was gruff and froggy, as if she were choking back sobs.

"I'm not *anyone*, Benna. I love you. Even if I didn't love you, you impress me as a woman who is unlikely to run about telling bizarre tales. A person would need a *very* compelling reason to abandon their life and home and impersonate another gender. Not to mention that trading a life of luxury and leisure for that of a servant's is not a decision I imagine you made lightly."

She blinked, her chin trembling as she gazed up at him, as if he were some sort of heavenly apparition.

"Shh, no more of that," he begged when a tear escaped. "I interrupted your story. Do go on."

"There's not much more. He found me once—my cousin, that is—almost a year ago, after the man I used to work for discovered my identity and handed me over for money—"

"Bloody hell, Benna! Do you mean this Fenton bloke? The one you worked for all those years."

She nodded.

"That's—" Jago shook his head. "What a vile *louse*. What happened? Did you have an argument of some sort—a falling out—or was he skint? Not that either reason would justify such despicable behavior."

"He sold me to my cousin after he asked me to marry him and I refused."

"I'm sorry—but what?" he asked, feeling as if he were missing something.

She chewed her lip.

"Benna? What are you saying? Were you—was he—" Jago ground his teeth, unsure of how to word such a question.

"He said he loved me, but love had nothing to do with it. I will inherit a great deal of money when I turn twenty-five. But if I marry before that time—without trustee approval—it will revoke the trust." She paused, frowning. "Or at least I believe it will. My brother explained everything to me after my father died, but it was so long ago and I was so young. And then after David died, well, Michael gave me a version of my brother's will, but it wasn't the one I remember. Quite honestly, I wouldn't be surprised if that will was a forgery." Her brows knitted together. "I know this sounds confusing—that's because it is. You see, I can't know what is really going on without talking to my family's solicitors. And that has been impossible with Michael claiming I am actually in a sanitorium in Sussex." She growled with frustration. "I've gone around and around and around on this for years. I decided that without money or help from somebody with power, I'd have no chance against Michael. So, my best hope has been to wait until I can make a legal claim on the trust. The rest of my inheritance—that which belongs to the dukedom—was under his guardianship until I married or turned twenty-five, whichever came first." She gritted her teeth. "I'm sorry, I know I'm babbling."

Jago couldn't help smiling at that. "I think you are justified, Benna. I feel a bit like babbling myself. So, Fenton asked you to marry him, you rejected him, and then he told Norland?"

"Yes. He said that he'd only planned to threaten Michael with marrying me—that he thought my cousin would pay him not to. But then he learned about the trust conditions, and that's when he handed me over."

"Bastard," Jago hissed. Something occurred to him. "This Fenton, why did he believe that you would marry him to begin with?"

She opened her mouth, and then hesitated. "We were lovers." Her voice was barely audible, but she raised her chin and looked directly at him.

Jealousy struck him like a kick to the gut, stunning him with its intensity. He'd been jealous before—lord knew Ria had always manage to rouse him—but never had it been so *visceral*.

She stared at him, both anxious and defiant, as if she thought he might judge her.

Well, in a sense he was, of course. But he could not fault her for taking lovers—even one who employed her—without being a bloody hypocrite.

"He knew your true identity all along?" He tried not to feel hurt that she would have confided in some other man, but not him.

Then again, he shouldn't be surprised that she had not trusted him—not after that swine sold her secret. It was astonishing that she could trust anyone after that.

"No, he found out by accident." She paused, chewing the inside of her cheek. "What happened between us is—well, it is not an edifying story to tell."

"You needn't tell me anything you don't wish to, Benna." He wouldn't badger her, no matter how badly he wanted to know. But knowing, he suspected, was only likely to cause him pain.

After a moment, she said, "No, I'd like to tell you. It will also explain why I was so angry with you earlier. You see, he treated me rather, er, callously for several years." She grimaced. "*Very* callously."

Jago decided that he didn't want to know what she meant by *callously*. He already wanted to kill the man. Thank God he was already dead.

"And then suddenly, about two years ago, he became much nicer. Several months after that he told me that he'd come to … love me

He had to ask. "You felt nothing for him?"

Her brow furrowed. "He saved me that night in Durham, so, at first I admired him and saw him as a savior. But he—" Her cheeks flushed. "Well, exposure to him over time eroded those early feelings. After I rejected him the first time he became far more—" She pursed her lips and then shook her head. "Let's just say he was charming, kind, and caring, but I wasn't thoroughly convinced, even though this went on for months. When he asked me again to marry him, I said *no*. I woke up the following morning to find myself tied up and waiting for a man to come and collect me."

Jago felt more than a little nauseated. "Good Lord, Benna. No wonder you were furious—and frightened—when I popped up after all but ignoring you for three days and said that I wanted to marry you."

She squeezed his hand in answer.

"You said that somebody came to take you away. What happened?"

Her jaws flexed. "I got away," she said flatly.

Jago waited, but she remained silent.

There was a story there, but she clearly did not wish to share it. Well, he could wait until she was ready.

Instead, he asked, "Do you still wish to wait until you are twenty-five to take action? Or would you allow me to help?"

Her eyes widened. "You mean you—that is—well, you would let *me* decide?"

"Lord, Benna—you've been your mistress all this time. I'm hardly going to start telling you how to handle matters when you've done an excellent job surviving."

She looked more than a little dazed by his response. "My plan is not really much of a plan, but then I haven't had many options." She met his gaze, her eyes suddenly vulnerable. "Until you."

Jago gathered her in his arms and she melted against him.

"I've wanted somebody to trust for so long, Jago."

The words were a hoarse whisper and he heard all the pain and fear behind them.

He squeezed her tighter. "I love and adore you, Benna. I will do whatever you want, however you want to do it. But you need to tell me." He released her just enough to look down at her. "If it was a broken arm you had, I'd know exactly how to help. But I'm afraid your lover is something of a dunce when it comes to legal matters. I am guardian to Catherine and Mariah—along with their mother—but I believe these things can be set up in a variety of ways." He hesitated, and then said, "If I might be permitted to advise you?"

She nodded eagerly. "Please."

"I think you should talk to Stephen Worth. When it comes to legal matters he is the most knowledgeable man I've ever met. He is also a lawyer. You know him a little—do you think you could trust him?"

"I like him," she said simply.

And then two tears leaked from her magnificent eyes.

"Oh, darling—why are you crying?" he asked, kissing away her tears.

"I don't know why I'm such a watering pot—I never cry. I'm just so … *relieved* that I'm no longer alone."

He rubbed her back. "Everything will be fine, Benna. I promise you."

Jago hoped to God that he was right.

Chapter Thirty-Three

Cornwall
1817
Present Day

*Y*ou *could* be a kind young gentleman and ask one of them to dance," Jago teased.

"I'm not sure that would be a kindness, my lord." Benna turned to find the earl grinning appreciatively at her.

They were standing together, not far from the refreshment table, watching the crowded dancefloor.

They'd arrived only half an hour later than they'd anticipated and Catherine and Mariah had immediately been solicited for dances.

Benna had no interest in dancing with or talking to anyone but Jago.

She knew that was an unrealistic hope. In fact, Jago had already done his duty and danced with two young women, likely he would do even more dancing before his evening was through. Even though he wore a half-mask, every mama in the room knew he was the newly minted Earl of Trebolton.

"There were too many people around earlier for me to tell you how stunning you look," he murmured softly. "When I saw you come down the stairs in that coat and breeches it brought back such happy memories. My parents were like gods to us that night—Cadan and I must have been four and seven—when they visited the nursery before going out. Never had my mother looked more beautiful. She had a tiara that looked like it had been made from a tiny rose hedge." He frowned, and Benna guessed that he was wondering where his mother's jewelry was, now.

"You look very nice yourself, sir."

He smirked. "You are revolted by my laziness."

"Not at all. How clever of you to come disguised as a country doctor."

He laughed at her acerbic tone and the sound drew interested looks from more than one woman in their vicinity—especially their hostess, who was standing not far away talking to a clutch of adoring young bucks Benna assumed to be houseguests.

Benna didn't know much about parties of any sort, but she was fairly certain they didn't usually include quite so many handsome, unattached young men.

"You dance, I presume?" Jago asked.

"Adequately. But my lessons were quite, er, different."

"Ah," he said, nodding in comprehension, his gaze on Mariah as she avoided a collision with a very youthful-looking George III. "My nieces say you helped them practice while Lady Trebolton played for you."

She had; it was the first time she'd taken the man's role dancing.

"The countess plays beautifully." Benna had been surprised that the normally languid woman had roused herself to join in the dance lessons. They'd only had four, but she'd been excessively merry at the first three, laughing and encouraging Lady Mariah's outrageous capering.

At the last lesson, yesterday, she'd looked so exhausted and gray that she'd scarcely been able to lift her hands to the keys. She had played for only a quarter of an hour before turning the instrument over to Catherine.

Benna felt Jago looking at her and turned. "What is it?" she asked.

"It just occurred to me that this must be *your* first ball—if you left before you were seventeen."

"I hadn't realized that," she admitted.

He clucked his tongue, the sound one of sympathy.

"Please don't feel sorry for me. I dug in like a stubborn mule when my brother broached the subject of a Season."

"Did you? Why?"

"Some of what I told you is true, my lord. I always have preferred horses to people."

"I hope you like *some* people better than horses."

"Are you … flirting with me, sir?"

He chuckled. "If you have to ask then I'm doing a dreadful job of it."

Mrs. Valera appeared beside the earl. "Jago, my dear, I *do* hope you've saved some of your dances." She turned to Ben and gave her a glorious but superficial smile. "Please excuse us, Ben, but I'm going to steal your employer."

Benna bowed her head, biting back a smile at the quick scowl of annoyance that flickered over Jago's face before his social mask slid into place.

Once he was gone, she studied the rest of the room. The ballroom at Stanford Hall was as cavernous as that at Wake House. And tonight it was full to capacity. Benna knew—thanks to intelligence gathered by Lady Catherine, that a good many of the guests were staying at the monstrous country house.

"There are over one hundred guest rooms," Catherine had confided in accents of wonder. "And Ria says they will all be occupied for at least some of the house party."

After working below stairs for so many years Benna was more impressed at the thought of serving so many revelers. Indeed, the house was larger than most hotels, she wondered if—

"Excuse me, sir, Mr. Piddock?"

A footman hovered beside her. "Yes."

The servant came closer, as if to impart a confidence. "I was sent to tell you that Lady Trebolton is unwell."

Benna glanced toward where she'd seen the countess sitting and watching her daughters only a few minutes ago; another woman now sat in her chair.

"Where is she?"

"If you'll follow me, sir."

Benna hesitated to leave Catherine and Mariah if their mother had gone, but the dance was currently in the middle of the set and Jago was in the huge room, somewhere; they should be safe.

She nodded and the footman led her through clusters of milling guests toward a set of double doors with a pair of liveried footmen posted on either side. He opened one door of the doors and waited for her to pass through before closing it behind them.

Benna saw they'd entered a long, broad gallery. "Where are you taking me?" she asked as they passed several guests who were promenading and enjoying the paintings.

"She's in the library, sir, where it is quiet and private."

"Did she faint?" Benna asked as they passed through another set of double doors, these opening into a hushed hallway.

"That is what I was given to understand, sir."

Benna wasn't surprised. Lady Trebolton had been in a strange— almost fey—mood during dinner. She'd startled everyone by showing up to the dining room dressed as a highway woman, complete with a tooled leather gun belt and pair of the heavily chased pistols, similar to those Benna had found in the crate.

Jago had looked a bit concerned by his sister-in-law's uncharacteristic vivacity, but her daughters had been enchanted by this unexpected version of their mother.

The footman stopped in front of a door, knocked softly, and then opened it.

Before Benna entered the room, she said, "Will you please find Lord Trebolton and tell him where we are?"

"Of course, sir."

Benna stepped over the threshold and the door closed quietly behind her, pausing while her eyes adjusted to the dim lighting.

Across the room somebody rose from a chair.

Benna squinted. "My lady?"

"She's not here, Benna."

Benna jolted at the sound of a voice she'd heard in her head thousands of times; she gaped like a fool as her cousin materialized from the gloom.

Michael was dressed in a black velvet robe that was trimmed with something that looked like spotted lynx fur. Around his neck was a large and elaborately worked gold collar studded with diamonds, rubies and pearls, an object of astonishing opulence which would have been designed, she guessed, to evoke wonder in all who saw it. On his hat was a brooch in the form of a Greek cross.

The only part of his costume that was not of the Plantagenet era was the pistol he was pointing at her.

Michael was one of the few men she knew who was taller than her, and Benna had to look up to meet his familiar blue eyes—de Montfort blue, people often called it.

"Let me guess," she said, "Richard III."

His smile never reached his eyes. "As clever as ever, I see. How relieved I am to learn that the years haven't ground it out of you." His gaze flickered over her body and it felt like the light, skittery legs of insects were crawling all over her. "If I'm Richard then you must fancy yourself one of the Tower Princes." His full lips curled into a smile bristling with spite. "How fitting. I suppose you would be the younger one."

"You mean because you already murdered my older brother?"

His eyes widened. "Ah," was all he said.

"Do you deny it?"

"Why would I?"

She took a step toward him and he raised the gun. "You stay where you are."

"How?" she demanded, barely able to force the word out from between her clenched jaws.

"How did I kill him?" He gave her an oily, smug smile. "It wasn't difficult. Poor David always did rush his fences. All he needed from me was a little ... *push*."

"You filthy bastard."

"I see you've broadened your vocabulary—and not for the better."

Benna heard a scuffing sound behind her and spun around.

Viscount Fenwick stood considerably farther away than Michael, the pistol he clutched trembling slightly. "Good evening, *Ben*."

"Good evening, my lord," she said, not surprised to see him. Strangely, she was not worried by the turn of events, either.

Instead, what she felt was a profound relief. At last. There would be no more running and hiding.

Fenwick, she couldn't help noticing, was swaying slightly.

"S'quite a rig you've got on," Fenwick slurred, eyeing Benna's salmon pink frock coat and breeches, three-quarter white silk loo-mask, and heavily powdered wig with an offensive smirk.

"Thank you." She gave his own costume a quick once-over. "Cavalier? How original."

She'd seen at least two dozen of the royalist supporters mincing around the ballroom in fancy red heels.

"Who're you meant to be?" he demanded.

"Just another pink of the *ton*."

He blinked owlishly, his forehead furrowing.

Benna turned back to her cousin. "Two guns for a mere female?" she taunted.

"You've killed two men with only a penny knife my dear. It is always better to be safe than sorry."

She raised her hands in a gesture of submission, amused when he stepped back. "I've got no knife on me tonight," she lied. If there was one thing Benna had learned over the past six years it was never to be without a knife.

He gave her a sour smile. "I think I'll keep the pistol, anyway."

"Well, whatever it is you have to say, you'd best get on with it because I just sent the footman to fetch Lord Trebolton, so he'll be here any moment."

Fenwick laughed in a way that made her flesh crawl. "Jago's gone off with the lovely Mrs. Valera. He won't be in any condition to talk once she's finished with him. I can personally attest to that."

Michael ignored his taunt. "Let's step away from the door, shall we?" He motioned with his gun hand and Fenwick moved toward the hearth, the two men keeping Benna between them.

"Sit." Michael pointed to a long brown leather settee that looked big enough to accommodate at least six people.

Benna sat and Michael lowered himself beside her, although not too near. Fenwick stood behind the sofa, his pistol aimed at Benna's head

Her cousin laid his gun in his lap, but he kept his finger on the trigger, the barrel pointing in her direction.

"What adventures you've had, dear Benna." Michael's lips curved into an unpleasant leer. "Tell me, have you spread those long legs of yours for the handsome earl—as you did for Morecambe? I'm guessing the answer to that is *yes*."

"Why do you ask, Michael? Does it bother you to know that I'd rather work as a servant than allow you to touch me?"

Michael's hand flexed on the gun handle and his face tightened, but he chuckled. "Too bad for you that fucking Trebolton didn't work any better than it did with old Geoffrey." He smirked at the confusion she knew must be showing on her face. "Don't expect Jago to rescue you, darling. How do you think I found you in the first place?"

Benna's head buzzed at his words. In her heart, she knew he was lying. But her brain—her traitorous, suspicious brain—began to make unwanted connections.

"Oh, I'm so sorry, my dear. I can see that's quite a shock. But poor Trebolton is only trying to save his wretched estate, Benna. You shouldn't blame the man for doing what he needed to do. Not that marrying the gorgeous Ria is exactly a sacrifice."

I'm not marrying Mrs. Valera. Jago's solemn words came back to her.

No matter what bile Michael was spewing, Benna knew he was lying about that.

"If it is any consolation, Jago can't really do anything except marry Ria. Not if he ever wants to get out from under the cat's paw." He glanced up at Fenwick. "Isn't that right, Dickie?"

Fenwick's mouth tightened. "Hold your tongue," he said through clenched teeth, looking quite sober suddenly.

Michael smiled at his friend's barely suppressed fury. "Yes, poor Doctor Jago can be excused for sacrificing himself for money. But Morecambe, on the other hand, he was flush when he sold you to me—did you know that?" He smirked when Benna didn't answer. "It's too bad that Geoff never got to keep any of that money."

"What did you do to him?" she demanded.

Michael laughed softly. "Good God, look at you—you actually care about a man who used you like a drudge and treated you like a whore and then sold you when he tired of you. Even after all that you're as loyal as a dog to its master. Bloody pathetic."

"You say the word *loyalty* as if it were a bad quality, Michael. But then, you *would* think that—wouldn't you?" She leaned closer to him and he jerked back, his face flushing when he realized what he'd done.

"You're going to hang for what you did to David," she whispered, forcing him to crane his neck to hear her. She looked up at Fenwick, who was observing their conversation in open-mouthed fascination, the tip of his pistol actually pointing toward Michael. He jolted when Benna met his gaze and reoriented the gun on her. "Fenwick knows what you did and I'm sure he'll give evidence to spare his own neck."

Michael snorted. "You have nothing; you're just casting for fish and hoping to hook something."

Benna smirked and shrugged. "Whatever plans you have for me—whatever thugs you have waiting outside to tie me up and haul me away—you should put them out of your mind. In fact, if I were you—after what you've done to me and my brother—I'd leave this place at a gallop and hop on the first packet to Dover."

His face twisted into an ugly sneer. "The only place I'm going, dear Benna, is back to Wake House. You, my murdering friend, have two choices: you can come with me—nice and quiet—or I can go to the local sheriff and mention how you are connected to not one but two murders."

"Connected how?" she scoffed, but her heart lurched in her chest.

"The sheriff found a penny knife lodged in a rather unfortunate part of poor Willy Karp's body." Michael gave a dramatic shiver. "I understand it gave the local magistrate *quite* a turn. It's a pretty thing—this knife—with 'BEN February 22, 1811 DEG' engraved on the silver handle. Isn't that sweet?" he mocked. "Benedicta Elizabeth Norah from her loving brother David Edward George on your last birthday."

Benna had thought about her knife hundreds of times since that night in the beach cottage; she should have gone back for it.

"I won't marry you, Michael. Ever."

He eyed her with intense dislike. "Don't flatter yourself that I'm lusting for you. As if I would even consider marrying another man's—no, at least *two* other men's—leavings." His lips twisted into an unpleasant grin. "But that is neither here nor there, since you have already married me. Indeed, you've been my darling wife these past five and a half years."

"What do you—oh my God." She raised a hand to her mouth, suddenly ill. "My sister. You married my half-sister," she said, her lips so numb she could barely get the words out.

"Ah, I see Morecambe told you about her—or about *you*, I should say. Yes, you are my wife—my possession to do with as I please, under the law. So much better than a mere guardian-ward relationship." His eyes brimmed with malice. "You will come with me now, calmly and respectfully and without knives, and I will see that you find somewhere quiet and peaceful to live; somewhere you will have ample time to reflect on your many transgressions."

Benna had to laugh. "Somewhere like a pine box? Or perhaps a cozy cell complete with chains? You must be even stupider than you look if you think I'll go anywhere with you. You'll have to drag me out of this house at gunpoint, past five hundred people."

Michael chuckled, unperturbed. "Oh, I daresay you'll accompany me obediently and willingly. Tell me, does your new employer—or why mince words, let's just call him your lover, because I know how you work—know that you've killed two men? How staunchly do you think he will defend you when you are tried in Lords for murder?"

"You won't do that because then the truth about you would come out."

"You have no proof of anything." His eyes narrowed. "If you think you can threaten me and I'll simply give up everything I've worked for—"

"You mean everything you've *killed* for."

"If you think you can threaten me and I'll simply give up everything I've worked for," he repeated, "then you are in for a nasty surprise. Not only are you my wife, but you've spent the last six years in a sanitorium, under heavy sedation and guards. For your own safety, of course. I have doctors, nurses, and other respectable people who will attest to that fact. You escaped only long enough to viciously stab the man I sent to apprehend you. Trust me, my dear, by the time I'm done putting forth evidence nobody will believe a word you say."

Horror seeped through her at his words. "Jago will believe me."

"What *Jago* believes doesn't matter. I have marriage lines to prove you are my wife. No court in the nation will take the side of your lover over your husband."

Benna's mind began to fracture and fly apart; it was her worst nightmare made real. It was—

Stop! You know how to bluff, so do it. This is your life you're fighting for, Benna.

She swallowed back her terror and met Michael's smug gaze, forcing herself to sneer. "I'll take my chances, Michael. I would relish telling my story in front of my peers. I'm sure they'd be fascinated to learn that you've abducted and locked up an innocent woman, forged a marriage document, and are scheming to murder a peeress of the realm." She paused and then added softly, "What they'd find *most* interesting is the fact that you've already killed one duke."

"You think to make wild accusations based on some conversation you claim to have heard? With not a single shred of evidence? I have a houseful of servants who will testify how violently you argued over anything and everything—no matter how minor. How you behaved like a deranged woman and conspired with your stable master to steal from your own brother's estate. How you and that same man killed a *Bow Street Runner*—" He laughed at Benna's horrified expression. "Yes, you didn't know that, did you?" He smirked. "You have nothing, Benna. Nothing. And if you don't—"

The door to the library flew open and a figure in skirts staggered into the room.

"Lady Trebolton?" Benna said stupidly, standing out of habit.

Michael stood along with her, holding the gun at his side, as if that would hide it from the countess's view.

Lady Trebolton pulled the door shut with a *bang* and then raised the hand that had been hidden by her voluminous skirts; she was holding a gun.

Michael gasped. "Christ! What in the name of—"

The countess's blue eyes were wide as she grasped the gun with both hands and then leveled the pistol at her target.

Chapter Thirty-Four

Cornwall
1817
Present Day

What is all this about, Ria? Why have you brought me here?" Jago glanced around at what was obviously a study.

She had led him here via several corridors, until they were so far away from the ballroom that he couldn't hear even a hint of the noisy revels.

Ria came toward him with a glass in each hand. "Sit for just a moment, Jago. I promise I shan't take much of your time."

He sighed, took the glass, and sat. "I can't stay any longer than a few minutes. You must know that I'm here to help Lady Trebolton mind the girls."

"Such a serious, protective uncle."

"As would any man be upon seeing the crowd you've assembled tonight. My God, Ria, is there a loose fish or unconscionable rattle in England you *didn't* invite? You may do what you wish in your own house, but I'm not comfortable leaving my nieces unprotected."

"They're just young boys, Jago—remember what it was like to be full of spirit and a zest for life?"

He ignored the jibe. "What did you want to talk about?'

"What else? A union between us."

"We've already been over this." Jago wanted to throttle the woman; why must she make him resort to incivility and cruelty to get his point across?

"I think I have some information that will change your mind."

He snorted, not caring how rude it sounded. "That almost sounds like a threat, Ria. Tell me, does it have something to do with those letters I found? Because I know that story you told me was nothing but a tissue of lies."

"Why, Jago! I can't believe you think that *I*"—she splayed an elegant hand across the draped silk bodice of her dress—"would even dream of threatening you." Her heavily kohled eyes glittered darkly at him, her smile brittle.

Jago had to admit, grudgingly, that she made a magnificent Queen of the Nile.

"Ria," he said, the word soft but stern. "Please make your point."

"Cadan was involved in something that was … well, not just unfortunate, but illegal."

Jago set down his untouched glass. "You'd better choose your words very carefully."

"Remember when you, Brian, and Cadan took your boat out to play at being *gentlemen* and were brought back by some *real* gentlemen—"

"Yes, yes, I remember the story—I was there. What about it?"

"Do you recall the man who brought you back?"

"Of course I do. It was Toby Bligh. Where are you going with this?"

"Cadan and Brian formed a business connection with Bligh."

He snorted. "That's a lie."

"Bear with me, please. It was years later, of course, during the summer of 1798. You weren't here. I *was*."

That summer—after his first year at Oxford—had been the first one he'd spent away from home. He had gone to stay with a friend in Scotland rather than return to Lenshurst. At the time he had regretted missing out on whatever larks his brother and Brian got up to, but he'd been relieved not to spend the summer caught between Cadan and Claire's hostilities.

"Go on," he said.

"It was Brian's idea. You know his parents could never deny him anything. I'm sure you remember the yacht they bought for him?"

"Yes, of course I recall his boat." The St. Johns had spoiled their only child and the yacht—sizeable and luxurious—had been a gift they could ill afford.

"Brian encountered Bligh somewhere while he was out boating, they reminisced, and he ended up begging the man to allow him to help with a run."

"I don't believe you." But his words lacked heat, even to his own ears. God damned Brian.

Ria ignored the interruption. "Bligh told him to make a solo journey, first—to prove himself. So Brian did, and he ended up with a nice bit of money for his labors. The next time he went, he took a larger, more valuable cargo—one that Bligh arranged. That run went off without a hitch, too. And so, when Bligh had another cargo for him, Brian asked Cadan if he wanted to come along. Your brother was skint and miserable at home; he thought it sounded like a great lark." She shrugged. "They did well and made money. And that went on all summer and into the fall."

"How do you know this?"

She gave him an amused look. "Because I was Brian's lover, Jago, and a man will tell you anything when he is in bed with you."

Jago snorted; no wonder Brian was so furious when Jago came back the following summer and proceeded to cut him out with Ria. He looked into her smiling eyes. "Finish your story."

"Things went exceedingly well—in fact your brother was able to cover the debts he'd run up the prior year and could afford to go to London again."

Jago remembered; Cadan had sounded so happy in his letters. He'd left Claire breeding in the country and moved to the London house—back when they'd still owned one—set up an expensive mistress, and, for once, he hadn't complained about either his wife or their lack of money."

"I remember," he admitted when he saw she was waiting.

"Just before Christmas, he received a letter—so did Brian. It turned out that the cargo they'd been running back and forth hadn't only been only of the bottle and bolt variety. One of the men who'd been on Brian's small crew was working for our government. Bligh caught the man and managed to extract some alarming information from him. It seems that somebody who made those runs with Brian and Cadan had been selling information."

"Good God. Are you claiming they were spying for the French?"

"Not directly, but they were the ones financing the purchasing of all that cargo. And they were doing it on Brian's boat. And *somebody* who went with them was selling information."

"Wait, you said Bligh *got* the information out of him? What do you mean?"

She nodded. "Bligh questioned him. And then he took care of the man."

"*Took care of,*" Jago repeated, bile flooding his throat. "Are you saying he killed a British agent?"

"That is exactly what I'm saying."

"Good God, Ria, Cadan and Brian would never have sanctioned anything like that."

"They did, Jago. They met with Bligh and agreed with him. It was his hand that did the killing, but they agreed with him and they were there to watch."

"This is—"

"Treasonous?" she suggested.

"I was thinking more along the lines of horrific. Where is the proof for any of this?"

"Oh, there is plenty. I'll get to that."

"Well, get to it quickly," he snapped.

"As you can imagine, Cadan and Brian ceased their activities immediately and Bligh disappeared, most of his men along with him. For a while, it seemed like it had been a tempest in a teacup. But then the letters came."

"You mentioned that before—what letters?"

"Somebody knew all about the smuggling, the secrets, and the murder. And they wanted money to keep quiet."

"Who?" he demanded.

But she ignored his question. "Brian sold his boat to pay the first time. The second time a letter came, he had to sell some things from his parents' house. But the third time? Well, you know the St. Johns were not exactly well-larded. So Brian asked Cadan for help."

"*Three* times? In how many months?"

"The third demand came not long after you returned from your second year at Oxford."

That had been 1799, Jago's last summer at Lenshurst Park. He'd been well aware of the tense, unpleasant atmosphere at home but had chalked it up to Claire not giving birth to the heir Cadan had so desperately wanted. Also, his brother had begun pressuring Jago to marry, going so far as to find him the *perfect* bride.

"I take it Cadan had no money for Brian?" he asked grimly.

"No. While the money from the smuggling had been pouring in, your brother had gambled more carelessly than ever. It was around that time that he sold your family's London house and began to run with Peter Cantwell, I'm sure you recall him?"

Cantwell had been a local landowner who gambled, exploited his miners, and raped the daughters of his tenant farmers and servants. He was a repulsive reptile whom Jago still could not believe his brother had tolerated.

"Cantwell drew Cadan into deeper and deeper play. He had no money to help Brian—he was too busy trying to pay the piper himself."

The truth struck him like a proverbial bolt of lightning. "Brian didn't kill himself over that duel."

"No, he didn't."

Jago stared, utterly stupefied. "All these years you and Cadan not only allowed me to believe it was my fault—you bloody well engineered it, didn't you?"

"Oh, come, Jago, you were eager to be a martyr."

Jago swallowed his disgust and fury. "Why are you telling me this now, Ria?"

"Because I know who was blackmailing Cadan. And they are not finished."

"Are you saying that whoever was blackmailing my brother now thinks to try that on *me*?"

"I know he does."

He snorted. "I had nothing to do with any of it."

"If that story got out, would it really matter if it were you or your brother who'd been involved with selling secrets to the French?

Would the government care if it had been you or your brother who agreed to the killing of a British agent? It's treason, Jago, and you—and what remains of your family—will suffer greatly by association."

"And you know who this person is? How?"

"I made it my business to find out. With enough money, all information is accessible." She smirked. "But that is not the point."

"What *is* the bloody point, Ria?"

"The point is, I can make it all go away, Jago—the blackmailing, the danger of exposure, the constant, slow bleeding."

Jago looked into her beautiful, but hard, green eyes. "How?"

"Because I have my own information against him."

"Ha! Blackmailing the blackmailer? How ... appropriate. Who is it?"

"I can't tell you that."

"How long have you had this information?"

She shrugged. "Perhaps six years."

"Are you telling me that you could have stopped what was happening to Cadan?"

Her lips curled into an unpleasant smile. "Your brother thought I was lower than dirt. Even after I married Henry and could have bought your wretched Lenshurst Park fifty times over he lifted his nose at me. Why in the world would I ever do anything to help him? Besides, I *did* help him, and more than once. Why do you think there is even anything left of your family's land or possessions?"

"Are you saying you are responsible for slowing—but not stopping—the blackmailer's demands?"

"I convinced him that a dead goose could lay no golden eggs." When Jago just stared in disgust she continued, "I also helped Cadan *immensely* that summer when Brian was preparing to go to his parents and confess everything."

"You *helped?*" His stomach had been roiling almost since the moment Ria had opened her mouth. Now, his dread almost choked him.

"I convinced the fool he would bring nothing but suffering on his family—and yours—which was no more than the truth. I painted him a picture of himself tried for treason and his parents losing everything they had. And before you spout some sanctimonious claptrap about how I'm the one who killed him, just think about his choices for a moment. Hanging himself was the only solution for him, and, in the end, he knew it. So did your brother."

Jago shot to his feet, staring at her with open-mouthed revulsion. "You actually believe you *helped* him. You heartless monster. And you think I would marry you?"

"I won't raise a finger to help you if you don't," she said, unperturbed by his insults.

"I wouldn't take your help—or anything else—for any amount of money. As for facing such a scandal, I have some faith in our leadership. I'm not a betting man, but I'll wager on the truth winning out, Ria. Even if it means we lose Lenshurst Park, so be it. I can live somewhere else quite happily. But being shackled to you for the rest of my days? No, thank you. I shall pass on a lifetime of hell." He strode toward the door and flung it open.

"She won't get her hands on her money until it's too late for you, Jago."

Jago stopped and spun around. "What did you say?"

She smiled. "The girl—your stable master."

"I don't know what you're talking about."

"Oh darling, you're *such* a dreadful liar. It's a good thing you never had a taste for cards like Cadan."

Jago didn't stop until he was right in front of her. He leaned over, his hands on the arms of her chair, his face inches from hers. "Where did you learn this?"

She gave him an amused look. "Don't worry, Jago. If you enjoy pretending that you are with a boy you needn't give up such entertainments once we are married. I quite enjoy sharing—or even just observing. Indeed, if you decide that you'd like to try a *real* boy—"

"Shut up." Jago had never been so close to striking a woman in his life; he took a step back, removing himself from temptation. "Stay away from her, Ria."

She gave an exaggerated shiver. "So possessive and primitive. But it's not me you have to worry about, darling. Your faithful little stable master has been a bad, bad girl. According to the Earl of Norland she's not quite right in the head."

"You know him?"

303

"Mmm-hmm."

"Well then you know he's trying to usurp her title—and steal her money."

She nodded agreeably. "Yes, I should think he is—your little toy is quite an heiress. Nothing to my wealth, of course. But that's not my concern." She pursed her lips. "It's not yours, either, Jago. She belongs to Norland."

"What the hell are you talking about? She's an adult—he has no authority over her person."

"He does according to the marriage license he showed me."

"What mar—wait, are you saying you've *seen* the man?"

"Of course, I've seen him—he's a guest here. I daresay your duchess has seen him, too. Indeed, they are likely already—"

Jago seized her by her arms and shook her. "Where?" he snarled.

"They're in the library. You're hurting me—"

He shook her until her teeth rattled. "Where is the damned library?"

"Two doors before the gallery on—"

Jago shoved her away and ran for the door.

Ria's earthy laughter rang out behind him. "You bruised me, you beast!"

He grabbed the handle and flung the door open.

"Come back and apologize after you regain your senses, Jago," she called after him. "I'll be waiting for you. We shall have the most glorious wedding that Cornwall has ever—"

Jago ran.

Chapter Thirty-Five

Cornwall
1817
Present Day

*J*ust stay where you are, you mad bitch!"

Michael and Benna jolted at Fenwick's menacing growl and Lady Trebolton stumbled to a halt as Fenwick raised his gun and pointed it at her.

Benna couldn't help noticing that his hand was almost as unsteady as Lady Trebolton's.

"Fenwick," Michael said between clenched teeth. "Perhaps you might explain what the bloody hell is going on?"

"I have no idea, Norl—"

Lady Trebolton laughed in a way that made the hairs on the back of Benna's neck stand up. "You have no idea?" she repeated shrilly, taking a few more steps toward him.

"You take one more bloody step and I'll shoot you through the head," Fenwick shouted, his voice several registers higher.

Benna seriously doubted that Fenwick would be able to hit the wall behind Lady Trebolton the way his hand was shaking, but the countess stopped. She was close enough that Benna could see that her pupils were mere specks.

"I received your *message*, my lord," the countess snarled, the gun jumping wildly in her white-knuckled hand. "And I'm here to deliver my answer."

Benna risked a glance at Fenwick; he'd forgotten her existence. His gaze, attention, and gun were all aimed at the countess.

"What message would that be, Dickie?" Michael demanded in a voice that throbbed with annoyance.

Benna slid her hand into the pocket of her frock coat and her fingers closed around the familiar wooden handle.

When Fenwick didn't answer, Michael gave a bitter laugh. "Please tell me you didn't disobey my order and decide to have just *one* more bite before we—"

"I'm not your bloody slave to be ordered about, Norland," Fenwick shrieked. "That harpy is draining me dry—even though she doesn't need a penny. I just needed one more—"

"Always one more." The countess spoke in a dreamy, sing-song voice, her smile … unsettling. "Just … one … more. That's what Cadan always promised, too."

"You can lower the gun, my lady," Michael said in a soothing voice. "Viscount Fenwick will not bother you again. You have my—"

The door flew open again, this time hard enough to hit the wall.

Jago froze on the threshold as he took in the scene. "What in the name of—"

Whether Fenwick fired first or the countess did, Benna would never know.

All she knew for sure is that by the time she drove her knife into Fenwick's arm three shots had been fired and two people were on the floor.

"Claire!" Jago ran toward his sister-in-law but hesitated before dropping to his knees. "Benna, are you—"

She had to raise her voice to be heard above the viscount's screaming. "I'm not hurt, Jago."

A footman ran through the doorway, his jaw sagging as he skidded to a halt.

"Fetch my black doctor bag from the ballroom. It's on a table near the refreshments. Go *now* and hurry!" Jago yelled when the footman paused to gawk at the carnage.

Benna glanced down at her cousin.

Michael's eyes were open and he was gasping for breath.

Lady Trebolton had hit him almost dead center in his throat. It was an amazing shot—although she suspected that the countess had been aiming for her own tormentor rather than Benna's.

Michael made a gurgling sound and reached a hand toward her.

Benna dropped to her haunches and took his hand in hers.

His lips formed the word *help*.

Benna shook her head. "There's no help for you, Cousin. But if you want to unburden your soul before you meet your maker you could tell me who actually killed my brother?"

His mouth moved but only blood came out.

"I thought not," she said. "I'll take this—I believe it is mine, anyhow." She grabbed the familiar ring on his little finger, having to yank hard before it came off.

Benna slipped the heavy gold de Montfort signet onto her own pinkie, where it fit perfectly.

She leaned close and kissed his temple. "I hope you go straight to Hell, Michael."

She stood and stared down at him. He gurgled for a moment longer and then stopped with astonishing abruptness, his mouth open, eyes still staring.

He had died and now she would never know who'd helped him kill David. She waited to feel something—anything—but there was nothing; she was empty. No hatred, no hunger for vengeance; nothing.

She turned and went to Jago. "Can I help?" she asked, dropping down beside him.

He held his folded coat pressed against the oozing wound in the countess's chest, and gave Benna a grim look, shaking his head.

"Jago—"

Blood bubbled out of the corner of Lady Trebolton's mouth.

"Shh, Claire, you shouldn't talk. Everything will be fine, I promise you," he soothed, his tone so calming and certain that even Benna believed him.

"It's in the trunk. All in the—" A cough wracked her body and blood poured from her mouth as well as the wound in her chest. Like Michael, her death was shocking in its suddenness.

Jago closed her wide-staring eyes, leaving bright red smears on her pale forehead.

He stared at the countess, his expression one of incomprehension. "Why?" He shook his head, as if to wake himself, and then jerked his chin toward Michael's body. "Is he—"

"Dead."

His gaze flickered to where Fenwick lay face up on the settee, keening loudly. "What about him?"

"Just a little cut on his arm. He'll be fine. Unfortunately."

Jago shook his head in amazement. "My Benna." He began to pull her toward him, but then stopped at the sound of voices. "You need to get out of here, Benna. *Now*." He stood and held out a hand, helping her to her feet. "You can't be found here with Norland's body. Take the carriage and go directly to Worth's house. Stephen and Elinor will help you."

The same footman as earlier thundered into the room, followed closely by several others. All were too busy gaping at the scattered bodies to notice Jago and Benna.

"But what about—"

"Not now," he hissed. "Just go." He shoved her ungently toward the door.

More people started to pour into the library—people in costume—as Benna tried to force her way out of the room.

A hand grabbed Benna's shoulder, stopping her before she could disappear into the rapidly swelling throng. "What happened?" an elderly Marie Antoinette demanded. "Who are the two on the floor? Are they *dead*?"

"I don't know," Benna said. She stopped and turned, hoping for one last glance of Jago.

But he was tending to Fenwick and his back was to her.

"I heard there were gunshots," the woman persisted, her gaze avid. "Was there a duel? Or was it murder?" the last word was barely a whisper.

Benna thought of Claire and the way she'd looked—so scared and yet so ... relieved—as she lay dying. Only now did she understand what had happened. Yes, there had been a murder—albeit the victim had been the wrong one—but there had also been a suicide. The countess had come to the library not only expecting Fenwick's death, but looking forward to her own. That was why she had two pistols.

Benna shrugged the woman's hand from her shoulder. "No, it wasn't a duel. It was an accident. A tragic accident."

And then she disappeared into the crowd.

Chapter Thirty-Six

*Y*ou have a visitor, Your Grace."

Benna looked up from the watercolor her half-sister was painting and took the card from the salver her new butler, Horne, held out to her.

She smiled when she saw the name. "Where is he?"

"I put him in the Garden Room, Your Grace."

She nodded her dismissal and turned to Gilly, who hadn't noticed the interruption and was painstakingly adding petals to one of the many flowers in her painting.

"Lord Trebolton is here, Gilly."

Her sister kept painting, but Benna knew, after living with her for almost five months, that the slight stiffening in her slender shoulders meant she was listening.

"You remember I told you about Jago?"

Gilly gave an infinitesimal nod but didn't look at her. She didn't like to make eye contact with anyone if she didn't have to, not even Benna.

"Jago's a good man," Gilly said in her strangely flat voice.

Benna smiled. "A very good man."

"We can trust him," Gilly added, mechanically.

"Yes, we can. I am going to talk to him right now, but I shall still be able to see you from the Garden Room terrace. You can look up and wave to me if you have a mind to do so."

Gilly nodded.

Benna turned to Mrs. Taylor, the older woman she'd engaged to help with her sister.

Mrs. Taylor's kindly face creased into a smile. "I'll take care of her, Your Grace."

"Did you hear that, Gilly? Mrs. Taylor will be here with you."

But Gilly had already gone back into the world of flowers.

"Those are lovely roses," Mrs. Taylor said, using a normal voice, rather than the patronizing tone people often employed with her sister—as if she were a child rather than a grown woman. Gilly wasn't stupid; she just had little need for people. After the life she had led, Benna couldn't blame her.

Benna had to force herself to walk slowly, even though she wanted to break into a run.

Not only was running undignified, but it was too difficult to run in skirts and flimsy slippers.

Besides, she needed a moment to calm her thundering heart. Even though she had been expecting him, her stomach was churning and her thoughts were fluttering like flustered pigeons.

It had been five and a half months since Benna had seen Jago that night. They'd not even exchanged letters for five of those months.

"Lord Trebolton and Viscount Fenwick have their hands full explaining the unfortunate incident that occurred at Stanford Hall that night, Your Grace," Jonathan Parker—Stephen Worth's frighteningly clever solicitor—had told Benna. "It would be disastrous if your name were associated with any of it until we've settled, er, everything. Letters might seem harmless, but—as you know—servants talk and secrets always leak out."

Benna thought about Lady Mariah—and her hobby of lurking in stairwells—and agreed to the solicitor's request, even though she hadn't liked it.

It turned out that she'd had little time to lament letter writing as Mr. Parker kept her extremely busy—and exhausted—cleaning up the mess that Michael had left.

For all except the last two weeks her only communication with Jago had been through Mr. Worth, who'd kept them both apprised of important developments.

Even after Parker told Benna that she could write to Jago, their letters had, by necessity, been circumspect.

There was still so much she didn't know.

And so much more that she did not want to tell …

Benna stopped beside the door to the Garden Room, her favorite of Wake House's sitting rooms, and checked her appearance in the glass.

The woman who looked back at her was still a bit of a stranger.

She'd stopped dying her hair and it had slowly faded to her natural color. Her dress was a simple white muslin but the addition of delicate pearl earbobs made her look, if not pretty, then at least more feminine. Even though she was now her own mistress and could wear whatever she liked, she wore gowns most days, but would never give up breeches or riding astride.

I'm dithering.

Benna swallowed, turned from the glass, and opened the door to the sitting room.

***

Jago was staring so hard as she dropped a graceful curtsey that he forgot to bow.

Rather than rectify his social solecism, he strode across the room with ungentlemanly haste, wrapped his arms around her, and crushed her mouth beneath his.

A mixture of relief and desire flooded him when he realized that Benna's hunger matched his own.

"Good God, but I've missed you," Jago murmured, only pulling away because he decided that she probably needed to breathe. "I want to look at you." He took her face in his hands and held her for inspection. Her hair was a little longer and it gentled the strong angles of her face, which was no longer as tanned. Her short, wavy locks were like fresh corn silk, a beautiful and unusual color; Jago now understood why she'd dyed it.

She blushed adorably under his scrutiny. "It's the same old me, just in a dress." She looked away, clearly mortified by his attention.

"I'm relieved—because that is who I was hoping to find: the same old you." He gave her a lingering kiss and then pulled away with a happy sigh.

She took his hand and led him out onto the terrace. "I need to stay where Gilly can see me."

"How is she?" Jago asked, sitting as close to her on the settee as he could without actually pulling her onto his lap.

"Better, I think. She is less anxious and not so easily frightened."

"I am glad you brought her to live with you."

"And you won't mind having her with us … after?"

"You mean when we are married?" he teased. "Go ahead, I want to hear you say it."

Her cheeks tinted pink. "You don't mind having her with us *when we are married?*"

"I look forward to having a bigger family. You won't mind having two nieces living with us?"

"I miss them both," she said, simply. "How are they managing after the countess's death?"

"They had so little of her before she died. Only after Cadan's death did Claire take any notice of them." He grimaced. "I know it sounds callous, but I'm glad—for their sakes—that they did not know her better."

"I'll never forgive myself for buying her the very drug you were trying to ween her from, Jago."

"Don't blame yourself, darling, you weren't to know. Besides, it didn't matter what either of us did because Ria kept her well-plied with laudanum. It still sickens me to think that Ria all but poured it down Claire's throat to manipulate her." He cut Benna a grim look. "It worked, too; just not the way Ria hoped it would."

"Do you think she wouldn't have done what she did without the drug?" Benna asked.

"Clearly we can never know, but I think Claire's courage to confront Fenwick came from a bottle that night."

"I'd always thought laudanum made people lethargic."

"It does, but it can also cause brief periods of extreme euphoria, which are always followed by melancholia."

Jago reached into his coat and took out a folded rectangle of paper. "This is a very long, convoluted tale. You should read this," he said, handing the letter to Benna, "it explains the first part of the story far better than I can."

Jago silently read it along with her, even though he'd read it at least a dozen times:

Jago,

You will know what I tried to do if you are reading this. I can only hope that I succeeded.

I simply cannot continue to live this way and killing Fenwick is the only way to end it.

I am sorry that I could never bring myself to tell you the truth, Jago, but it was all so sordid—so endlessly sordid—that I was ashamed.

Cadan did a foolish thing, a long time ago, and we have been paying for it ever since. Your brother hated me from the first, but even he could not keep the truth from me once matters became truly dire.

I only know what little Cadan told me. He and Brian got involved with the smuggler Bligh and his men. One among them—they never knew who—sold information to the French. The government sent an agent to investigate and Bligh caught, tortured, and killed the man. Still they learned nothing. But, somehow, the dead agent's diary fell into Viscount Fenwick's hands—the one before the present viscount.

The older Fenwick bled us dry for years.

Cadan sold the London house, the hunting lodge in Scotland, the manor in Buckinghamshire that your mother left him, and even the industrial properties my father left me. He sold the Trebolton rubies—the set in the vault is paste—and then he sold all the rest of the jewels that were worth anything. He sold at least a dozen paintings—including the Holbein—your father's illuminated manuscript collection, his string of hunters, the carriages—all except his curricle and that broken-down old boat of a coach—and on, and on, and on.

Then, after five years of hell, that bastard died and the torment stopped.

Only to start up again six years ago, when his brother discovered the diary and began putting it all together.

Apparently the diary contains detailed information about Cadan and Brian's involvement in the smuggling, complete with the agent's opinion that all three men—with Bligh as the ringleader—knew about the spying.

I don't believe Cadan knew anything about that, Jago, but he certainly knew what Bligh intended to do to that poor man.

The new Viscount Fenwick was far less greedy. At first.

And then, a few years ago, the demands began to come faster. Finally, two months before Cadan's death, Fenwick asked for an enormous amount of money. He gave his word that that would be the last time and he would hand over the journal.

313

Your brother actually believed him. To pay him, he took out the three loans. I argued with him, but of course he didn't listen to me.

And so when Cadan brought home the money, I took it.

"Oh my God," Benna said, looking up at him.

"Keep reading; it only gets worse."

"Cadan went mad when he couldn't find it. He had promised to bring it to Fenwick by the end of that month.

Why did I do it?

Because I knew it would never end. Fenwick would come back again—or the wretched book would fall to somebody else. It would go on and on and on.

There was only one way to end it: your brother needed to take the honorable way out. He needed to do what Brian had done all those years ago. It would be for the good of the earldom and his daughters. Once he was dead, it would end.

No matter how much he raged at me, I would not give him the money. Cadan had never hit me before that night.

But I refused to tell him; I knew it would be the end of us.

He was in a fury when he ordered his curricle brought round so that he could tell Fenwick that he didn't have the money. I overheard poor Nance try to talk him out of it, but Cadan was in no mood to listen.

I didn't know that he would die that day, Jago, but I was glad when it happened.

Finally, it would be over.

For eight blissful months I believed the nightmare was at an end. I knew the estate was going to be a dreadful burden on you, but you are so much stronger than Cadan ever was. I knew the loans were not due until next year. I wanted to tell you about the money—to ease your mind—and decided to tell you when you moved home to Lenshurst for good.

But then Fenwick came to me.

I know you will think me a fool, but I honestly thought he would feel remorse for driving Cadan to his death. I—stupidly—believed that he only wanted to give me the book and that would be the end of it.

I never imagined that he would resume his demands. He gave me until the end of the year to sell what I could to raise the money.

After you came home, I wanted to tell you the truth so badly. But I know you, Jago. You would have done the right thing—the thing Cadan and Brian and I should have done long ago: you would have gone to the authorities and told them the truth.

I am weak, and I couldn't do it. I had decided that I would give him the money when Gloria Valera came to me. She told me that she could make Fenwick stop. All she wanted in return were some letters that she'd written Cadan.

She wants to marry you—you know that—and worried that you might come across those letters and learn of her involvement all those years ago.

If I gave her the letters, she promised to deal with Fenwick.

You were always so kind to me when I was a young, lonely girl; I couldn't condemn you to life with such a heartless viper. But I also couldn't refuse her help. So I made a compromise with my conscience: I gave her five of the letters I found, but left a few—the most damning—in with the other papers. I hoped that you would find them before you offered for her.

But, once again, I miscalculated. She was furious when you confronted her directly about the letters. She told me I had destroyed any chance my daughters had for a future. She told me that rather than dissuade Fenwick, she would encourage him.

I know I've chosen a coward's way out, Jago, but I hope that I have at least managed to stop him. I have left you to deal with yet another mess.

You will find the money in two trunks in the east wing attic.

Please take care of my daughters. I love them both dearly.

With affection,

Claire

Benna looked up. "Those were the trunks that I had the footmen bring down to the library just before I left."

"Yes, I didn't even have to go and find the money, it was sitting right in front of my own desk." Jago shook his head. "I wish Claire had told me all of this. If she had, she would still be—" He broke off and shrugged. "But there's no point in wishing. I've returned the money to the banks and have negotiated yet another loan to pay the interest back. The estate will survive and—I hope—eventually flourish."

He pulled his thoughts away from poor Claire and smiled at his love. "I told you the story was long and convoluted. Let's put the rest of my tale aside for the moment. Why don't you tell me a bit about your dear, departed husband."

Benna smiled. "Well, I have to admit that Mr. Parker's solution to my, er, problem, didn't sit right with me when he first suggested it, but the more we found out about what Michael had done, the more it was clear that I'd never recoup what he'd stolen from the dukedom if I didn't allow the marriage to stand."

"It is actually a fiendishly simple solution to all of it."

She nodded. "By allowing the marriage to stand and accepting my role as Michael's widow—as repellant as that might be—I also avoided the expense and effort of overturning a fraudulent marriage and eliminated the need to explain a six-year absence."

"Did he do a great deal of damage?" Jago asked.

"Enough," she said, shaking her head. "All these years I worried that he'd gotten to the trust and it turns out that it was everything else that was in danger." She swallowed and gave him a haunted look. "My father was wise to make inheriting contingent on me turning twenty-five—regardless of my marital status. My God, Jago. If that clause hadn't been in the trust Michael would have killed Gilly."

Jago pressed her hand between his. "But it *was* in there and she is safe, darling. Stephen said it was easy to get Gilly out of that private asylum?"

"Only after Parker threatened to bring a case for false imprisonment against them." Benna smiled grimly. "And then they couldn't get rid of her fast enough."

"I understand that she received some monetary compensation?"

"They gave back all the money Michael paid to keep her there and paid the same again in restitution." Her jaw flexed, her blue eyes burning. "I wanted to destroy them, but Parker warned that the case would become public if we did." She sighed. "I left the decision to Gilly; she just wanted to forget about it all. The only thing she wanted from a settlement was to make sure there was nobody else in her situation locked up there. So we made an impartial investigation part of our agreement."

"Did they find any abuses?" Jago asked.

"No, thank God."

Jago could see the subject still upset her, so he said, "Are you ready for part two of my story?"

She nodded.

"I know that Stephen told you a little bit about that, already."

"Just that you spent nine days in London at the Home Office going to meetings."

"*Meetings.* That's rather a bland euphemism for interrogations." Jago didn't tell her that they'd actually taken place in a cell so grim and dismal he'd wondered if he would ever again see the light of day. As it was, they had kept him overnight for three nights.

"How did you manage to convince them that you had only just learned about it all?" she asked.

"Believe it or not, Fenwick helped prove that."

Her lips parted with surprise. "He spoke to them? But Stephen said that he disappeared the week after the masquerade ball."

"He *did* scarper." Jago grinned. "But Worth had his brutally efficient henchman—John Fielding—flush the viscount out of his hole, shove a sack over his head, and bring him in kicking and screaming." He laughed. "Well, he would have been screaming if Fielding hadn't gagged him. Anyhow, let's just say that Fenwick didn't speak to them voluntarily."

Benna chuckled and shook her head.

"By the way," Jago said, as something occurred to him. "Worth said you asked Fielding to help you with something—about your brother's death? Did—"

"He didn't find anything," she said, her smile draining away.

"I'm sorry," Jago said. "I know you were hoping to find out something."

She shrugged. "It's been over six years and I'm sure Michael was careful to cover his tracks. In any case," she said, clearly wishing to change the topic. "I'm still astounded that the Redruth authorities believed the story you and Fenwick concocted—that Michael and the countess accidentally shot each other while play-acting a duel because they didn't realize the pistols were loaded."

"I was amazed, too," Jago admitted. "But Worth threw some money—and influence—around and of course Ria wasn't eager to be attached to such a scandal and brought more influence and money to bear. My position in the community didn't hurt, either. All of that combined to make both the sheriff and magistrate quite, er, persuadable. Not to mention there was no rational explanation for why those two would have wanted to kill each other since they had only met that night. It was fortunate that I had a few minutes alone with Fenwick while I patched him up. By the time the sheriff arrived we'd set our stories straight and agreed to pass off his injury as a nick from the same bullet that passed through Norland."

"You showed great presence of mind getting me out of there, Jago."

Jago shuddered at the thought of what might have happened if she'd been discovered there. "I don't even like to think about that," he said quietly.

She lifted his hand and kissed his palm.

Jago groaned at the erotic gesture. "Wicked, cruel, temptress."

Benna smiled. "Finish telling me about the Home Office."

"There isn't a whole lot more to tell. It was a deeply unpleasant experience. The whole time I was there I felt ashamed, as if I had been involved in the sordid enterprise. The diary actually wasn't as damning as I'd feared. It turned out that Fenwick had shown Cadan the worst of it. The agent wasn't convinced they were involved, at all. It was Bligh, and the agent had apparently found evidence to prove it." Jago shook his head. "What my brother and Brian and Bligh did was unforgiveable. I am so fortunate the authorities believed me, Benna. If they hadn't …"

She squeezed his hand. "I'm sure that you coming forward with the information was a point in your favor."

"Yes, they said as much," he agreed. "I hope at the very least that they'll be able to find Bligh and get some justice for their murdered agent."

"Poor Jago, you did nothing to deserve all that."

"No, lucky Jago. Because I had you to look forward to at the end of it all."

He saw the slight tightening around her eyes and frowned. "What is it, love? Why do you look anxious?"

Benna's eyes moved to something beyond the terrace and Jago turned to see her sister approaching.

Her resemblance to Benna was startling at first glance, but the closer she came, the more he saw it was superficial.

She was shorter—although still tall at perhaps five feet eight or nine inches—and her hair was a golden blond rather than Benna's striking silver. Her features were softer, and, objectively, Jago supposed, she would be considered prettier than her older sister.

Like Benna, she wore a simple white muslin gown.

Benna took her hand and smiled—the gentlest expression Jago had ever seen on her somewhat severe features. "Have you come to meet Lord Trebolton?"

Gilly nodded, but stared at the ground.

Benna turned to him. "My lord, it's my pleasure to introduce you to my sister, Miss Gillyflower Danvers. Gilly, this is Lord Jago Trebolton."

Gilly dropped a shallow curtsey but did not offer her hand. "A pleasure," she said in an almost inaudible voice.

"The pleasure is mine," Jago assured her, bowing low. "I hope you will do me the honor of calling me Jago."

Her lips quirked slightly and she nodded. "But not until next month, when you become my brother."

Jago turned to Benna and gazed into her bottomless blue eyes. "Yes, that's very proper, Gilly, er, Miss Danvers—since I shan't be your sister's husband for another long, endless, thirty days."

He added in a far softer voice, for Benna's ears only, "I don't think I can wait that long."

Chapter Thirty-Seven

Wake House
1817

That same night ...

enna had dismissed her maid fifteen minutes ago and had been pacing ever since. She was about to go down to the conservatory and look for Jago herself when the door opened and the man himself slipped into the room.

Benna had seen him only an hour earlier, down in the library where they had sat after dinner with Gilly, but she was still robbed of breath by the sight of him. His coat and pantaloons were a sinful black, his waistcoat a creamy ivory, and his cravat snowy white. He wore no jewelry except for the gold and onyx signet.

She gave a sigh of relief. "I was beginning to worry."

He pulled a wry face. "I'm ashamed to admit I got lost." He held out his hands as he strode toward her.

Benna took his hands and squeezed them. "Let me remind you that it was *you* who insisted on staying in the Dower House, rather than here at Wake House."

"It would hardly be decent to stay under the same roof as my betrothed before we are wed."

"Oh? Does that mean you won't be staying the night?"

"Ha! I'm definitely staying the night. But I shall quietly scuttle away unnoticed before first light."

"Are you really going to *scuttle* back and forth for an entire month, Jago?"

"Mmm-hmm." He drew her close for a long, languorous kiss.

Benna slid her arms around his body and allowed her hands to roam freely, amused by the series of grunts and purrs her beloved made as she explored him.

Just when Benna began to think she might escape the ordeal she'd been dreading for five and a half months Jago released her and pulled away. "If I didn't know better, I would think you are trying to distract me?"

"Maybe."

"Oh come, I spilled out my endless story almost upon arrival. But we were interrupted before you had a chance to tell me about the rest of your adventures."

Benna had given the matter of her past a great deal of thought and had come to the unpleasant conclusion that she would have to tell him about Tom and Diggle.

And also about Willy Karp.

Benna had poured the entire story out once already, to Parker, who'd demanded to know everything about the last six years. Parker had not looked at her any differently after what he'd learned.

"I will see to retrieving your penny knife," was all Parker had said when she was finished.

But then Parker was her solicitor, not her lover.

Jago was a doctor—it was his sworn duty to save lives. This might be the last evening she spent with him if he could not forgive her for being a murderer, twice over.

Benna swallowed; it felt like there was a rock lodged in her throat. She had to have him one last time before the dreadful truth was known.

She had to.

"I'll tell you about everything," she blurted, lifting her shaking hands to his neatly, but not fancily, tied neckcloth. "But first I want to strip you naked and sate my wicked appetite with your body."

His lips parted in surprise and his pupils ballooned. "As Your Grace commands."

One moment Benna was removing his neckcloth, the next she was facing the wall.

He seized her wrists in a gentle but unbreakable grasp and raised them above her head. "I'm afraid I'm too impatient to allow myself to be stripped just now. Later—after I've given you what you need—I

321

will have you undress and bathe me." He bit her neck and then added in a rough voice, "you will wait on me hand and foot."

Benna's sex clenched fiercely and she bit her lip, but not before an animal grunt slipped out.

"Ah, I can see you like that thought." He kissed the place he'd just bitten and nuzzled her ear before nipping the lobe. "Does it make you wet to imagine serving me—tending to my every need?"

She shoved her hips back at him, earning an evil chuckle.

"I'll take that as a *yes*. But for right now, hands flat on the wall, darling," he whispered, the words hot against her skin as he thrust his shoe between her slippers and kicked her feet apart. "Spread for me like a good duchess."

Blood thundered in her ears at his hungry tone and demanding words.

"I pleasured myself shamelessly this past week thinking about what we would do tonight," he said in a conversational tone, grinding his erection against her bottom while kissing and nibbling her neck

"Only this past week?" she taunted in a breathy voice.

He laughed. "All right, I might have been abusing myself a bit longer than that."

She shivered at the thought of him stroking himself to thoughts of her.

"You like that, don't you? Imagining me suffering and yearning for you, touching myself to those well-worn memories of our only night together."

Cool air drifted across her legs and a warm firm hand slid over her hip and then push between her thighs.

Instead of stroking her core, he only teased her lower lips, his touch maddeningly elusive. "Have you missed me, Benna?"

"I've missed you."

He pushed a finger up her, not stopping until his knuckles were pressed against her sensitive flesh. "Mmmm—you're so tight."

"Jago, please," she groaned, spreading wider and canting her hips to give him better access.

He pumped her slowly and deeply, easing a second finger beside the first. "Tell me this isn't another dream, Benna—that I'll wake up alone in my bed again tomorrow morning. Tell me you're real."

Benna let her head fall back, exposing her throat to his hungry mouth. "I'm real, Jago. And I need you inside me."

He caressed her aching bud with his thumb and she whimpered and thrust back at him.

"So eager for me, aren't you?" He worked her harder, deeper, relentlessly circling her core. "Shall I make you come on my hand, Benna?" he demanded, his voice rough with arousal, and then he thrust her over the edge of bliss.

His fingers disappeared from her clenching body, but even as she groaned at the loss of him, she felt the scalding heat pushing between her swollen lips.

"Yessss," she hissed.

"Hot and wet and so soft," he murmured, pulsing his hips so that his blunt crown stroked her sensitive flesh. "I want to be inside you, Benna."

She reached between her thighs and wrapped her fingers around his slick shaft.

His sucked in a harsh breath and shuddered at her touch.

Benna wanted to stroke him—to tease him—but the angle was too awkward. Instead, she stood on her toes and positioned him at her opening.

They both groaned as he entered her, invading her slowly. It had been months since she'd had him inside her and the sensation of being stretched and filled was almost painful.

"You're so damned tight, Benna." He didn't stop until he was in her as deeply as he could go. And then he stilled, his chest heaving against her back.

"Good?" he asked a moment later, his voice taut and his hips tensing as he flexed inside her.

"Very good," she whispered, clenching her inner muscles in response.

He hissed in a breath. "And you're very, very bad." He pulled out with agonizing slowness, and then thrust hard enough to lift her off her toes.

Benna braced herself against the wall with both hands as his hips began to move.

"I missed you so much," he gasped, his pumping rhythmic and deep. "I'm never letting you go again, Benna. Never"

She canted her hips, offering him everything; opening herself to pure sensation as he rode her, pounding into her without mercy, driving her toward yet another peak.

"I'm already too damned close, darling," he grunted, his thrusts becoming savage and less controlled.

Benna came apart just as her lover drove himself home, his body spasming as he spent deep inside her.

"I love you, Benna" he said in a voice hoarse with passion. "I love you so much."

Joy spread through her at his words.

But lurking behind her elation—like a sneakthief ready to snatch away her happiness—was a crippling fear.

Would he still feel the same way when this night was over?

***

"Brandy?" Benna offered, gesturing to a nearby tray with a decanter and two glasses.

"Please," Jago said, even though he didn't particularly want one. But tension had replaced the bliss that he'd seen on her face only moments earlier.

He took the glass she offered and patted the seat beside him when she looked as if she might sit in one of the chairs.

She hesitated.

"You don't have to tell me anything you don't wish to, Benna. I'll love you no matter what I learn about your past." He paused, and then plunged ahead. "If this is about Fenton, I know you were lovers—perhaps you were even *in* love with him. I'll admit I'm jealous, but it isn't as though—"

"I'm a murderer."

Jago blinked. "I'm sorry?"

She raised the glass to her mouth with a trembling hand and drained the contents in one swallow.

"Careful, darling—not so fast," he murmured, taking her empty glass from her shaking fingers. "Everything will be all right," he soothed. "You don't have to—"

Benna turned to him, her gaze oddly flat. "No, I need to tell you."

Jago nodded. "Very well. I'm listening."

And then he held her hand while her story poured out of her.

She told him about a lonely, willful girl who'd grown up loved but neglected by her absent father. About a brother who'd once been her best friend but had slowly drifted away as he'd come of age, and about an old man—a servant—who'd been her best friend and had probably saved her life.

By the time Benna finished describing Tom's death in that spinney the tears were running down her cheeks. "I repaid his friendship by stripping him of his valuables and leaving him there," she said, squeezing Jago's hand so hard that the bones shifted. "I don't even know where Michael buried him—I doubt I'll ever find out so I can never tell his brother or give him peace."

"You did what you had to do Benna," he said, his words woefully inadequate. "And it was exactly what Tom wanted you to do. As for Diggle?" Jago scowled. "Well, that sounds like an accident, not murder."

"It *was* an accident; I hadn't meant to kill him." Her expression shifted from desolate to feral in a heartbeat. "But after what happened to Tom, I was *glad*, Jago," she said, her eyes fierce.

Jago pulled drew her to his side, holding her tightly. "You did what you had to do," he repeated.

"I don't even remember leaving the spinney that night." Her words were hot against his shoulder, where she was resting her head. "I couldn't go to the village—it was the first place Michael would look for me. So, I just started walking south. I walked for days. And every time I heard a carriage or horse behind me, I dove into the nearest hedge or bush or ditch; I was *terrified* that it was Michael. Or the sheriff."

She sat up, dabbing at her eyes with a dainty handkerchief that had materialized from somewhere. "I was so scared those first days, Jago. Everything was strange, people were so—so *harsh* and life move so much faster. It was easy to make mistakes, and the mistakes had dreadful, dangerous, consequences. I never knew any of that growing up." Her pained blue eyes finally met his. "I spent my money foolishly when I got to Newcastle. I took rooms at inns and ate meals that didn't seem expensive at the time, but…" She sighed and then shrugged. "Well, I ran out of money so fast."

Jago had known that she had run away, but he'd not allowed himself to imagine the enormity of what she had done. "You are so brave, Benna."

"No, I'm—"

He took her chin, keeping her from turning away from him. "*Yes, you are.* I, too, ran away from home. I still recall how frightening it was to leave everything I knew with only a few of my possessions. And I wasn't in fear for my life, forced to masquerade as somebody else, and hunted by an unscrupulous man who was supposed to protect me." He kissed her lips softly. "You are utterly astonishing."

Her cheeks darkened, and she pulled away, putting some distance between them. "There is more," she said, the set of her jaw grim.

"You don't need to—"

"I *do* need to tell you, Jago." She turned to him. "You see, Diggle wasn't the only man I killed."

***

The alarm in his eyes was there and gone in a heartbeat, but Benna had seen it.

But it was too late to turn back now.

"The man I worked for wasn't named Fenton. His name is Geoffrey Morecambe and he's not dead."

Jago's eyes widened. "Morecambe? Was he related to—"

"He is a younger son of Baron Morecambe."

For the first time, Jago wouldn't meet her gaze and Benna saw the slight tightening in his jaw.

"You know him?" she asked.

He nodded. "Yes. He was two years ahead of me in school." He looked up at her, his mouth twisted into an odd smile. "A handsome and engaging rogue. I can certainly understand your attraction to him."

"It wasn't love, Jago—never that. I was infatuated—but even that didn't last long. He was not an easy man to work for and live with." Benna saw Jago's nostrils flare and recognized jealousy on his beautiful face.

"There is nothing to be even remotely jealous about, Jago. He was—"

He took her hand. "Don't fret about me, darling—I was just … surprised." He gave a self-deprecating smile. "My jealousy is not logical—and I don't know why it bothers me that I actually know the man—but I promise you I will not let it ruin what we have. Go on with your story."

"I told you that Geoff—er, that's Morecambe—tied me up and sold me to Michael?" Jago nodded. "Michael didn't come himself, he sent a man called Willy Karp to fetch me from Geoff. His orders were to take me to a remote cottage and wait for Michael." Benna swallowed and cut him a nervous glance.

"I am a grown man," he assured her, reading her anxious look correctly. "I can handle whatever you have to tell me."

Several Minutes Later ...

"My God," Jago said.

That was the third time he'd said the words since Benna had described where she'd stabbed Willy.

"My God," he said again, and then gave a flustered laugh. "Lord, I sound like a demented parrot. I'm sorry, Benna, but that's just, well ... my God." He swallowed, and then nodded, as if he'd settled some matter with himself. "As horrific as it is, I have to admit it is *appropriate* for what he was about to do."

Benna might have fibbed a little when it came to how far things had progressed before she had pulled out her knife. He didn't need to know the entire truth; nobody did.

Jago, still a bit greenish, smiled at her. "Er, as much as that would hurt like—well, like nothing I want to even imagine—being stabbed in such an area wouldn't necessarily have killed him. In any case, if not for the metal bedpost, there is a good chance that he might still be alive." He winced. "Although he probably wouldn't have been, er, functional." He cleared his throat. "Do go on."

"I was nerving myself up to retrieve the knife when I heard something outside the cottage and became frantic."

Half-mad would have been a better way to describe her state of mind.

"Instead of taking the knife, I grabbed the poker and ran for the door." She swallowed. "What I would have done if it *had* been Michael waiting for me, I'll never know," she said.

"It wasn't your cousin?" Jago asked, confused.

"It was Geoff; he had followed me."

Jago merely stared, looking as amazed as Benna still felt—even all these months later.

"I almost brained him with a poker," she admitted.

"Good God! What's all that blood from?" Geoff had blurted, his eyes wide with horror. Geoff had a great dislike of blood and had once almost fainted when he'd seen Benna cut herself while carving.

He had quickly held up a hand. "Never mind, don't tell me; I don't want to know."

"What are *you* doing here?" she'd demanded.

He'd ignored her and strode back to the horse he'd tethered at the post. "We don't have time to argue right now, Benna," he called over his shoulder. "You can hit me or cut me later."

"I'm not going anywhere with you."

"You don't have any choice," he said as he swung himself into the saddle, "I believe I just passed your cousin's carriage on the road no more than ten minutes ago." He held out his hand. "We don't have much time."

When she'd hesitated he'd given her an exasperated look. "I'm all you've got." His gaze flickered over her blood-soaked arm. "And it looks like you're going to need some help."

"I knew he was right," Benna said to Jago. "And so I went with him."

"Where did you go?"

"First, we headed down the beach rather than the road. Michael must have seen us, but there was no way he could follow over the mudflats and sand in a coach. Geoff knew we couldn't go to a small village—we'd be too easily remembered. So, he looped back around and we returned to Carlisle, to the townhouse."

"What happened then?" he asked when she paused.

Benna met Jago's curious gaze. "I cleaned myself up, packed my valise, and left."

He blinked. "And he didn't try to stop you?"

"No, he knew it was over," she lied, shoving away her memory of her last conversation with Geoff. Not because it was painful, but because she simply didn't know what to make of it.

He had begged her while she packed. "I made a mistake, Benna—a horrid, dreadful mistake. Can't you forgive me?"

That had been one question she could honestly answer. "I will never forgive you, Geoff."

He'd flinched as if she'd shouted.

"Doesn't me showing up to help you mean anything?"

"Do you really expect me to praise you for doing the decent thing, Geoff?"

"Please, Benna. I—I—" His expression had been one of pure anguish. "I love you." He'd said the words with quiet, desperation.

"I hope that's true, Geoff. Because you deserve to suffer."

"You don't have to marry me—I don't care if you ever claim your inheritance. I just … I want you with me, Benna. Wasn't our life together good?"

"Benna?"

Benna blinked and saw that Jago was looking at her, his brow furrowed with concern. "Are you all right?"

She cleared her throat. "Yes, of course, I am." She recalled where she'd left off with her story. "I knew I couldn't go on the mail coach, so I parted with a great deal of money to hire a post chaise." Her lips twitched into a smile.

"What?" he asked.

"You won't believe this, but I was robbed not far out of Carlisle—in broad daylight."

"You were robbed a *third* time?"

Her face heated. "Actually, this was the second time. I, er, changed some of the details when I told you the story before. Although they really did take everything I had—that was the truth."

"You do seem to get more than your share of trouble, don't you?"

Benna studied his face, looking for any sign of disgust or apprehension.

"What is it?" he asked her, inching closer, until their thighs were pressed together. "Why are you looking at me like that?"

"I love you, Jago. But I will understand if what I've done is just too—"

He jerked her against him so abruptly that Benna squeaked with surprise. His arms closed around her like the iron rings of a barrel. "If you say one more foolish thing—if you apologize one more time for what you did to survive—I shall put you over my knee and spank you." He held her away so that he could look at her. "Er, that is—you don't have that blasted penny knife in the pocket of your dressing gown, do you?" he asked, giving her an exaggerated look of worry.

At least Benna suspected it was exaggerated. Mostly.

"No, I don't have my penny knife on me." She hesitated and then added with a straight face. "I keep it on my nightstand."

Jago threw back his head and laughed. "Life with you, my love, will never be boring."

Epilogue

Wake House
One Month Later

*J*ohn Fielding stood on the terrace attached to the small sitting room and watched as guests arrived from the church in the village, where the wedding had just taken place.

They were gathering in the perfectly manicured garden and drinking champagne as they waited to attend the wedding breakfast of the Duchess of Wake and Earl of Trebolton.

If somebody had told John fifteen years ago—when he was living in a one-room flop in St. Giles with a dozen other boys and ten thousand fleas—that he'd one day be a guest at a duchess and earl's wedding he would have laughed in their face. Right after picking their pocket, of course.

He lifted the glass of champagne to his mouth and downed the contents in one gulp.

"If you keep drinking like that I shall have to crack open another case, Mr. Fielding."

He turned to find the bride smiling at him.

John smirked, impressed when she didn't flinch away from the nightmare that was his face. "You should have thought of that before you invited a ruffian like me to your wedding, Your Grace."

She came toward him, holding a bottle and an empty glass. "I brought reinforcements."

Even though she was wearing a dress she still moved with the loose-limbed gait of a man. She wasn't a pretty woman—not even an expensive dress, careful grooming, and a king's ransom in jewels could make her that. But she had a face that made a person look twice—whether she was dressed as a man or a woman.

She handed him the bottle and held his glass while he opened it. "I need to thank you, Mr. Fielding."

He glanced up from the stubborn cork. "For what?"

"If you'd not given me the sack I probably wouldn't be standing here today."

He snorted. "Somehow I think you would have gotten what you wanted no matter what I did."

She chuckled. "I'll take that as a compliment."

John just grunted; he'd meant it as a compliment. He'd met some fine women in his thirty-two years, but the Duchess of Wake was definitely at the top of the list. Jago Crewe was one lucky son-of-a-bitch.

The cork popped and she held out both glasses for John to fill.

Once he'd put down the bottle, she gave him his drink and raised her glass. "I propose a toast."

"Oh? To what?"

"To second chances, may we recognize a golden opportunity when we are faced with one."

John hesitated, narrowed his gaze at her, but nodded and took a drink, not draining the glass this time—he had *some* couth, after all.

They turned and looked out over the terrace at the crowd of people who'd gathered for the wedding, which had been held in the sizeable chapel attached to Wake House.

"How does it feel to be married?" he asked, his eyes wandering from person to person and lingering on Stephen Worth, who was staring in their direction.

"It feels … right," she said, her low voice heavy with contentment. "I'm glad that you are here, Mr. Fielding," she added.

John grunted, even though he knew it was as rude as hell. Her invitation had been for the festivities the week before the wedding, but his business in London was too pressing, so he'd only arrived yesterday evening.

"How is your room? Are you comfortable?"

He smirked at her studiedly casual tone. "Why don't you get to the point, Duchess. What did Worth send you to say?" He turned to find her watching him.

She smiled wryly. "I guess I need to work on my conversation skills."

"Your skills are just fine, you're just not a weaseling manipulator."

She gave a surprised laugh. "Er, and Mr. Worth is?"

"Absolutely. Worth is the king of the weaseling manipulators. But I can't think why he believes that you might be able to convince me to seize an opportunity, golden or otherwise." He threw back the rest of his glass and then met her startled blue gaze. "Why would that be, I wonder?"

"Fine," she said, a look of resignation replacing her smile. "It's true that he sent me to talk to you. He thought that perhaps you might see how happy a person can be even if they don't, er, wreak vengeance on a wrongdoer."

"A wrongdoer—like your cousin the Earl of Norland, you mean?"

"Yes."

"And you're happy even though you never got your pound of flesh from him? Even though he probably killed your brother?"

Her long slender fingers tightened on the glass and she swallowed.

John took a step toward her. "Worth got his revenge—did he tell you that?"

She nodded.

"And now he thinks he's some kind of expert on the subject because he regretted what he did. But I'm *not* Worth. Neither are you." He cocked his head, suddenly curious. "Tell me this, Duchess, if Norland was standing right here where I am and you had a gun in your hand would you just let him walk away?"

Her breathing quickened and John knew what she was thinking.

"Or what if I'd actually found the man Norland paid to bash in your brother's head?" She flinched, but he didn't stop. "Would you let a man like that live if the law couldn't touch him?"

She opened her mouth, and then closed it again, her pale blue eyes glinting with a poisonous blend of fury, frustration, and desolation.

John knew the feeling. He nodded, even though she hadn't spoken. "I thought as much."

The truth was, John *had* found Gerry Barnett, the man the Earl of Norland had paid to arrange the young duke's *accidental* death. It hadn't actually been that difficult. Norland had paid Barnett well, but you could never pay well enough to silence somebody. No, there was only one way to guarantee that.

John had considered bringing Barnett back to the Duchess of Wake—as she'd hired him to do—but he'd decided to spare her having to kill the man. Especially when killing was so very easy for him.

And so he'd settled the debt for her—a wedding gift, of sorts.

He looked at her shattered expression and frowned, vaguely ashamed at having caused her pain on her wedding day.

It was time for him to go—in fact, he never should have come. He was nothing but a specter at the feast.

John took her hand, the one not clutching her glass, and bowed over it. "I wish you and the earl happy, Your Grace. Thank you for inviting me. I'm sorry that I need to leave so soon, but I have pressing business in London."

She nodded dumbly.

John left her alone and strode toward the door of the small sitting room. Before he could grab the handle, the door swung open.

The Earl of Trebolton gave him a surprised look. "Er, Fielding. Good to see you." His eyes darted to where his duchess stood and then back to John. "I was just looking for my wife." His pale cheeks darkened as he said the word *wife*.

John held out his hand and the other man startled.

It always amused him how much the American ritual of shaking hands confused the average Englishman. "Congratulations, my lord. And thank you for your hospitality."

Trebolton blinked. "Oh, er, thank you. And you're quite welcome. Are you leaving already?"

"Yes." John stepped past him and left without a backward glance.

***

Jago walked over to the terrace, to where Benna was standing with an odd expression on her face.

"Is something wrong, my love?" he asked.

She seemed to shake herself. "No, nothing."

He took her half-full glass and set it on the table before wrapping his arms around her. "You seem distracted. Did Fielding say something to upset you?"

"Not really."

He smiled at the strange answer and kissed her right cheek. "What did you two talk about? I can never get a word out of the man, myself."

"Nothing much. I just passed a message to him from Stephen."

Jago kissed her left cheek. "Why didn't Stephen pass it along himself?"

"He thought I might have a better way to phrase it—something that might get through to him."

"Hmm," he kissed the tip of her nose. "And did you—get through to him, that is?"

"I don't think so."

"Well, at least you tried, darling." Jago kissed her mouth. "That's all anyone can do—try."

Benna's gaze sharpened and focused, as if she were only now seeing him. She gave him a smile that send blood thundering south. "Yes, I tried."

He kissed her again, this one longer, more lingering. When he pulled away he said, "The guests don't seem to be leaving."

Benna laughed, amusement transforming her, making her so lovely that he was momentarily robbed of breath. "The breakfast hasn't started yet, Jago."

"Oh. Well, do you think anyone would notice if *we* sneaked away?"

"I think since we're the guests of honor we probably have to stay."

He frowned. "What if I dropped a few subtle hints that they should go? Or would that be terribly rude."

"No, you probably shouldn't do that—we promised them a wedding *and* a meal, after all."

He heaved a put-upon sigh. "Well, I supposed I'd better go back out there and face them, then."

Benna took his hand, raised it to her mouth, and kissed it. "I'll go with you, how about that?"

Jago smiled. "I can do anything if you're with me, Benna." He squeezed her hand and then opened the door for her. "Shall we, my darling duchess?"

"Yes, let's face them together, my dearest lord."

And then she stepped out of the room and Jago shut the door behind them.

Hello my romance reading friends! First off, I'd like to say:
THANKS SO MUCH FOR READING.

I hope enjoyed THE POSTILION and are looking forward to
John Fielding's story in THE BASTARD.

If you've just read THE POSTILION the chances are good that
you've read the first book in the series, THE FOOTMAN. If so, then
you are the sort of reader who likes unconventional tales of love and
adventure. You're my kind of reader, in other words.

THE MASQUERADERS is a 3-book series (*maybe* 4, I haven't
decided yet …) about characters who aren't immediately what they
seem.
The series grew from a standalone novel, THE FOOTMAN,
when I decided I wanted a hero from the working classes.
Only after I started writing THE FOOTMAN—and Jago and
John—showed up did I think about more *masqueraders.*
Benna only makes a brief appearance in the first book, but she
immediately captured my attention. Who was she? Yes, I'm that crazy
kind of writer who never knows what characters will show up in my
books. The only way to learn more about a character is to write their
story.
I'll admit I was blown away by Benna's story—I wasn't expecting
her adventurous past.
Anyhow, I'm about ¾ finished with THE BASTARD as I write
this little note. John's past is every bit as interesting as I expected—
and his future is surprising not only me, but him!

If you liked my story, I'd really love even a one sentence review
on:
AMAZON
or
GOODREADS
Or anywhere else you like to review.
I especially love to get emails from readers. Drop me a line at
minervaspencerauthor@gmail.com if you would like to see a specific
character get their story. Or tell me the sort of story that YOU'D like
to read. I am always open to good ideas!

Please read on for a peek at THE BASTARD, Book 3 in THE MASQUERADERS series …

Chapter 1

Norfolk Island Penal Colony
1812

No beard could ever conceal the scar that bisected his face, the same way no glove could ever hide his right hand. John Fielding was, and always would be, a freak. That knowledge fueled him like coals heaped on a roaring fire and he bunched his six-fingered hand into a fist and connected it with the other man's chin. The resulting crack of bone and spray of blood fed his rage and nourished his hatred. It was a punch in the face of every person who'd played a part in sending him on this journey to the far side of Hell.

And it also earned him another handful of coins.

John watched with disinterest as his opponent went down with a dull thud. The crowd reacted with a primitive roar and John turned away and pushed through the maddened throng, ignoring congratulations and jeers alike.

Riddle, the man who managed John's fights, waited in back with all the rest of his ilk: Men who sported cheap, too-colorful clothing and noses that had never been broken. Men who spoke in quick, sharp sentences as their watchful eyes roamed in constant, shiftless motion.

Riddle grinned at John, the money he'd spent on his suit ruined by the black gap in his front teeth. "Well done, lad," he yelled over the din, reaching up to clap John on the shoulder.

John shrugged away his hand and snatched his shirt off the wooden cart where he'd tossed it a short time earlier. He pulled the rough-spun garment over his head and turned back to Riddle as he tucked the tails into leather breeches as battered and scarred as he was.

"Where's my money." It wasn't really a question.

"Aye, aye. Not so hasty, my boy. I've got yer pay. But I've got something else, too. Something maybe worth even more to you."

John looked down a good eight inches into the other man's eyes. "My. Money."

Riddle's swallow was audible even over the din behind them. "Aye, here 'tis." He placed a small pouch in John's bloody fist. John didn't need to count it. Riddle would be a fool to cheat him; a bleeding, bruised fool with broken bones. He turned away.

"Wait, Fielding, don't you want to know who's looking for yer?"

John didn't hesitate. What convict with even a teaspoon's worth of brain would want to know such a thing?

"He says he has information about you—about your Da."

Riddle's words hit him like grappling hooks, sinking into his memory like it was flesh. John's feet became heavy, as if they still bore the manacles and heavy chains that had encircled his ankles all those years ago. The metal rings had chafed his adolescent legs until they'd bled. They'd left scars.

Always more scars.

He whipped around and demonstrated the skill that had earned him the nickname *Lighting John*. Riddle's throat felt like a dry corn stalk beneath his hand: thin, delicate, breakable. John squeezed. "Name."

The smaller man's Adam's apple fluttered against his fist, like a tentative, anxious knocking against a door. John loosened his grip a little.

Riddle gasped and choked and then gasped again. "Worth, Stephen Worth. The banker from Siddons. The one who's come about the timber."

Riddle's high-pitched squeak made John realize he'd squeezed the man tighter, this time in surprise. He released the weasel-faced manager and turned away.

The crowd was already dissipating as he made his way back to town.

John smiled bitterly at the word: town. Only a true savage would consider the pathetic collection of shacks a town. It was nothing but a prison that had spread beyond its borders. He, like just about everyone else around him, was one of its inmates. Of course he'd heard of the arrival of Stephen Worth—who hadn't? Visitors to the wretched penal colony, at least voluntary ones, were rare. Rich Americans visitors were even rarer.

John had been living outside the prison even before his seven-year sentence ended. He'd been deemed an exemplary prisoner in his fourth year and, as such, allowed to live in his own hovel. The gesture was more to shed the expense than to reward a prisoner. As he was allowed only a pittance of what he earned the notion that he'd have enough to rent quarters—not to mention feed himself—was a fiction maintained by all. He wouldn't have lasted a week without the money he made from fighting. It was better than most others, many of whom made their money off whoring. Women were almost non-existent on Norfolk and some men were not choosy.

John frowned at the unwelcomed thought as he entered the building where he lived, a ramshackle structure that had been divided into four tiny rooms. The short hall was dim and he almost didn't see the person leaning against the door to his room. A large, well-dressed man; a big, red-headed bastard, to be precise.

"John Fielding?"

John eyed the tiny, cramped corridor behind the other man. He had come alone, unprotected. And unwise.

"Aye, 'oo wants to know?" John asked, even though he already knew.

The American extended a hand, something convicts did not do. John stared at it until the other man dropped it back to his side.

"Stephen Worth, I'm with Siddons bank."

John waited.

The other man smiled, amused, rather than annoyed, by John's belligerence. "I've heard a great deal about you, Mr. Fielding."

John raised one eyebrow.

"Of course I already knew you were a good man to have beside you in a fight." He paused and the smile dropped off his face. The look that replaced it chilled John's bones, a thing he wouldn't have believed possible anymore. This man was dressed like a gentleman, but he was not one: This was not a man to cross. "You don't remember me, do you, John?"

Something about the other man teased at John's memory, but it was a wisp, a tendril of smoke and too tenuous to grasp. "No."

"I've spent a great deal of time and money looking for you, Mr. Fielding. You should trust me—it is in your best interest to give me a few moments of your time."

Something about the man's face, maybe it was the expression on it—could that be honesty? Not that John could remember what such a thing looked like after nearly a decade in this hellhole—helped him make up his mind.

"Trust? That be scarce as 'en's teef 'ere. But time? Well, you're in luck there, Mr. Worff. I 'ave all the time in the world." John grinned, the action calculated.

Stephen Worth's eyes dropped to the savage scars on his cheeks, but his expression remained impassive. It was rare a man who could look John Fielding full in the face and show no fear. This banker was intriguing, as well as dangerous.

John flung open the door to the dark, cramped hole he called home and gestured the other man inside. "Welcome to my 'umble castle."

Chapter Two

London
Six Years Later

John leaned against the lamppost and watched the three women alight from the carriage. He had left his horse on the next street over and walked the short distance to avoid the chaotic congestion that always marked Bond Street, the *ton's* favorite fashion haunt.

He had been watching the women for weeks; watching *her*, really. Somehow it had become a habit. He told himself that was because he had nothing pressing to do. For the first time in fifteen years—hell, for the first time in his life—he was his own man and able to do whatever he pleased.

Apparently, this was how he wished to spend his time: stalking a spinster and her two youthful charges.

John barely noticed the younger women—Ladies Melissa and Jane—even though both of them would be considered far more physically attractive than their aunt, Miss Cordelia Page.

But it hadn't been Miss Page's face or body which had first drawn his interest. To be honest, John had barely noticed her when he started watching the three women and he never would have put himself to the bother of spying on them ever again if Miss Page had not intrigued him by stopping a group of boys from torturing an old dog.

It was the type of scene played out all over London all day, every day, for centuries. Poor boys picking on something weaker than themselves and being cruel for reasons of their own—or no reason at all. There had been perhaps five of the lads just a few feet down a narrow alley that ran beside yet another millinery shop—the three women's destination.

Miss Page had been the only one in her small party to notice the disturbance: the yelping dog and the boys pelting it with stones, their voices loud and raucous. She had stopped in the center of the walkway and cocked her head to locate the sounds while her companions walked on, unaware that they'd lost her.

Indeed, by the time the two girls and their footman, laden with packages, noticed she was gone, Miss Page was confronting the jeering boys, her hands on her hips, her body between them and the cowering dog

She had no clue about the danger she was facing.

John had started running toward her when he'd guess what she was doing, but he was too far down the block and would never make it in time.

It was fortunate the footman realized something was wrong and reached the fray in time to launch himself between Miss Page and a sizeable rock. The servant took the projectile in the chest and the young ruffians ran when they saw what they'd done.

The footman would have a bruise on his chest but was otherwise the worse for wear.

Meanwhile, the woman—utterly oblivious to the danger she'd just faced—picked up the cringing animal and cradled it in her arms, regardless of dirt and disease, holding it as if it were the most precious thing on earth.

John had stood frozen at the opening of the alley, as though he'd been hit dead between the eyes with a brick. A dog. She had risked her safety for a filthy old dog. Women of her class didn't do such things.

Except now he knew they did. Or at least *one* of them did.

And so John had found himself following the trio again the following week. And the week after that.

Today they were going into some modiste's shop. Last week it had been a bookseller. The week before a modiste *and* a bookseller. Upper class women seemed to do little other than shop. Even ones like *her:* unmarried impoverished gentlewomen who were dependent on their wealthy relatives' whims and kindness.

John was bloody fed up with arguing with himself about his foolish interest with the woman.

He'd bedded dozens of women in his life and had never been even a fraction as fixated on a female before—or anyone or anything else, really, either objects or people.

He'd learned early in life that wanting things was the fastest road to disappointment. The more you wanted something, the more disappointed you were when it was taken away, or when you couldn't have it in the first place.

John might have been dirt poor, but that hadn't meant he was stupid. Why set himself up for unnecessary pain?

But this was … different. The usual arguments weren't working and he was left wanting her more than ever.

He had no idea what it was about her. He didn't just want to bed her, although that thought had begun to take up more and more of his mind, he also felt a compulsion to—God forbid—learn more about her.

Whatever the hell that meant.

It was not John's habit to get to know anyone, man or woman. Knowing people just meant more responsibility and more possibility for disappointment.

In the weeks following the incident in the alley she had not rescued any other dogs, but he'd seen other acts of kindness: always a penny for a street sweeper, a smile and kind word for the servants who fetched and carried and hovered, and she was sweet to her nieces even when they were snappish with her.

She was a poor relation—a woman tolerated only so long as she was useful—yet she seemed to face her servitude with humor and good-natured acceptance.

If there was one thing in life that John knew about, it was servitude.

But he'd never faced it with good humor or acceptance.

To John, the woman was like a shiny object he could see, but never quite well enough to make out the details. It wasn't just a matter of want; he *needed* to get closer.

It was bloody annoying.

He paused beside a lamp post to watch her from beneath the brim of his hat. She was wearing the same dark gray carriage costume she'd worn the last time. As far as John could tell, she possessed only a handful of dresses.

The two girls she shepherded from place to place—his stepsisters, not that anyone would ever believe such a relationship existed—never wore the same garment twice. It wasn't surprising the girls did not resemble him. Not only did they have a different mother, they'd also had a very different life.

The notion that the two slight things in muslin were related to him in any way made John smile—a gruesome sight that caused an approaching pedestrian to stumble and career into an oncoming pair of young bucks.

One of the young bloods stopped and called after the frightened older man. "On the tipple this early?" And then the dandy spotted

John and his sarcastic smile slid from his face faster than a whore dropped her knickers.

John ignored the other man's horrified stare and kept his eyes on the three women, who were disappearing into the milliner's shop, where they would most likely be for hours. And when they came out? Well, they would climb directly into their carriage and go to some other shop.

Was he really going to wait hours for a glimpse that lasted no longer than a few seconds?

John sighed, pushed himself off the post, and crossed the street to one of tea shops that catered to the throngs of Bond Street loungers.

The hum of conversation inside the crowded shop leaked from the room like water trickling down a drain when he entered.

John paid no attention to either the sudden silence or staring eyes and lowered his big frame into a rickety chair near the bow window.

He ordered a pot of tea that he had no intention of drinking from the stammering, wide-eyed waiter and commenced to wait.

***

Cordelia smiled at her niece's reflection, careful to mask her true thoughts on the hat that Melissa was currently modeling. It was not a difficult thing to do. In fact, masking her feelings was a thing she did well. She had found it was wiser to ignore Melissa's whims rather than confront them head on.

"It *is* a fetching bonnet, my dear." *For a lady of the night*, she could have added, but did not. "However, that particular shade of red will flatter the sprigged apricot muslin you are planning to wear to Lady Northumberland's indoor *fête champêtre*."

Melissa frowned at her reflection before sighing and plucking off the dreadful hat and handing it back to the hovering shop clerk. "I daresay you are correct, Aunt Cordy. What about that one?" She pointed to a far more appropriate straw and pale green voile concoction and the clerk went to fetch it.

Satisfied that Melissa had been gentled into a more suitable direction Cordelia turned to her younger niece, Jane, who sat slouched on a settee, her nose in a book. Her pelisse, bonnet, gloves, and reticule lay scattered about her on the plush divan, as though she were a female volcano that had erupted, spewing women's garments far and wide.

"Jane, darling, won't you please consider looking at a hat?"

Jane looked up, her blue eyes unfocused behind thick, smudged spectacles. "I beg your pardon, Aunt Cordy?"

"A hat, my dear. That is why we are here, among all these hats. You must select one."

Her smooth brow wrinkled. "Must I?"

"If you care to attend Lady Northumberland's tomorrow."

Jane appeared to be giving her words serious consideration.

Cordelia sighed. "You have already accepted the invitation, Jane, it would be unkind to change your mind at this late date. Besides, you wanted to see the conservatory for yourself. There will never be as good an opportunity as having a party inside one."

Jane pursed her lips and grudgingly closed her book. "Can you not choose something for me?"

The shop bell jingled and she turned to find Eldon Simpson, the new Earl of Madeley, standing in the doorway, looking very much like a fox inspecting a henhouse.

Drat.

"I *thought* I recognized His Grace's carriage in that dreadful snarl outside." He spoke to Melissa, although his eyes flickered to Cordelia, to whom he gave the slightest of nods to acknowledge her existence.

Melissa flushed in a way that made Cordelia's heart sink. How could her niece not recognize a hardened rake and cold-blooded fortune hunter when she saw one?

That was a foolish question and Cordelia knew it. Her sister's children had been protected and cosseted from the moment they'd been born. They had no clue what dangers the world held for pretty—seemingly wealthy—girls.

Cordelia smiled at the handsome Lord Madeley, whom she knew to be one step away from being chased by shopkeepers bearing pitch forks and torches.

"Good afternoon, my lord." She masked the chill in her voice with a pleasant smile.

"Good afternoon, Miss Page." He glanced at Melissa and then Jane. "Will you ladies be gracing Lady Northumberland's conservatory party tomorrow?"

"That is why we are here, to select new hats," Melissa said.

Jane had already inserted her nose back into her book and appeared unaware of the handsome lord's existence.

The earl's eyes widened, all the better to show off their sky-blue color. "Hat shopping? I adore it above all things."

Melissa laughed. "Will you be going to the party, my lord?"

"An alfresco party in a conservatory? Why, I wouldn't miss it for the world, Lady Melissa."

Cordelia knew the earl would rather be boiled in oil than attend such an insipid affair. But he was so strapped as to make finding a wealthy bride—immediately—a necessity.

"Oh, dear," Cordelia said in the harried but accommodating tone she knew people expected of spinster aunts and chaperones. "What has happened to the time? I'm afraid we are running terribly late. Have you made your selection, Melissa?"

Her niece cut her a narrow-eyed look. "Surely we needn't leave just yet, Aunt."

"Hmm." Cordelia was adept at appearing not to notice slights, irritated, sighs, or withering looks, and doing so with a vague smile. "I seem to recall seeing something the exact shade of your gown in Madame Lisette's window, Melissa. If we make haste, we might be able to see if the hat is still there." She didn't wait for an answer and instead turned to Jane. "Come, my dear, we must be on our way." She helped Jane collect her scattered possessions and ushered her toward the door. "It was a pleasure seeing you again, my lord." She gave her glowering niece a pleasant smile. "Shall we go, Melissa?"

Lord Madeley bowed over Melissa's hand and smirked. "I shall look forward to seeing you again soon, Lady Melissa."

Cordelia herded the girls out of the shop before her.

"That was very *rude*, Aunt Cordy," Melissa hissed beneath her breath, sounding remarkably like her mother, the Duchess of Falkirk.

Jane pushed her smudged spectacles further up her small nose and tucked her book beneath her elbow before scowling at her elder sister. "Oh, don't be such a cat, Mel. Anyone can see Lord Madeley is nothing but a hedge bird."

Cordelia had to bite her lip to keep from laughing. "Jane, that is hardly a polite thing for a lady to say."

Melissa glared at the youngest member of the family. "I'm sure she learned it from Charles."

So was Cordelia. The duke's son and heir, Cordelia's only nephew, was close to his youngest sister. Unlike most young men his age, Charles Merrick did not find it unmanning to socialize with a female.

Cordelia was waiting for the two girls to climb into the barouche when a shadow fell over her.

She turned to find a vast expanse of great coat-covered chest in front of her.

Cordelia looked up and up and up. The man was so big his towering form blocked the sun and left his face in shadow.

"I believe you dropped this." The voice was a deep rumble and did not sound entirely English. The footman, Marcus, who'd been helping Jane settle into the carriage turned, saw the stranger, and puffed up like a belligerent rooster.

"Here then, what do *you* want?" he demanded, attempting to thrust himself between Cordelia and the other man and failing when the far bigger man did not budge.

Cordelia had always believed young Marcus to be large, but that was before he stood next to the giant. The stranger turned in profile to glance at the younger man and Cordelia gasped as sunshine illuminated his face. Heat like the blast from a furnace surged up her neck and into her face at her ill-bred response.

His full lips twisted into something that might have been a smile, although it was difficult to say given the way the muscles in his scarred cheeks pulled in such odd directions. The footman took a step back and the stranger's gaze turned back to Cordelia, his black eyes burning into her.

"Is this yours?" he said again, this time lifting his hand between them.

She knew she should pay attention to whatever it was he was attempting to return, but she could not look away. Aside from the savage scars radiating out from both corners of his mouth his face was handsome in a stark, harshly hewn way. His nose was the regal falcon's beak so prevalent in many of England's oldest families—or at least it had been before it had been broken and poorly set, at least twice from what she could see. While she was too consumed with his face to study the rest of his person, she had the hazy impression he was dressed like a gentleman.

His most unusual characteristic after his scarred visage was his hair, which was black, wiry, and long enough to be worn in a queue. Outside of a few military units who still adhered to the custom it was unusual to see long hair on a man.

"Ma'am?" He cocked a jet-black eyebrow at her and she wrenched her gaze from his face and looked down to see he held a rose-pink glove in his huge hand. She blinked; his huge *six-fingered* hand.

"Aunt Cordy?" Jane poked her head outside the carriage. She looked from the giant to his hand and then back to his face. "Oh, that is my glove." She reached out a small, bare hand and her sunny, open smile made Cordelia even more aware of her own rude gaping.

The stranger cut Jane an almost dismissive look and handed her the glove.

"Thank you, sir," Jane said, pulling the glove onto her hand.

But his eyes were already back on Cordelia, who realized she had been holding her breath.

She exhaled and fixed a gracious smile on her mouth. "Yes, thank you, sir." She was pleased that her voice sounded so much calmer than her flustered brain.

His nostrils flared slightly and he gave an abrupt nod and turned, his graceful movements a surprise for such a massive body.

He cleaved oncoming pedestrian traffic like some sort of human axe, the people he passed cutting him furtive, anxious glances.

And then he turned down an alley and disappeared.

"Goodness," Cordelia murmured. She climbed into the carriage, her mind a chaotic whirl, and settled into the forward facing seat beside Melissa, who, she realized absently, was glaring out the opposite window to communicate her unhappiness at having been dragged away from Lord Madeley.

Jane leaned toward Cordelia, her blue eyes wide. "Did you *see* that, Aunt Cordy?"

She was formulating a gentle chastisement about ladies not commenting on the disfigurements of others, when her niece continued. "I have never met anyone other than me, Charles and Papa like this, have you?" She held up her right hand.

Cordelia looked at Jane's six-fingered hand, grateful she had misjudged Jane's interest in the stranger. She shook her head and sat back against the plush velvet squabs, oddly exhausted by the brief encounter.

"No, Jane, I haven't."

***

John waited until he'd turned into the alley to look at the small square of embroidered linen in his hand, *C. F. P.*

Thanks to his investigation of the duke's family, he knew that the initials stood for Cordelia Frances Page.

He also knew she was the Duchess of Falkirk's much younger sister and had come to live with her sister several years before. Cordelia and her sisters had grown up in a genteel but poor country manse not far from the Duke of Falkirk's country seat.

Cordelia was close to John's age—whatever his exact age was, he wasn't really sure—and had no beau in either London or at the duke's country house, where she spent most of her time when she wasn't launching a niece into society.

He ran his thumb over the raised needlework. It had been only the work of a moment to pluck the handkerchief from where she kept it tucked in the wrist of her left glove. While he was not a particularly skilled cly faker he had done his share of dipping when he'd been a lad, until he'd grown too large and conspicuous to work as a pickpocket.

Tiny violets and even smaller green leaves encircled the initials. The workmanship was exquisite. Before John realized what he was doing, he raised the handkerchief to his nose and inhaled. The small cloth did have a scent, although not of violets. The smell was sharply aromatic but John could not identify it. To his untutored nose the fragrance reminded him of lavender, but not quite as floral. And it certainly was nothing so cloying as rose or lilac. He inhaled deeply and held the breath in his lungs, savoring it like he would a fine brandy.

He knew women of her class—when they were not shopping or attending balls or parties—spent their time employed in activities like needlework.

But not the type of needlework his Mam had done—stitching garments for a tailor by the dim light of a tallow candle until her eyes were too weak to see, her fingers too bent and stiff to ply a needle.

John shoved aside the broken shard of memory and pictured instead the woman who must have labored on this tiny square of fabric.

John had spent years with nothing other than his own mind and imagination to entertain himself. And when a man lived among criminals, he learned to pay attention to details or he didn't make it to a very great age.

John's past had left him skilled at constructing mental images of any person, place, or thing. More than once in his life his power to recreate with his imagination was all that had stood between him and the yawning maw of insanity.

Before his ex-employer, Stephen Worth—had taught him how to read, his imagination had been the lifeboat his mind had clung to when he'd been in such physical agony that he'd not wanted to go on living.

It had been what remained of light and life and color when he'd believed he would die in the dark belly of a convict ship.

It had kept him going when he'd been so alone, so stripped of everything he was—like an onion that had been peeled layer by layer by layer—that nothing remained.

Right now, John used his formidable imagination to picture Cordelia Page. He reconstructed her face until she hung in his mind as clearly as a portrait in some rich nob's gallery.

The sun had been at his back and had thrown her face into relief. Her eyes were a kaleidoscope of greens and browns with a hint of gold. But it wasn't the color that made a man take notice so much as their shape and the expression in them. Large and slightly tilted, they seemed to be smiling.

Even when they had looked up at John.

People generally did not smile when they looked at him.

Her lips were not bow-shaped like those so admired by poets, but full and mobile. Although she probably didn't know it, hers was a mouth made for sensual pleasures.

They'd stood so close that he'd seen small brackets at each side—lines from smiling.

Her figure was not the slim, fragile type so admired by the *ton*, but then he was not a member of that august assemblage.

The word to describe her figure was voluptuous—his preferred type of female body. He could imagine her in his arms and had done so far more often and far more vividly than was comfortable for his mental state.

Her wide hazel eyes had swept his cheeks and taken in his scars with an expression of cool contemplation that had enflamed him. It wasn't the look he normally saw on women's faces. No, the normal reaction was one of horrified fascination, the expressions usually a combination of morbid attraction and sexual curiosity. Being with a man with such a savage visage allowed them to experience danger, even if it was only second hand.

John had long ago become accustomed to people gawking at his face and it had ceased bothering him, if it ever had. He had never put much value in appearances. How could he when he'd seen such pretty, handsome people do such vicious, cruel things?

And why wouldn't people stare at him? He was hideously scarred. Most people only looked out of curiosity, not malice.

But she had looked at him like a kindly school mistress assessing a troublesome student.

John had felt like a book she'd opened and begun flipping through. Could she see the things he had done? The things he was still doing? The things he had planned for her family?

The notion was foolish, whimsical, and unlike him. It was far more likely the woman was merely more self-possessed than most people. What had looked like cool contemplation had probably been her polite mask of shock and revulsion. He knew women of a certain class—*her* class—were taught to control and conceal their feelings.

His reaction to *her* reaction told John he'd become far too reliant on using his scars to intimidate and manipulate people. Some people required more subtlety.

And why was he standing there thinking about her? Again.

He wanted her.

Why did he want her? He had no earthly reason.

It didn't matter how often he told himself, that she was just another impoverished spinster, a woman of average beauty who was well past her prime. That she was nothing special.

No, that argument was as toothless as an old crone.

John pushed away any thoughts of the woman he'd just left and tucked the fragrant cloth he'd stolen into his pocket. He made his way to the far end of the narrow alley, where he'd left his horse. He tossed a coin to the boy holding his mount and reached for the reins.

The lad, no older than ten or twelve, tilted his head back and stared up a good two feet at John.

"'E bit me, sir." He held out a scrawny limb as proof. His arm was stick-like with pasty skin stretched over bone, the half-starved body of a street urchin. The undeniable U-shaped mark of equine teeth reddened his small forearm.

John swung himself into the saddle and then looked down at the lad's upturned face. "He bit you, but you did not let him go?"

"No, gov." The boy's pinched face was serious and his dark-circled eyes were steady. He held his ground even though most grown men quailed beneath John's stare.

John tossed him another coin. "If you want to get bitten again come to St. James's Square; I have need of a stable hand."

The boy grinned and the expression transformed his homely face while exposing a set of teeth that were two short of their normal complement.

"Aye, gov."

John snorted at the boy's enthusiasm and wheeled his mount.

"But which 'ouse?" he asked, trotting alongside him.

"The biggest one on the street."

His soot-smudged forehead wrinkled. "But ain't that the Duke of Falkirk's house?"

John smiled and kneed his horse into a canter. "Not anymore."

<u>Hope you enjoyed the sneak peek!</u>

If you haven't read my SEDUCERS series you should check it out ...

Melissa Griffin is quite literally sick and tired. She's the owner of one of London's most exclusive brothels, but her failing health is telling her she can't continue to keep working at her current pace. A relaxing stay in the country is exactly what she needs. Falling for the small town's gorgeous young vicar—a virgin, no less—was never part of her plan. Their love is scandalous, forbidden…and everything Melissa never knew she wanted. Denying her feelings is unthinkable. Avoiding devastation when her past inevitably drives them apart? Impossible.

Magnus Stanwyck never resented his vow of celibacy…until meeting Melissa. As beautiful on the inside as she is on the outside, the mysterious woman captures his heart in a way he never could've anticipated. No matter what stands between them, no matter the cost, he'll do whatever it takes to possess her—heart, body, and soul.

By day, they're opposites who were never supposed to be together. By night, their passion threatens to overtake them. When all is said and done, can Melissa and Magnus overcome the obstacles (and enemies) that stand between them? Or will fate deny them their happily ever after?

Looking for more unusual heroes and heroines? Have you tried THE ACADEMY OF LOVE series?

Finding out that her husband was a bigamist didn't devastate Portia Stefani; she held her head high when she forced him out of her life. But losing her beloved music school as a result of the traitorous bastard's gambling debts almost destroyed her. The only way she'll be able to make ends meet is to accept a lucrative tutoring position in remote Cornwall. What Portia hasn't anticipated is the life-altering impact that her mesmerizing new employer has on her.

Stacy Harrington learned the hard way to keep people at a distance. Playing the piano is the only thing that makes his solitary life enjoyable these days, and he'll be damned if he allows his albinism to keep him from everything he loves. Bringing a private music tutor into his home is disruptive, but it's the only solution. Unfortunately, nothing could have prepared him for the overwhelming attraction he feels toward his fiery new employee.

It's not long before a shared passion for music develops into something infinitely deeper. But when ghosts from the past—along with some very dark secrets—emerge to threaten everything they've built, can Stacy and Portia continue to make beautiful music together? Or will their happily ever after end on a painful, discordant note?

Who are Minerva Spencer & S.M. LaViolette?

Minerva is S.M.'s pen name (that's short for Shantal Marie) S.M. has been a criminal prosecutor, college history teacher, B&B operator, dock worker, ice cream manufacturer, reader for the blind, motel maid, and bounty hunter. Okay, so the part about being a bounty hunter is a lie. S.M. does, however, know how to hypnotize a Dungeness crab, sew her own Regency Era clothing, knit a frog hat, juggle, rebuild a 1959 American Rambler, and gain control of Asia (and hold on to it) in the game of RISK.

For news about upcoming books, free excerpts, and awesome giveaways check out: www.MinervaSpencer.com